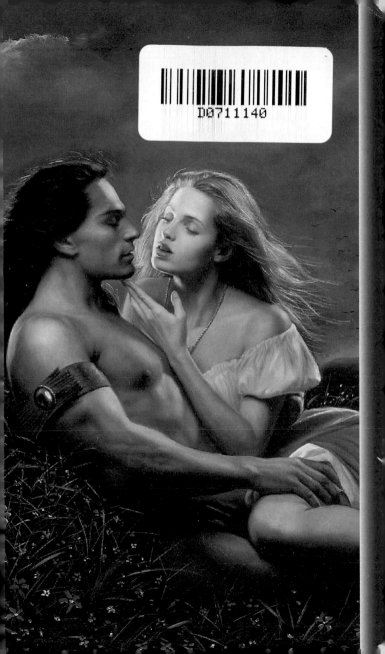

ALL THE RIGHT MOVES

"I can't stand with you against my men, Cass. I can't let myself believe that Buck, Pete, Nash, Baird, or any of the other boys could be responsible for your brother's death. They don't deserve that. I can't do it, and I won't!"

"You said you love me."

Cass's words broke her heart.

"Have your feelings changed?"

Purity's reply was a rasping whisper. "Here and now? No. There's no conflict between us here, no hatred. But there's no reality, either. There's no wrong or right..."

"No, that's not true."

Cass touched his mouth to hers. "To return my kiss is right, Purity."

He stroked her cheek. "To know my touch is right."

He drew closer. "To indulge the beauty when our flesh meets is right."

His lips brushed hers, and then he whispered, "To believe there is no one else in the world when I hold you in my arms could never be wrong."

"No..."

"Look at me, Purity, and listen." His eyes seemed to mesmerize her. "Your breath is my breath. Your heartbeat is mine. We are one now, Purity."

"But tomorrow—"

"Tomorrow is hours away."

Other *Leisure* books by Elaine Barbieri:
DANGEROUS VIRTUES: HONESTY
DANCE OF THE FLAME

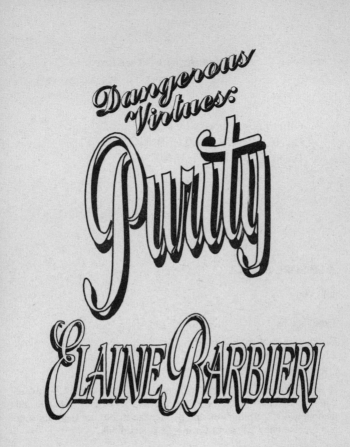

Dangerous Virtues:

Purity

ELAINE BARBIERI

LEISURE BOOKS NEW YORK CITY

To my family, with all my love

A LEISURE BOOK®

July 1997

Published by

Dorchester Publishing Co., Inc.
276 Fifth Avenue
New York, NY 10001

Printed in the United States of America.

There is no light so fair or bright,
To cast upon the darkened night,
As a ray of purity.

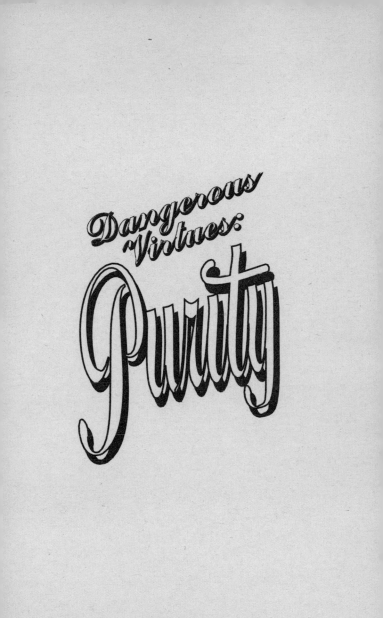

Dangerous Virtues:

Purity

Prologue

1867

The trail herd moved at a brisk pace, stirring a cloud of dust that shrouded the setting sun despite rains recently fallen. Riding alongside it, Stan Corrigan raised his neckerchief, cursing softly when a calf stumbled out of sight over the high riverbank nearby. He spurred his mount toward the edge, acutely aware as he spotted the animal that he could not afford to lose a single head if the Circle C were to survive its latest financial threat.

Guiding his mount cautiously down the steep incline, Stan was a few feet from the bawling calf when an object in the flooded river caught his eye. He squinted against the glare of the glittering surface.

Stan's heart began a slow pounding. Could it be?

It was!

Reacting spontaneously, Stan turned his horse into the rapids and spurred him forward. His gelding swam strongly as he neared the small body and snatched it from the water. His throat tightened at the blue color of the child's skin as he turned back toward shore.

The girl was so still.

She wasn't breathing.

Damn it all, *she wasn't breathing!*

Panicking, Stan turned the child over his arm and pounded her back. The sick feeling inside him expanded as he pleaded, "Breathe, little darlin'... breathe."

He heard it then ... first a sputter, then a loud belching as a stream of water shot from the child's mouth with a burst of sound that ended in a wail.

Exultation swept through him. She was alive!

Stan turned the child toward him, cradling her in his arms.

She was crying.

But she was *alive*.

"My name's Stan. What's yours, darlin'?"

The child's light eyes returned Stan's gaze as she lay on the makeshift pallet quickly assembled for her in the cook's wagon. She could be no more than four or five years old. Her long, fair hair was almost dry and her tattered nightdress had been exchanged for a warm shirt that covered her fragile frame from head to foot, but she did not respond. Stan searched the child's angelic countenance as he crouched beside her, seeing small, delicate features and pale skin bruised by her terrifying experience.

Where had she come from? Whom did she belong to? They had seen some wreckage in the river, but had found no one else. He touched her forehead, then turned anxiously toward the drover standing at the rear of the wagon.

"She's burnin' up with fever, Buck. Damn it, where's Pete with that medicine?"

"Here I am!"

Wasting no time as he climbed into the wagon, the cook crouched beside the pallet and uncorked the bottle in his hand. His low grumbling was easily audible in the pervading silence as he poured the thick liquid onto a spoon.

"Beats me how that damned fool, Horton, could get so attached to this stuff that he don't want to give it up, especially when it tastes as bad as it does." He looked up, spoon poised, as he directed, "Lift her head up so's she'll be able to swallow."

"You're sure that medicine will do the trick?"

Pete's bloodshot eyes flashed. "I ain't sure of nothin', but I don't think we got much choice but to try it, seein' as it looks like this little gal might not make it otherwise!"

Right.

Stan slipped his arm under the child's shoulders and raised her cautiously. She had been conscious for over an hour. He knew she heard every word spoken to her, but she had not responded to a single question asked. He remembered hearing about a fellow who had been rescued from drowning, only to

13

have his brain so affected that he had not lived a normal day since.

But that couldn't happen to this innocent little girl . . . could it?

The child's expression grew anxious as Pete thrust the spoon toward her lips.

Stan forced a smile. "Don't go gettin' scared now, darlin'. Pete's goin' to give you some medicine. It don't taste too good, but it's goin' to make you feel better."

The child's expression did not change.

Pete joined Stan's attempt at reassurance. "What the boss says is true, all right. You just open up and swallow, and in a little while you'll be feelin' just as right as rain."

The girl's lips remained closed.

"Open your mouth, darlin'."

No response.

"You heard what the boss said. Open up!"

The girl's mouth locked tight.

"Don't holler at her, Pete!"

"I ain't hollerin'!"

"Yes, you are!"

"Seems to me you're both hollerin'."

Silenced by Buck's sober comment from the rear of the wagon, Stan turned back toward the silent child. His heart aching at her obvious fear, he tried again.

"I didn't mean to scare you, little sweetheart, and neither did Pete. We're just tryin' to get you to take this medicine. You need to take it to make you better."

The child began trembling. Her eyes filled the moment before she closed them, releasing two large tears that trailed slowly down her heated cheeks.

Damn it all!

Stan stared at the girl. He was thirty-one years old. He had fought in and lived through four years of a merciless civil war that had left scars on both his body and his soul. He had come home to Texas at the war's end to find that the sanctuary he had left no longer existed, and to discover that a war of another kind had only just begun. In the six years most recently past, he had been threatened, starved, wounded, trampled, forced to experience the humiliation of surrender, robbed of his dearest possessions, and left to wallow in useless rage and self-pity at the devastation that had once been his home. But in all that time he had never felt more helpless than he did at this moment.

Leaning closer to the shaking child, Stan stroked away her tears with his callused palm. The heat of her skin added a fearful earnestness to his tone as he whispered, "Open your eyes, little darlin'." His gaze intent on the fragile lids framed with incredibly long brown lashes, Stan urged again, "Open your eyes. Otherwise I won't know if you can hear what I'm sayin'."

Hope surged as the girl's eyes slowly opened. Her gaze fastened on his, and Stan's heart melted. He whispered, "You're afraid, ain't you?"

No response.

"Is it me you're afraid of?"

The child stared.

"Answer me, little darlin'."

Incredible joy surged within him as the girl shook her head in a weak, negative response.

He pressed cautiously, "Is it the medicine you're afraid of?"

The child's eyes again filled. Her head moved with a barely discernible nod.

"If I take the medicine first and show you it ain't really that bad, will you take it, too?"

Hesitation. Another nod.

"Promise?"

Consent.

Stan turned back toward Pete. "Give that spoonful to me."

Pete scowled. "We ain't got enough of this stuff that we can waste it on somebody who don't need it at all!"

Stan's full brown mustache twitched with suppressed agitation. "We could have a barrel of it and it wouldn't do this child no good if she won't take it! So stop arguin' and do what I said!"

His victory was short-lived as Pete shoved the spoon into his mouth and he swallowed the syrupy liquid in a gulp, then fought to control his reflexive gagging.

He coughed.

He wheezed.

He gasped for breath.

Damned if he had ever tasted anything worse!

Aware of the child's silent scrutiny, Stan managed a weak smile. He spoke in a choked voice.

"That medicine don't taste too good, darlin', but

it's goin' to have to do." He glanced at Pete, noting that the spoon was refilled and poised. Regaining his normal tone, he urged, "Open your mouth like you promised."

Stan stared at the girl. He held his breath as she blinked, then parted her lips.

Pete thrust the spoon into her mouth and smiled victoriously as the child swallowed.

Stan watched and waited.

No gagging reflex.

No grimace of distaste.

And unless his mind was deceiving him, he saw the flicker of a smile.

The girl's eyes closed. Within minutes she was sleeping.

Stan touched his palm to her forehead. He frowned at the heat there.

"Well, what did you expect? There ain't no medicine in the world that can bring down a fever that fast!"

A scathing glance was his only response to Pete's comment. Then Stan ordered, "Call me if you notice any change in her at all, you hear?"

"Does that mean you're leavin' and makin' me her nursemaid?"

Stan's weathered face hardened. "Looks like it's goin' to be that way until we can find her people or someplace safe to drop her off."

"What if I said I don't want the job?"

Stan did not bother to reply.

"That's what I thought."

17

Stan's gaze narrowed. "Just make sure you take good care of her."

"Of course I'll take good care of her! I ain't no monster, you know!"

"Call me as soon as she wakes up or if there's any change in her at all."

"I heard you the first time!"

"Come on, boss. It's gettin' late and the boys are waitin'."

Nodding in Buck's direction, Stan climbed out of the wagon. He looked back as Pete grumbled, "How many times do I have to tell him that I'll call him like he said? He must be gettin' hard of hearin'."

Stan walked to his horse.

"She won't take her medicine again, dammit!"

Stan stared at the child, who looked back at him with eyes wide. It was midway through the night. He had been standing watch over his sleeping herd when Buck rode up with a frantic call from Pete. His heart pounding, he had raced back to the chuck wagon to find Pete fuming over the girl as she lay rigidly silent, her lips locked closed again.

Stan reached out automatically to touch her forehead.

"Sure, she still has a fever!" Pete's frown deepened. "She needs another dose of medicine, and she won't take it."

"I told you to call me when she woke up."

"I did."

"I told you to call me *as soon as* she woke up."

"You was on watch!"

"Damn it, Pete, you—"

"It don't make no never mind no how. She take her medicine, and that's the crux of it!"

Stan turned back toward the silent child. Big, powerfully built, and endowed with earnest concern and a natural confidence that had never failed to inspire trust in those under his command, he leaned toward the girl, again feeling as helpless as a child.

"Pete says you don't want to take your medicine."

No response.

"You have to take it in order to get better. I thought you understood that, darlin'." He paused, dreading what he knew he must say. "Do you want me to take the medicine first like we did the last time—is that it?"

Still no response.

Stan touched the child's warm, bruised cheek. Despite the abrasions, her skin was as smooth as silk. He offered, "Tell me what you want me to do, little sweetheart. It's up to you."

Long, silent moments passed before the child took a short breath, then turned toward Pete and opened her mouth. She made no protest when he slipped the spoon inside, swallowing the medicine without flinching.

The relief that surged through Stan changed to surprise when the girl slipped her small hand into his.

Stan looked at the child to see her pale eyes fill with tears. He could not bring himself to withdraw his hand, even as her eyes gradually closed and she dropped off to sleep.

... the snap of a log on the
... of a drover's droning song
... rection of the sleeping herd ...
... d to the silver light of the moon
... to the chuck wagon. Reluctant to leave
... side while she still clutched his hand, he
ha... ally fallen asleep.

Abruptly conscious of a weight on his chest, Stan
looked down to see that the child had slipped off her
pallet to curl against his side and that she slept with
her head resting on his chest. Her face was peace-
fully composed, despite the heat of fever that still
radiated from her body. He attempted to shift the
child back to her pallet, but she burrowed nearer. He
tried again, only to have her clutch him closer.

Stan went still.

He had no choice.

Curling his arm around her, he closed his eyes.

Anxious dreams.

She saw the interior of a wagon. She heard familiar voices.

*"There, there ... don't be frightened, girls. Your
papa will find a doctor. You'll all be well soon."*

"I'm hot, Mama. I'm thirsty. My stomach hurts."

"I'm thirsty, too."

"Me, too."

The fragmented pictures whirled, changing.

She heard a roar like thunder.

The sound grew louder ... closer!

A wall of water was sweeping down the river while their wagon foundered midway across!

Chastity was screaming!

Honesty was calling her name!

Mama scrambled toward them! She reached for them, but the river came between them.

The world tumbled!

Water filled her nose and mouth!

It drowned her screams.

It stole her breath.

It ripped her from her sisters' clutching arms, enveloping her in a world of liquid darkness that stifled all.

There was no light.

There was no sound.

There was no life.

Only . . .

"Mama!"

She awoke with a start, shuddering and crying, pressing herself against the broad chest that pillowed her head. She felt a strong arm slip around her. She heard a deep voice speaking words of comfort.

"Shhhhh. Don't cry. You had a bad dream, little darlin', but you're all right. You're safe. I won't let anythin' happen to you now."

She looked up into a craggy face filled with concern. She remembered that face, that voice. It had parted the darkness and restored the light when Mama and Papa . . . when her sisters . . . when all had been swept away.

His name was Stan.

He said he would take care of her.

She knew he would.

She burrowed against Stan and closed her eyes as his arm tightened around her.

Stan would keep her safe. She would not have to move.

Stan would keep her secure. She would not have to think.

She opened her eyes and looked up again at Stan. Belatedly, she whispered, "My name is Purity."

1881

"Damn that maverick!"

Tall, whipcord-slim and dressed in drover's gear, Purity drew her mount up sharply, ignoring its snort of protest as she scanned the brush for a sign of the longhorn that had again eluded her. She cursed under her breath. She had been chasing the oversized brute for longer than she cared to admit as it zigzagged across the sunswept landscape. Crafty and belligerent, it had run her a merry chase until she was now separated from the main portion of the herd, left behind in the trailing cloud of red dust that presently hid the animal from view.

There it was!

Her teeth clamped tight with determination, she dug her heels into her mount's sides, her blood rushing as the steer spotted her and resumed its race across the wild terrain. Spurring her horse to life-threatening speed, she leaned low over the saddle, a sense of victory surging through her as she gained steadily on the obstinate beast.

Finally within range, Purity swung her rope over her head and threw the loop.

Missed again!

Still riding hard and cursing her luck, she gasped as a rope looped unexpectedly around her own shoulders. She was too late to avoid the sudden tightening of the coil that jerked her from her saddle to hit the ground with a stunning crack. She was still disoriented when a buckskin-clad figure fell suddenly upon her, knocking the breath from her lungs. She looked up to gasp a single word.

"Kiowa!"

With a knife pressed tightly to her throat, she was unable to move. She felt the tightly muscled length of the savage tense the moment before he ripped her hat from her head, spilling out the pale mass of unbound hair beneath. She gasped again as he twisted his hand in the strands and grunted, "A woman!"

But the voice held none of the guttural tones of the primitive tribe. Instead, it sounded almost—

On his feet in a flash of movement, the Indian dragged her upright. Grasping her by the shirtfront to hold her fast, he pressed the knife to her stomach and hissed, "Tell me what happened to him!"

She stared into the face of her attacker. Sun-reddened skin . . . sharply chiseled features . . . black, shoulder-length hair secured by a headband . . . but *green* eyes . . .

She rasped, "I . . . I don't know what you're talkin' about!"

The tip of his knife pierced her shirt. She felt her blood trickling. She heard his grated warning.

"I'll ask you one more time."

She heard a shot!

She saw the Indian's body jerk with the impact of the bullet that struck him.

She saw the look in his eyes, a promise that sent shudders down her spine as he fell to the ground at her feet.

And she knew she would never forget the chilling warning he breathed the second before his eyes closed—"I will remember. . . ."

"Are you all right, Purity?"

Too shaken to protest Buck's use of the given name she had discarded years earlier, Purity nodded. She stared at her attacker lying motionless on the ground. She touched the point where his blade had pierced her skin. Her shirt was wet with blood.

"He cut you, didn't he!" Buck's weathered face tightened. "Damned savages! They're havin' some kind of powwow around here somewheres. It's supposed to be peaceful." He made a short, scoffing sound that twitched his thick gray mustache. "Ain't a one of them that's worth the price of a bullet!"

Glancing up, Purity saw that Carter, Rome, and Baird had ridden up to join them. The three wranglers stood defensively beside her, their guns drawn as they scanned the nearby foliage. They advanced slowly to search the bushes.

Purity took a shuddering breath. "I think he was alone."

Buck scrutinized her more closely as he jerked off the rope still coiled around her shoulders. "Roped you from your horse, did he? Ain't never seen an Injun do that before." He grunted. "Ain't likely I'll see one do it again, neither, now that this one's out of the way."

Purity looked down at the man at her feet.

Clear, chiseled features, Indian dress . . . but he had *green* eyes . . .

Tell me what happened to him!

"He asked me what happened to him."

"What happened to who?"

Purity did not respond.

"Purity?"

"I don't know."

Buck gave another snort. "Ain't likely he did, neither. He was probably comin' off of one of them vision quests that turns them Injuns half crazy."

Purity's head snapped to the side as Carter emerged from the foliage, followed closely by Baird and Rome.

"It don't look like there's no more of them savages around." Carter's youthful face tensed. "I'm thinkin' we'd best get back to the herd and get as far away from here as we can before somebody comes lookin' for this one."

A sound from the Indian lying prostrate at her feet snapped Purity's eyes back toward him as Buck grated, "Still alive, is he? Well, I'll be damned if I'll waste another bullet on him. Let's get out of here."

Green eyes glaring into hers . . .

Purity took a stabilizing breath. "No."

"What are you sayin'?"

"I'm sayin' he's still alive and we can't leave him here to bleed to death."

"He tried to kill you, didn't he? Leave him where he lies! Nobody's goin' to pay attention to another dead Injun in this country!"

"I'm the boss here, and I said no. We're goin' to take him as far as the nearest town and drop him off."

"You're crazy, you know that, Purity!"

"My name is Boots."

Drawing his wiry frame up to its full height, Buck responded tightly, "Your name's Purity to me, and there ain't nobody goin' to make me call you by that silly nickname you took when you was a kid. And, I'm tellin' you that if Stan was here, he'd say the same thing I'm sayin' now—leave that Injun where he lies!"

"I'm the boss here. Stan isn't."

"But he—"

"Stan trusts my judgment, or he wouldn't have put me in charge of this drive."

"Yeah, but—"

"So, the decision is mine." Purity turned to address the others, who stood silently nearby. "Pick him up, boys. We're takin' him with us like I said."

"You're makin' a mistake."

Purity's delicate features hardened. "If I'm makin' a mistake, it's *my* mistake. Now do what I said!"

Watching as the Indian was lifted from the ground and thrown over his horse, Purity could not seem to draw her eyes from the blood that flowed steadily from the wound in his back.

Mounting, she started back toward the herd.

"He ain't goin' to make it."

Pete's countenance revealed no sign of regret as he glanced up briefly from tending the bloody wound in the Indian's back. They had met up with the chuck wagon a short time earlier. Her attacker had been lifted from his horse and unceremoniously dumped onto a blanket on the hard ground where Pete had dug the bullet out of his back with a skill earned over years of dealing with similar medical emergencies. But Pete had performed the service with undisguised resentment, which did not lessen as he remarked dispassionately, "I ain't never seen nobody bleed as much as this fella and still have a breath left in his body."

"Hell, he'd do us all a favor if he just stopped breathin'!"

Purity shot Buck a reproachful glance that turned his trail-weary face red.

"Don't you look at me like that, young lady!"

"I'm not a *young lady!*"

"That's half the trouble, here!" Buck glared. "You're forgettin' just who and what you are! And as much as you try gettin' everybody else to forget it, too, you're still a woman! I'm the first to admit you can outride and outrope just about any wrangler here, but there's no way you'd be a match for this fella in a fight when he's at full strength! Hell, look at the size of him! He's bigger and packed with more

27

muscle than any Injun I ever seen! But it didn't make no difference to him—not how big he was, or if you was a woman—when he knocked you from your horse for no reason at all and put a knife to your belly!"

"He had no way of tellin' from a distance that I was a woman."

"Oh, really? Then it would've been all right if he'd put a knife to Carter's belly—or Rome's, or mine—instead of yours?"

"I didn't say that!"

"He knew you was a woman as soon as he got close to you, and he didn't back off one bit!"

"I don't want to discuss it."

"And if he got the chance, he'd do the same thing again!"

"I said I don't want to discuss it!"

"You're wastin' your time arguin', you two." Pete's interruption turned all eyes around the campfire toward him as he straightened up beside the Indian's prostrate form. "He ain't goin' to last the night. Hell, he's hardly breathin' now."

Strangely shaken by Pete's comment, Purity strained for control. She supposed she was so affected because she had looked death directly in the eye in a flooded river many years earlier and was incapable of dismissing the specter lightly.

Purity felt Buck studying her. He spoke abruptly.

"All right, what do you want us to do with this Injun for the time bein'?"

Surprised by Buck's unexpected turnabout, Purity instructed, "Put him in the chuck wagon."

"I ain't takin' care of him!" Pete's shoulder-length gray hair flew out almost comically as he shook his head. "Hell, he just might live, and I might wake up one mornin' with my throat cut!"

"He won't be with us long enough to do any damage. We'll drop him off at the first town or Indian agency we pass."

"I already done the best I could for him! We can leave him here. If he lives, he lives. If he don't . . ."

Pete completed his statement with an indifferent shrug. The others standing around the campfire nodded their agreement and Purity was momentarily silent. Cold-blooded? No. There wasn't a man present who hadn't had some kind of personal experience with an Indian rampage in the past. As for herself—Purity touched a hand to the bloody spot on her shirt—she knew firsthand what this particular Indian was capable of.

A chill ran down Purity's spine. Disregarding it, she ordered, "Pick the Indian up and put him in the chuck wagon."

"I ain't takin' care of him, I tell you !"

Ignoring Pete's declaration, Purity swept the men standing around the campfire with an unyielding stare. She spoke three words.

"You heard me."

He felt sick. It hurt to breathe. A fire burned in his back, leaving him so weak that he could not lift his head.

The woman—light eyes, light hair, light skin—*the enemy*.

29

He had followed the tracks.

They led directly to her.

He had asked her what happened.

She did not answer.

The pain surged anew.

He struggled to open his eyes. He saw the interior of a wagon. He glimpsed a night sky. He heard voices at the campfire beyond.

He remembered those voices. . . .

He ain't goin' to last the night. We can leave him here. If he lives, he lives. If he don't . . .

He heard a sound at the rear of the wagon. He closed his eyes.

Someone moved to his side. He heard low grumbling.

"Damned if I know why I'm doin' this. . . ." Then louder, "Open your eyes! You ain't foolin' me. I know you're awake. I brought you some soup I cooked up. You'd better eat it now,'cause I ain't comin' back."

He recognized the voice. *We can leave him here. If he lives, he lives . . .*

He opened his eyes.

"Open your mouth, and do it quick,'cause I'm runnin' out of patience."

He accepted the offering, knowing he must regain his strength. He continued swallowing, despite his weakness.

"Finished it all, huh? Maybe you ain't as weak as I thought." The man's small eyes pinned him. "What's your name, Injun? What tribe are you from?"

He did not respond.

"Don't play dumb with me! I know you understand me. I asked you what your name was."

Silence.

"Damned savage."

Another sound. Another face. The woman.

"What's goin' on here, Pete? I could hear you hollerin'."

"This damned savage . . . He let me feed him, all right, but he won't answer no questions."

"What did you ask him?"

"I asked him his name and I asked him what tribe he was from, so we'd know what to look out for!"

The woman looked at him. She leaned closer.

She spoke.

"What's your name, Indian? Your tribe's Kiowa, isn't it?"

"He won't talk, I tell you!"

Yes, he would talk. He wanted this woman to know his name. He wanted her to remember it.

But his tongue was heavy, his lips stiff. It was hard to speak.

She saw his struggle. She leaned closer.

The tracks had led directly to her.

Hatred burned.

He responded with the last of his waning strength.

"My name . . . Pale Wolf. You will remember. . . ."

Darkness.

His name was Pale Wolf.

And he hated her.

Shaken, Purity drew back from the Indian's side.

"Damned savage! He tries to kill you, you end up

31

savin' his life, and he looks at you like—like he's goin' to make sure he gets you good the next time!" His face hot with anger, Pete continued, "Boss or no boss, I'm givin' the orders now. I want you out of this wagon, and I don't want you comin' back until we drop this Injun off somewheres!"

"Pete, I—"

"Don't say nothin'! Just listen! I saw the way that Injun looked at you. He was picturin' that hair of yours on his scalp pole!"

"Pete, he—"

"You ain't listenin'! This Injun is out for blood— *your* blood! Stan would tar and feather me if I didn't talk some common sense into you, and he'd skin me alive if I let anythin' happen to you. If you won't listen to me, I'm goin' to Buck!"

"You can go to Buck if you want."

"All right, I will!"

"But it isn't necessary."

"What?"

"It isn't necessary to go to Buck, because you were right in everythin' you just said."

"I was?"

Purity saw the wariness in Pete's expression as she continued, "I'll do what you said. I'll stay away from this Indian until we drop him off if you'll make me a promise."

"What kind of promise?"

"If you'll give me your word that you'll take the best care of him you can."

"Why should I if he's out to—"

"Promise me, Pete."

"But—"

"I need to hear you say it."

"All right! I'll take care of him like he's a baby! Now, you get out of here and don't come back 'til we're rid of him!"

Sealing their agreement with a brief nod, Purity slid to the rear of the wagon. She paused for a final, backward look at the unconscious Indian.

Pete was right. For some reason, the Indian hated her. It was for the best.

Night had already fallen when Purity stepped into the doorway of the doctor's office. A long three days filled with tension had passed on the trail with the Indian lingering between life and death, but the herd had reached a town at last. She had spoken to the sheriff and the semi-conscious Pale Wolf had been delivered into the doctor's care. Relieved to be free of him, her drovers had celebrated briefly, then returned to the herd as directed.

Only she remained.

The gaiety of evening rebounded on the street behind Purity, but all was silent within the office as she entered and walked slowly toward the cot where the Indian lay.

The doctor glanced up from his position seated at the desk nearby. "I thought you and your men had left town."

"I wanted to stop back."

Halting at his bedside, Purity stared down at the sleeping Indian. He had refused to speak, revealing nothing more about himself than his name. But there was something about him. . . .

Who was he? Why had he attacked her?

Purity leaned closer. Her gaze trailed Pale Wolf's shoulder-length black hair, stripped free of its headband. She studied his strong, sharply sculpted features. He was thinner than he had been, but the innate power he exuded had not diminished. It was there in the expanse of his shoulders and chest, and in the long, muscular length of his body. She recalled the weight of that body pinning hers, the strength of arms that had jerked her to her feet without effort and held her captive. She recalled that beneath the lids now closed were green eyes that appeared eerily light in contrast with skin of warm russet. She remembered that—

Pale Wolf's eyes opened abruptly. Purity gasped as his hand clamped around her wrist to hold her fast with unexpected strength. She froze as he spoke in a grating whisper.

"You made a mistake." His light eyes pinned her. "You let me live. . . ."

The doctor's step sounded behind her the moment before he jerked her arm from Pale Wolf's grasp.

Free of Pale Wolf's grip, Purity was not free of the chilling promise in his voice as he rasped, "We will meet again."

Chapter One

1882

"It ain't no good, you know."

She didn't like the tone of his voice.

Pausing in the doorway of the ranch house, Purity turned back toward the man seated at the desk behind her. It had been a damned hard morning. It was unusually hot for spring, and she had been up since daybreak. She was tired and sweaty and not up to the discussion she sensed was again about to begin as she surveyed the man's sober, craggy face and voiced the question he was waiting to hear her ask.

"What are you talkin' about, Stan?"

"You know very well what I'm talkin' about." Waving a broad hand across the papers scattered on his desk, Stan Corrigan shrugged. "It ain't no good pretendin'. There's no way around it. No matter what you want to believe, the Circle C ain't goin' to make it through another year."

"Stan, we've been through all this before."

"That's right, we have."

Rolling his wheelchair out from behind the desk, Stan guided it toward her with a skill reluctantly developed after his horse went down in a stampede and he learned he would never walk again. Three years had passed since then, and the pain of that day was with her still—an anguish that often knotted so tightly within that the distress was almost physical. Strong, invincible Stan, the rock on which she had rebuilt her life.

"Are you listenin' to me, Purity?"

"I answer to the name Boots."

"I'll call you what I want! And don't try to change the subject!"

A smile tugged at Purity's lips. Crippled as he was, and ranchbound as he was, Stan was still as sharp as ever and wise to her every ploy. And he hadn't lost his spunk, not by a long shot, which was the reason she couldn't understand his persistent pessimism about the financial status of the ranch.

"Purity . . ."

"All right. Say what you've got to say. I'm listenin'."

Stan paused. In that moment of silence Purity was acutely aware of the changes that these three, difficult years had wrought on his physical appearance. Stan was thinner, and his hair was now totally gray. The wide stretch of his shoulders had rounded, the chest against which she had so often rested her head in consolation had lost its muscular tone, and the strong arms that had granted her protection and comfort over the years now occasionally trembled. But that wasn't the worst of it. The pallor of Stan's skin and the shadows and angles that were new to his pleasant, homely face were beginning to frighten her. Doc Williams said there was nothing to worry about, but—

"I thought you said you was listenin'!"

Purity frowned. "I am."

His skepticism clearly displayed, Stan began slowly, "You know how things was with the ranch when I found you in the river that day when you was a little girl . . ."

"You were just about holdin' on, with the carpet-baggers and all takin' over the land around these parts."

"Right. Well, the truth is, I never did get back on my feet completely." Stan paused again, and then laughed wryly. "It's beginnin' to look more like I never will now, in more ways than one."

"I know about all that, Stan."

"No, you don't." Stan's expression suddenly softened. He motioned to the chair beside him. "Come over here, darlin'. Come sit by me so I can explain." Waiting until she complied, he continued, "I'm not goin' back over everythin' that happened over the years to tell you how we barely made it from one spring to the next without the bank takin' over. It's enough to say that I was just beginnin' to believe we could get ahead of it all when that damned horse of mine fell and put me in this chair."

"But I took over for you!"

"Right. And you did a good job. Hell, there ain't no foreman in Texas who could've done better. But it wasn't enough."

Purity remained silent.

"We was just in too deep. Then that quarantine on our herd cut our profit to the bone. The trail drive last year didn't bring in enough to get us out of the hole we was in." Stan motioned toward the papers piled on the desk behind him. "Those are all bills, Purity, darlin'. It ain't no fault of yours or mine, but there ain't no way we're goin' to get them all paid."

"The bank will extend our credit."

"No. They won't."

"I'll talk to them."

"I already talked to them."

Purity nodded. "They'll listen to me."

A smile tugged at Stan's lips. "You're meanin' Roger Norris will listen to you."

"It's his pa's bank."

"And he's got eyes for you."

Purity unconsciously grimaced. "Yeah."

"Goin' to lead him on to buy us a little more time, are you?"

Purity's clear eyes locked with Stan's. "If I need to."

"What if he wants to marry you?"

"Marry me!"

"Or some such thing."

"I'm not *marryin'* anybody!" Purity shuddered at the thought. "I'm not one of those gigglin', eyelashflutterin', hip-waggin' town women with nothing more important on their minds than the lastest fashion catalogue about to be delivered, or the newest man who came to town! And I'm not about to get a ring put on my finger and let some fella think he's got the right to tell me what to do. Hell, that'd be the same as puttin' a ring through my nose!"

"A woman needs to get married."

"Why?"

"Because . . . because she needs to, in order to have a full life!"

"Who told you that? Some woman somewhere?"

"Nobody had to tell me!"

"*You* never got married."

"I ain't no woman!"

Purity grimaced. "I'm a match for any man in Texas. You said so yourself."

"That don't mean—"

"That means I'm not gettin' married."

"Purity . . . darlin' . . ." Stan took Purity's hand, his gaze sober. "I ain't goin' to last forever, you know."

Purity was suddenly furious. "Don't talk like that!"

Stan held her hand tight. "Your family was all killed in that river." He ignored the negative shake of her head, continuing, "When I go, you'll be all alone. And if I lose the ranch—"

Purity snatched back her hand and stood up on legs that were abruptly trembling. "I'm done talkin'."

Obviously frustrated that he could not stand up as well, Stan snapped, "Well, I ain't!"

"Then you can talk to yourself, because I'm done listenin'!"

"Purity . . ."

"And for your information, I'm goin' to town to see Roger Norris right now. The word is that the price of beef is goin' up, and with the herd we'll be drivin' to market this year, we'll be all right. All we need is a little more time."

"I don't want you doin' that."

"I'm goin'."

Stan's jaw hardened. "That Roger's a sly one. Don't you let him talk you into nothin' you don't want to do."

"Stan . . ."

"Don't 'Stan' me! I seen the way he looks at you, and I don't like it one damned bit!"

"But you would if he put a ring on my finger."

"That's different."

"Is it?"

"You heard me, Purity."

Purity stared at Stan for a long, silent moment, then walked abruptly to the door. Pausing there, she turned back briefly to add, "I told you, my name is Boots."

"No, it ain't!"

Stan gave a grunt of disgust, realizing that he had shouted his response to a closed door. He paused, listening to Purity's gruff commands to the hands outside. He heard Carter and Rome respond, and he knew they'd waste no time doing what she told them to do. Besides the fact that she was considered the boss's daughter, there wasn't a man on the Circle C who didn't respect her enough on merit alone to follow any order she gave him.

And there were also some who fancied her.

Stan unconsciously shrugged. Hell, why not? Purity was a beautiful woman, even if she'd go to her death denying it.

Stan sat back in his chair. He remembered the day he'd pulled her from the river years earlier. He hadn't realized it then, but that was the luckiest day of his life.

His throat tightening as it often did of late when memories assaulted him, Stan recalled the first weeks after the beautiful gray-eyed little girl entered his life in such an unusual way. He remembered his growing attachment to her on that drive, and the tension that knotted his stomach each time they reached a new trail town and asked if someone had inquired about a lost child. And he recollected with a tinge of shame his silent relief each time the response was negative. When the time came to make a conscious choice whether he would keep little Purity Buchanan or give her up, he found that the decision had already been made for him.

That had been Purity's name—Purity Buchanan. It occurred to him that she probably hardly remembered it now. In looking back, he supposed it wasn't exactly right for him to let her take his name without any legal proceedings, but it had all come about so naturally. And the truth was that he had been proud to have her use his name, with her being so pretty and all, with her attaching herself to him the way she did . . .

. . . and with him finally admitting to himself that

he couldn't love her more if she was his own flesh and blood.

But it hadn't all been easy! Once the fear and the memories drifted from her mind, the spirited, mischievous side of little Purity emerged. Smart as a whip and stubborn as a mule, she had both amused and delighted him, while almost driving him to distraction when she set her mind to something—as she did when she adopted the name Boots.

Boots—hell! He'd never heard a more stupid name!

No more than nine years old, lacking in confidence, and trying desperately to be "one of the boys," Purity had taken a transient wrangler's ridicule seriously when he said her name made her sound like a "sissy." Stan still cursed the day shortly afterward when Purity was strutting around in a pair of hand-tooled boots he had bought for her birthday and someone jokingly called her "Boots."

She had insisted upon being called "Boots" from that day on.

Stan sighed. He supposed things might be different right now if he had married. Purity might have been different with a female to influence her. She might not have been determined to discard her femininity and prove she could best any wrangler on the ranch. She might let herself think about marrying instead of insisting she would make her way on her own. And despite his growing premonition that his days were numbered, he might even be sitting in his wheelchair now with his mind at rest, knowing Purity would have a husband to take care of her when he, and possibly the ranch, were gone.

But he hadn't married.

And his mind wasn't at rest.

There was only one reality that gave him hope. Despite the male clothing she chose to wear, the truth was that if Purity looked any more of a woman than she did now, it might be downright *dangerous*.

A smile picked at Stan's lips.

Purity—a dangerous virtue. Now that was a thought!

Stan's smile became full-fledged. Purity did not realize, however, that she had outsmarted herself! Her determination to look like one of the boys had backfired. The boys' clothing she had adopted as a child had served her purpose well then, but the male clothing she wore now had an effect that was totally opposite the one she strove to achieve.

Granted, Purity's figure wasn't fashionable by the standards of the day. She was too tall for a woman, standing at least seven or eight inches over the mark of five feet, he was sure. And to some minds, she was too slim and firmly muscled. But he knew damned well that the sight of her long, slender legs and rear end in tight pants had near to snapped the neck of many a man. And the baggy shirts she wore to conceal a generous bosom unhampered by any corset were equally distracting. Then there was Purity's hair, her only concession to femininity. She kept the long, silver-blond locks confined in a braid at most times, but the severe style only served to call attention to her delicate features and flawless skin, and to a rare smile capable of breaking a man's heart.

It concerned him that Purity was a more formidable woman than she realized. She made the mistake of discounting the fact that men would be drawn to her without her even trying.

Among their own wranglers, young Nash Carter was proof of that. As was not-so-young Jake Baird.

Stan scowled. Purity was on her way to talk to Roger Norris. As handsome as the fellow was, and as successful as he was rumored to be with the ladies, there was only one woman that fellow really wanted. But Stan wondered if marriage entered these fantasies he saw dancing in Norris's eyes whenever he looked at Purity. He had already determined that, crippled or not, he'd find his way to town to set the fellow straight if the situation demanded.

Stan squared his shoulders, taking a moment to draw his concerns under control. Purity was sure she could handle young Norris. Maybe she could. Maybe she'd return from town in a couple of hours and tell him that their loan would be extended again. She was too smart to let Norris talk her into anything. Besides, he had warned her about the banker's son, and if he knew her as well as he thought he did, his warning was now ringing inside her head.

Damn, he wished he could see Norris's reaction when Purity walked through his office door.

Purity stood in the doorway of the First Citizens Bank, pausing to gather her thoughts. The sunlight of mid-morning baked the rutted main street behind her as she scanned the interior of the formal estab-

lishment. She noted that there were only two customers at the tellers' windows and that Walter
Graham, the senior clerk, was busy at work behind
his desk.

She glanced at the clock on the far wall. Ten-thirty.
She would have ample time to talk to Roger before
lunch. That was important. Had she arrived later,
Roger would have had the excuse to invite her to eat
with him, which would allow him to put the business
discussion on a more personal level. She intended to
avoid that possibility. She needed to save that edge
as a last resort.

Suddenly acutely aware of her appearance, Purity
lifted her hat from her head and wiped the perspiration from her forehead. Nobody had to tell her how
she looked. It hadn't occurred to her to change from
the work clothes she had donned that morning when
she started for town. Still clothed in the faded shirt
and worn pants that were her usual attire, she was
aware that the long ride to town in the unusual
morning heat had left the fabric clinging uncomfortably to her moist skin, and that she probably appeared totally trail-weary.

Three years of running the ranch had freed her of
the thought that she needed to dress like a man in
order to be treated as an equal in a man's world.
Rather, she now dressed as she did for comfort and
ease in her work. She did not own a dress. She had
no use for one.

But she knew this situation was different.

Purity frowned. Stan had said that Roger had an
eye for her. She knew he did—an eye that followed

her wherever she went when she was in town—and she was puzzled by it. She had never encouraged him. She knew he was considered the most eligible bachelor in the county and that every woman with an unmarried daughter looked at him with a gleam in her eye. She had been truly shocked to realize that Stan had joined that avid brigade. She had thought he knew better!

All the same, she knew Roger wanted to pique her interest in him. That was fine. She was prepared to present a forceful argument for the extension of Stan's loan, but if reasoning didn't work, she would make use of Roger's attraction to her.

She owed Stan that much, and a lot more. For that reason, she supposed she should have given more thought to her appearance.

An interior office door opened abruptly and Purity silently cursed. It was too late to worry about the way she looked now.

"Purity Corrigan!" Roger Norris approached with obvious pleasure. He was immaculately tailored and dressed, his brown hair and fine mustache trimmed to perfection. His appearance contrasted sharply with her own present untidiness, a fact of which he appeared totally unconscious as he took her hand. "I haven't seen you in town in weeks. I hope you were intending to come in and say hello."

"As a matter of fact, it was you I came here to see," Purity replied.

"Really!"

Damned if she couldn't see Roger's mind racing! She forced a smile. "That's what I said."

"Let's go directly to my office then." Roger took her arm. His palm was warm as he cupped her elbow and urged her forward. The desire to shake her arm free of his grip was almost overwhelming—but she didn't.

Her first concession.

Purity gritted her teeth. This was going to be harder than she'd thought.

She was smiling.

Roger almost laughed aloud, recalling the countless times he had attempted to elicit a smile from Purity Corrigan and failed . . . the innumerable occasions he had attempted to engage her in pleasant conversation, only to be rebuffed . . . the endless hours he had spent at his window, watching the street when he knew she was in town, waiting for an opportunity to approach her.

She was looking at him now. She was wondering what he was thinking. She removed her hat, exposing pale hair that was a paler gold than the heart-shaped locket she wore at her throat. Her skin was even smoother and clearer up close, her eyes almost translucent. Her clothing was dampened with perspiration. Her shirt clung to her body in a way that sent the heat within him soaring. Almost his match in height, she had an aura about her, a power, a womanliness beyond common female affectations that clawed at his innards like a rake.

He had never wanted any woman more.

He seated her and sat beside her. He spoke in his most sincere tone.

"How may I help you, Purity?"

He watched her lips as she spoke, fascinated by them as she replied, "It's about Stan's loan."

Feigning ignorance, Roger repeated, "Stan's loan?"

"Your father decided against extendin' it."

"Oh, did he? I hadn't realized that. Father decided against extending a number of loans. It was purely a business decision."

"I wanted to talk to you about that. I have new market information from one of the newspapers back East. The price of beef is expected to go up, and things are lookin' better than ever for the fall drive. I hoped I could make you see that the Circle C just needs a little more time. Do you suppose you could talk to your father on Stan's behalf?"

Roger suppressed a smile. Purity Corrigan was actually soliciting his help! Realizing that he could not allow the opportunity to escape him, he pressed his advantage.

"Do you mind if I ask you why you came to me instead of going directly to my father with this new information?"

"I came to you because I thought you'd be more willin' to listen to what I had to say."

"Why did you think I would be more willing to listen than my father?"

It was obvious that he had caught Purity off guard. She had not expected such a direct question. He saw the battle that went on behind her clear eyes. He saw them changing. He recognized the moment when she cast all attempt at pretense aside to speak with unexpected candor.

"I knew you wanted to get to know me better. I thought you'd consider this a good opportunity."

Silence.

"What are you proposing?"

"I know it'll be hard to convince your father to extend Stan's loan, and I know you'd be doin' both Stan and me a real favor if you'd try. I haven't had time for anythin' other than work in the past, but if you decided to help us, I'd expect to show my appreciation by makin' time for us to get better acquainted."

Suddenly aware that the wrong word would put Purity beyond his reach forever, Roger responded cautiously.

"Are you making me *an offer*, Purity?"

"I'm not about to sell myself to any man, if that's what you're thinkin'." Her gaze did not waver. "I meant exactly what I said."

"No promises."

"No promises."

A slow anger swelled inside Roger. The temerity of the long-legged witch! Looking him straight in the eye, she had coldly informed him that she knew he wanted her, and she had then offered him a bold bargain that was lopsided at best! Yet, it was obvious that she thought he wouldn't be able to refuse her!

Roger held her gaze. He should teach her a lesson! He should tell her he could have any woman in town he wanted. He should tell her he *had had* any woman in town he wanted.

Yes, he should do that!

But he wouldn't.

Because the beauteous witch also knew there was only one woman he *really* wanted.

With that silent admission, Roger responded in the only way he could.

"This new information . . . tell me all about it."

Purity smiled. Did she know how hard his heart was pounding?

He would put a passion in her smile that matched his own, damn her! He would, if it was the last thing he ever did!

The evening meal had been uncomfortably quiet. Purity had returned from town in the early afternoon, her disposition foul. She had gone straight to the branding corral and had snapped at the men in a way that was unlike her. The supper table had been silent as a result, with one wrangler after another getting up and leaving as soon as his plate was emptied. She was ashamed of her behavior and aware that she owed each of those decent, hardworking men a sincere apology. She was not looking forward to it.

Looking up as Pete entered the dining room, Purity prepared herself for the disapproval she would see on the aging cook's face when he picked up her barely touched plate.

True to her expectation, Pete darted her a fulminating glance.

"I wasn't hungry, Pete."

"You should be hungry."

"Maybe, but I wasn't."

Pete did not bother to reply, leaving Purity to the mercy of Stan's somber stare. She knew what was coming.

"Are you ready to talk now?"

Purity sat back stiffly in her chair.

"I asked you, are you ready to talk?"

"I heard you the first time."

"Well?"

"There's not much to say."

"I'd say there is, damn it!" His face flushing a deep red, Stan exploded, "What in hell went on between you and Roger Norris this mornin'? You came back growlin' like a bear and near to bit the head off everybody you looked at!"

"Yeah, I know."

"Well?"

"Well, what?"

"What happened?"

"We had a long discussion." She unconsciously grimaced. "We went to Maude's Place and had somethin' to eat."

"You did."

She nodded.

"And . . ."

"And what?"

"Did he say he'd help us or didn't he?"

"He's goin' to try."

Silence.

The second explosion wasn't long in coming.

"All right! What did it cost you?"

"What do you mean, what did it cost me?"

"I meant exactly what I said! What kind of a deal

51

did you make with that sidewinder to put you in such a snit?"

"A snit . . ."

"Purity . . ."

"All right!" Despite herself, Purity could feel her face flaming. "I told Roger that if he talked to his father and got the loan extended, I'd make time for him and me to get to know each other better."

"*You'd make time* for you two to get to know each other better?"

Purity nodded again.

"Yeah . . . and what else?"

"That's it."

"That's it?"

"That's what I said!" Unable to bear more, Purity jumped to her feet. "No promises . . . just gettin' to know each other better."

Stan's stiff face twitched. "I guess I don't have to ask you how you feel about that bargain."

"I think it's fine . . . fair."

"No, it ain't."

"It is."

"The hell it is! The thought of havin' Roger Norris out visitin' and fawnin' over you—or whatever else he has in mind—is makin' you so sick you can't eat!"

"That isn't true."

"Go to bed, Purity."

"It's early."

"You look like you're about to drop. Do what I said."

Purity nodded. Strangely, she didn't have the strength to argue.

Climbing into bed minutes later, unwilling to let herself think, Purity forced herself to sleep.

He didn't have the strength—or maybe the heart—to move.

Stan rubbed a weary hand over his face. The dining room table had been cleared of the evening meal and reset for the following morning, all without a word being exchanged between Pete and him. Even the clanging of pans in the kitchen had stopped, indicating that Pete had finished his chores there and had probably left for the bunkhouse.

Stan glanced at the wall clock. It was close to nine. Purity was most likely asleep by now. The boys would doubtless be in their bunks soon, too. And if he knew them as well as he thought he did, they'd be relieved to be free of the silence that had probably prevailed even after they had left the table. He'd bet his life that despite their anger at Purity's short temper, there wasn't a one of them who would suffer a word spoken against her.

An annoying moistness crept into Stan's eyes. The truth was that each and every one of his hands had a true affection for Purity. Most of them had watched her grow up and had seen her struggle to pull her own weight on the ranch without concessions being made for the fact that she was female. After he was crippled, they had taken Purity's orders out of regard for him, because they knew he wanted it that way, but she had earned their respect a day at a time. He knew they were almost as proud of her and what she had achieved as he was. And although it might rile Purity if he said it aloud, he knew that despite her independence and ability, the men felt protective of her. He was glad of that. He depended on it.

Which all boiled down to the fact that his wranglers hadn't deserved the way Purity had acted toward them that afternoon. They knew it and Purity knew it. And they were all miserable because of it.

Hell!

Stan slammed the flat of his hand down on the table in front of him. It was all because he couldn't get out of the damned chair he was sitting in! He never should have laid the burden of his debt on the shoulders of a seventeen-year-old! And now, three years later, it was even more unreasonable for either Purity or him to expect her to get the ranch out of the trouble it was in!

Stan ran a weary hand through his heavy gray hair, unconsciously shaking his head. He should never have let Purity go to town to talk to Roger Norris. That fella looked at her like she was some kind of pastry that he was dying to sink his teeth into! Stan supposed he had hoped that by some miracle, Purity might actually take a liking to Roger once she spent some time talking to him. One look at her face when she came home, however, had blasted that prospect to blazes.

Making an abrupt decision, Stan turned his chair and wheeled himself toward the living room and the large, bill-laden desk in the corner. He took only a moment to stare at the papers piled there before pushing them aside and drawing a sheet of writing paper from the middle drawer. It galled him that his hand shook as he picked up the pen and dipped it in the inkwell. Realizing there was nothing else he could do, he forced himself to control its trembling and started to write.

Purity awakened with a start. She glanced anxiously around her room, fighting to expel the last shadows of an anxious dream she could not quite remember. Her composure gradually returned as she gazed at the familiar wallpaper with faded blue flowers; the mirrored dresser covered with personal incidentals; the washstand with a white, chipped pitcher; and the wall rack where her few articles of spare clothing hung in clear view.

It occurred to Purity that she had few personal possessions that she truly valued. There was the first pair of hand-tooled boots that Stan had given her, which she stored in a chest under the bed. They had been the most beautiful boots she had ever seen. She took them out to look at occasionally, and they never failed to make her smile. They were so small. She was certain Stan didn't know she still had them or that she was somehow unable to part with them.

Also stored in the chest under her bed was the red ribbon from a box of candy that the boys had given her for her last birthday. The candy had come directly from St. Louis, and it had tasted better than anything she had ever eaten. She suspected the reason was because it had come from them.

Then there was the gun and gunbelt, also hand-tooled, which Stan had given her on her sixteenth birthday. She remembered she had not been able to take her eyes off it once she had seen it in the gunsmith's shop. She had never expected it would be hers one day.

And, of course . . .

Purity reached for the locket that rested at the hollow of her throat. It was gold, small and heartshaped, and she treasured it more than anything she owned. It was all she had left of the family that had been swept away in the river that day so long ago.

Purity strained to recall the faded images of her family, a smile gradually growing. Her mother's name was Justine, and she had been fair and blonde, like Purity. Her father's name was Clay, and his hair had been a deep red. Strangely, all she could clearly remember about her mother was that her mother's hand had been cool and comforting when it smoothed away her tears, and that it had seemed to brush away the fever burning her. As for her father, she recalled his smile most clearly, and the sound of his deep voice saying her name.

But she remembered her sisters well. Honesty was dark-haired, the oldest, the prettiest, and also the *bossiest*. She had come next in age, her blond hair the palest of the three. Chastity, with curly red hair like Papa's, was the youngest in the family. She recalled that she had longed desperately to have hair the color of Chastity's, and that she always suspected Honesty did, too.

Purity unconsciously stroked her locket. Papa had given each of "his girls" a similar locket. She remembered how proud she'd been to wear it; it made her feel special in a way she could not quite describe. She recalled that the last thing her father had said to her was that her mother would be driving the wagon when they crossed the river, but she shouldn't be afraid because Honesty was the oldest and she would take care of Chastity and her. She had never told anyone, not even Stan, but she was convinced her locket would one day lead her back to the sisters she had lost.

The heat of tears unexpectedly warmed Purity's eyes, but she brushed them away with annoyance. She was long past tears. They accomplished nothing, and she would not allow them. Instead, she had found a secret consolation as she had grown. When troubled in the silence of the night, she held her locket and talked to her sisters. She was certain they were alive somewhere and that they heard her somehow and knew she was thinking of them.

Purity sighed. Did they hear her now? If Honesty were she, what would she do if she knew the ranch was threatened . . . if she knew that Stan had no one but her to help him . . . if she knew there was only one way to get Stan the time he needed?

Honesty's youthful, determined face flashed before Purity's mind, and Purity had her answer.

Honesty would do whatever she had to do.

And so would she.

Purity forced her eyes closed.

But no wedding ring, damn it! Not ever!

The remembered mists of the sweatbath again swirled in Pale Wolf's mind. They glowed with the colors of the painted sky overhead, tinted by the shafts of golden sunlight beating down on his bared head. His heavy, unbound hair lay wetly against his scalp. Each strand scalded him, reminding him of the power he solicited. Sweat dripped from his temples in streams. It beaded his skin, enveloping him in moisture. The heat consumed his thoughts, his flesh, leaving only the seeking spirit.

Pale Wolf opened his eyes to observe the hilltop of power where he sat, the place where the omen had led him for his quest. Daylight had vanished, leaving only night. The sun—life-giver—had turned its back upon the world below. It had cast all into darkness, leaving only a pale globe in its stead, a shadow of its power to dominate the darkened sky.

Shafts of silver luminescence touched Pale Wolf's skin, cooling him. He beheld lights in the sky above him. They blinked as they sought to raise the darkness, but he knew that they could not. He looked up, awaiting the dawn, recalling the three dawns already spent in this same prayerful posture. He beseeched the light, remembering the smoke and the fasting that had purified him for his holy quest. He raised his hands in supplication, recollecting the songs he had sung to the spirit above as he awaited the visions that had not yet appeared.

He would wait. He would pray. He would smoke. He would fast . . . for his need was great. His physical wound had healed—a deep wound, a cruel wound—but his spirit had not. His direction was not clear.

He saw it then, a vision distinct against the night

sky! A woman with hair so gold, with skin so fair, with eyes so clear! He saw blood flow around her, and he knew it was not his own. He felt a cry rise within him as he sought to stem its flow, but it was too late!

Blood spilled, never to be recovered.

The vision drew nearer.

The woman's face grew clearer.

He recognized her.

Light hair, light eyes, light skin . . . the enemy.

And he knew what he must do.

Chapter Two

"Damn, how did it get so late?"

Jack Thomas glanced at the horizon, still muttering under his breath. The sun was setting in a glorious display of red and gold that was an integral part of the day in north Texas. The beauty of the sunset was far from his mind, however, as he called out to the men nearby.

"All right, boys, gather up the rest of those critters and get them movin' or we'll lose half of them in the dark before we get to the corral!"

Grunts of acknowledgement sounded from all sides of the herd. They didn't have far to go. The corral they had set up was just over the rise, and this was the last of the calves in the area to be driven there. They would cut out the cows and start branding tomorrow.

Relieved when the corral fence came into view, Jack halted. He knew no further orders would be necessary when Cass's familiar, broad-shouldered figure moved into sight. Slipping the corral gate free of its closure, his son swung it open, shouting, "You heard the boss, boys! Get those cattle in there!"

Jack watched as the gate finally swung closed. He felt suddenly weary. He snapped to attention at the sound of Cass's deep voice by his shoulder.

"We can start the branding tomorrow." Scrutinizing him too closely for comfort, Cass added, "It's a good thing we're heading home. You look like you could stand a good meal."

Aware that there was not a trace of fatigue in his son's bearing, Jack attempted a smile. "I've never had a day in my life when I wasn't ready for a good meal, and this day's no exception." He kicked his mount forward, calling over his shoulder, "Come on. Julia's waitin', and so are those apple pies I saw her puttin' together this mornin'."

Riding beside him minutes later as the men fell in behind, Cass did not bother with preamble.

"What's wrong, Jack?"

Jack.

Jack could pinpoint to the day the last time Cass had called him Pa. It was the day he married Julia, when Cass was eight. Losing his mother so young—and so tragically—had left his son an angry boy ready to battle the world, a boy unwilling to accept Julia in his mother's stead three years later.

A sardonic smile pulled at Jack's lips. He had voiced no objection to his son's use of his given name that first day, despite his initial anger. He had been certain that Cass would eventually accept the situation and everything would return to the way it had been. But he was wrong. He had gradually come to realize that by marrying Julia he had forced Cass to the premature realization that his father had a life separate from his own.

Cass's childhood had ended that day. Jack knew that now. Julia had eventually won Cass over, but his own regrets were many—not for having married Julia, who had never wavered in her determination to provide the home and love that had been stolen so precipitously from both him and his son, but for his lack of understanding when his son had needed understanding so badly.

"Jack?"

Snapped back to the present as Cass pressed for a response he was not yet ready to give, Jack replied with unintended sharpness.

"What makes you think anythin's wrong?"

"So, you don't want to talk about it."

"I said, nothin's wrong!"

Cass's stare did not waver.

"Damn it all, doesn't a man have a right to private thoughts once in a while?"

Spurring his mount forward again, Jack left his frowning son behind him.

Purity sat her mare easily, despite the long day spent in the saddle. She allowed her gaze to roam the south Texas range around her as she followed the familiar trail home. The new green of the grass was already darkening, and the former, glorious display of bluebonnets and wild mustard now only tinted the landscape. Spring had settled firmly onto the land and summer would soon sear its way across the landscape in the march of seasons that never failed to exhilarate her. Oh, yes, she loved this land—this beautiful, debt-ridden ranch whose future was still in question.

A burst of laughter from the wranglers riding beside her turned Purity toward Nash Carter. She smiled, seeing that his boyish features were flushed and drawn into a scowl. The men were teasing him again. She wondered if Carter realized that most of the fellas teased him because they were envious of his youth and good looks, and of the attention he received from the ladies in town every time he showed his face. She supposed the men all wished they were Carter, who, despite his proven dependability, was always ready for a good time and who was young enough to go in any direction he was inclined to take. She supposed that to an extent, she envied Carter, too.

Purity sighed. It was damned hard being female. She couldn't count the times she had gone to town, yearning to follow the boys into the nearest saloon to wash the heat of the day from her throat with a cold beer and enjoy the easy camaraderie they took so much for granted. It galled her that although she had earned that diversion as much as they, she couldn't take advantage of it, simply because Stan said the saloon was no place for her. She recalled the shouting matches that had resulted when she challenged him, always ending with her declaration that she would do as she damned well pleased! But, somehow, she never did.

Protective Stan, loving Stan, always watching out for her. . . . She was fully grown and was running the ranch, but nothing had really changed. The reason was simple. She loved Stan too much to add to his feeling of impotence by disregarding his wishes now that he was helpless.

Yes, it was tough being female.

It was almost as tough as apologizing.

A few weeks had passed since the morning she had visited the bank and returned in such a foul mood. She had apologized to the men for her behavior that day, silently determining not to repeat that mistake . . . but it hadn't been easy.

The reason was Roger Norris.

Purity withheld a groan. To her dismay, Roger had taken to visiting her several times a week since their talk. The men were snickering, Stan was growling, and her disposition was suffering—all to little avail since the matter of Stan's loan at the bank had not yet been resolved.

Purity fought to subdue her frustration. Were she of a suspicious mind, she might believe that Roger was buying himself time by holding the loan over her head, but she knew that couldn't be true. He couldn't possibly sink so low. Besides, she knew Willard Norris's reputation. He allowed no one and nothing to get in the way of his bank's security. It was a measure of Roger's effort in Stan's behalf that he had managed to convince his father even to consider the loan's renewal.

". . . and we was thinkin' you might want to join in."

Suddenly aware that Carter was talking to her, Purity looked at him questioningly.

Carter repeated, "I said, some of the boys are gettin' up a card game after supper. I was thinkin' you might want to join in."

"Well . . ." Pleased at the invitation, Purity smiled. "That sounds like a good idea to me."

Treacher snickered. "What about you, Baird? You goin' to be playin', too?"

"That's none of your damned business!"

Treacher pressed, "I figured with the way things are, you wouldn't want Carter gettin' ahead of you."

Baird's face reddened. "I'd shut my mouth if I was you, Treacher!"

Purity was suddenly angry. Damn that Treacher! He wouldn't be saying anything about a simple, friendly invitation if she was a man!

The ranch house came into view over the rise, and Purity's thoughts came to an abrupt halt. She stared at the chestnut gelding tied to the hitching rail in front, hearing as if from a distance the mumbled comments around her.

"Oh . . . looks like Purity's got company."

"He's here *again?*"

"He sure is . . ."

"Looks like there'll be one less at the poker game tonight."

"Too bad, Carter."

"Shut up, Treacher!"

Purity closed her eyes.

Yeah, shut up, Treacher!

And go home, Roger!

Damn, it was hard being female!

The whir of a nighthawk's wings momentarily distracted Cass as he squinted into darkness alleviated only by the pale light of a quarter moon. The shadows of the trees undulated gently in the evening breeze, drawing his attention to his father's silhouette where he stood motionless amongst them.

As silent and stationary as a statue, Jack had been standing in that same spot since he'd left the supper table. He had not touched his apple pie. That had been a dead giveaway. Despite Jack's denials, something *was* wrong.

"You're not about to give it up, are you?"

Jack's unexpected question broke into Cass's thoughts. Approaching his father, Cass responded, "That's right, I'm not."

The lines of strain on Jack's face became clearly visible despite the shadows as he neared. The lines tightened as Cass halted beside him and Jack reached into his pocket to withdraw a sheet of paper.

"Well, I suppose it's time to lay it all out for you, now that I've made my decision." Jack paused. "I received this letter yesterday."

Jack clenched the sheet tightly as he continued. "It's from an old acquaintance I haven't seen or heard from in more than fifteen years. He's in trouble. He needs my help."

"You haven't heard from this 'old acquaintance' for fifteen years, but he's asking for your help?"

"Right."

"And it upsets you."

"It does."

"Why?"

"Old memories."

"Old memories . . ."

"We were in the war together." Jack's wiry brows knitted in a frown. "Hell, we fought side by side, watchin' the fellas around us drop one by one until there was only the two of us left!"

"You were friends."

"No, we weren't. We couldn't be. Your ma had come between us years earlier." Jack paused, suddenly exploding. "I could never understand why your ma chose me over him! He was bigger and better lookin' than I was! He had one of the best ranches in South Texas. Everybody was impressed with him, includin' your grandfather. I was just beginnin' to build my spread, and I didn't have much to offer for your ma's love. I suppose that was what made me so jealous. I was afraid he might convince her to change her mind about me one day. I knew he'd never change his mind about her. That was the kind of man he was."

Jack's growing distress was obvious as he continued. "I suppose that's what grates on me. He never married. It says so in this letter. That shames me because I won the woman we both loved, and when I lost her, I just went out and found somebody else."

The torment was old, but Jack would not let it die.

Cass offered the only words of comfort possible. "Julia's a good woman."

"I know that."

"She loves you."

"I know that, too, but—"

Cass interrupted, purposely changing the subject. "So, what are you going to do? Are you going to help him?"

"I don't see as I have much choice. He saved my life."

"What does he want?"

"He wants to see me . . . right away."

"Now?" Cass's dark brows rose with surprise. "He should know this is a bad time of year to break away."

"He does. That's why I know this request is urgent. He's got a lot of pride. He wouldn't ask for my help, especially now, if he wasn't desperate."

"But—"

"I'm goin'."

Cass did not respond.

"And I want you to come with me."

"I think I should stay here and keep an eye on things. You can take Powers with you."

"No. I want you to come with me."

"Why?"

"Because . . . you're my son."

The unexpected emotion in Jack's simple response filled the ensuing silence. The words resounded strangely within Cass. The reverberations reached a cold, untouchable well within him that left him powerless against the only response he could give.

* * *

There was no doubt about it. Roger Norris was a handsome man. There was also no doubt that she couldn't stand much more of him.

The pale light of the moon lit the path in front of them as Purity walked beside Roger, maintaining as much distance as she dared between them. A few hours earlier, she had greeted Roger with strained warmth and invited him to dinner, despite Stan's glaring looks. She had hoped against hope that Roger had come to tell her that his father had decided to extend Stan's loan. She had even hoped for a moment that Roger's father had decided *not* to extend the loan, just so she would be free of their agreement.

But a decision had not been reached.

Oh, she was so tempted. . . . Were so much not at stake, she knew she would tell Roger that she had neither the time nor the patience to continue this farce. The truth was that she had done her best to discourage him without being obvious. Certainly no woman could look less appealing than she did right now. She had been grimy and disheveled upon returning from the day's work. Pausing only to wash the dirt of the trail from her face, she had not even bothered to tidy her braid before she came to the table.

But Roger just kept on smiling.

Damn it all, *how* could he look at her that way? Her clothes were work-stained, she smelled like a horse, and she looked no better than the six other wranglers seated around the table! And *why* couldn't he dispense with all the silly pleasantries she so despised and tell her straight out what it would take to convince his father to extend that damned loan!

They had been walking for a distance when they reached the stream where she had played as a child. She had loved the spot for the privacy it afforded, for the whisper of the trees that shaded its banks, shielding her from sight and enabling her to indulge in childish games. But the trees were silent tonight in the absence of a breeze, and the spot somehow lost its charm in her present company.

Purity noticed the twitch of Roger's jaw and the subtle shift of his eyes and realized he was angry, more angry than he wanted to reveal.

"You haven't heard a word I've said, have you, Purity?"

"What?" Purity's smile weakened. "I . . . I guess my mind was wanderin'."

"Why don't you say what you're thinking?"

"What I'm thinkin'?"

Roger's expression turned suddenly venomous. "I'm damned sick of this game you're playing! If you're that disinterested in what I have to say, just tell me what it'll take for me to get what I want and I'll go away!"

Startled into speechlessness by Roger's unexpected anger, Purity did not respond. Infuriated by her silence, he grasped her arms and shook her roughly. "Do you want me to say it straight out? All right, I will! I want you, Purity. And I want you to want me back. But you don't want me, do you? You don't want any damned part of me!"

"Let me go, Roger."

"Tell me what it'll take to make you want me!"

"I said, *let me go.*"

"Not until I'm ready!"

Purity felt a hot flush rising. Roger's hands were bruising her upper arms, and her patience was growing short.

She grated, "You're makin' a mistake, Roger."

"Am I?" Roger's voice dropped to a low snarl, "Yes, maybe I am. Maybe you aren't interested in me because you're the kind of female who finds women more appealing than men . . ."

"I'm warning you . . ."

". . . but I don't think so. I think I've been taking it too slow and you've grown impatient. Well, the waiting is over."

Jerking her up against him in an unexpected embrace, Roger ground his mouth cruelly into hers. His thrusting tongue separated her lips with passionate fervor, almost gagging her as his seeking hands sought her breasts. Disgust rose up in her and Purity shoved hard against his chest, forcing him a step back as she spat, "Go home, Roger! And don't come back!"

"Oh, no! You're not getting away that easily!"

Her pale eyes bright with fury, Purity warned, "I'm not one of your little town floozies who'll swoon at your feet! If I didn't feel partially to blame for this . . . if I didn't think I might've led you on by askin' for your help the way I did, I wouldn't even bother talkin' right now. So I'm goin' to make everythin' perfectly clear, once and for all. Gettin' Stan's loan extended isn't worth the price you're askin'."

"It isn't about money, Purity."

"Yes, it is. It always was for me. If I made you think anythin' else, I'm sorry."

"Apologies are cheap!"

Purity tensed. "Maybe so, but an apology is all you're goin' to get from me."

"That's where you're wrong!"

Roger's sudden blow was unexpected. Staggering backward, Purity fought her spinning vision, refusing to surrender to the throbbing pain in her jaw as she struggled to square her stance. Her fists were clenched and she was prepared to meet him head on when a voice grated from the shadows, "Get away from her, Norris! Now! I won't warn you again."

Purity turned toward the familiar voice, suddenly furious. "Stay out of this, Buck! He caught me off guard, that's all. I'll show him he's not dealin' with one of those town hussies who's afraid to fight back!"

Roger's sudden move toward Purity was halted by the ominous click of the hammer on Buck's gun.

"All right, you win!" Roger took a step back, and then turned hotly toward Purity. "I'll leave, and I won't come back if that's what you want. That *is* what you want, isn't it, Purity?" He gave a short laugh. "You also want Stan's loan extended, don't you? Well, there's not much chance of that now." He paused, adding with a sneer, "But then again, things could change . . . depending on what you're prepared to offer the *next* time you come begging."

"You're on borrowed time, Norris!" Buck advanced into clear view, his expression threatening. "Get out of here, fast!"

"I have one more thing to say."

"Another word," Buck warned, "may be your last."

Buck's trigger finger twitched, and Purity gasped. The draining of Roger's color was apparent even in the limited light as he turned abruptly and started back toward the ranch house.

Releasing her breath, Purity rasped, "Buck, you—"

"If Stan knew what just happened here, wheelchair or not, he'd shoot that fella dead!"

"I know."

"And if Norris ever comes near you again, I'll kill him myself."

Her eyes cold, Purity responded through stiff lips. "Don't worry about that—and don't worry about me, either. I appreciate your help, but I could've handled that bastard myself!" Her fists again tightening, she added, "And if there is a next time . . . I *will*."

"Purity . . ."

Disregarding the warning in Buck's voice, Purity stomped off into the darkness.

Jack's expression was rigid. "I have to go, Julia. I owe it to the man."

Standing in the living room as night sounds echoed in the shadows beyond the ranch house door, Julia glanced between Jack and Cass. The concerned knit of her graying brows revealed her surprised dismay at Jack's unexpected announcement that they would both be leaving at a time when every hand was needed at the ranch.

She knew what that meant.

A strange realization flashed through her mind. Despite fading hair and maturing proportions, she had changed very little over the years. Inside, she was still the only child of an itinerant preacher who had never lived in one place for any longer than six months at a time. She was still the daughter who had accepted spinsterhood with grace, expecting to spend her life supporting her father's vocation. She was still the lonely woman who'd fallen so unexpectedly and hopelessly in love with a widower and his angry young son that she burned her bridges behind her by marrying against her father's wishes—her father, whom she had not seen or heard from since that day so many years ago.

Did she have regrets?

She supposed she had some. Her thoughts had often returned to her father over the years, and it still pained her that she had not been able to bear Jack a child. And during the dark hours of the night, her silent sorrow was her certainty that although Jack loved her in his way, he would never love her with the passion that he had given his first wife, the woman he still—

Refusing to allow her mind to finish that thought, Julia asked instead, "When will you leave?"

"Tomorrow."

No, she didn't want him to leave so soon . . . especially not now.

Jack's response turned Julia toward Cass. The angry child had become a handsome man who stirred in her a maternal pride. Cass touched her arm lightly

74

in an instinctive gesture he had used since childhood when she was distressed. The warmth that simple gesture evoked brought the heat of tears briefly to her eyes as he addressed her softly.

"This is important to Jack, Julia. You don't have to worry about him. I'll take care of him, and the boys will take care of you while Jack and I are gone. They'll have to answer to me if they don't."

Gaining strength from Cass's supportive touch, Julia forced a smile, then turned back to address her husband. "How long do you think you'll be gone?"

"I'm not sure. If we're goin' to be gone any longer than a few weeks, we'll get word back to you."

"I . . . I suppose you'll want me to get some things ready for you then."

Jack's expression softened for the first time. "That would be fine."

Forcing her chin high, Julia left the room, accepting as she had always accepted, knowing as she had always known, that love held her powerless to change the situation in any way.

Clouds moved across the night sky, blocking the meager light of the quarter moon as Roger rode in rapid retreat from the barrel of Buck's gun. His horse stumbled briefly on the rutted trail and Roger cursed aloud. He jerked the reins roughly, his mount's pained response allowing him little satisfaction as thoughts of the volatile encounter lingered.

Purity's face flashed vividly before his mind and Roger's passions soared anew.

Damn her! Damn that beauteous witch for the

tease that she was! She knew what she did to him! She knew how he had struggled against the swelling proof of his desire when she swung down from her horse with that long-limbed grace that was hers alone! She knew that the scent of her body heat, the drop of perspiration that had trickled down her throat and disappeared into the soft swells beneath her coarse shirt excited him almost past control. She knew that a glance from her pale eyes had left him all but salivating.

She knew that he ached to have her!

And she knew that the frustration only whetted his appetite.

Roger's patrician features contorted with sudden rage. He had maintained control during his visits to Purity by venting his salacious needs on the debauched women at Sophie's Place in the interim. He had allowed himself only a light kiss on the cheek and an occasional arm around Purity's waist—*when he would have liked nothing better than to devour her!*

He wasn't certain what had pushed him over the edge a short time earlier. Perhaps it was the glint of the silver moonlight on Purity's faultless cheek as they walked together, the shimmer of the pale rays on her glorious hair, or the innate female allure that was hers alone.

Or perhaps it was her distracted manner, which suddenly made him feel that she wished she were anywhere else in the world at that moment but with him.

If Purity only knew . . . Approval for the extension of Stan Corrigan's loan had been in his pocket since the day she first approached him. His father had turned the matter over to him with a knowing smile and instructions to handle the loan however he chose. He had chosen to hold that approval in abeyance, uncertain whether he would eventually use it as an inducement or as a reward.

His delay had been a mistake—he knew that, now. The situation had become further complicated by the fact that Buck Parsons had witnessed his unfortunate lapse. That hard-nosed old wrangler would not forget, and the momentary pleasure of the blow he had struck Purity had not been worth the setback it would afford his plans.

But he was still certain he would eventually get Purity to come around. Roger nodded in silent confirmation of his thoughts. Yes, he would have Purity yet. She would soon be lying naked beneath him, where she belonged.

And when that happened, he would make her pay . . . and pay . . . and pay. It was just a matter of time.

Jack forced himself to lie still in bed, despite his sleeplessness since retiring for the night. Julia had accepted the announcement that he was leaving, but her feelings about his and Cass's departure in the morning were obvious. She felt there was something more to his decision to make the untimely trip than he had been willing to reveal. She had always been sensitive to his feelings, a quality about her that was both endearing and disconcerting. He knew the love that had caused Julia to put her former life behind her had not diminished. He was certain of that, just as he was certain that Julia loved Cass as if he were her own son. She had proved those truths over the years.

Honest, loyal, loving. Julia was all those things. But she was not—

"Jack? Are you awake?"

The uncertain tremor in Julia's voice tore at Jack's heart. His first inclination was to pretend he was asleep, but he knew Julia would sense his deceit. Instead, he replied softly, "Yes, I'm awake."

"I couldn't sleep, either."

Jack did not reply.

Julia's voice was hesitant. "I'll miss you, you know."

"I'll miss you, too."

"Will you, Jack?"

Jack turned toward Julia, saddened by her distress. "You know I will, dear. I'm not leavin' by choice, you know. I told you, there are some debts that a man must pay."

"I know. You're an honorable man."

Jack shook his head. "Not always."

"Yes . . . yes, you are! You're the most honorable man I've ever known."

"Julia . . ."

"I love you, Jack. You know that, don't you?"

"Of course, I do. I love you, too."

"You . . . you will come back to me, won't you, Jack?"

"Julia . . ."

The dim light of the room did not hide the tears that had sprung into Julia's eyes. A thickness formed in Jack's throat, lending a rasp to his voice as he whispered, "Of course I'll come back."

Suddenly realizing that he had made that promise as much for himself as for her, Jack took Julia into his arms.

The faint light of the moon his only guide in the darkened house, Cass walked across the living room. His soundless steps did not impinge on the silence as he drew open the front door and walked out into the shadows of the yard. Stripped to the waist, the broad expanse of his chest bared to the shifting currents of the night breeze, he allowed the darkness to envelop him.

Cass knew instinctively that his father was as wakeful as he. Jack could not forgive himself for his belief that he had failed Cass's mother, the woman he loved beyond all else. The letter Jack had received from his old "friend" had only served to burn that belief more deeply into his heart.

Cass silently acknowledged the truth that there had been a time when he also believed his father had betrayed his mother. Years and maturity had brought those conflicts to rest in his mind, yet the letter had raised mixed emotions.

Cass ran his hand through his dark hair in an unconscious gesture that betrayed the disharmony of his thoughts. He could not put a name to the strange sense of premonition gradually expanding within him. Nor could he expel it.

Raising his eyes to the night sky, Cass sought an answer there. It eluded him.

No answer.

No rest.

Cass slipped into the shadows, permitting the night to consume him.

The hushed darkness of her room suddenly felt oppressive, and Purity sat up abruptly in bed. It was hot, unusually so for spring. The air was still. It lay against her skin like an invisible weight she could not shed.

Throwing her feet over the side of the bed, Purity stood up and walked to the window, noting that the image flashing briefly in the washstand mirror as she passed was in sharp contrast with the appearance she normally presented. She had told herself over and again that she had not chosen the simple white cotton nightdress trimmed with narrow lace because of its beauty. She silently maintained that she had bought it simply because it was practical—the coolest garment she could wear on nights such as the present one when her room became stifling and the night breeze afforded little relief. But she knew that was not totally true. The garment had originally caught her eye because it had recalled an image of her mother that had lain dormant in her mind. As for the way she had allowed her hair to remain unbound that night, streaming past her shoulders, duplicating to perfection the likeness she recalled, she told herself that she had been too tired—or too impatient—to do other than brush it free of tangles before seeking relief from her smoldering emotions in sleep.

But she could not sleep.

And there was no relief from the anger simmering within . . . or the persistent throbbing of her jaw.

Purity's hands unconsciously balled into fists. She had underestimated Roger Norris. She had not anticipated the violent side of his personality. His blow had been totally unexpected. She still itched to return it in kind, but she knew she dared not chance another encounter. Buck had meant every word he'd said, and she could not afford to further complicate an already dire situation with possible bloodshed.

Purity raised a weary hand to her brow. What was she going to do now? Stan was helpless. She could not bear the torment behind his gaze—the realization that each day brought them closer to disaster. Stan had so little to cling to. It would kill him to lose the ranch.

But then, that all depends on what you're prepared to offer the next time you come begging.

The snake! She'd never get that desperate. Would she?

Purity rested her temple against the windowpane as she contemplated the day to come.

A shadow moved unexpectedly in the yard, and Purity froze into motionlessness. Her heart leaped as she strained to identify the shape she saw there.

No, it could not be he! Instantly, she recalled sharply chiseled features, a blade pressed to her throat, green eyes glaring hatred.

The shadow moved again.

Purity's breath caught raggedly in her throat the second before a large buck bounded out of the darkness, dispelling the vision she had created in her mind.

Still trembling, mentally berating herself for her irrational fear, Purity closed her eyes.

You made a mistake. You let me live.

Pale Wolf . . .

A chill ran down Purity's spine. Months had passed, yet she was still unable to banish his savage image or the strangely conflicting feelings accompanying it from her mind.

Questions haunted her. Had Pale Wolf survived his wound? Where was he now? Was he lurking in the darkness, watching her window? Would she close her eyes to awaken with a knife again pressed to her throat? And this time, would he—

No, damn it!

Purity forced a halt to her escalating fear. She was through suffering the anxieties her mind invented! She would not allow them, most especially now, when more urgent problems pressed.

Purity turned abruptly back toward her bed, refusing to submit to fear. She lay down, the irony of the situation suddenly striking her.

Two men wanted her. One man wanted her body. The other man wanted her blood. While she struggled merely to survive. . . .

Chapter Three

The morning sun had already risen when Purity walked briskly down the steps toward the first floor and the breakfast that she knew would be waiting. She grimaced at the realization that she was late, knowing that the men would never let her hear the end of it. Always out of bed at the crack of dawn, she was normally the first to greet Pete for the day, and the first to boast that she had beaten the biscuits to the table. But dawn had sneaked past her that morning. The reason was obvious. She had not had a decent night's sleep since Roger's visit more than a week earlier, when her hope for a loan extension had collapsed forever.

And no one had to tell her that the stress was beginning to show. Her mirror did not lie. It boldly reflected the dark circles that now ringed her pale eyes, making them appear eerily light, and the narrowing of her waist that had forced her to make another notch in her belt in order to hold up pants that had formerly fit well. As if that wasn't enough, Stan's gaze had taken on an assessing quality of late, and the sound of Pete's voice urging her to take a second serving at every meal was getting downright maddening.

Hardest of all, Stan had not asked a single question about Roger—not the reason for his hasty departure on his last visit or why Roger had not returned. She hadn't volunteered any information, either. How could she? To tell Stan that Roger was not coming back would be tantamount to telling him it was all over.

But it wasn't all over.

She had made her decision last night. She was ready. She would go into town today to see Roger. Whatever his reaction to her appearance might be, he would need to maintain a semblance of decorum when she faced him in his office at the bank. She would make herself perfectly clear to him there—the loan must be extended, the agreement signed and sealed, and then—

Bile surged to Purity's throat, and she swallowed convulsively.

Oh, hell, how bad could it be? She was a strong woman, and strong women had stood worse before! Just because the memory of Roger's searching tongue in her mouth still made her gag, and just because the thought of his eager hands roaming her flesh made her all but retch, well . . . well . . .

Purity paused midway down the stairs and closed her eyes. The truth was, she wanted Roger only close enough for her fist to settle his lascivious desires for some time to come.

That thought brought a brief smile to Purity's lips. She had promised herself that pleasure. She had *vowed* to keep that promise.

But first . . .

Oh, damn, there went her stomach, again!

What would her sisters do in a situation like this?

Chastity? Chastity had been only a sweet, loving little girl when Purity last saw her.

Honesty? Purity did not need to ponder that question very long. If her determined older sister were here right now, she'd doubtless say that she'd rather rob a bank than go crawling to Roger Norris.

Rob a bank . . .

Purity considered the thought.

No. She'd never get away with it.

Purity continued down the stairs, gradually realizing that the dining room was silent, too silent. She heard no easy banter or gruff morning complaints, no scraping forks and knives, or even the shuffling of booted feet.

Taking the last few steps at a run, Purity turned the corner of the dining room to find it empty, with breakfasts lying partially consumed and abandoned on the table. Her heart began a frightened pounding at the same moment that she heard the rumble of angry voices in the yard.

Covering the distance to the door at a run, Purity jerked it open to see Stan on the porch. His expression frozen, he sat motionless in his chair. The men stood stiff-faced nearby, watching a horseman ride away.

The sheriff.

Beside Stan in a moment, Purity pulled the official-looking document he clutched out of his hand. The words jumped out at her, hitting her with the strength of a blow: NOTICE OF FORECLOSURE

Stan snatched it back and hot color flushed Purity's face. She stated flatly, "This isn't goin' to happen, Stan."

She turned away, only to be caught by Stan's surprisingly strong grip on her arm as he demanded, "Where do you think you're goin'?"

"To town."

"You ain't goin' nowhere!"

"You can't stop me!"

"You try ridin' away and I'll rope you off your horse and drag you to the ground if I have to!"

"This is my fault. I made Roger angry. We . . . he . . . we had a fight, and he's just gettin' back at me."

"I know about that 'fight'." Stan's hard jaw tightened. "I made Buck tell me . . . and if that fella comes back here for any reason at all, I'll put a bullet right between his eyes."

"Buck, damn it!" Purity shot the sober wrangler a furious glance.

Buck retorted, "Stan knew somethin' was wrong. He had a right to know."

"To know what?" Carter interrupted. His youthful face growing hot, he stepped away from the other men and strode closer. "I asked a question!"

"A question you ain't got no right to ask!"

Stan's sharp response had no effect on the young wrangler's determined expression, or on the men gathering behind him.

Purity's temper snapped.

"Nothin' happened—nothin' I can't handle myself!"

"That's where you're wrong!" Rapidly paling, Stan ordered roughly, "I want you to come inside with me, Purity. I have somethin' to say—somethin' I've been holdin' back in case—"

Stan took a short, choked breath that sent a tremor of fear coursing through Purity. "I want you all comin' inside," he continued. "You got a right to hear what I'm gonna say, too. I was goin' to wait, but this paper changes everythin'." Clutching the foreclosure notice tightly, he snapped at Purity, "Push me inside where we can talk like civilized people, damn it!"

Push me inside.

Purity nodded, shaken by the request that was more revealing than Stan intended. He was getting weaker.

Close to tears, Purity pushed the chair into the living room and sat close by as the men filtered in behind them. She held her breath as Stan started to speak.

"All right, somethin's makin' you feel uneasy and you're not talkin' about it. So it's my turn to ask. What's wrong?"

Cass turned briefly toward his father when he spoke. Declining response, he hooked the cinch on his saddle tighter and tested it cautiously. His gelding was young, obstinate, and tired. They had been riding steadily for more days than he cared to count, and the big animal was about ready to start trying some of his tricks. Inflating his stomach when saddled was one of them, and Cass had no desire to find himself on the ground with his horse looking down at him when he attempted to mount.

Satisfied that he would have no surprise in store, Cass turned back to his father. The morning sun had just risen, they had already cleaned up their night camp, and they were ready to continue with their journey. Jack looked tired. Long days on the trail had taken a lot out of him, but Cass knew the true reason for the deep lines that creased his father's face. Jack had spoken little since the inception of their journey. He was not looking forward to this meeting with his "old friend." Cass knew that if Jack had any other choice, he would turn around and head back, even now when their journey was so close to its conclusion.

Jack wasn't the only one. The peculiar feeling that had risen that first night, when Jack had announced his intention to leave immediately for south Texas, had grown stronger with each mile they traveled. He was at a loss to explain it.

Jack repeated, "You aren't answerin' me."

"Because I have nothing to say."

Jack gave a low snort as Cass rolled up his blanket and strapped it to the saddle. "Nothin' to say, huh? It seems to me I'd have plenty of questions about this whole thing if I were you."

"I know all I need to know."

"Yeah? And what's that?"

Dousing the ashes of the campfire with the remaining coffee, Cass shoved the pot into his pack, then turned resolutely back toward his father. "I know this visit is important to you. That's enough for me."

"You mean that, don't you?"

Cass did not respond.

"Hell, that was a stupid question!" Jack shook his head. "I don't even know why I asked it . . . except I guess I could never quite believe that you didn't hold it against me all these years, knowin' about your ma and all."

Cass remained silent.

"You know how I felt. You know I didn't want to let her go."

"You don't owe me any explanations."

"I do, because I stole somethin' precious from you that I can't ever give back."

A familiar agitation rose within Cass. He didn't want to discuss a past that could never be altered.

"You're wonderin' why I brought this all up right now, aren't you, especially since we'll be reachin' the Circle C sometime today."

Cass maintained his silence.

"Damn it, boy, I'm tryin' to tell you somethin'!" Jack's gaze tightened. "You don't want to hear it, though, do you? That's because you got secrets of your own that you don't want to share."

Cass mounted abruptly. When he turned back, his

expression was cold. "We're wasting time. We could've been on the trail an hour ago."

"You don't want to talk."

"No."

"All right. If that's the way you want it."

His expression tight, Jack mounted just as abruptly and kicked his horse into motion.

Silent, Cass allowed his father to lead the way.

The living room of the small ranch house was unnaturally quiet as Stan prepared himself to speak. He wiped his arm across his brow. He was warm, too warm. It made him feel even weaker than he had been feeling for the past few weeks. He was slipping fast. He could not lie about it to himself any longer. The anxiety in Purity's eyes when she looked at him made it clear that she realized it, too.

Damn! He had so many regrets! He should have realized this was coming. He should have provided better for Purity's future! He should have *made* himself marry some nice woman so Purity would have a family to fall back on. Or he should have paid more attention to what she had to say when she was little.

That last thought nagged viciously at Stan's mind. He remembered that he had thought it somehow strange that Purity had grieved for her parents almost immediately after the accident, accepting from the start that they had drowned in that flooded river, but that she had begged him to help her find her sisters. She had been so certain they were alive.

Maybe they were.

Maybe he should have tried.

Stan unconsciously clenched the foreclosure notice tighter. But he couldn't go back. He could only go forward. And everyone was waiting.

Stan glanced around the room. The men were standing apprehensively. Carter had assumed a position to Purity's left, situating himself as close to her as he dared. His mouth was tight, and his youthful face was still flushed. The agitated young cowpoke would give Buck no rest in trying to discover what had happened between Purity and Roger Norris, he was sure. Buck wouldn't tell him. He was sure of that, too. Buck knew that the Norris family was too influential, and Carter would be the one to suffer in the end if he lost his head.

Stan continued his silent survey. Buck, dependably stalwart, was at his right. Pete, apron still wrapped around his waist, stood nearby. The others were grouped silently a few feet away: Baird, looking at Purity with noticeable concern; Treacher, his expression uncharacteristically sober; Rome, Pitts, and Horton, motionless, as if awaiting direction.

Grateful for the support of men whose loyalty had never wavered, Stan glanced down at the notice in his hand.

Two weeks to clear out.

Stan squeezed the official paper tighter, then looked up, eyes suddenly blazing.

"Whatever you're all thinkin', this here notice don't mean nothin'—nothin' at all! Old Willard Norris at the bank thinks he's got himself another nice spread to cut up into parcels and sell to the first available bidders, but he's *wrong!* There ain't goin' to be no foreclosure, and there ain't goin' to be nobody but a

Corrigan runnin' this spread, not ever! You've got my word on that!"

Silence greeted his impassioned statement, and Stan gave a mirthless laugh. "No, I ain't crazy. And I ain't got money buried somewheres that I'm goin' to dig up to pay my bills." He paused. "But what I do have is . . . somebody who's goin' to be my new partner."

Stan felt the shock that rippled across the room, holding it in temporary silence. He looked at Purity as she straightened up. He saw resentment in the stiffness of her shoulders when she spoke.

"You never mentioned takin' in a partner to me."

"No, I didn't. I'm sorry, darlin'. I suppose I was waitin' until the last moment, hopin' against hope that some miracle might happen and it wouldn't be necessary, after all. When I finally made the decision, I figured it might be best not to say anythin' until he got here."

"Until who got here?"

"Somebody I knew a long time ago. We was in the war together. His name is Jack Thomas."

Purity shook her head. "I never heard you mention him."

"I . . . we ain't had much contact since the war."

"Since the war?"

"Yeah, I know, that was a long time ago. But that don't make no difference. I've been hearin' about him. He's doin' real well up north, so I wrote him a letter."

"You wrote him a letter."

"That's right."

"And he agreed to cover your debts in return for a share in the ranch."

"Not exactly . . ."

Purity stared at him for a long, silent moment before she stood up and started toward the door.

"Stop where you are!" Stan's shout halted Purity in her tracks. She turned back toward him as he continued tightly, "I know what you're thinkin'. You're thinkin' everythin' that's happened has touched my mind and that Jack Thomas probably don't even remember who I am anymore—but you're wrong! You're thinkin' I'll never get an answer from him—but you're wrong again! Because he's on his way here right now!"

Wheeling himself to the nearby desk with hands that shook visibly, Stan jerked open the drawer. He pulled out a clipped sheet and held it up.

"Here's his answer, a wire that was delivered when you all was out huntin' up steers. Read it, if you want. He says he's startin' right out. That means he'll be here any day."

"Any day . . ."

"That's right."

Purity accepted the wire Jack offered her. She read it and looked up.

"This wire only says that he's comin'."

"That's all it needs to say."

"Well, it don't make any difference to me what that wire says." Buck interrupted the sober exchange unexpectedly. His deep voice filled the room as he stated flatly, "As far as I'm concerned, I'm behind you, Stan, whatever you decide to do. And I think I can speak for the rest of the fellas when I say they feel the same."

Grunts of acknowledgement sounded in reply, and Stan nodded, his throat tight. "Thank you, boys."

Suddenly realizing that Buck's statement had eliminated the need for any further discussion, Stan allowed himself a stabilizing breath before turning abruptly to Pete. "Seems like I remember that these fellas didn't have a chance to finish their breakfast this mornin'. I'm thinkin' some hot coffee might taste real good before they start out for the day."

Pete moved toward the kitchen in silent response, and the men followed. Only Purity remained behind. The uncertainty in her clear eyes pained him.

Beautiful Purity, his dear, darlin' little girl . . .

Waiting until the men had cleared the room, Stan took her hand.

The mid-afternoon sun shone with dazzling brilliance on the Circle C as Jack and Cass approached the main buildings. The heat of the day demanded a leisurely pace for their tired mounts, allowing Cass the opportunity to assess the scene cautiously as they neared the ranch house. The modest, two-story structure, obviously constructed of hand-hewn lumber many years earlier, was well maintained, as were the barn and bunkhouse situated respectable distances away.

Cass unconsciously nodded. He would not have expected anything else. The approach through Circle C land had revealed a dedicated ranching hand that allowed little neglect. The cattle he had viewed on the way in appeared healthy and active, the fencing and equipment were well tended, and if the branding corrals he had passed were any indication, the herd was expanding rapidly.

A second sense nudged him, contradicting the silent serenity of the scene, and Cass glanced at his father. Jack sat his horse rigidly. He had not spoken a word since they had broken camp that morning. It was obvious that his emotions were running high.

Cass tensed. Subtly shifting his reins, he allowed his free hand to drop into the area of the gun he wore on his hip. His fingers twitched expectantly at a sound of movement in the ranch house doorway. They were within a few yards of the door when it snapped open and a wheelchair moved into view on the porch.

Cass sensed more than heard his father's sharp intake of breath at first sight of the man in the chair. The fellow's broad shoulders were rounded with age and infirmity. The thick, gray hair that seemed to overwhelm his gaunt face was balanced only by the full gray mustache that hung heavily over his unsmiling mouth. His work-roughened hands clutched the metal wheels of the chair, knuckles white, and his long, obviously lifeless legs were awkwardly propped. He did not speak as they drew up at the hitching post and dismounted.

A step behind his father, Cass watched the fellow's expression as they approached. He knew the man was Stan Corrigan. From his father's reaction, it could be no one else. It was also apparent that Corrigan had no more taste for this meeting than Jack did, and he was equally uncertain what the outcome would be.

Disregarding words of greeting that would be superfluous under the circumstances, Corrigan broke the strained silence with a flat statement.

"I need your help, Jack."

Cass saw the emotion that flicked across his father's face as he came to an abrupt halt. He saw the control his father exerted as he swallowed with obvious difficulty, and he felt the unexpected pain in his father's hoarse, unequivocal response.

"Whatever you need, it's yours."

The two men reached out simultaneously for a handshake that bridged the years—and so much more.

The sun was rapidly dropping toward the horizon as the exhausted Circle C wranglers headed home. Riding a short distance ahead of the others at Purity's right, Buck sat his saddle stiffly, his jaw tight. The low-voiced bickering behind them resumed, and he turned his mount abruptly, raising a gritty cloud of dust as he spurred the surprised animal toward the two men straggling at the rear of their group.

Purity frowned. The reason for Buck's sudden, angry sprint toward Treacher and Baird was obvious. The two of them had been at it all day. A burly fellow approaching middle age, Treacher was steady and dependable, but he was also a burr under the saddle of every man around him when the notion possessed him. Why he had chosen a day that had started out so disturbingly to taunt Baird relentlessly and further shatter nerves that were already frayed, she could not quite understand.

Purity looked up at a sky streaked with the glorious pink and gold of the setting sun. They had gotten a late start after the sheriff's visit, had put in a full day, and were late in returning. The men were hungry and their spirits were low. Buck had taken a few minutes to talk to her when they paused at midday, but there had been little he could say to relieve her anxiety. The other men had said little but were thinking much, and she knew they were as worried as she—because the truth was that there was not a one of them who shared Stan's confidence that his old acquaintance would put an end to their problems at last.

Purity's stomach twisted into familiar knots of despair. Her heart ached for Stan! His hands had trembled when they held hers earlier that morning. He had promised her that everything would be all right, but she knew he was more worried than he cared to reveal. She also knew his main concern was not for the Circle C. The truth was that as much as Stan loved the Circle C, he loved her more. Somehow, in all the years of uncertainty behind her, she had never doubted that truth.

"Purity . . ."

Purity looked up to see that Carter had replaced Buck at her side. In that moment, she recognized the true reason for Carter's popularity with women. Even features, curly brown hair, and muscular frame aside, there was an innate honesty about him that lent him endearing warmth. That warmth encompassed her as he spoke again.

"I've been wanting to talk to you all day, Purity."

"Have you?" Purity shook her head. "I'm sorry. I guess I've been caught up in my own thoughts. What did you want to talk to me about?"

Carter's dark brows knitted appealingly. "I guess it's none of my business what happened between you and Roger Norris."

Purity slowly stiffened. "That's right, it isn't."

"But then again, maybe it is."

"Carter . . ."

Carter's jaw hardened. "I've been workin' for Stan since I was seventeen years old, and I never had a better boss. He made that bunkhouse seem like home to me."

Purity nodded. She shared that same appreciation.

"You were fifteen years old when I came, and I watched you grow up." He paused, continuing more earnestly, "But you're a woman now, and . . . and . . . I want you to know that my feelin's for you are special. I know this ain't no time for me to be talkin' about these things, but I want to say that if I had the money Stan needed, there'd be no way either one of you'd have to look to somebody else for help." Carter paused again. "And while I'm at it, I want you to know that there's nothin' I wouldn't do for you. Nothin' at all. All you'd have to do is ask."

"Carter . . ."

"No, don't say nothin'. You don't have to. I just needed to say it, because . . . well, because I had to."

The tightness in Purity's throat constricted to the point of pain.

"Thanks."

Purity purposely averted her gaze as the ranch house came into view. She stiffened at the sight of two unidentifiable horses tied up in front.

Visitors.

Purity felt Carter tense. She heard low mumbling behind her as Buck rode up to resume his place at her right. Her gaze straight ahead, she rode directly toward the house, hardly conscious of the men following her as she studied the brands on the horses tied up there.

The Rocking T. She had heard of it. It was a big spread up north.

Stan's friend . . .

Dismounting, Purity looked up as the door opened and Stan pushed himself into view. His face was startlingly smooth, almost free of anxiety, and Purity's throat constricted tightly with relief. She started toward him as a gray-haired man she knew could only be Jack Thomas followed Stan out onto the porch. She was smiling, reaching for Stan's hand when she saw—

Purity went stock still.

Another man stood in the ranch house doorway. Caught in the shadows of the overhang, the fellow's features were not clearly discernible—but the size of him, the breadth of his powerful shoulders and chest, struck a chord of frightening familiarity that stole her breath.

No . . . it couldn't be!

Purity mentally shook herself. What was wrong with her? The fellow was a wrangler, just like any one of her men. The hat he wore pulled down low on his forehead was as well seasoned as his clothes and boots, and the gunbelt slung low on his narrow hips rested there naturally. The shadows were playing tricks on her.

As if reading her mind, the man started toward her. A quiver moved down her spine.

"What's wrong, darlin'?

Stan's question echoed hollowly in Purity's mind as the big stranger came into clear view. He removed his hat with slow deliberation, finally allowing the pink rays of sunset to eliminate all uncertainty.

Purity's throat choked closed.

Sun-reddened skin . . . sharply chiseled features . . . black, shoulder-length hair . . . green eyes . . .

Oh, God, those same green eyes!

It was *he*.

"What's that Injun doin' here?"

The man called Buck stepped toward him, but Cass saw only the woman who stood rigidly still a few feet away.

Light hair . . . light eyes . . . light skin . . . *the enemy*.

The woman did not speak. Instead she stared at him, frozen into motionlessness as her men rallied behind her—the same men who had declared their hatred for his Kiowa blood as it had spilled onto the ground.

"Get that savage out of here before I shoot him dead!"

"What's the matter with you, Buck?" Stan's thin face paled. "What's the matter with all of you? This fella is Cass Thomas, Jack's son!"

"No he ain't!" Buck stood his ground. "He's that Injun we told you about, the one on the drive last fall who tried to kill Purity!"

Cass saw Stan's incredulity. He heard Jack mumble his name. He felt the enmity swell around him, but he did not respond.

"You're mistaken!" Stan shook his head. "You're confusin' him with somebody else!"

"No, I ain't. Tell him, Purity!"

Her name was Purity. . . .

"Tell him, Purity!"

The woman's light eyes blinked as they stared into his. Her lips moved as she struggled to speak. He felt the tension mounting around him, but he did not relinquish her stare.

"It's him." The woman spoke at last, her voice a hoarse whisper. "His name is Pale Wolf."

Burning emotions flamed to life within Cass, igniting a living, palpable hatred that drove him another step closer to the woman. He allowed long moments of silent confirmation to register clearly in her eyes. He indulged his satisfaction at her horror. When he spoke at last, his familiar words were meant for her ears alone.

"You made a mistake. You let me live."

*   *   *

Elaine Barbieri

"All right, out with it! What's this all about?"

Jack addressed his silent son, his harsh demand ringing in the silence of the Circle C living room. He awaited Cass's response, intensely aware of the gravity of the moment. Stan and Purity Corrigan sat stiffly nearby, as tense as he. He did not have to look out the window to confirm that Stan's wranglers stood in the yard, waiting.

Jack took a shaky breath. It had been a day of surprises unlike any other. First had been the jolting impact of seeing Stan again. Stan Corrigan, big, sound, indefatigable in all he did, had been one of the strongest fellows he had ever known. He had never expected that when he met his old acquaintance again, he would find little left of that man beyond the spirit that still shone so vividly in his eyes.

The conflict of the past had dissolved the instant he saw Stan. He had listened attentively as Stan outlined his difficulties in great detail. There had been no question in his mind what his own response would be.

The solution to Stan's problems had seemed clear-cut until Purity Corrigan returned. Then all hell had broken loose!

Jack shuddered. If he lived to be one hundred, he knew he would never forget the hatred in the eyes of the Circle C wranglers when Cass stepped forward into clear view.

Nor would he forget the moment when he glanced at Cass—to see the eyes of Pale Wolf staring back at him.

Pale Wolf, with his Kiowa blood surging hotly . . .

Everything had happened so quickly then that he was not truly certain what had transpired! Cass whispered something to Purity Corrigan, and her face turned chalk white. The drawing of guns, angry threats, and impending violence that ensued were abruptly halted by Purity herself when she ordered her men back.

The truce that followed temporarily relieved the tension and allowed them to leave the agitated wranglers behind as they moved into the house for rational explanations.

But bad blood still boiled. The threat of violence was like a heavy cloud encompassing them all. He knew he needed to dispel it before it was too late.

Jack pressed, "I asked you what this is all about, Cass."

"His name's not Cass. It's Pale Wolf," Purity Corrigan responded, her lips tight. "He tried to kill me."

"My Kiowa name is Pale Wolf." Cass sneered, "If I had wanted to kill you, you would be dead."

Purity jumped to her feet, retorting, "You roped me off my horse! You held me at knifepoint!"

"The tracks of the horse thief I was following led directly to you."

"If Buck hadn't ridden up in time, I would be dead!"

"You mean, if Buck hadn't shot me in the back . . ."

"You drew blood with your knife!"

"A scratch—a warning that I would not accept your lies."

"Lies?" Purity shook her head. "I didn't know what you were talkin' about!"

"I didn't believe that."

"You didn't *want* to believe it!"

"I believed you were lying."

"Lyin'! You didn't give me a chance to explain—or to talk!"

"Your man didn't give me a chance, either."

Purity's fair skin flushed. "We could have left you for dead, but we didn't. Pete nursed you back to health."

"So willingly . . ."

"Willingly or not, he took good care of you! He saved your life!"

"He removed your man's bullet."

"Buck was protectin' me!"

"He shot an Indian."

"No, he—"

"An Indian 'whose life wasn't worth the price of a bullet'."

Purity's face flamed.

"All right, that's enough!" Stan interrupted from his chair, his face equally hot. "This ain't gettin' us nowhere." He turned to face Jack squarely. His expression was rigid. "I'll be truthful with you, Jack. I don't like what I'm hearin'. If things was different and I had my legs under me, I ain't got a doubt in my mind that I'd have your son by the throat right now. But as things are, I'll tell you this—if I saw somebody threatenin' Purity with a knife, I wouldn't stop to ask questions no more than Buck did! I'd shoot first and ask questions later, the only difference bein' that I'd make sure I finished off the bastard after I took him down! And I'll tell you another thing! It wouldn't make one damned bit of difference to me if he was Injun or white!"

Stan's jaw was tight as he continued with an obvious effort at control, "But you're lookin' at this from the other side, and I know what you're thinkin'. You're thinkin' that however this whole thing came about, the fact is that Buck put a bullet in your son's back. You don't like that no more than you like me backin' Buck up for what he did." Stan's chest heaved with agitation in the few seconds before he grated, "We've got a problem here, and right now I'm not sure we can work it out—even if we want to."

The silence of the room stretched painfully long as Jack sought to control his anger at Stan's bold statements. He looked at Purity Corrigan. She did not flinch under his stare. With her halo of light gold hair, silver-blue eyes, and small, perfect features, she had an almost angelic appearance at first glance, but nobody had to tell him that nothing could be farther from the truth. Fire and an iron determination blazed in those heavenly eyes. She was a young woman accustomed to giving orders, and she didn't back down easily. He had no doubt she could hold her own against any man, with one possible exception.

"You're right," Jack said. "I'm damned mad, but I want to discuss this with my son before we do any talkin'."

"That's fine with me." Stan turned toward the balding cook, who appeared suddenly in the kitchen doorway. "Put supper on the table, Pete, and call the boys in so they can eat while Jack and me do some separate sortin' out here."

Jack strode abruptly toward the door. He turned back, addressing Cass tightly.

"Are you comin'?"

His anger did not abate as Cass fell in behind him.

"I ain't goin' to do it, you know." Stan stared a silent moment longer at Purity's pale face. He hissed a curse, continuing, "I don't care what happens, I want that Cass Thomas off my land!"

Purity looked at Stan where he sat a few feet from her in the small living room. They were alone. The clinking of dinnerware echoed from the dining room where the men were eating, their customary boisterous conversation noticeably absent. Jack Thomas was outside somewhere with his son.

Jack's son. Pale Wolf.

The shock of meeting Pale Wolf again was with Purity still. His clothing, the hat that shaded his distinctive features, the shoulder-length hair tied at the back of his neck—none of it had fooled her for a minute! Awareness had prickled up her spine the moment she had seen him. Fury . . . apprehension . . . uncertainty . . . a strange excitement . . . He raised all those emotions with the silent promise in his eyes that chilled and disturbed her in ways she could not clearly define.

She spoke unconsciously. "His name is Pale Wolf."

"Pale Wolf or Cass Thomas . . . I don't give a damn what he calls himself! I want him off this ranch!"

Stan's face flushed an almost apoplectic color. The

106

lines of strain deepened cruelly, further emphasizing the physical deterioration so evident there. He looked angry, worried, infirm. Desperation was again clearly visible in his eyes. All was in sharp contrast with the picture of the man who had greeted her on the porch only a short time earlier when he'd believed all would soon be well.

She could not bear it.

"Wait a minute, Stan." Purity forced herself to be calm. "We both have to think this through. If you throw Pale Wolf off the ranch, his father's goin' to leave with him."

"Let him!"

"Do you realize what you're sayin'?"

"I know what I'm sayin', all right!"

Purity's lips tightened. "It was all set before I came home, wasn't it? Jack Thomas had agreed to the partnership."

"So what if he did?"

"I knew it."

Stan's gaze pinned her. "Tell me somethin'. Do you really think I'd let that fella stay in this house after what he tried to do to you? I don't give a damn if Jack walks out and never looks back. I'll save the ranch some other way!"

Some other way . . .

The foreclosure notice, with two weeks to clear out . . .

You made a mistake. You let me live.

Damn that Pale Wolf! He didn't scare her! And she would not let him get between Stan and his last hope to save the ranch!

Purity's jaw locked with determination. "That would be a mistake, you know."

"What are you talkin' about?"

"The mystery is over. We know the reason why Pale Wolf . . . Cass Thomas . . . whatever he chooses to call himself, attacked me. He mistook me for some horse thief he was trailin'. He had no way of tellin' that I was a woman the way I was dressed."

"It didn't make a bit of difference to him when he found out!"

"Should it have? He didn't know me. He was trailin' a horse thief. I might've done the same if I was in his shoes."

"He put a knife to your throat, Purity!"

"And Buck shot him in the back for makin' that mistake. He got the worst of that exchange. He almost died."

Stan stared at her, his gaze knowing. "You ain't foolin' me, you know."

Purity stared back at him. "I'm not afraid of him."

"I know. You ain't got the sense to let yourself be afraid."

"Stan . . ."

"What makes you think he won't try somethin' again?"

"Why would he?"

"You said it yourself! Buck shot him in the back because of you. He don't look like the forgivin' type."

"He'd never get away with it, and he doesn't look like a fool, either."

"Do you think the fellas are goin' to stand for him bein' around here after what he did? Not the way they were lookin' at him, they won't. And I'm damned proud of them for the way they're standin' up for you!"

Purity's jaw stiffened. "I don't need anybody to protect me. I can take care of myself."

"Maybe you think so."

"Did you ever stop to think"—Purity hesitated, reluctant to voice her suspicion—"that maybe the boys might have other reasons for the way they feel about Cass Thomas?"

"What are you sayin'?"

"You know how most of them feel about Indians."

Stan remained silent.

"They wanted me to leave him to bleed to death!"

Stan frowned. "Most of the boys have a reason for the way they feel about Injuns."

"You agree with them?"

Stan's frown darkened. "I didn't say that. I meant what I said before. It don't mean nothin' to me that Cass Thomas is part Kiowa. Hell, how could it, after the way I felt about his mother?"

Purity's thoughts jarred to a halt. She questioned slowly, "The way you felt about his . . . mother?"

Stan did not respond.

"What about his mother?"

"Nothin' . . . nothin'."

Stan's complexion turned suddenly gray, and Purity reached spontaneously toward him.

"Don't go gettin' scared." Stan's reprimand was unexpectedly gentle. "I ain't goin' to die right here and now, if that's what you're thinkin'."

"Stan, please . . ."

All his anger seemed to have drained away with his color, and Stan took Purity's hand and drew her down onto the chair beside him. He attempted a smile. "I suppose I haven't really been fair with you."

"That's not true, I—"

"Let me finish." Stan sighed. "The truth is that you've got a right to know, especially after all that's happened. It's a long story, and it ain't that interestin', but I suppose it's got to be told."

Sensing his determination, Purity did not respond.

Stan began hesitantly, "Didn't you ever wonder why I never got married, darlin'?" He gave a short laugh. "Hell, I wasn't bad lookin' when I was younger. There was some ladies who took a real fancy to me."

"No, I never wondered." Purity spoke sincerely. "As far as I was concerned, there wasn't any woman good enough for you."

"Hell, that couldn't be farther from the truth!" Stan's smile was brief. "The truth is simpler than that. There was only one woman I wanted, but she didn't want me."

"She must've been a fool!"

"No, she wasn't. She was very wise. Her name was Whisperin' Woman."

"Whisperin' Woman . . ."

"I was doin' some tradin' with the Kiowas when I met her for the first time. She wasn't no more than a girl, probably fifteen or sixteen. She was little and kind of delicate lookin', with big eyes and shiny black hair. And when she smiled, well, she was the prettiest thing I ever saw. She spoke real soft and she had a way of makin' a man feel special, a way of listenin' like there wasn't nothin' more important to her in the world than hearin' what he had to say. It only took me a week to make up my mind that I was goin' to ask her father for her. I didn't expect to have any trouble there. I knew she liked me, and I figured I could meet any price her father set, because I was doin' real well then."

Stan paused, a frown gradually growing. "But she was so young. I decided I'd better take it slow. I figured I should give her another year to grow up a little. It was one of the hardest things I ever did, goin' home to the ranch without her, even if I was already lookin' forward to the day I would come back in the spring." Stan paused. "I made a mistake leavin' her behind—a mistake I've regretted all my life."

Stan's gray brows tightened. "I went back to the village the followin' spring, all right. Young fool that I was, I brought all kinds of gifts for her father—blankets and trinkets, and some of the best ponies my ranch had to offer. It never occurred to me that I might be too late."

"Too late?"

"Whisperin' Woman was in love with somebody else, a white man who had wintered at the camp. That fella didn't have much to offer her, but she didn't care."

Purity did not respond.

Stan shrugged. "Her father was real angry when he saw all the gifts I brought him. He didn't like it one bit that Whisperin' Woman wanted somebody else. He told her that she had to marry me. I was

happy about that for a while, until I found her cryin'
. . . them pretty eyes of hers all red and puffy. She
told me then that she loved me, but not the same way
she loved the other fella. She said the other fella was
already a part of her heart, and that if she had to cut
him out of it, her life would bleed from the wound."

Stan's eyes filled unexpectedly. "That brought me
to my senses, because the truth of it was, I felt the
same way about her."

Stan took another breath. "I didn't like that other
fella much, but I wanted Whisperin' Woman to be
happy. So, I offered all the gifts I had brought for her
father to my rival. But he got mad. He didn't want to
take them—his pride and all. That was when I told
him that if he didn't use my gifts to buy Whisperin'
Woman for his wife, it would mean he loved himself
more than he loved her. And I told him that if that
was the way it was, I wouldn't care if Whisperin'
Woman loved me or not. I'd marry her anyhow! That
turned him around. He married Whisperin' Woman
and brought her back to live with him on the ranch
he was startin'. He was good to her, too."

Stan paused again. His face stiffened. "A couple of
years later, he sent a few of his men to the ranch to
pay me back everythin' I gave him that day—the ponies, the blankets, the trinkets. The bastard! He
wouldn't let me have even that much!"

Stan's expression darkened. "That ain't the whole
of it, you know. The war came along some time after
that, and who do you think ended up fightin' right
by my side?" He nodded at the realization that

dawned in Purity's eyes. "That's right. And what was worse, I ended up havin' to save the bastard's life!"

As the implications of Stan's story dawned on her, Purity whispered, "The man who married Whisperin' Woman was Jack Thomas." She swallowed, continuing hoarsely, "And Pale Wolf is Whisperin' Woman's son."

His incredulity appearing to equal hers, Stan nodded his head. "Strangest thing of all is that I was damned glad to meet the young bastard! I knew Whisperin' Woman was gone and that Jack had remarried. I made it my business to know it. But as soon as I saw Cass—Pale Wolf—I knew whose son he was, and it was like I was seein' a part of Whisperin' Woman again. Truth is, I was thinkin' that with me meetin' him for the first time, with the ranch about to be saved, and with the weight of all that trouble bein' lifted off your shoulders, this was probably one of the happiest days of my life!" Stan's voice softened. "Damn . . . how wrong can a man be?"

Silent tears rose inside Purity. She could not bear Stan's distress. His shoulders were bowed with exhaustion. His expression was drained. His happiness of a short time earlier had been so brief, and he deserved so much more.

Damn it all, she'd die before she'd let Pale Wolf take everything from him!

Determination renewed, Purity began cautiously, "It can still be a happy day, Stan. The ranch can still be saved, don't you see? Everythin' was a mistake from the beginnin'. Pale Wolf mistook me for a horse thief, so he attacked me. Buck thought he was goin'

113

to kill me, so he shot him. Two mistakes that don't change the fact that Jack Thomas still owes you his life."

"I don't know . . ."

"I'll be perfectly safe and everythin' can still work out fine, now that all the mistakes are cleared up." Purity took a breath, adding the words she knew would clinch the matter. "And the ranch can still be saved . . . for *both* of us."

Hardly able to speak when Stan's eyes again filled, Purity rasped, "You know Jack Thomas best of all. Do you think he's reasonable enough to be able to go on from here with the partnership?"

Stan did not respond.

"Please, Stan . . ."

"I don't know."

Forcing aside her conflicting emotions, Purity stood up abruptly, "I suppose there's only one way to find out."

"Why didn't you tell me?"

Jack's question hung on the night air. Silent, Cass surveyed his father's furious expression. They had adjourned to the privacy of the Circle C yard where the twilight that shaded his father's face failed to hide a jaw as hard as granite. The tick that pulled the corner of Jack's eye was equally revealing. His father was close to losing control.

"Answer me, damn it! Why didn't you tell me what happened last fall when you went to that Kiowa pow-wow? That's when you were shot, wasn't it? I knew somethin' happened to make you stay away so long.

And what was all that nonsense about trackin' a horse thief to the Circle C herd? There had to be more to it than that to make you attack a woman!"

"I didn't know she was a woman until I had her down."

"And when you did, you still didn't back off! No, there had to be more to it than you said." Jack's gaze narrowed. "It had somethin' to do with Flyin' Eagle, didn't it?"

The mention of Flying Eagle knotted Cass's stomach tight.

"I knew it!"

Cass did not respond. No, his father *didn't* know, and that was the crux of it. Jack had never really known what he felt, and he never would. But Whispering Woman had understood.

Half-breed!

Squaw woman!

The image of his mother's sober, determined expression flickered briefly before Cass's mind. He remembered the dignity with which his mother faced the jeers and slurs no one dared utter within his father's hearing. He remembered that he drew from her strength in ways his father never could or would understand. And he remembered that his mother had instilled in him a pride in his Kiowa heritage that his father was unable to share completely. Even now, memories of the limited time he had spent in his mother's village filled him with warmth. He had known only happiness there—until that fateful day.

He remembered it all as if it were yesterday. He was five years old and his father had brought Whispering Woman and him to visit his grandmother in the Kiowa village. Jack knew that Whispering Woman's attachment to her ailing mother was strong and that she wanted to spend time with her. He also knew Whispering Woman felt strongly about the training her son would receive in the Rabbit Society with the rest of the Kiowa boys while he was there. Never able to refuse her anything she truly wanted, his father had reluctantly left them there, promising to return in a week as was his usual custom.

The familiar warmth again swelled within Cass. His arrival at the village always signaled the immediate shedding of "white man's clothing," the donning of the traditional breechcloth, and the onset of a sense of freedom he felt nowhere else. He remembered how determined he had been to become a true Kiowa brave like the other boys his age, so he would make his mother proud.

His father had been gone for no more than a few hours when it began.

Gunfire!

The thunder of pounding hooves!

Panic!

Terror!

Scorching fire!

Choking smoke!

The screams of the maimed and dying!

He remembered the horror on his mother's face as she swept him from his feet and carried him, running breathlessly to escape the attacking soldiers as others fell all around them. He recalled his relief when they were safely concealed at last and the gunshots were behind them. He recollected with utmost clarity the look in his mother's eyes when she turned to him and warned him to stay hidden, then his shock when she left him to run back in the direction from which they had come, toward the tepee of her ailing mother.

His shouted pleas were lost in the escalating sounds of the holocaust. When she disappeared within the black smoke, fear swept his mind.

The gunfire gradually stilled. Screams of panic and pain became dwindling wails as a black cloud of death finally descended, leaving only scorched earth and choking silence.

He did not recall how many days passed before his father found him . . . but he remembered watching as his father sifted through the blackened debris of the village, tears falling unrestrained.

The two charred bodies found amongst the remains of his grandmother's tepee were unidentifiable.

Standing beside his father at last, he had refused to believe that one of those blackened bodies had been his mother.

His life had changed forever that day, and he—

"Answer me, Cass! It had somethin' to do with Flyin' Eagle, didn't it?"

Brought back to the present by the agitation in his father's voice, Cass frowned. He was two men now. He was Cass Thomas, his father's son, and he was Pale Wolf, true to the Kiowa within.

"Cass!"

"Does it matter?" Cass's voice was void of emotion. "The incident with Purity Corrigan was a mistake— on their part and mine. It's best forgotten."

"And what if I don't want to forget it?" Jack's voice was cold.

"That's your choice and Stan Corrigan's." Cass paused. "You said you owe him your life."

"They almost killed you!"

"No. I was never in danger of dying. I was determined to live."

Jack looked at him strangely. "What are you sayin'? Are you tryin' to tell me that I should forget that bastard wrangler put a bullet in your back, and every damned one of the other men here looks at you like they're sorry that bullet didn't do the job?"

Cass repeated, "You said you owe him your life."

"You're tellin' me that I should forget everythin' that happened just because Stan Corrigan was faster with his gun than some fella who had me in his sights durin' the war?"

Cass did not reply.

"What if I won't?"

"The decision is yours."

"No, it isn't. Because if *I* agree to this partnership, *you're* a part of it . . . every step of the way."

Silence.

"I want to hear you say it, Cass." Jack's expression grew thunderous. "I want to hear you say that you'll put everythin' that happened between you, Purity Corrigan, and those wranglers behind you if I go on with this partnership as planned. I want you to tell me that you'll be startin' fresh from this day on, and that you'll do everythin' needed to make this partnership work. I want you to say that you've put the past behind you forever."

His expression unrevealing, Cass nodded. "The past is behind me, where it belongs."

Jack waited a long moment, then demanded, "Why?"

"Why what?"

"Why this sudden forgiveness? Why this sudden decision to put the whole affair behind you?"

Cass held his gaze unflinchingly. "You said you owe Stan Corrigan your life."

"All right, damn it! I owe Stan my life and it's time to pay him back! If he'll agree to it, the partnership is on, but I'm tellin' you now—this is the hardest debt I'll ever pay!"

Turning, Jack started back toward the house with a stride that was rigid with resentment.

Cass followed slowly behind. He had known from the beginning what the outcome of their conversation would be. His father was an honorable man. He paid his debts, no matter how high the cost.

A hard smile tugged at Cass's lips. He was like his father in that way. He paid his debts.

As for the rest, the assurances he had given his father . . .

Regret briefly twinged his conscience.

He had lied.

Purity twisted and turned in her bed. She heaved a heavy sigh and turned to look at the shadows beyond her window, acceding to her sleeplessness at last. She had been abed for hours—or so it seemed. During that time she had avidly courted sleep, if only to escape her thoughts and anxieties. But it was to no avail. The events of that evening played over and again in her mind, disallowing rest.

It's settled.

Stan's voice had been gruff. His face had been pale and tight with strain. Purity knew she would never forget the silence that followed, or the air of disquiet that prevailed as the ranch hands waited for him to continue.

Jack and I are agreed. We're puttin' the past behind us, and he'll be takin' on a full partnership in the ranch as soon as we can get to the bank and settle all the papers. We haven't worked out all the details yet, but I wanted you to know that you'll all have a job here as long as you want to stay.

Another silence had ensued as the men exchanged looks, as each glanced toward Jack's son standing in a corner of the room. Her own glance had followed. A chill had trailed down her spine, and she had questioned herself silently. Why had she talked Stan into accepting such an impossible situation? She had made her decision that morning, hadn't she? She had been prepared to crawl to Roger Norris if that was the only way to get the loan extension. Surely one night with Roger could not be so bad that she—

Momentary nausea had launched a familiar attack then, and Purity had known she was kidding herself. *Anything* was preferable to the subjugation she would have been forced to accept at Roger's lecherous hands. In that moment she also accepted another truth—she was more comfortable facing physical threat from Pale Wolf than she would be facing Roger's amorous advances.

In looking at Stan then, she had seen that the signs were all too clear—the trembling of his hands that he could not quite control, his fading color . . . The tension of the last few weeks had stolen precious time from him. He needed to know that all would be well. She made up her mind in that moment to talk to the men as soon as possible and explain that to them. If necessary, she would plead for their help in making the situation work.

As for Pale Wolf . . .

She had looked again at him then; his expression was unchanged. Standing in the corner of the room as he had since his father and he had returned to the house, he remained enigmatically silent.

Damn him! She was still uncertain what he was thinking!

We need to forget all the mistakes and hard feelin's if this thing is goin' to work, Stan had continued. *Jack and I are agreed that his partnership in the Circle C will pay off for everybody in the end. The drive this year is goin' to be a good one, and you'll all get paid back for the hard work you've put in.* He had forced a smile. *That's all I got to say for now.* He had looked at Jack Thomas. *You want to say somethin'?*

Jack had not immediately responded, allowing Purity the time to assess him more closely. She had attempted to think of him as he had once been, the man who won the woman Stan loved, but she had seen only the shadow of resentment that still clouded his eyes as he eyed the men around him and spoke abruptly.

I have only one thing to say right now, and it's this. I'm thinkin' that Stan's a lucky man to have men as loyal to him as you fellas seem to be. I suppose he deserves it, but it speaks well of you. I'll be expectin' good things from all of you.

Purity had looked at the men. Their faces were grave, and their expressions were easy to read. Words meant little. Realities remained.

Her gaze had again snapped back to Pale Wolf, and it occurred to her then that it might be best if she attempted to think of him as Cass Thomas.

Another chill rolled down Purity's spine.

Yes, words meant little. Realities remained.

Determined to force from her mind the nagging uncertainties that would give her no rest, Purity moved restlessly in her bed. Finally facing the darkened corner of the room, she closed her eyes. It was warm and the air was still. Her nightgown clung moistly against her and her hair was hot against her neck. She was uncomfortable and tired. Tomorrow would be a hard day and she needed her sleep.

Another thought badgered her. She had told Stan that she was certain the hostility still remaining would gradually fade.

Purity's discomfort increased.

She had spoken that reassurance so earnestly. But she had lied.

The household was asleep.
Night shadows encompassed all.

Purity's bedroom was silent . . . but she was not alone.

Cass looked down at Purity as she lay sleeping. His chest bared to the night air, his hair streaming freely against the broad width of his shoulders, he had slipped out of the bunkhouse and entered the ranch house without being heard. It had not been difficult. His step was silent, darkness was his ally, and the inevitability of the moment now before him had been made apparent by his vision quest.

An indefinable awareness rippled along his skin as Cass crouched beside the bed. He contemplated Purity's hair, which was strewn across the pillow in a swath of glittering silver-gold. He observed dark lashes lying against skin that was flawless and smooth. He studied features that were small and delicate. Clothed as she was in a white nightshift that lay softly against her, the woman appeared almost angelic.

But she was the enemy.

And the time for retribution was at hand.

Cass touched the golden flow of her hair. He wound his fingers in its silken length. His lips tightened abruptly as he twisted the strands with a soft command.

"Wake up, Purity."

Purity stirred. Her eyes flew open, reflecting the fear she fought to control as she caught her breath.

He felt the heat of her. The sweet scent of her skin assaulted him. He breathed it in as she rasped, "Wh . . . what are you doin' in my room? What do you want? If Stan knew you were here—" She halted, then continued, "I thought everythin' was settled, that the past had been put to rest."

"Did you?"

"How many times do we have to go over this? Buck shot you to protect me. He believed he was doin' the right thing. I could have left you to bleed to death, but I didn't. I took you to a doctor."

"A doctor . . . who didn't give a damn if I lived or died."

"The doctor said he'd take care of you."

"An empty promise."

"Well, what did you expect? You didn't tell anyone who you were. You were dressed like a Kiowa!"

"I *am* Kiowa."

The smooth skin so close to his lips paled as she muttered, "You survived."

"Because others came to seek me out when I was missed at the powwow nearby. They brought me back to camp."

The fine line of Purity's jaw stiffened. "All this has nothin' to do with a stolen horse, does it?"

Cass did not reply.

"It's somethin' else." Her breasts heaved beneath the sheer garment she wore . . . the fine cotton revealed an outline of the soft female flesh beneath. The gold locket at her throat glinted as she spat, "I'm not a mind reader! Tell me what this is all about, damn it!"

Cass breathed heavily as well. It would be so easy. She would not cry out. She wanted Stan to believe all former hostility had been dismissed so he could put his mind at rest. Her concern for the old man left her vulnerable to him in every way.

Cass tightened his grip on her hair, drawing her closer. His mouth only inches from hers, he hissed, "You aren't fooling me. I found Flying Eagle's horse wandering loose. His saddle blanket was soaked with blood. I tracked him to your herd, and I found your horse's tracks."

"I don't know what you're talkin' about."

His hand twisted tighter. "Tell me what happened to him."

"I don't know what you're talkin' about, I tell you! You're the only Indian I saw that day."

Fury and another emotion he dared not identify flamed hotter still, testing Cass's control as he grated, "Tell me . . ."

Purity's eyes flared with unexpected heat. "You don't know the truth when you hear it!" He saw anger replace fear the moment before she commanded unexpectedly, "Let me go." She waited, then demanded, "I said, let me go!"

Taken by surprise when Purity's anger erupted abruptly into flailing arms and pounding fists, Cass struggled to subdue her. She was stronger than he'd expected and more determined. Her fire stirred a responsive heat within him as he pinned her with the weight of his body, gripping her wrists to secure them against the bed over her head.

Holding her powerless beneath him at last, Cass grated, "You're wasting your time trying to fight me. Your struggles are as useless as your lies. I promise you, no matter what you're thinking now, you'll tell me the truth in the end."

"Get out of my room."

She was shuddering with rage. Her breath fanned his lips. Her breasts heaved under his chest. The taut female length of her scorched him.

"I said, get out!"

"Why don't you call for help?"

"I don't *need* help."

Cass did not bother to reply.

Releasing her abruptly, he drew himself to his feet. Finding his separation from her flesh more difficult than he wanted to acknowledge, he repeated, "You'll tell me the truth, in the end."

He was gone.

Alone again in her room, Purity released a quaking breath. But the image of the man who had disappeared into the darkness of the hallway remained: black, shoulder-length hair unbound; massive shoulders and chest bared to the heat of the night; strong features shadowed with darkness; power and menace held tightly in check.

A cold knot of fear tightened inside her.

The savage within Cass Thomas had revealed himself once more.

Flying Eagle. The name emerged from Purity's racing thoughts.

Pale Wolf had said she knew the truth.

The frightening reality was that she did. She knew that the man known as Cass Thomas was merely a veneer. She knew that Pale Wolf was the true man within.

And she knew that neither of the two would allow her to escape him.

Chapter Four

There was no doubt about it. Willard Norris wasn't happy.

Stan glanced around him. Norris's office was large and well furnished, but its size was diminished by the number of people presently crowding its confines.

Stan frowned, recalling the tension in Purity's demeanor as she'd descended the ranch house staircase that morning. There was little need for conversation between them. They knew what the first business of the day would be.

The ride into town was more arduous than he had expected it would be. It tested his strength to the limit, despite the fact that everyone was so intent on his comfort that it was almost irritating.

Upon arrival, they went directly to the office of the

town's only lawyer, Jonathan Weaver. There that amiable fellow proved his longstanding friendship by drawing up the partnership agreement between the Thomases and the Corrigans on the spot. Despite his desperate circumstances, it was harder than Stan had dreamed possible to sign away half of the Circle C.

To his credit, Jack accepted the terms exactly as he had offered them—equal partnership between the two families, with Jack meeting all payments due on the loan until the specified amount was satisfied. Nor did Jack dispute the provision that neither partner could sell his portion of the ranch for ten years.

But the strain had sapped Stan's strength. It galled him that he had barely been able to conceal his exhaustion as they made their way from the lawyer's office to the bank. Buck had pushed his chair, Purity walking silently beside him, with Jack and Cass Thomas slightly to their rear. Telling himself that he need persevere only a little longer, he was never happier that his strength had held up than at the moment when they walked through the door of the bank and he saw Roger Norris's face.

The bastard . . .

Even in retrospect, the fury of the moment set Stan's heart to pounding. It had taken all he had to maintain a civil facade.

It occurred to him that he was never more proud of Purity than he was when she met Roger's eyes squarely, with a gaze so cold that he could swear he saw Roger shudder. Viewing the deadly promise in

Purity's gaze, he knew that if he had been Roger, he might have shivered, too.

He remembered Roger's expression when he told the bastard that he wanted to talk to his father. He was almost able to see the fellow's mind racing. The assessing glance Roger gave Jack and Cass was returned in kind. There was no need to guess what they thought of each other when Roger turned abruptly and led them toward his father's office.

As for Buck . . . well . . . as Roger stood across the office from them, reading over his father's shoulder, it was safe to say that the younger Norris was not among friends.

His ample bulk filling his chair, Willard Norris looked up from the legal document Purity had handed him. He was not smiling. It occurred to Stan that he had never liked the fellow much. Norris's face was shiny, flat, and finely shaved. With his puffy pink features, Norris always reminded Stan of a sow—a well-dressed, well-spoken sow who sported a fine gray mustache and a questionable disposition. He suddenly realized that the only time Willard Norris's smile appeared genuine was when someone was in financial difficulty.

Stan suppressed a snort. He had viewed that genuinely happy smile too many times for his own comfort. But today was different.

Willard Norris addressed him abruptly. "This agreement says that Jack Thomas and his son are your new partners and they'll be meeting the payments on your loan."

"That's right. Jack will advance the next payment, too, just for good measure."

Norris frowned. "That isn't necessary."

"Yes, it is."

"Whatever you say." Norris's frown deepened. "I'm pleased that the foreclosure won't be necessary."

He didn't look pleased.

"Roger and I were saying just yesterday that it would be the end of an era if the Corrigan land were to be swallowed up."

Roger, the bastard . . .

"I hope you'll understand that I must verify the funds on this letter of credit."

"Those funds are available." Speaking for the first time, Jack stepped forward. Stan could not help being amused at the look in Jack's eye when he continued, "And I don't mind tellin' you that I don't appreciate either my name or my word bein' doubted."

"No personal offense intended." Norris managed a nervous smile. He stood abruptly and extended his hand. "I'm pleased to have met you, Mr. Thomas." He glanced at Cass after Jack's cool handshake. He nodded, as if duplicating his comment when he extended his hand toward Cass as well. "You may be sure we'll be pleased to serve your needs in the future, but right now I have an appointment to keep." He turned toward his son. "You'll take care of the details, won't you, Roger?"

"I'll be pleased to."

A wave of unexpected weakness suddenly assaulted Stan, and he lifted a hand to his temple.

"What's the matter, Stan?"

Purity's voice sounded in his ear and Stan realized abruptly that he had almost blacked out. Purity leaned closer, her expression concerned, and he was suddenly certain that if her face were the last one he saw before his eyes closed the final time, he would consider himself the luckiest man in the world.

That thought stimulated a smile as he replied, "I'm more tired than I thought, darlin'. I'm thinkin' I'll let Jack and you take care of the details so Buck can take me back to the wagon."

"You're sure you're all right?"

Those clear eyes . . . such beautiful eyes. Yes, he was a damned lucky man to have been riding beside the flooded river that day.

"Stan?"

"I'm fine. Buck will take care of me."

"Stan . . ."

"I'm all right." He forced a stronger note to his voice. "You just take care of business, and when you're done I'll be rested up and we can start back home."

Purity hesitated.

"Your father's right, Purity. He needs to rest and we have some business to settle. Just step this way."

Purity's head snapped up at the sound of Roger's voice. Stan knew he would never forget the look on her face, the contempt that was accompanied by an almost indiscernible curling of her lip as she replied with exaggerated slowness, "Business to settle . . . yes, we do."

He felt Buck stiffen behind him. He was prepared

131

for his old friend's voice in his ear as Buck rasped, "You ain't goin' to let that bastard—"

Interrupting Buck, Stan spoke a flat, definitive statement that bore not a trace of uncertainty.

"Purity will take care of it."

"But—"

"Let's go."

Buck turned his chair toward the door with a last grunt of protest, and Stan smiled. Despite his conviction that his days were numbered, he wouldn't trade places with Roger Norris right now for all the money in the world.

Stan almost laughed out loud.

He'd be damned if he would!

Purity's eyes bored into Roger's back as she followed him toward his office. His well-tailored, broad-shouldered, *unprincipled* back . . .

She clutched the partnership agreement in her hand, disdain for the man walking in front of her rising as keenly as bile in her throat.

It had not been an easy morning.

The stealthy visit from Pale Wolf—Cass—in the dark of the previous night had left her shaken. Strangely, she had awakened with a lingering uncertainty if his visit to her bedroom had been a nightmare or reality. It had taken only one step down into the dining room and the clash of a hard, green-eyed gaze with hers to confirm the reality of that visit. It had taken only one step more for her to read in those eyes that despite the importance of the partnership to be signed that morning, Pale Wolf—Cass—had only one true mission in mind.

The ride into town had been endless. Despite his attempts to conceal his discomfort, Stan had grown more weary with every mile. Then had come Stan's obvious distress in signing away half his ranch.

But, strangely, all other thought had disappeared when they stepped through the doors of the bank and she saw Roger. The memory of his hand striking her cheek returned in that moment with abrupt and stunning clarity, and her determination to make Roger rue that act was renewed.

The time was now at hand.

Roger paused at his office door. He turned toward her as he pushed the door open, allowing her to precede him. She looked behind her, surprised to see that she was alone.

"It seems the others left with Stan. I suppose you'll have to take care of the details yourself." His voice dropped an intimate note lower. "You're not afraid to be alone with me, are you, Purity?"

So he was going to play that game.

Purity inwardly smiled.

"No, I'm not afraid. Are you?"

With slow deliberation, Purity linked her gaze with his. She saw the instantaneous heat that surged to life in his eyes. It was visible in the subtle twitch of his cheek, in the immediate darting of his gaze to her lips, and in the almost indiscernible tensing of his frame. Satisfaction surged within her. Whatever the reason for his attraction to her, she knew he was helpless against it.

Not waiting for his reply, Purity walked past him into his office. She turned abruptly toward him as the door snapped closed.

"You didn't expect this turn of events, did you, Roger?" She took a deliberate step closer to him, her voice dropping to a husky whisper. "You thought the next time you saw me that it would be under different circumstances, that I'd be desperate for your help. You thought that you'd snap your fingers and I'd be in your arms. You thought I'd forget that you hit me."

Roger's jaw tensed. The line of his body grew rigid. "I lost my temper. What I did was regrettable. I didn't expect things to get out of hand."

"It almost happened, you know." Purity inched closer to him, her gaze intent. "After Stan received the foreclosure notice, I made up my mind to come to you and beg you to save the ranch. I knew you could do it. I knew it was just a matter of persuadin' you to convince your father to extend the loan. I was prepared to do whatever I had to do."

Purity paused, her lips parted. She noted the gradual acceleration of Roger's breathing as his gaze darted again to her mouth.

She moved closer. Her breasts brushed his chest as she whispered, "What would have happened if I had come to you, Roger? Tell me. Would you have dragged me to your bed? Would you have torn off my clothes so I couldn't hide anything from you? Would you have mounted me like a stallion and shown me that you were my master? Would you have whipped me into submission and made me *beg?"* Roger's cheek ticked spasmodically as she prompted, "You're not answerin' me, Roger."

Silence.

Purity laughed softly. "It almost happened. *Almost . . .*"

The silence grew taut.

"I've been thinkin' about it. . . ." Purity allowed her voice to trail away. She felt a surge of triumph as perspiration appeared on Roger's brow, as his face twitched again and his breathing grew increasingly strained. "I've wondered what it would've been like to let you do what you wanted with me . . . to be submissive to whatever whims crossed your mind." She fought the swell of nausea the thought raised, continuing, "I couldn't fall asleep last night. I *ached* inside with the thought of it."

Roger's only response was a telltale locking of his jaw that betrayed his rapidly waning control. Purity moistened her lips with the tip of her tongue and asked, "Have you been thinkin' about it, too, Roger? Have you been wonderin' what it would've been like if Buck hadn't stepped in that night at the ranch, if you'd been able to follow through, to pull me off into the shadows and show me who's really the master? I dreamed about it, Roger." She took a stabilizing breath, determined to continue, "And then I wondered if—" She allowed a calculated pause. "But that's all changed now."

"No, that's not true." A visible tremor shook Roger the moment before he gripped her arms abruptly. His hands were shaking and his body was rigid. Purity felt victory within her grasp as he rasped, "It

135

doesn't have to end here. Not if you don't want it to. I can come to you. I can meet you somewhere away from the ranch where we'll be alone and we can do it all, just as you described. You'll love it. You'll love the sense of power, the ecstasy that only pleasure mixed with pain can provide. I'll give you all you can withstand, and then I'll give you more until you're gasping with the rapture of it. Then I'll let you lay your hands on me." His expression grew intense. "You have strong hands. I'll let you use them however you wish. I'll let you use your hands, your body, your mouth, until you're writhing with a passion that matches mine. We'll be good together, Purity." Roger's brown eyes were hot with desire. "I sensed the heat inside you the first time I saw you, and I've dreamed of the moments you described over and over again until I'm crazy with wanting it."

"You want me, Roger?"

"Yes . . . yes."

Purity pressed herself against him. She felt him shudder as she urged, "Beg me."

"Wh . . . what?"

"Beg me." She slid her fingers between them and loosened the button on her shirt. She released it slowly. "We'll lock the door and make them wait. We'll do it right here . . . right now."

Roger glanced at the door. He licked nervously at his lips, then started abruptly toward it.

"No!" He turned at her command. "Beg me, Roger. I want to hear the words."

Roger's face shone with perspiration. A single bead of moisture trickled from his temple, streaking his cheek. His lips trembled with the visible difficulty of his effort as he forced out the word.

"Please."

"More." Purity stared levelly into his eyes. "Plead with me."

He took a shuddering breath. "Please. I want it to be just the way you described it—pleasure with pain. You won't be sorry, I promise you."

Purity withheld response.

"*Please!*" Roger's face grew livid. "Please, please, please! Is that what you want to hear? I'm begging you!"

Roger's hoarse pleas rang in the silence of the room. Purity paused to savor the moment. She then spoke a single word in reply.

"No."

Roger blinked. He shook his head, as if disbelieving his ears.

"Wh . . . what did you say?"

"I said, *no*. That word shouldn't be too hard for you to understand. You want me . . . but I don't want you."

"But you said—"

"What did I say? I said I've been thinkin' about what it might have been like to be with you. I have. What I didn't say was that the thought of it nearly made me sick." A smile as cold as her words touched Purity's lips. "But you can still have it all, just as you described it. Sophie's house of pleasure is up the street. You know that place well enough. One of the whores there will be happy to oblige you."

"What are you saying?"

"I'm sayin' I don't want you. I never did! I sayin' I can think of nothin' worse than havin' you touch me in any way. Too bad, isn't it, considerin' how much you enjoyed hittin' me that last night at the ranch. You did enjoy it, didn't you, Roger?" Her smile grew frigid. "You enjoyed it almost as much as I enjoyed *seein' you beg.*"

"Bitch . . ."

"But you still want me, don't you, Roger?"

"Bitch! I'll make you regret—"

Roger's threatening step toward her was halted by a sound behind him the moment before the office door swung open abruptly. His lips snapped closed as Cass's broad frame filled the doorway. She saw the effort Roger expended to control his rage as Cass spoke in a voice that was low and void of emotion.

"Stan's in the wagon. The others are with him." His light eyes narrowed. "Where are the papers?"

Roger nodded stiffly and walked to his desk. He took a folder from his drawer without speaking a word. The folder bore Stan's name, and Purity inwardly sneered. He had been waiting for her, all right. He had been expecting her to come crawling on her hands and knees. Well, she had shown him what begging really meant!

Roger cleared his throat, then spoke. "I had these papers already prepared in the eventuality that Stan would find a way to meet the payment."

That *Stan* would find a way to meet the payment . . .

Roger scratched his name across the bottom of the last sheet, then looked up. "This will take care of it.

My father already has Mr. Thomas's letter of credit."

"That's it?" Cass's expressionless demeanor did not alter. "This cancels the foreclosure notice?"

"Yes."

"That's all I need to know."

Snatching the papers from Roger's desk, Cass gripped Purity's elbow unexpectedly and turned her toward the door. A protest rose to her lips, but Purity swallowed it, unwilling to allow Roger the satisfaction. She did not look back as Cass ushered her outside and closed the door behind them.

The snap of the latch resounded in the small alcove that concealed them from view, signaling a release of her fury as Purity hissed, "Let go of my arm!"

His gaze frozen, Cass returned, "That bastard may have gotten when he deserved in there—"

Purity gasped with outrage. "You listened at the door?"

"—but if I hadn't come in when I did—"

"If you hadn't come in when you did, I would have handled Roger myself!"

"You pushed him too far!"

"That's *my* business, not yours!"

"That's where you're wrong!" His gaze glittering, Cass grated, "From now on, if someone approaches, you, he walks in my shadow. If someone speaks to you, I hear the words. If someone touches you, I make him pay the price . . . because your life's no longer your own. *It belongs to me.* Life for life . . . blood for blood."

"You *are* a savage!"

Cass jerked her close. "And I warn you now—don't

139

try any of your tricks on me. If you do, you'll live to regret them."

Shrugging off his grip, ignoring the chill that ran down her spine at the intensity of Cass's gaze, Purity did not bother to respond. Nor did she wait for the sound of his footsteps behind her as she turned abruptly and headed for the street.

Halting beside the Circle C wagon minutes later, Purity felt all anger fade when she looked down into Stan's exhausted face. She forced a composure she did not feel when Cass handed him the paperwork. She stated flatly, "The foreclosure notice has been cancelled."

Stan studied her expression, his gaze searching as he addressed her.

"Is everything all right?"

"Yes."

"Everythin's settled with Roger?"

"It is."

"There's nothin' left undone?"

Purity's single word of response emerged with a hard smile. "Nothin'."

"All right. Let's go home."

Riding out of town minutes later, Purity positioned her mount as close to the wagon as possible. She frowned as Cass boldly assumed a place at her side.

Turning her face forward, Purity bit back the words that rose to her lips. Her time would come. Stan deserved the peace of mind that this day and Jack Thomas had availed him. She would allow nothing and no one to tarnish the moment for him.

As for Pale Wolf—or Cass Thomas—whichever he chose to be, he would soon realize that he had met his match in every way.

She wasn't going to get away with it!

Roger straightened his well-tailored shoulders, forcing a steadiness to his trembling frame as he stared at the doorway through which Purity and the hard-eyed Cass Thomas had disappeared minutes earlier. They were a fine pair—a merciless bitch and an arrogant half-breed! Damn them to hell, both of them!

Withdrawing his handkerchief from his pocket, Roger mopped his brow and upper lip. His rage rose anew as he reviewed in his mind the stinging humiliation Purity had dealt him. How could he have been such a fool? How could he have abandoned common sense and played into her hands?

Experiencing a familiar hardening, Roger cursed aloud and adjusted his trousers with a rough hand. The truth was that common sense had flown out the window when another part of his anatomy assumed control.

Purity Corrigan . . . cool eyes that were almost level with his, a firm, hard body he longed to feel lying naked against him . . . He had lain awake, reliving his last visit to the Circle C countless times as he cursed his flaring temper and lack of control. It infuriated him that he could not strike her from his mind. Her image taunted him, tainting the moments he spent with women who offered themselves willingly to him.

141

Damn her—she even haunted his dreams!

Roger threw his handkerchief onto the desk and began pacing. She had done it deliberately! She had led him on, knowing that his body swelled at the mere sight of her, that he ached to have her. She had tormented him! She had gotten her revenge.

Roger's step halted abruptly. But it wasn't over yet.

Cass Thomas . . . Roger's low snort was filled with contempt. The man was a half-breed . . . a brute! No decent woman would even look at him!

His stomach twisting, Roger remembered Thomas's proprietary manner when he took Purity's arm. She did not protest. Was there something between them? Had she lain with him? Had she let him sink himself deep inside her? Had she given that half-savage everything she had refused to give him?

Roger walked stiffly to his desk and sat abruptly. He stared sightlessly forward. His jaw clenched as Purity's image rose again before his mind, her pale hair glittering, her smile mocking. She had made him beg. She had made him crawl, and then she had turned her back and left on the arm of her new lover!

No, damn her! She wouldn't get away with it! He would still get her where he wanted her, and then he would humble her. He would get her down on her knees. He would take her body as many times and with as many perversities as he could manage, and when he was done—when he was so tired of her flesh that he could stomach the sight of her no longer— he would throw her away!

Yes, he would!

Roger stood abruptly. Purity Corrigan would rue this day.

As for Cass Thomas . . .

The countryside rolled past at a frustratingly slow pace as Cass maintained his position riding at Purity's side. He surveyed their small party briefly. At the reins of the wagon, Buck maintained a sober silence that did not conceal his concern. Riding alongside, Jack had not spoken a word during their return journey, although his expression spoke volumes. Beside him, Purity preserved a stone-faced facade that altered only when she spoke to Stan.

They had been traveling for what seemed ages under the pitiless afternoon sun. Stan's condition had forced them to halt several times, and it was obvious, despite the lack of conversation, that everyone was becoming increasingly concerned.

Cass saw the glance that was exchanged between Purity and Buck the moment before he again drew the wagon to a halt and Purity dismounted. She climbed up beside Stan in a moment and crouched next to him, holding the canteen to his lips. She wiped Stan's forehead and cheeks with a dampened bandanna. Cass could read her determination to protect Stan from anxiety at all cost.

Devil or angel . . . which was she?

Mentally chastising himself for that last thought, Cass fought to maintain an impassive facade. He knew who and what Purity Corrigan was! He had known when he found Flying Eagle's horse and tracked it to the site where its hoofprints mingled

143

with those of an unknown rider—unmistakable tracks with a notched shoe that could not be mistaken. He had followed those distinctive tracks over terrain that might have made the task impossible were it not for the determination that drove him. He had remained concealed, awaiting his opportunity, watching the rider rope and ride with a skill and tenacity that could not be denied. He had no doubt, then or now, that the rider was equally adept with a gun and not averse to using it.

Strangely, considering the rapidity with which events had unraveled that day, he remembered with utmost clarity his shock at looking down into Purity's pale eyes. Incredulous, he had held her immobile with the weight of his body and ripped her hat from her head, releasing hair that was a finer gold than any he had ever seen.

Images faded from that point on, but the voices remained.

Still alive, is he? I'll be damned if I'll waste another bullet on him!

I'm the boss here. Stan isn't!

. . . Leave him where he lies! Nobody's goin' to pay attention to another dead Injun in this country!

Cass's jaw stiffened. *Another* dead Indian . . .

Cass's stomach knotted tightly.

He had searched his mind for the reason he had been allowed to live. The answer eluded him until that day on a scorching hilltop when the path of retribution became clear.

With his visit to Purity's room the previous night, he had set the pattern for what was to come. He would make her tell him the truth, one way or another.

But he had not been expecting Roger Norris. Cass's lips tightened. He had sensed the tension between Purity and that fellow immediately. It had crawled up his spine in a silent warning that had forced him to follow her to Norris's office in Jack's stead, and to pause outside the door where he overheard their whispered conversation.

Cass's stomach twisted. She had made Norris salivate with desire. She had made him crawl, and she had then brought everything crashing down around him. But she had underestimated Norris's rage. He knew with unfaltering certainty that if he had not entered the office when he did—

Cass halted that thought. He would allow nothing to happen to Purity. He would protect her with his life until the day when the truth was revealed at last.

Cass glanced at the wagon as the team resumed its slow progress, at the frail old man who had slipped into a semi-sleep. Stan would not live much longer, but that would be for the best considering what was to come.

Purity had remounted and was again riding beside him. Her shoulders were squared, her jaw set, her gaze straightforward. She had taken her revenge on Roger Norris fearlessly and without regret. She was now dealing with an equally difficult situation. Throughout, she revealed not a sign of weakness.

Cass's gaze narrowed. However black it was, Purity Corrigan's heart was that of a warrior.

Prompted by his sixth sense, Cass turned to catch

Buck's heated stare. The fellow did not like seeing him at Purity's side.

The sound of hoofbeats raised Cass's gaze abruptly to a rider fast approaching. Reining up beside them moments later, Nash Carter surveyed the situation at a glance, his expression stony. He addressed Purity directly.

"Is everythin' all right?"

"Everythin's fine." She did not smile. "The foreclosure notice has been cancelled, but Stan's worn out. He needs to rest."

"The boys were wonderin' what was keepin' you."

Purity glanced at Stan, frowning. "We had to stop a few times, but Stan will be all right once we get home."

Carter nodded and wheeled his horse up alongside the wagon. Refusing to yield his place beside Purity, Cass saw the looks Carter and Buck exchanged. He saw the heat that flushed Carter's face as his hands tightened into fists on the reins.

So, that was the way it was . . .

Were the sun not so hot, were he not frustrated by their slow pace and by the nameless, nagging unrest he could not seem to shed, Cass knew he would be tempted to laugh at the battle lines that were being drawn up. All centered around the woman so ironically named Purity.

Roger Norris, the lecherous bastard, wanted her body.

Carter, obviously smitten, wanted her heart.

Buck, a greying watchdog, wanted to protect her.

As for himself—the man who had come back from

the grave for one purpose alone—he would not be satisfied with anything less than her soul.

All trace of amusement slipping away, Cass urged his mount closer to Purity's.

He had no doubt who the victor would be.

"How are you feelin', Stan?"

Purity's voice echoed strangely in the silence of Stan's room. The setting sun beyond the window cast the room into shades of pink and gold that lent a trace of color to Stan's deeply grooved cheeks, but Purity was aware of the deception perpetrated by the light. She did not fool herself. The trip to town had almost been Stan's undoing. She knew she would never forget the gray tinge to his skin as he attempted to raise himself to a seated position upon their arrival back at the ranch, or the look on his face when he realized the effort was beyond him. Buck had come immediately to his aid, but it had been Cass, with his superior size and strength, who had brushed everyone else aside and lifted Stan down without visible effort and carried him to his room. To his credit, Cass had left immediately, allowing others with whom Stan was more comfortable to settle him in.

Purity steeled herself against the painful emotions assaulting her. She was intensely aware of the silence that prevailed beyond Stan's bedroom door, although most of the hands still milled in the living room. She understood that they were somehow reluctant to quit the house for the evening despite the fact that supper was finished and the table had already been cleared. The apprehension she had read in their eyes mirrored her own as she placed a cup on the nightstand and forced a smile.

"Pete sent you some coffee. It's a little stronger than usual, likely to make your hair stand up on end, but there wasn't a one of us who had the nerve to complain. You remember what happened the last time we did. He nearly burned out the linings on our stomachs with those chile peppers he used in everythin' he cooked for the rest of the week."

Stan's smile was weak. "How could I forget? My stomach ain't been the same since." Purity saw the effort Stan expended to maintain his smile as he patted the bed beside him and urged, "Sit down. I feel like talkin'."

"Are you sure?" Purity hesitated. "We can talk tomorrow if you're tired."

"Sit. Hell, I'd rather look at your face than sleep anytime. Besides, there's some things I want to talk to you about."

Purity sat. Her throat closed painfully as Stan took her hand. He looked so frail. She remembered a time when she had thought him the biggest, strongest man alive. She had been soaked to the skin, shivering, almost drowned, and more frightened than she had ever been in her life the day he pulled her from the river, but the sound of his heart thumping heavily under her cheek as he held her in the protective circle of his arms had given her strength. Her terror had calmed the instant she had looked up into his eyes, and although her childish heart had nearly broken when she realized she might never see her parents or sisters again, Stan's presence had consoled her.

But that was long ago. Everything had changed. There was little left of the man who'd rescued her from the river that day other than the heart that shone with such beauty from his eyes. She could not bear to think that he might—

Squeezing her hand with surprising strength, Stan whispered, "Stop worryin'. I'm not goin' to die yet." At her spontaneous protest he said, "I gave you a scare today, I know, but I've still got some time left. I'm intendin' to use it to get things straightened out."

Stan paused for a breath. Despite his pallor, his gaze was keen as he pressed on. "First things first. The ranch is taken care of now. Things ain't exactly like I'd want if I had a choice, but you won't have to worry about scramblin' for the money to meet them loan payments when they come due, and that's what's important. Ten years is a reasonable amount of time for everythin' to get on a firm footin' again, and you won't have to worry until then."

"Stan . . ."

"Quiet." Stan's smile showed a trace of his old humor. "Let a sick old man have his say." His scrutiny intensified unexpectedly. "I want to know what you think of Cass Thomas now that the dust is settlin'."

Purity stiffened.

"That bad, huh?"

Purity shrugged, aware that an outright lie would be pointless. "It's not as easy as I thought it was goin' to be to put the past behind me." She chose her words carefully. "I think he feels the same."

Stan did not respond.

She offered speculatively, "I suppose it'll work out once we get to know each other better."

A fleeting frown passed over Stan's face. "Hell, I was hopin' you was startin' to feel better about the whole thing. The truth is . . . well, I've got a feelin' about that fella. I can't get it out of my head that even if he's more Kiowa than the boys and maybe even you can be comfortable with, there's honor in his blood. I'm thinkin' that maybe this is goin' to work out better than you think, and when I'm gone—"

Purity halted him abruptly. "Don't talk that way! I won't listen if you do."

"Nobody lives forever, darlin'." Stan squeezed her hand again, then patted it lightly. "Anyways, I wasn't softenin' you up without a purpose. The thing is, I want you to make me a promise."

"A promise," Purity responded with an unsteady laugh. "That's not fair. You're takin' advantage of me."

"I guess I am. I never was a fella to let an opportunity pass, and I'm not about to let you off the hook. So, listen close." His gaze locked with hers. "I want you to promise me that if anythin' goes wrong, you won't hide the truth from me. I want you to come and tell me, no matter how sick you think I am."

"Stan . . ."

"This old man needs that reassurance, darlin', 'cause the truth is, there ain't nothin' in this world more important to me than you—"

"Stan, please—"

"—and there ain't no force on heaven or earth that

will keep me from standin' with you if you need me."

Purity could not respond.

Stan's eyes bored into hers. "I got my regrets, you know." At her look of surprise, Stan explained, "I didn't do as much as I could have to look for your family . . . I know that now. I suppose in the back of my mind, I was afraid of losin' you if I did."

Purity's throat squeezed tight.

"I'm sorry about that, darlin'."

Purity unconsciously raised a hand to the locket at her throat. It was warm to the touch. It comforted her, allowing comforting words in reply.

"You did all you could, Stan."

"No. Lookin' back, I don't think I did." Stan's eyes suddenly filled. "You're the best thing that ever happened in my life, you know. I suppose I ain't said that often enough to you."

Struggling to conceal her emotion, Purity chided, "You didn't need to say anythin'. You spoiled me rotten. That was a dead giveaway."

"You ain't spoiled."

"Oh, I'm not? I remember a time when you bought me hand-tooled boots. You paid more for them than you ever paid for boots of your own. Then when I wanted that sorrel mare—"

"I said you ain't spoiled, and you ain't." Stan's eyes narrowed assessingly. "And neither are you puttin' anythin' over on me, tryin' to change the subject again. I ain't about to forget that you ain't given me your promise yet." He waited. "Well?"

Purity continued to hesitate, and Stan's frown

deepened. "You ain't hidin' nothin' from me, are you?"

He was too close to the mark for comfort and Purity exploded, "All right, you win! I'll promise you anythin' you want!"

"Don't like me infringin' on your independence, do you? Well, that's the privilege of a dyin' man."

"Stan . . ."

"Even if I ain't ready to kick the bucket right this minute." Stan's smile was weak. "But I am tired. I'm thinkin' we've both had enough for a while, so maybe we'll finish talkin' some other time." Abandoning their conversation just as abruptly as he had begun it, Stan urged her gently, "Go finish your chores. And while you're at it, tell them fellas waitin' outside my door that they can get rid of them long faces. This old man's too ornery to die yet."

"Oh, Stan . . ."

"I do love you, darlin'."

Tears welled.

"Hell, you ain't goin' to cry!"

"Oh—" Purity bit the tears back. "Go to sleep!"

Purity kissed him quickly on the cheek and turned toward the door. Emerging outside, she had not a moment's respite as she met the silent scrutiny of the waiting men.

She swallowed against the tightness in her throat. "He said to tell you that he's too ornery to die yet."

Incapable of saying more, Purity strode toward the yard.

* * *

"It's time you stopped avoidin' me, don't you think?"

Jack's question turned Cass abruptly toward him, allowing Jack to study his son's unrevealing expression briefly in the darkening shadows of the yard. It had been a difficult day, with the visit to town and the settling of affairs that had used up so much of Stan's meager reserve of strength.

Poor Stan. He supposed it was best that the fella had slept most of the way and was oblivious to the strain among the group. No one had to tell Jack that Cass and Purity had had some kind of run-in at the bank. Hell, Cass's jaw had been rock hard, and Purity's shoulders had been ramrod stiff when they came back. Stan might have missed it, but he knew Buck hadn't. That fella had barely taken his eyes off Cass on the way home, and if looks could kill . . .

As for the ranch hands, they had all but ignored both Cass and him at the supper table. Purity had been understandably distressed by Stan's condition, and the truth was that Cass had done little to help matters.

Jack stared at his son, his gaze narrowing. He didn't like the way things were going. Cass had changed somehow. He didn't remember his son's silence ever being so stoic, his eyes so cold, or his demeanor so unyielding.

Jack forced himself to view Cass with the eyes of a stranger. He frowned. He saw the indefinable qualities that had set his son apart from others since childhood: the proud bearing, the keenness of his startlingly light eyes, inherited from the Thomas side of the family, the surprising silence and agility with which he moved. Jack was uncertain when those qualities had become menacing in the eyes of others. There was only one thing of which he was sure as he returned his son's enigmatic stare. The transition was now complete.

That thought prompted Jack's next words as he stated flatly, "Looks like you put somethin' over on your old man." And when Cass did not respond, he went on. "I don't suppose there's any use in askin' you what your real reason was for encouragin' me to go through with the partnership in this ranch."

Cass did not respond.

"You're makin' a mistake, you know."

Cass's eyes narrowed.

"You're settin' everybody against you instead of clearin' the air. There's not one wrangler on this ranch—much less Purity, or even Stan—who has any idea that you're the one who talked me into goin' through with savin' the ranch."

"That isn't important."

"Oh, isn't it? You know I was ready to walk out on the whole deal until you spoke up. But I guess you're right." Jack squinted assessingly. "What's really important is *why* you talked me into goin' through with the partnership. It wasn't a matter of my owin' a debt of honor, was it?"

Silence.

Jack could feel his patience slipping. "I asked you a question."

No response.

"All right, damn it! If you don't want to talk, I will!

Let me make somethin' clear to you. Whatever your reasons, we *both* entered into a contract today—a partnership—and we're goin' to live up to it! It's not just a matter of 'honor.' We've got a substantial investment here. It'll be drainin' the profits from the Rocking T for some time to come. Stan's sick. We both know there's no guarantee how long he'll last . . . and I'll be damned if I'll go home and leave my investment in the hands of an inexperienced woman, no matter how competent Stan thinks she is."

The brief flicker of Cass's expression did not escape Jack.

"I'm gettin' tired of this. You've got somethin' to say, so say it!"

"You're mistaken if you believe that Purity Corrigan is just 'a woman'. She's as smart and determined as any man, and there's not a hand on this ranch who'll buck her."

"Only because Stan's advising her."

"You're wrong."

"I don't think so . . . which brings me to the reason I'm talkin' to you now. I was foolin' myself when I made myself think everybody was goin' to put the past behind them on this ranch. I've seen the way the hands still look at you, and I've seen the way you still look at them—not to mention the fact that that young woman turns to ice every time she glances in your direction." Stan shook his head. "But it's too late for that kind of hindsight, now. I'm stuck with things as they stand." He paused again, adding, "And so are you."

Jack waited a moment, watching his son's face for

a reaction that did not appear. Annoyed, he continued, "I'm turnin' our partnership in this ranch over to you. You're the one responsible for it now. It's up to you to make it work, one way or another—and you'd damned well better *make* it work!"

"Jack . . ."

"Don't 'Jack' me! I'm your father, and I'm tellin' you now that I expect you to take over here until we can both be sure that things are headin' in the right direction. And don't you go lookin' at me that way, either! There's no way I can stay here long enough to make certain things are goin' right. We're short-handed at the Rocking T, and you know how Julia worries. I can't leave her alone there indefinitely. This thing's goin' to be up to you."

No response.

Jack's cheek ticked with vexation. "You're a hard case, you know! Well, I am, too, and I'm not changin' my mind! I just want you to remember—you attacked that woman on the trail drive last fall. Whether you thought at the time that you had good cause or not, the fact is that everybody here has a right to the way they feel about you."

"Nothing I can say will change that."

"No, but Purity can make a difference. Talk to her. Hell, the tension between the two of you is so thick you could cut it with a knife! I can feel it, and the men can feel it too. If Stan wasn't so sick, he'd be the first to face you down about it. So, I'm tellin' you now, straighten things out, because I'm goin' to be headin' out tomorrow, and I want to do it with a clear mind."

"Tomorrow . . ."

"That's right." Jack waited. "Cass, damn it . . ."

"All right, I'll talk to her."

Jack studied his son's expression. Something about it nagged at him as he urged, "She's in the barn now, tendin' to her horse. I saw her go in a few minutes ago. There'll never be a better time."

Jack studied his son more closely. He could almost believe he saw a smile behind those light eyes as Cass turned toward the barn. Jack realized that he was still worried, despite his son's compliance.

Why?

The question lingered.

Cass approached the barn, alert to the sound of Jack's footsteps heading back in the direction of the house. One thought in mind, he scanned the shadows of the yard. The men had gradually filtered out of the house and gone back to the bunkhouse. He had never seen a more sober bunch. They had deliberately avoided the barn. He supposed he knew the reason. They were avoiding Purity. By the look of them, they were thinking that Stan might not make the night.

Cass's lips lifted in a brief smile. Not that tough old man! He had seen the scrutiny in Stan's eyes when he had lifted him from the wagon and carried him to his room. As weak as he was physically, his mind had been keen and assessing. It had made Cass wonder just how much more difficult matters would have been if the fellow were on his feet and at his best. But he wasn't. And as circumstances presently stood, things were going his way.

Cass paused at the barn doorway, allowing his eyes to adjust to the darkness within. A lantern was lit in one of the far stalls. He heard sounds of movement and saw a shadow flickering against the rear wall . . . a slender shadow. He took a bold step forward, only to halt abruptly when an object glittering on the ground nearby caught his eye. He bent down to pick it up.

A locket.

A remembered scene from the night before stole his breath: gold hair strewn across the pillow; small, perfect features motionless in repose; a white cotton gown adhering damply to gentle feminine curves beneath; a small heart-shaped locket, lying against creamy skin that called for his touch. He remembered the scent of that skin, the sensation of the silky, gold strands sliding against his palm.

Suddenly angry at his thoughts, at the responsive hardening of his flesh, Cass clenched the locket tightly. No! He had waited too long for retribution to allow his body to rule his mind.

Cass strode angrily toward the rear stall. Purity did not hear his approach. Involved in a frantic search of the area that apparently blocked all else from her mind, she scoured the ground anxiously with her gaze. She kicked aside saddle blankets piled in the corner, knocking over a stool and bucket in her haste as she grasped a feedbag hanging there. She dug down into the bag, filtering the grain through her fingers repeatedly before casting it aside with a soft curse. Her gaze fixing again on the floor, she then dropped to her hands and knees to begin a more intensive search.

He knew what she was looking for.

Cass clenched the locket tighter.

He was unprepared for the sob that escaped Purity's lips as her movements became more desperate, as she slid her hands over the ground in widening circles, without apparent concern for the nervous mare tied there and the restless hooves so close to her head. He did not expect the emotion that rocked him when she sat back abruptly on her heels and covered her face with her hands to cry in earnest.

Deploring his sudden desire to stride forward and draw Purity to her feet, to stroke away her tears, Cass reminded himself that this woman now overcome with emotion had shown no remorse for the pain she had caused others. He forced himself to remember that while this woman had lost a locket, Flying Eagle had lost his life.

Those thoughts added a harshness to his tone as Cass spoke abruptly.

"Did you lose something?"

Purity stiffened at the sound of his voice. The haste with which she wiped her eyes and raised her chin before she stood up and turned toward him did not escape him. But he was not ready for her pallor, for the damp streaks that still marked her cheeks, and the trace of a quiver that lingered in her voice as she responded, "It's nothin' important."

The locket seared the skin of his palm as Cass held

159

it in a crushing grip. "It seemed pretty important to me from the way you were searching."

"Did it? Well, the fact is, it's none of your business what I was lookin' for."

Cass's jaw hardened. If that was the way she wanted it . . .

Cass slipped his hand to his pocket and dropped the locket inside. He continued coldly, "I can see you're upset. Is Stan all right?"

"He's fine."

Purity started past him, only to halt abruptly as he added, "Jack will be leaving tomorrow."

"Tomorrow!"

"He can't spare any more time away from the Rocking T."

Purity's relief was obvious as she responded, "I didn't think you'd be leavin' so soon. I thought there'd be things you'd want to settle before you did."

Pausing for effect, Cass responded as casually as he could manage, "*I'm* not leaving.

"What?"

"Jack wants me to stay to oversee things."

"To *oversee* . . . ?"

"He wants me to take an active part in running the ranch until it gets back on its feet again."

"That'll never happen!"

"Oh, I assure you, I can make this ranch get back on a paying basis."

Purity took a furious step, her eyes blazing. "You know damned well what I meant! This is Stan's ranch . . . and *mine!* We give the orders here, not you or your father, and two small payments made to the First Citizens Bank aren't goin' to change that!"

"If it weren't for those 'two, small payments,' both you and Stan would've found yourself on the outside of a padlocked door."

Purity flushed. Her emotions obviously under tenuous control, she spat, "All right, let's settle this once and for all. What do you want from me?"

"I told you."

"And I told you, I don't know anythin' about what happened to anybody named Flyin' Eagle! You were the only Indian I saw that day last fall! I don't even know who he was!"

Cass locked her gaze with his. "He was nobody important . . . 'just another Injun not worth the price of a bullet.' "

Purity went stock still. Her lips stiff, she replied, "I'll say this one last time. If this Flyin' Eagle you're talkin' about disappeared, I had nothin' to do with it."

"If you didn't, you know who did."

"My men are wranglers, not killers! If they had seen an Indian skulkin' around the herd, they would've chased him, and then they would've warned the others to be on the lookout."

When Cass did not respond, Purity snapped, "Believe what you want! I'm tired of this conversation."

Cass gripped Purity's arm as she attempted to brush past him. A lightning jolt of heat surged through him at the touch, lowering his voice to a grating rasp as he whispered, "I'm going to find out what happened that day, and you're the one who's going to tell me."

"You're wastin' your time."

"I have all the time in the world."

"Let go of me!"

Jerking her arm free of his hold, Purity strode out of the barn without looking back. Watching until she stepped out of sight, Cass slid his hand into his pocket and gripped the locket tightly.

Purity had lost something she valued deeply.

So had he.

She needed to find out what had happened to it.

So did he.

She would not stop searching.

Neither would he.

Stalemate.

"Purity ain't goin' to like this one bit."

Stan's brief comment hung on the air of his small bedroom. He stared at Jack, who was standing beside his bed. He was tired. He had wanted to rest, but there had been something about the tone of Jack's voice when he knocked lightly on his door a few minutes earlier and asked if he could come in. He had known it couldn't wait. Jack had not minced words upon entering, but he was finished talking, and now it was his turn.

Stan continued, "I should've cleared this all up with you before the agreement was signed. Maybe I wasn't thinkin' as clear as I thought."

"You were thinkin' clearly enough." Jack was frowning. He was obviously uncomfortable with the situation, and just as obviously unwilling to back down. "You needed to save the ranch and you made the right move by takin' in a partner. I have to go back to the Rocking T." Jack avoided his eye. "Julia . . . well, she doesn't like handlin' the ranch alone. She gets nervous if I'm away too long."

"Julia—your wife."

Jack's eyes snapped defensively to Stan's. "That's right. I met her three years after the massacre at the Kiowa village. She needed somebody, and we needed somebody, too."

"We?"

"Cass and me. He was only eight years old and bitter as could be. Hell, he hated every new white face he saw. We needed somebody soft in our lives, to put things back on an even keel."

"You don't have to explain nothin' about that to me."

"I'm not."

"Yes, you are. And I'm tellin' you that I understand. Hell, maybe Purity ain't my own flesh and blood, but she's my daughter just as much as if she was. And I'll tell you somethin' now that you might not like, but the truth is that I would've seen that padlock go up on my door rather than ask you for help if it was only for me. But there was no way I was goin' to my grave without knowin' that Purity was goin' to be all right. I damned near choked on it, but I swallowed my pride—for her—just like I would've done anythin' else I needed to do to protect her."

Eyeing Jack as he remained silent, Stan felt an unexpected surge of envy. Jack was about the same age as he was, yet except for gray hair and a face as lined as old leather, he hadn't changed a bit from the man he had been. He still walked tall and with a sense of purpose. His body was still strong and tight with working muscle, and there was the brightness of health in his eyes, no matter how sober they were right now. The fella had a score of years and more left in his life, while he was one step away from looking his maker in the eye. Damned if he hadn't come out on the bottom again!

Stan shook his head, his expression wry. "You know, I have to tell you, I remember a time when I was so damned jealous of how everythin' seemed to go in your favor that it near to killed me." He continued despite Jack's frown, "I couldn't understand how life could be so lopsided. First Whisperin' Woman chose you over me. Then she gave you a son. Then things started goin' real well for your ranch up north while everythin' kept goin' from bad to worse for me down here. I kept thinkin' it wasn't fair that you should have everythin' and I should have nothin'. When I heard what happened to Whisperin' Woman at that Kiowa village—well, I told myself that at least you had good memories and Whisperin' Woman's son to help you get over your grief, when all I had was a failin' ranch that was takin' up all my time and a lot of thoughts about what could've been." Stan paused. "Then I found Purity, and everythin' changed."

Mumbling a low curse when his throat choked with emotion, Stan continued, "Maybe you don't want to hear none of this, but I'm thinkin' we should get everythin' out in the open before you leave." Jack avoided his gaze again, causing Stan to comment,

"Only thing is, I got the feelin' you got somethin' to say that you ain't sayin'."

Jack's gaze snapped back to his. "All right, maybe I do. Everythin' wasn't as rosy from my end as you thought it was. I had to look at Whisperin' Woman—the woman I loved—every day we spent together knowin' she knew that we owed everythin' to you. Then, when I thought I had finally paid back the debt I owed you, you saved my life and I ended up owin' you again, this time a debt I figured I'd never be able to repay!"

"Yeah, maybe I should've just turned around and walked away when that Yankee had you in his sights. As for that dowry . . ."

"I gave Whisperin' Woman the best life I could give her!"

"I never doubted that."

"But Julia's my wife now. She put Cass's life and mine back on an even keel when we were both flounderin', and I've got a responsibility to her."

"I never said nothin' about that, neither."

"Part of that responsibility is to take care of her now, the way she took care of us."

"I told you, I understand that. But I already explained what's happenin' on the ranch. Purity's been doin' a real good job. Barrin' hell or high water, we should be in good financial shape in the fall."

Jack's gaze hardened. "Yeah, well, maybe I don't have the same confidence in Purity that you have."

"What?"

"You just as much as told me that she can't do anythin' wrong in your eyes."

"Purity's as good a hand as any man you can put against her!"

"She's a woman."

"What difference does that make?"

"Look, Stan, I don't want to argue. Cass is stayin' until things start runnin' smoothly around here."

"Things *are* runnin' smooth!"

"Sure." Jack nodded. "That's why you needed to call me in."

"That didn't have nothin' to do with Purity!"

"Cass is stayin'."

"I'm tellin' you, Purity ain't goin' to like it! She don't like takin' orders. And from what I've already seen of the two of them, there's goin' to be fireworks."

"Then you're goin' to have to handle it."

Stan stared. "Handle it? Look at me. I'm a dyin' man!"

"Talk to her."

"Why should I? It may be half your ranch now, but it's half mine, too!"

Jack drew himself to his feet. "I know it isn't goin' to be easy. Cass has resentments that he hasn't been able to put aside."

"*He* has resentments, huh?"

"I'll talk to him again."

"It won't work out, I tell you!"

"Look, whether you like it or not, I'm leavin' to-morrow, and Cass is stayin'. The rest is up to you."

Left to stare at the door after Jack closed it behind him, Stan cursed softly under his breath. So, Jack had been resentful of him all these years—Jack, the fella who had won it all. What he couldn't figure was why those resentments still remained, with Jack having the upper hand and all.

As for leaving Cass behind to oversee everything for a while, he guessed he should have expected something like that. But the truth was, he hadn't. There was going to be hell to pay.

Stan closed his eyes. If he wasn't so damned feeble . . . if he wasn't so damned tired . . .

Damn it all, he couldn't even die in peace!

With that sorry commentary not far from his mind, Stan allowed sleep to claim him.

Purity was in his arms, and Cass knew what he had been longing for. He heard her short intake of breath as his mouth closed over hers. He felt her melt against him. She separated her lips, and he tasted the sweet moistness within. His heart began a thunderous pounding as he carried her to her bed, then raised the wisp of cotton that was the only barrier to the meeting of their flesh. She made no protest when he tossed it to the floor. Instead, she reached for him and drew him down upon her.

Sighing when their bodies touched, Purity whispered into his ear, words that echoed the hungry mutterings that rose to his own lips. He could not get enough of her. She was loving to the touch, sweet to the taste.

She spoke softly. "Give me the locket, Cass."

He stared at her. How had she known?

"It's important to me. I need it." Her gaze locked with his. The glorious gray-blue of her eyes singed him as she whispered, "Fasten it around my neck. It's the only thing I want to feel between us."

He could not resist her. He reached to the nightstand, aware that his hand trembled. He slipped the locket around her neck and fixed the catch. The fine old gold sparkled against her skin.

She was beautiful and she belonged to him.

But she drew back from him. Her expression changed. She pushed him away, struggling. Her fingers clawed at him.

"What's the matter, Purity? Purity, please . . ."

"Please?" Purity held his gaze. "Say *please* again, Cass."

No.

"If you want me, you'll say please."

Never.

Purity clenched the locket tightly in her hand. Glorious in her naked splendor, she was a vision that stole his breath with desire.

He wanted her. He needed her. He must have her.

"Please . . ."

"Please? Did you say, *please?*"

She was laughing at him then, her head thrown back, her gold hair glittering. Cass stiffened as the sound rebounded around him. She had made him beg. She had gotten what she wanted, and then she had made him beg!

Damn her!

Rage flooding through him, Cass grasped Purity's shoulders with a threatening curse. He felt the breath catch in her throat. He saw the fear in her eyes.

He was uncertain when his cruel grip became a

caress. He was not sure when Purity's protest became a sigh.

Purity was underneath him. Her flesh was hot and acquiescent. It welcomed him in. It closed around him as he sank inside her. Her arms encircled his neck. She raised her mouth to his. Their lips touched . . .

Cass gasped aloud as Purity's teeth bit sharply into his lower lip! He felt the blood flow.

Her teeth sank deeper. Her laughter grew. The sounds of laughter grew louder, wilder . . .

Cass awoke with a start.

His heart pounding, his body bathed in perspiration, he sat up abruptly in his bunk. He stared into a darkness alleviated only by the pale silver light of the moon. There was no sound in the bunkhouse beyond the snores and shifts of movement that indicated the men were sleeping. There had been no witness to his turbulent dream.

His jaw tight, Cass lowered himself back onto the narrow cot. Explosive emotions lingered as he closed his eyes. Purity's image flashed again before him, forcing him to accept a truth that had become all too clear. He had made a mistake. He had looked too deeply into Purity's eyes, and the seeds of desire had been sown.

That thought a gnawing ache within, Cass slid his hand under his pillow and withdrew the locket he had placed there. He studied it in the dim light. It was a simple piece, heart-shaped and worn with age, yet she had been frantic to find it. He remembered Purity's sobs. He knew how much they had cost her.

The precious metal warmed to Cass's touch and unexpected jealousy surged. The locket was a gift of love. That love heated his palm as he closed his hand around it.

She had to find it!

Purity walked silently across the moonlit yard. Her clothes carelessly donned, her hair unbound, she glanced around her, grateful for the full moon that allowed her to see she was alone. She wanted no one to witness her mission. She wanted no one to know that the loss of a locket could leave her so shaken.

Raising a hand unconsciously to her neck, Purity felt her throat constrict. She could not remember a single day of her life when she had not turned to the consolation of her locket in one way or another. So much had it become a part of her that she had almost come to believe the simple gold heart was linked to her own. It was her past, the key to fading images she cherished. It was a hope for the future and her link to love that would remain ever constant and unchanging. It was her sense of self. It was her identity. Without it she was somehow defenseless.

Walking rapidly to the barn door, Purity traced her earlier actions in her mind. She had left the house after her disturbing conversation with Stan and gone directly to the corral for her mare. She remembered that the animal had protested being led back to the barn, and that she had needed to maintain a firm hand. She was uncertain how long she had been in the barn when she realized that her locket was missing. She only knew that when she reached up to touch it, she had frozen with disbelief to find it gone.

Then had begun the frantic search which had been interrupted by Cass's appearance.

Purity reached for the lantern that hung at the barn entrance, her hand shaking as she held a match to the wick. Her thoughts heated with its glow. She had no doubt that Cass had come to the barn to taunt her, just as she had no doubt that he believed everything he'd said was true. But she had had no patience for their conversation. Foremost in her mind had been her lost locket, and she knew that even were she of a mind to attempt to explain the reason for her distress, he would not have understood.

But then, who could possibly comprehend how she felt? Who could understand that she was somehow certain that if she lost her locket, she would lose all chance of finding her sisters again? And who would believe that after all the years that had passed, she would even care?

Holding the lantern high, Purity stepped into the barn. She walked carefully, retracing her steps as she scoured the narrow walkway between the stalls. Frustrated when she found herself at the back stall for the second time without any result, Purity hung the lantern on a peg and dropped to her knees. She was determined. She would find her locket if it took all night. When she did, she would be renewed and ready to face whatever came.

Close to despair, Purity raised a trembling hand to her cheek. Unmindful of the dirt that coated her palm, she wiped away a frustrated tear, sat back on

171

her heels, and looked around her again. The shadows swayed in the flickering light. She had searched every inch of the path, crawling as she slid her hand into each dark corner, beneath every tuft of straw, under and around every pail and implement that had been cast thoughtlessly aside in the course of daily work. The locket was not there.

Purity closed her eyes in an attempt to regain her composure. Her back was breaking, her head ached, her knees were sore, and her palms were rubbed raw. She was exhausted and aware that the new workday would begin in a few hours. She drew herself to her feet. It was useless to search any further.

Purity took a step, then halted. No, she wouldn't give up! She would start looking again, and she wouldn't leave until her locket was in her hand!

Turning with new determination, Purity caught her breath at the sight of a tall figure standing behind her. She instantly regretted her small step in retreat when Cass spoke.

"What are you looking for?"

Purity shook her head. "Nothin'."

Purity caught her breath as Cass walked closer. The lantern light accented the size and breadth of him. It danced on the bared skin of his shoulders and tightly muscled chest, gleaming on the black hair that hung loosely against his sun-darkened skin. It lent new sharpness to the taut contours of his cheeks, emphasizing the light eyes that studied her so intently.

Purity's heart began a slow pounding.

Cass pressed. "You aren't telling me the truth."

Pushed beyond endurance, Purity snapped, "What difference does it make to you what I'm lookin' for? Maybe I come here every night when I can't sleep! Maybe it's my favorite pastime!"

"Purity . . ."

"It's none of your business, damn it!" Suddenly shaking, Purity continued shrilly, "I'm lookin' for somethin' that I can't find, and I'm goin' to keep lookin' for it if it takes me all night!"

"It must be something important."

"It isn't."

"Tell me."

"Damn it . . . damn it . . ." Purity closed her eyes. "Go away. I don't want you here. I need time . . ."

"Tell me, Purity."

Purity opened her eyes. "My locket. I lost it. Now will you leave?"

"Why is it so important to you?"

"It just is."

"Why?"

"My father gave it to me!"

"Stan . . ."

"No, my *father*. He gave identical lockets to each of us . . . my two sisters and me."

Purity fought the shuddering that began to overwhelm her. She could not take much more. She whispered, "Just . . . leave me alone."

Cass struggled against warring emotions. Purity's whispered appeal was almost his undoing. She was standing in front of him, just as she had been in his dream. He wasn't sure how he'd known she had left the house to search the barn again, but he had somehow known she was there. She hadn't seen him enter. Nor had she seen him watching from the shadows as she retraced her steps again and again, finally getting down on her hands and knees to cover every inch of the passageway with her hands.

But dream and reality differed. Purity wasn't wearing a sheer gown that allowed a tempting view of the curves beneath. She was dressed in worn work clothes that hung limply on her. Her hair was unbound and tangled. And she was not smiling. Instead, her face was dirty and marked from tears.

She looked small and helpless, despite her height, and a slow yearning began inside Cass.

"Where are your sisters now?"

Purity closed her eyes. "I don't know. I haven't seen them since the day Stan found me in the river."

"They drowned."

"No!" Purity's eyes flew open. "They're not dead! I'll find them . . . someday."

He paused. "But you have to find the locket first."

The short, jerking nod of Purity's head tore at Cass's waning control. She shuddered again and his resolution began crumbling.

Warning signals flashed in Cass's mind. The night was too silent. His dream was too fresh in his mind. Purity was too vulnerable . . . and so was he. He could not afford to linger much longer.

Reaching into his pocket, Cass closed his fingers around the locket. The worn metal seared his skin as he withdrew it and dropped it into Purity's hand.

Dream and reality differed as Purity stared at the

gold heart lying in her palm. There was no laughter, no withdrawal, only incredulity as she looked up at him, momentarily speechless.

"Wh . . . where did you find it?"

Cass forced a coolness to his tone that he did not feel as he responded, "Does it matter where I found it? It's getting late. Jack will be leaving at dawn, and he'll want to talk to you and Stan before he does."

"What does he want to talk about?"

"His plans for the ranch."

Purity's chin rose. "*His* plans? Your father may be a partner here, but he's not my boss."

Cass did not respond.

"Neither are you."

The silence grew taut. All sign of her previous emotion had vanished.

"I'm goin' to sleep," Purity said abruptly.

His gaze narrowed, Cass watched as Purity strode out of sight.

She had sandpaper under her eyelids and a pounding headache that would not abate. Morning had come too soon.

Purity walked down the staircase to the first floor of the house as the early light of morning dawned. She stopped short at the sight of Cass standing near the doorway in conversation with his father. Stan sat in his chair nearby, fully dressed and looking more like his old self. Her relief to see him there was tempered by her annoyance at the realization that she had been the last to rise. She hated disadvantages, almost as much as she hated—

"Here she is."

Purity barely suppressed the curling of her lip. All Jack Thomas needed to add to that impatient statement were the words *at last*. That point was further emphasized when the elder Thomas looked at each one of them in turn, then stated flatly, "I don't have the time to mince words, so this is what I want to say. I'm leavin', and Cass will be actin' for me in my absence. He knows what to do to put this ranch back on its feet again."

Purity's forbearance snapped. "So do we, Mr. Thomas."

Purity held the gaze Jack turned sharply toward her. It was he who first broke the contact as he addressed Stan.

"Like I said, Cass will be actin' in my stead."

Stan nodded and Jack turned back to address his son.

"I'm leavin' everythin' in your hands. I'll tell Julia you'll be back as soon as things straighten out here. Stan said you can move your things out of the bunkhouse and put them in the empty room upstairs."

A knot tightened in Purity's stomach. "That's Stan's room!"

"I can't use it no more, darlin'," Stan soothed. "There's no sense in keepin' it empty now that I'm sleepin' downstairs."

Purity glanced at Cass, meeting cold green eyes that were unreadable.

"I'll be leavin'." Jack turned toward Stan and extended his hand. "Cass will take care of things."

Purity suppressed her spontaneous comment.

Hesitating, Jack extended his hand toward her. She accepted it and shook it stiffly as he added, "I'm sure everythin' will work out fine."

Purity watched as Jack motioned for Cass to follow him, then walked out the doorway.

Stan spoke abruptly, turning her toward him. "You're lookin' tired today, darlin'."

Purity forced a smile. "Whereas you're showin' me up by lookin' just fine. I hope you're feelin' as good as you look, but in any case, I know we'll both feel better after we eat. Is Pete in the kitchen?"

"Is Pete in the kitchen?" Popping his head around the corner, Pete revealed that he had missed little that had transpired. "Ain't I always? And before you ask, the coffee's ready."

"How about the biscuits?"

"Hell, there ain't been a day that you ever beat the biscuits to the table, no matter how much you bragged that you did, and today's no different!"

Her smile fixed, Purity pushed Stan's chair into the dining room. Despite herself, her thoughts returned to the two who had disappeared out into the yard. She resisted the urge to raise her hand to her locket. It had taken only a few words for Jack Thomas to make it clear that he expected Cass to manage the ranch after he left.

Well, he was wrong.

As for those few moments in the barn the previous night when she somehow thought she saw those hard green eyes soften, she knew now she had merely imagined it. She didn't owe Cass anything for finding her locket, either. She would have found it

177

herself, sooner or later. She would make sure he understood that, just as she would make sure he understood that she did not intend to take his orders.

Purity's smile hardened as she glanced toward the yard. She could just imagine what Jack was saying . . .

"I'm countin' on you, Cass."

Sunrise was making inroads into the morning sky as Jack mounted, then looked down at his son with a frown. "I'm expectin' you to put the past behind you and get along with those two in there as best you can."

Cass nodded.

"It isn't goin' to be easy." Jack shook his head. "You got your work cut out for you with that young woman. Don't sell her short. She had a grip like a man when I shook her hand."

"I'll take care of it."

Jack accepted the hand his son extended toward him. "Let me know if you need my help with anythin' here."

"All right."

Jack turned his horse and urged him forward. He had only gone a few feet before Cass added, "Make sure you tell *her* I said hello."

Chapter Five

The afternoon sun was high in a cloudless sky, and the air was heavy. Lifting his hat from his head, Jack glanced upward at the unrelenting sun, then ran his hand through his perspiration-soaked hair. He replaced his hat with a muttered curse. It had been more than a week since he had left the Circle C behind him, and the trail had been hard.

Stan's frail image came suddenly to mind and Jack frowned. The shock of seeing Stan in such a deteriorated condition was with him still. He had not realized how closely he had associated that fellow with himself, with his youth and manhood, and with a love they had both lost. Strangely, seeing Stan weak and wasted had forced him to take stock of his own life. He had envisioned his mortality in that moment, and the cruel twists of fate he had formerly managed to shrug aside had tightened into knots of true pain.

The questions had come unbidden: How many years did he have left ahead of him? How did he want to spend them? Whose face did he want to be the last he saw before his eyes closed forever?

Oh, hell . . .

Jack squinted into the distance. Maybe Stan was luckier than he was, after all. His choices were limited and his path clear. He had put aside thought of his own future and was concentrating on the life his daughter would lead after he was gone.

Jack unconsciously shook his head. He wondered how things were working out on the Circle C. There were more than hard feelings involved, and he sensed that Cass's concentration on Purity Corrigan was too intense for comfort on either side. It made him uneasy, the way Cass looked at that young woman. The truth was that there was a part of his son that would always remain a mystery to him, but one fact had become increasingly clear. The Kiowa side of his son was growing stronger. He supposed that was the reason he had felt pressed to leave so quickly. . . .

Jack halted that thought. Who did he think he was fooling? He knew why he had left the Circle C in such a hurry.

All thought coming to an abrupt halt, Jack squinted more intently into the distance. His heartbeat accelerated when a familiar landmark came into view. The heat of the day and his physical discomfort forgotten, he kicked his horse into a gallop.

Drawing his laboring mount back when tall, poled

tepees came within sight, Jack continued at a walk. He perused the stoic faces of those emerging from the tepees.

Then he saw her.

The tight constriction in his chest, the sense of yearning, were painfully familiar. He had felt that way the first time he saw her. Time had not altered his feelings. He knew now that it never would.

Dismounting, Jack approached the camp on foot. Unaware of others who observed in silence, he saw only her face.

She smiled. She said his name. Her voice was soft, a sweet whisper.

He took her into his arms.

Purity reined her mount to a halt. The glory of the unblemished Texas range was lost on Purity as she glanced at the partially constructed corral in front of her. She scanned the faces of Rome, Baird, Pitts, and Treacher as they looked up.

Seething, she dismounted beside them.

"All right, what's this all about? Do I have to be with you fellas every minute in order for you to follow a few simple instructions? I told you what to do when you left the ranch this mornin'. You're supposed to be makin' a sweep of the eastern hollow to flush out any calves that might be hidin' there. I didn't say I wanted you to build a corral to put them in! Hell, what were you thinkin'?"

"It wasn't our idea!" Treacher showed no trace of a smile as he continued hotly, "Your new partner got it in his head that we needed another brandin' corral, and that's what we're doin'."

"My new partner . . ."

Purity fought to restrain her flaring temper. In the short week since his father had left him in charge, Cass had not given her a moment's peace. Looking over her shoulder, questioning her with his gaze, wordlessly challenging her every command, *effortlessly surpassing her in every task she undertook*, he had wielded his authority at every opportunity. Tensions were high. The men had maintained their silence for the most part, but she knew them well enough to realize that the situation could not continue as it was much longer.

And the nights . . .

A chill ran down Purity's spine. A locked door between them had provided little comfort in the darkness while thoughts of Cass taunted her—the heat of his body as it had held her captive with its weight . . . the warmth of his breath as it had fanned her lips, his fingers sliding through her hair to grip it suddenly tight. Each creak, each whisper of sound had been enough to disturb her sleep. She knew it was no coincidence that Cass made his presence known in the hallway between their rooms when he retired to his room each night. His brief hesitation outside her door was deliberate. She had no doubt that he knew she waited for the sounds of his movements to stop and for the creak of his bed before she could take an easy breath.

Galling her even more, however, was her realization that her senses had become acutely attuned to

Cass's presence throughout the day. His nearness disturbed her composure in a way she could not quite define. She could not seem to forget that moment when Cass dropped her locket into her hand. Despite herself, she strained for a glimpse of the man she thought she had seen then, refusing to acknowledge her disappointment when it was proved to her time and again that that man had never existed at all.

She had made a mistake in allowing Cass to witness her desperation when she lost her locket. She knew that now. She had allowed him a glimpse of weakness that he would doubtless use against her. She would not make that mistake again.

The conflicts were draining—the pressure of Stan's worsening health and her need to keep him free of worry; the men's resentment of Cass; her need to show everyone, including herself, that she could run the ranch as well as any man; and her driving need to prove to Cass that she would not allow him to intimidate her.

Now he had a new tack—taking advantage of her absence to employ the men in useless tasks that frustrated both them and her.

Treacher stared at her, his face flushed, awaiting her response. Her voice flat, she ordered, "Forget the corral. We don't need it." Ignoring the frustrated mumbling that ensued, she continued tightly, "Start searchin' those hollows like I told you."

The sound of approaching hooves behind her was too opportune to be coincidental. Turning toward the sound, Purity already knew who was approaching. Her gaze narrowing, she watched as Cass dismounted. She noticed that Nash rode reluctantly at Cass's side—another of Cass's deliberate ploys to increase her frustration.

Purity's jaw locked with determination as Cass strode toward her. He towered over her, overwhelmingly close. The bastard . . .

Purity struggled against the breathlessness that beset her as his gaze locked with hers. "I gave the men their orders this mornin'," she said. "They didn't include buildin' a corral that wasn't needed."

Cass's gaze raked her face as she struggled to conceal her agitation. She thought she saw satisfaction flash in his eyes as he responded, "Setting up a corral here will save us time and money in the long run."

"We don't need it."

"I say we do."

A slow shuddering beset Purity. She saw the ice in those light eyes looking down into hers. She recognized that look—an almost savage ruthlessness. It had been in his eyes that first day when he held a knife at her throat. He knew the men were behind her, and he knew how the men felt about him. He was trying to push someone into making a move that would give him an excuse to shed blood. She'd be damned if she'd fall into that trap!

Purity forced a smile so brittle that it almost cracked. "All right, we need a corral." She turned toward the men. Her words clipped, she ordered, "Build it. Then, when you're done, search those hollows like I said." Ignoring the men's muttered protests and refusing to allow Cass a total victory, she turned toward Nash. "I'm goin' up to the northeast waterhole. It needs to be cleaned out. I want you to come with me."

Indulging a moment's satisfaction at Cass's obvious displeasure, Purity remounted. Nash's expression said it all when he drew his horse up beside hers without a glance in Cass's direction. She felt a stab of triumph when she spurred her mount forward and Nash took up unhesitatingly alongside.

But her triumph was short-lived. It died at the sound of Cass's short barks of command to the men who remained behind, and the clatter of his horse's hooves when he rode up to claim a place at her side.

Not a moment's peace, damn him!

Night had fallen. The lonely howl of a wolf rent the silence of the sleeping camp—a silence broken within Whispering Woman's buffalo-hide shelter by the soft sounds of ardent lovemaking.

Drawing his mouth from hers, Jack looked down at Whispering Woman where she lay in his arms. The flickering flames in the fire pit illuminated the sloped planes of her face, and he silently marveled. She was beautiful. Her small features had not hardened with age, the contours of her cheek were still taut, and her eyes—black velvet pools that spoke to him more clearly than words—were still filled with love. And when her flesh was pressed to his, passion still blossomed between them.

He loved her.

He would always love her.

It had been so long . . . too long to deny the driving urge any longer.

Shifting in a subtle movement, Jack slid himself inside her. He heard Whispering Woman's sigh, and her beauty filled him. It soared to burgeoning life, growing stronger, more heady as the rhythm of their lovemaking increased. He wanted to tell her . . . he wanted to say that he lived for these hours when they could be together. He wanted to explain that the time in between was merely existence, that only with her was he truly alive. He wanted to declare his love loudly for all to hear, even while he knew he could not. And he wanted her to know that he wished with all his heart that he need never leave her.

But the rhythm of their lovemaking stole his breath. It claimed his mind, expelling all other thought. He heard her ecstatic whimper and his joy soared even as he groaned his protest against the sudden explosion of climax that brought his joy to a quaking end.

His breathing ragged, his eyes strangely moist, Jack spoke at last.

"I'm sorry. It was too fast."

"No." Whispering Woman raised her callused hand to his lips. Her palm was coarse against the sensitive surface. Her touch tantalized him. Hers were hardworking hands, gentle hands, hands that touched him with love as she continued, "Do not torment yourself. Your haste was born of a need that I, too, shared. We will go more slowly next time. This tepee is now mine alone. No one will disturb us here."

Whispering Woman's gaze strayed briefly toward the rough hide walls surrounding them, her eyes rising to the many poles that supported the tepee, to the pallets on either side of the fire, and the food stocks stored so neatly in place. He knew what she was thinking.

Jack stroked her cheek, his hand slipping down to her shoulder and on to the deep grooves of jagged scars marking her arms. He rested his palm against them, his gaze dropping to legs still slender and gracefully formed that were similarly scarred. He looked back up to meet dark eyes that reflected his pain.

"Do not suffer at the sight of wounds that were self-inflicted. Such was my grief. So was my mourning expressed. It was as it should be."

Jack could not restrain his protest.

"I shouldn't have left you alone here! If I had been with you, I wouldn't have let you do that to yourself! I would've stopped you!"

"No, you would not."

"But you aren't even sure he's dead!" Jack slipped his fingers into the heavy strands of hair that had once been long and flowing, but which now reflected the shearing Whispering Woman had administered in her grief. "You savaged yourself without bein' sure."

"I am sure." Whispering Woman's eyes filled. "Flying Eagle came to me in a veil of smoke during the night. He came, not to bemoan his fate, but to tell me to send help to Pale Wolf, so he might live."

Jack's anger surged.

"You sent others to rescue my son, but you didn't send for me. You tended his wounds, but kept them secret from me while I thought Cass was just stayin' with you for a prolonged visit. You told me only that Flyin' Eagle was dead. Why?"

"It was Pale Wolf's wish."

"And you wouldn't betray his wishes . . . even to me."

Whispering Woman raised her palm again to his cheek. "Forgive me, husband, but I could not. Where once I had two sons, now only one remains."

Two sons . . .

Jealousy burned.

"It is in the past." As if reading his thoughts, Whispering Woman continued, "The past cannot be changed. Only the present is ours to mold."

Jack drew her desperately close. The musky scent of Whispering Woman's skin filled his nostrils as he whispered, "I've gone over it all so many times in my mind. I keep wonderin' why I didn't sense danger all those years ago, the day when I left you and Cass at the village to visit with your mother. I should have! I knew the soldiers were rangin' out farther and farther in their searches. I didn't find out that the village had been attacked and burned for two days. When I did, I raced back to find you both. I couldn't believe my eyes when I saw what was left! Charred rubble, blackened bodies, animals slaughtered and left to rot in the sun . . ."

Jack took a shuddering breath. "I found the spot where your mother's tepee was. There were two bodies. They were burned so bad that I couldn't tell who they were. I didn't want to believe what I saw. Then I heard Cass call my name. I couldn't believe he was alive. He was so damned scared after the soldiers left that he had just started runnin' in the opposite direction and didn't stop until he dropped. It took all the courage he had to finally come back. I'll never forget the look on his face when he said you had left him to go back for your mother."

Silent tears filled Whispering Woman's eyes.

"We buried the bodies that were in your mother's tepee, Cass and me." Jack took a stabilizing breath, "But even when we did, we didn't believe one of them was you. We kept lookin' for you everywhere we went."

Whispering Woman's gaze held his. "I, too, suffered. My wounds were many, but the physical pain was not my greatest misery. When I awoke in the tepee of my rescuers, smoke and fire clouded all memory of the past."

Whispering Woman closed her eyes. When she opened them again they were filled with remembered grief. "With all memory lost to the haze that filled my mind, I clung to the kindness of Buffalo Hunter."

Jack fought to subdue the jealousy that rose within him as Whispering Woman continued, "He was a good husband to me, and when I bore him a son, life was good again. My torment was left in the shadows . . . until you returned to my life once more."

Jack drew Whispering Woman close. "Seven years . . . and I knew the moment I saw you again at that powwow that nothin' had changed for me." He took a steadying breath, "Then I saw Flyin' Eagle . . . and Buffalo Hunter . . . and I remembered that I was married to Julia. And I knew that nothin' was the same."

Whispering Woman's voice grew husky with distress as she pressed her lips to his. "Buffalo Hunter was my husband and father to my son. I owed him much. I could not shame him by turning to you while he was alive." Her voice grew softer. "But my heart was again yours from the moment the cloud was lifted from my mind—a heart that was rent in two when Pale Wolf stood in front of me, tall and strong, twelve summers old."

"He didn't understand what had happened. He couldn't forgive . . ."

"Until Flying Eagle took his hand." Tears spilled down Whispering Woman's cheeks. "Flying Eagle— only five summers old—who erased Pale Wolf's anger and healed his wounds with the bond that sprang between them."

"Cass had you back then—for all those years that followed—years together that *we* lost."

"Buffalo Hunter is gone, now."

But there was still Julia. . . .

Conflicting emotions drew Jack's strong features into a frown. "Julia was good to Cass. She helped soothe his pain and lessen the hate."

"Pale Wolf speaks well of her."

"She gave up all she knew for Cass and me."

"She is a good woman."

"I . . . I can't turn her out."

Whispering Woman's dark eyes flickered briefly.

"There is no dishonor if a man takes a second wife to his household."

"It's not the same in our culture. Julia would never understand."

"You need not explain these things again, my husband. . . ." Whispering Woman's eyes held his. "Your heart is good. You must do what it demands."

The thickness in Jack's throat allowed only his rasping whisper. "My heart is yours, darlin'."

Whispering Woman did not respond.

His torment almost beyond bearing, Jack rasped, "Tell me you love me, woman!"

Her small breasts warm against his chest, her smooth skin caressing his, Whispering Woman murmured, "I am your wife. I will always be your wife, and I will always love you."

Beyond speech, Jack clasped Whispering Woman tightly against him to bury his torment in the warmth of her lips.

The difficult day had come to an end not a moment too soon. Her endurance all but depleted, her head hurting and her body aching, Purity had finished her chores after leaving the dinner table and had then climbed the stairs toward her room.

Waiting silently in the shadows of the upstairs hallway, Purity tossed back her heavy gold braid and raised her chin. She was tired of smiling for Stan's benefit. She was weary of calming the men's agitation. And she had had her fill of listening for the sound of Cass's footstep behind her. She wanted nothing more than to lie down on her bed and let sleep overwhelm her. But she did not, knowing she had yet one more task to perform—one that had already been put off too long.

Conditions between Cass and her had gone from bad to worse after their confrontation at the corral that afternoon. Sensing her tension as he rode beside them, Nash had grown increasingly belligerent in his attitude toward Cass. Too late, she had seen the error of involving Nash in the ongoing contest between Cass and her. She had inadvertently played into Cass's hands by providing him with an opportunity to push Nash to the limit. Cass's words rang in her mind.

I'll make you tell me the truth . . .

And she recalled other words.

I followed the tracks of Flying Eagle's horse to your herd . . . to the spot where they met with the tracks of your horse.

Impossible . . .

Straining to recall every detail, Purity reviewed that fall day again in her mind. There was not a single detail that stood out in memory before the moment when Pale Wolf burst so violently into her life.

As if on cue, a familiar step sounded on the staircase. Purity drew back into the shadows as the footsteps drew closer. She waited, holding her breath for the right moment.

Cass was a few feet from the landing when Purity took an aggressive step out into the light and commanded softly, "Stop there." She sensed his surprise when she raised the gun in her hand and pointed it at his midsection. "Come up the rest of the way slowly . . . that's it." Waiting with growing agitation as Cass took the final step up onto the landing and turned to face her, she ordered, "Stand where you are. There're some things I want to make clear between us, right here and now."

Cass's presence overwhelmed the narrow hallway as he stood opposite her. The familiar scent of him filled the space between them. She could feel his heat and the power he held at bay as he maintained his silence.

Purity's hiss shattered the hush between them. "I figured you might think you won some sort of victory today in showin' the men that I bowed to your wishes about buildin' that corral. You didn't. I thought you also might believe you've got the upper hand here because all of us are scramblin' to keep Stan believin' things are goin' fine. You don't." Purity continued in a low tone that signified the fury within, "And you're makin' an even bigger mistake if you think Stan played into your hands when he gave you his room across the hall from mine."

Her eyes a glacial grey, Purity proceeded. "I'll take it one step at a time, so there'll be no mistakin' the meanin' of what I'm sayin'. Your father left you behind to run this ranch, but the men here will take my orders over yours anytime I ask. I haven't been tellin' Stan much about how things are workin' out because I don't need to. I can handle things by myself. And as far as losin' any sleep worryin' what you're intendin' to do since you moved in up here"— Purity's lips tightened—"your room may be across the hall from mine, but it might just as well be on the other side of the world for all the good it's goin' to do you. You see, I don't sleep alone." Purity raised her gun a notch higher. "This friend of mine shares my bed, now—and it's a friend I can depend on."

Purity sensed the responsive tightening of Cass's frame. "Your father made it clear that he thinks I'm just a woman, but what both of you didn't take into account is that this gun makes me a match for any man. It fits my hand real well, and I'm not afraid to use it!"

Speaking for the first time, Cass grated, "I never doubted that for a minute."

"Think what you like," Purity spat, "but I'm makin' this clear. Whatever else you do, one step through my bedroom door and you're a dead man!"

Not awaiting a response, Purity turned abruptly toward her room. She closed the door behind her and turned the lock. Silent, somehow unable to move, she waited for the sound of Cass's retreating steps and the click of his door before she released the breath she did not realize she had been holding.

A nagging unrest disturbed her dreams, awakening Whispering Woman with a start. Reassured by the familiar warmth of the man lying beside her, she allowed her gaze to linger on the night shadows of the tepee. She saw saddlebags lying a short distance from the entrance, where they had been dropped in haste. She saw clothing discarded in a careless heap where it would doubtless lie until dawn. She saw the remains of the meal that had been abandoned when hunger of another kind had assumed control.

A flush touched Whispering Woman's skin as her husband's arms tightened around her in sleep. She knew his love soared, even in his dreams, just as she knew his true passion was hers alone.

But he also loved another.

Disturbed by the pain that thought evoked, Whispering Woman studied her husband as he slept. Gray hair framed a face that still bore traces of sorrow. Myriad lines marked a countenance that had once been bright with youth. The passage of years had left indelible marks there, but time had not bowed his broad shoulders. It had not diminished the chest against which she rested her head, the strength of the arms that held her close, or the physical proof of a love he ardently declared. But even if that were not so, Whispering Woman knew, as she had known from the first moment she saw her husband so many years earlier, that her heart was his forever.

Bittersweet emotions rose. The words Pale Wolf had spoken of Julia would remain with her always.

Julia had been kind to Pale Wolf when his youthful heart was filled with hate. She had cared for him while receiving little in return. She had loved him as a son even though he denied her.

A familiar anguish stirred. Julia would not accept the status of second wife . . . if she knew.

The painful secret scorched Whispering Woman's heart, but she knew she could not betray Jack's trust.

Jack stirred beside Whispering Woman. He drew her closer and she turned toward him. She heard his sigh, and her heart echoed the sound. She looked up to see her husband's eyes opening.

"Pale Wolf"—her husband frowned—"he knew I was comin' to see you. He asked to be remembered to you."

The words lit her heart. "Pale Wolf is a good son."

"He's determined to find out what happened to Flyin' Eagle. He won't stop until he does."

She'd once had two sons.

"I tried to talk to him about it, but he won't listen to me."

Pale Wolf, who had been close to death the day he was brought to her a year earlier.

"Whisperin' Woman . . ."

A dormant rage sprang to life within her. "Pale Wolf will do what he must!"

"It's gettin' dangerous for him! I want you to talk to him. I want you to tell him to let it go."

"I will not."

"You lost Flyin' Eagle. Do you want to lose Pale Wolf, too?"

"Do not speak such words!" Fighting to dispel the horror of that thought, Whispering Woman rasped, "Pale Wolf will do what he must . . . as will I."

Whispering Woman slid her arms around her husband and drew him close. She halted her husband's response with her lips. Their time together was short. In a few days, he would leave again. She could allow no thought of death or vengeance to come between them. Nor could she allow herself to dwell on thoughts of a brave son who sought rightful retribution . . .

. . . or of the woman called Julia to whom her husband would return.

* * *

Cass pushed his bedroom door closed behind him. Standing in darkness lit only by the pale light of the moon that streamed through the window opposite him, he remained stock still, emotions raging. He raised his chin, remembering the gun Purity had leveled at his stomach a few minutes earlier. The brief words he had spoken during their exchange had been delivered with total honesty. He did not doubt for a moment that Purity had the courage to use that gun on him.

Cursing aloud, Cass recalled Purity's image as she had stood opposite him in the dimly lit hallway— smooth cheeks flushed with fury, shoulders rigid, eyes spitting hatred. It made no sense to him that he both despised and desired Purity Corrigan. There was no logic to his admiration for the will of iron she had demonstrated during the week past, when that iron will fought him every step of the way. There was no reason to respect the determination that drove her, when she was determined to withhold the truth he sought at any cost.

Nor was there an excuse for the memories that haunted him—the tears that marked Purity's cheeks when she had turned angrily toward him in the barn; the beauty of luminous, silver eyes raised to his as she clutched her locket tightly.

Opposing passions raged. Cass raked a hand through hair that was black, straight and bluntly cut—a Kiowa's hair. His heart pounded—a heart that was hard and pitilessly relentless—a *warrior's* heart.

Purity was his enemy, but he had never wanted any woman more.

He did not know why.

But he knew what he must do.

Awakening at a squeak of sound, Purity went rigid. She squinted into the darkness of her room, realizing that she had fallen asleep. She slid her hand under her pillow and clutched the handle of her gun.

She waited . . . listening.

Silence.

Suddenly furious with herself, Purity muttered a curse. There was no one lurking outside her door! For all her denials, she was again allowing her imagination to defeat her just as Cass intended, with one restless night after another leaving her body exhausted, her disposition soured, and her thinking blurred.

The nightmare would not end. Stan was ill. The men's resentment against Cass grew greater each day, but the partnership was the ranch's only salvation. She had to make it work.

Purity reached unconsciously for her locket. The warmth of the old gold stirred a familiar reassurance as blue eyes she remembered so well flashed angrily before her mind.

Fight him, Purity! Don't let him get the best of you!

Yes, Honesty.

Don't worry, Purity. Everything's going to be all right.

Dear Chastity, of the glorious red curls and dauntless smile . . .

Another squeak of sound in the hallway interrupted Purity's thoughts.

Her hand snaked back to the handle of her gun.

The silver-eyed witch haunted him.

Abandoning sleep, Cass drew himself up to a seated position in bed. The hour was late. The room was hot, the air heavy. Standing up abruptly, he walked to the window, his thoughts returning to the woman who lay in the bedroom across the hall.

He remembered the gold locket he'd found in the barn. It had been warm from the heat of Purity's flesh when he touched it. That heat had singed him.

He recalled the sound of Purity's desperate sobs. The echo reverberated within him still.

He remembered the anguish Purity had sought to conceal when she spoke of the sisters whose deaths she could not accept. That anguish had become his own.

. . . And he remembered the gun she had held leveled at his heart . . .

No, he could not wait much longer.

Chapter Six

Purity jerked her reins toward the wild-eyed calf making another break for freedom. Her patience short, she pursued the panicked calf at breakneck speed, dodging and weaving between the shrubs that dotted the rough terrain. She dug her heels harder into her horse's sides. Her mount responded with another leap forward that outdistanced her quarry and turned him abruptly back toward the herd.

Pulling back on the reins when the calf was again moving docilely forward, Purity released an agitated breath. She glanced briefly upward at the sky, almost disbelieving the position of the sun that indicated it was not yet noon. Lifting her hat, she wiped her arm across her moist forehead, frowning as the gritty residue of a full morning's work abraded her skin. She was hot and tired. Her shirt clung damply against her skin, and every muscle in her body was crying out in protest.

Damn that Cass Thomas! It was all his fault. Morning had come too soon after a night with little rest. Despite her claims to the contrary when she had faced him down in the hallway a few days earlier, she had not had a decent night's sleep since he'd arrived on the Circle C. Neither had that confrontation had the effect she had intended. Cass's attitude had not changed, and the men's resentment had only worsened. The tension whenever Cass was near had reached unbearable proportions, and tempers were at flashpoint. So relentless was he that she wondered now if Cass had deliberately lingered inside his bedroom that morning, waiting to step out onto the landing at the exact moment she did.

She had been more conscious of his step than she cared to acknowledge as he had followed her down the staircase to the breakfast table. Try as she might to ignore him, she seemed only to succeed in instituting him more firmly in her mind. His natural, fluid rhythm as he rode beside her had become as familiar as the sound of her own breathing. The scent of him, subtle and distinctively male, had become as recognizable as the fragrance of the wildflowers growing along the trail.

Purity glanced again around her. The section of range where they had found the cattle they were now driving was particularly rough. It was riddled with holes, providing dangerous footing for their mounts as they continued toward the branding corral set up a few miles away.

Purity surveyed the unruly animals moving pro-
testingly onward. This last group of calves was particularly contentious and aggressive. Sudden breaks
for open country had provided a persistent challenge
for their small group of four wranglers.

Nash Carter was included in their number. Purity
turned to look at him as he moved alongside the
herd. She could not help noticing that his boyish
countenance was devoid of its usual smile. She
missed that smile sorely.

Buck's grunting curse revealed his location behind
a clump of foliage as he urged a reluctant steer back
into the herd. It had not escaped Purity's notice that
although Buck was occasionally out of sight, he was
never far from her side.

Purity's smooth cheek twitched. She was the third
member of their group.

And then, of course, there was Cass.

Purity restrained the urge to look around her
again. She did not see him, but she knew he was
there. As tired as she was, she could not clearly define the feeling—somewhere between fury and a
strange excitement—that stirred inside her each
time their glances crossed. She was confused and
weary. Hardest of all was the realization that there
was no relief in sight.

A chill crawled up Purity's spine. She could feel
those cold, green eyes upon her even now.

What was he thinking?

Purity paused at that thought.

Why did she care?

Frustration exploding within, Purity jammed her

hat back on her head and kicked her mare into a gallop.

The willful witch! She was riding like a maniac!

Cass watched as Purity raced across the dangerous terrain with reckless speed. His hands squeezed into tight fists on the reins as she drew her mare to a skidding halt beside the herd, scattering the stock nearby. Uttering a few practiced grunts and clucks that urged the animals back in line, she then turned to assume a moderate pace beside them.

Cass felt the slow rise of fury. Purity Corrigan, for all her declarations of being equal to a man in every way, was behaving like a thoughtless child! She knew that one false step on terrain like this could easily bring her mount down, yet she was pressing the animal to the limit.

Cass's raging thoughts came to an abrupt halt as Purity shifted her position in the saddle, inadvertently allowing him to glimpse her face clearly. Exhaustion, frustration, and anger were visible there.

A knot tightened within Cass. He was winning. Purity could not hold up much longer under the pressure he exerted.

You'll tell me the truth, in the end.

That was what he wanted, wasn't it?

Purity spurred her horse into an aggressive gallop toward a straying calf in the distance.

A familiar tension knotted within Cass. What was the matter with her? She knew better than that! All she would accomplish by chasing the calf that way would be to force him to run. Didn't she care that she was risking her neck?

Cass dug his heels into his horse's sides.

Purity pressed her mount to a faster pace. She recognized the bull calf that had separated from the herd. It was the same one that had been giving her trouble all morning.

Almost gratified when the animal reacted to her rapid approach by breaking into a run, Purity clamped her teeth shut. She might be helpless against all else that plagued her, but she'd be damned if she'd let a stubborn beast get the best of her!

She was elated by the feel of pounding hooves beneath her, hot morning air rushing against her face, a sense of power and control as she rapidly gained on the racing calf. But her euphoria shattered abruptly as her mount missed a step. The moment blurred into an uncertain flurry of scrambling hooves and dawning fear as her mare stumbled, and then struggled to regain her footing.

A shrill whinny.

A sudden lurch forward.

She was going down!

Purity's spinning world jolted to an abrupt halt as a strong arm locked around her. Momentarily disoriented as she awaited an impact with the ground that did not come, she looked up to see a flashing glimpse of angry green eyes as Cass swung her up on his saddle in front of him. As he held her in a crushing grip, Purity felt his heart pounding against hers.

She saw the effort he expended to quell his rage. His breath was hot against her lips when he hissed at last, "I'm warning you—don't try that again. I won't let you get away from me that easily."

Lowering her abruptly to the ground to stand on legs that wobbled beneath her, Cass rode off and disappeared over the rise.

Whispering Woman dipped her feet into the glistening ripples of the stream. The sand of the bank was warm beneath her, a gentle breeze cooled her skin, and a sweet silence encompassed all. She glanced up at her husband where he was seated beside her, her happiness dimming at the sadness she glimpsed in his eyes.

They had arisen that morning in the quiet of her tepee. They had eaten and they had loved. They had talked and they had worked silently, side by side. They had renewed the pattern of their lives that had existed before the smoke and flames came between them.

Whispering Woman inwardly sighed. For years she had dreamed of returning to that life, to the husband and son she had left there. But that dream had been impossible. Her sole consolation for the loss had been the joy of Flying Eagle . . . her handsome son who was no more.

Pain stabbed brutally within her.

"What's wrong, darlin'?"

Her husband's gaze was loving as he stroked back her hair, and Whispering Woman felt the bliss of his touch. While all else changed, she knew that would remain forever true.

She whispered, "How much longer will you stay?"

The sadness in her husband's eyes spread to his lips. "A few days. I've been away from the ranch too long already."

"You will return to Julia."

He did not reply.

Whispering Woman's anguish erupted. "Is Julia as sweet in your arms as am I, my husband?"

"Darlin' . . ."

"Does she make your heart race as it does when our flesh touches? Does joy light your heart?"

"Please . . ."

Remorseful, Whispering Woman raised her hand to lightly trace the grooves that time had worn into her husband's cheek. "I am sorry. I speak of things better left unsaid. I have renewed the paths of sadness where earlier they were swept away. It was wrong to do so."

"It doesn't seem right, does it, darlin'?" Drawing her against his chest, her husband held her close. Whispering Woman heard the frustration of helplessness in his voice as he continued, "I mean, I loved you from the moment I first saw you, all those years ago. I never wanted anythin' more than for us to be together for the rest of our lives, yet life somehow came between us. I keep thinkin' how crazy it is that everythin's so turned around, with me wantin' to be here and bein' forced to be there, and with me spendin' precious time longin' for somethin' that's here at my fingertips to take."

Whispering Woman listened as her husband spoke earnestly. "I don't want to leave you alone again, darlin'."

"I am not alone. Pale Wolf visits often."

"It's not the same."

"It is good."

"It's not enough!"

"It is what will be."

"I could tell Julia."

Whispering Woman closed her eyes. She closed her heart. "No."

"I could explain to her. I could tell her that there are too few years remainin' for me to spend them apart from you."

"No, Julia does not deserve that blow."

"I need you."

"And I, you."

"I could take you back with me now."

"You cannot."

"I can, I tell you!"

"No, your heart is too kind."

"I'm not as kind as you think I am."

Whispering Woman smiled at his denial. "I am more fortunate than Julia, after all. I have a husband and a son. Were I to lose one, I would still have the other. Were Julia to lose you, she would lose all."

"If I lost you, I'd lose everythin', too."

"You will not lose me. I will be here, waiting."

Her husband's eyes moistened and his mustache twitched. Her heart echoed the words that emerged from his lips.

"Waiting . . ."

* * *

"I don't care what you say, I ain't goin' to let him get away with it anymore!"

Nash glanced in the direction where Cass had ridden off a short time earlier after Purity's near fall. She was keenly aware that the sun was not responsible for the flush that heated Nash's face as he continued, "Who does he think he is? He shows up here bold as brass, despite what he tried to do to you on the trail drive last fall, and then he thinks we'll let him take over the ranch you and Stan worked for all your lives. I know what he's been tryin' to do to you, followin' you around like he does and all. You don't owe him nothin' for savin' you from that fall, either! He cut in front of me or it would've been me who pulled you off that horse, not him!"

"Nash . . ."

"He ain't goin' to get away with tryin' to make your life miserable—not while I've got a breath left in my body."

Purity glanced nervously around her. Cass had not returned to the herd after her near accident. He had not witnessed Buck and Nash's concern, or her guilt when her shaken mare limped cautiously back to her side.

Submitting to Buck's demand, she had reluctantly agreed to an early midday halt, partially because she knew that Buck was as much in need of time to recuperate from the fright of her near accident as she was. They had sat in the shade of a tree nearby, toying with their food in silence until Buck had ridden off to check the herd. Nash had faced her then, too

Thrill to the most sensual, adventure-filled Historical Romances on the market today...

FROM ⌊ *LEISURE BOOKS*

As a home subscriber to Leisure Romance Book Club, you'll enjoy the best in today's BRAND-NEW Historical Romance fiction. For over twenty-five years, Leisure Books has brought you the award-winning, high-quality authors you know and love to read. Each Leisure Historical Romance will sweep you away to a world of high adventure...and intimate romance. Discover for yourself all the passion and excitement millions of readers thrill to each and every month.

Save $5.⁰⁰ Each Time You Buy!

Each month, the Leisure Romance Book Club brings you four brand-new titles from Leisure Books, America's foremost publisher of Historical Romances. EACH PACKAGE WILL SAVE YOU $5.00 FROM THE BOOKSTORE PRICE! And you'll never miss a new title with our convenient home delivery service.

Here's how we do it. Each package will carry a FREE 10-DAY EXAMINATION privilege. At the end of that time, if you decide to keep your books, simply pay the low invoice price of $16.96, no shipping or handling charges added. HOME DELIVERY IS ALWAYS FREE. With today's top Historical Romance novels selling for $5.99 and higher, our price SAVES YOU $5.00 with each shipment.

AND YOUR FIRST FOUR-BOOK SHIPMENT IS TOTALLY FREE!

IT'S A BARGAIN YOU CAN'T BEAT! A Super $21.96 Value!

⌊ *LEISURE BOOKS* *A Division of Dorchester Publishing Co., Inc.*

GET YOUR 4 FREE BOOKS
NOW — A $21.96 Value!

Mail the Free Book Certificate Today!

Get Four Books Totally FREE – A $21.96 Value!

▼ Tear Here and Mail Your FREE Book Card Today! ▼

PLEASE RUSH
MY FOUR FREE
BOOKS TO ME
RIGHT AWAY!

Leisure Romance Book Club
P.O. Box 6613
Edison, NJ 08818-6613

AFFIX
STAMP
HERE

disturbed to hold back his feelings any longer. Strangely, as young and earnest as he was—and as angry—she feared more for his safety than her own.

With that thought in mind, Purity replied, "What happened a little while ago was my fault. I was ridin' like a damned fool."

"No, it wasn't! Thomas had you so upset that you weren't thinkin' straight."

"I'm a grown woman. I'm supposed to be runnin' this ranch. I should've known better."

"It was his fault. I ain't goin' to let him get away with the way he's treatin' you, I tell you!"

"This doesn't concern you, Nash. It's somethin' I have to settle with Cass myself."

"No, it ain't!" Nash's jaw hardened. "You know how I feel about you, Purity. You know I'd do anythin' for you. You're just too proud for your own good. Somethin' inside you makes you think you have to handle Thomas yourself if you're goin' to prove that Stan's confidence in you ain't mistaken. But you ain't got nothin' to prove anymore, not to Stan or nobody else. Every last one of us on this ranch knows what you're made of."

Nash's expression darkened. "And every last one of us knows what Thomas is made of, too. He's a hostile half-breed, whatever way you look at him. He may dress like a white man and act like a white man, but he's out for some kind of crazy Injun revenge for somethin' none of us had anythin' to do with."

Purity frowned. "So you know about Flyin' Eagle."

"I know what he *said* happened to some Injun named Flyin' Eagle."

209

"What do you mean?"

Nash scowled. "I don't trust him, is all I mean. How do we know there ever was an Injun named Flyin' Eagle? How do we know Thomas didn't know you were a woman that day when he roped you from your horse, that he hadn't been watchin' you and decided to try to—well—" Nash's jaw ticked revealingly. "I see the way he looks at you. He can't keep his eyes off you!"

"He thinks I know more than I'm sayin' about Flyin' Eagle."

"Yeah?" Nash's expression tightened. "Well, whatever he's got in mind, he ain't goin' to get away with it."

"I can handle him, Nash."

"It ain't a fair match."

Irritated by his unexpected response, Purity snapped, "I'm a match for any man!"

Nash nodded. "You are . . . in most ways. But you only have to open your eyes to see that there's some things you can't overcome. Hell, Thomas stands at least a foot taller than you! He outweighs you by over a hundred pounds of solid muscle, and he moves as quick and silent as a shadow. If he wanted, he could snap your neck like a twig before you even heard him comin'!"

Purity's hand slipped to the gun at her hip. "That may be so, but I grow a few inches in height as soon as I curl my finger around this trigger . . . and when a fella's in my sights, all difference in size is erased."

"I ain't goin' to let it come to that, Purity."

"You don't have any choice."

Nash reached out a tentative hand to brush a flying wisp back from her cheek. His touch lingered. "Don't I?"

The emotion in Nash's eyes left Purity without response. She was somehow unable to move as he slid his hand into the hair at her temple. She saw his lips part. She felt the trembling that began inside him as he lowered his mouth toward hers.

"It's about time you get back to the cattle, ain't it, Nash?"

Purity jumped with a start at Buck's gruff question.

Nash's hand dropped to his side. He took a reluctant backward step, looking at Buck as the older man dismounted. Purity saw the promise in Nash's eyes when he turned back to speak in a voice meant for her alone.

"I meant every word I said, Purity."

Mounting, Nash rode off without a backward look. Purity did not speak as Buck approached. She saw his concern as he addressed her softly.

"You ain't told Stan nothin' about what's been happenin' between you and Cass Thomas since his father left, have you?"

"What do you mean?"

Buck gave a disgusted snort. "You're forgettin' who you're talkin' to, again. I've seen how Thomas has been doggin' you. He's tryin' to get to you . . . to wear you down. I don't know what's goin' on in that Injun head of his, but I know I don't like it."

"Don't say anythin' to Stan, please, Buck. I don't want to worry him."

"I heard what Nash said to you."

"He . . . he's worryin' for nothin'."

"He's got special feelin's for you that might color his judgment some, but everythin' he said was true."

Purity shrugged.

"Purity . . ." Buck's voice grew softer. "I was with Stan that day he found you in the river . . . and I was by his side all them years while he raised you like you was his own. Stan ain't able to do what he might if things was different, so I'm sayin' what I know he would if he was here now." Buck's voice chilled. "You just say the word, and I'll take care of Cass Thomas, once and for all."

"Buck . . ." Purity shook her head, incredulous. "You don't mean that!"

"Yes, I do."

No. He couldn't.

She would never let that happen, anyway.

Would she?

Purity took a shuddering breath.

Stifling a momentary desire to step into Buck's consoling embrace, to lay her head on his shoulder and shift her concerns there as well, Purity searched for the strength that had temporarily deserted her.

Forcing a steadiness into her voice that belied her inner turmoil, Purity repeated, "I can handle Cass Thomas. I don't want you or anybody else gettin' in the middle of all this."

"You always was hard-headed."

"Buck . . ."

"Say what you want. I make my own decisions. But I'll tell you one thing. That fella may think he's got things goin' his way, but he ain't. I'd tell him just exactly that, too, but I know he wouldn't believe me. So, I'm tellin' you, instead. Don't worry about him. If the need arises, I'll take care of him."

"I don't want that, Buck! Buck—"

But Buck was already remounting.

Cass's hand twitched on the reins. Concealed in the foliage some distance from Purity, he snapped a sharp reprimand as his mount moved restlessly beneath him. Motionless, he watched as Buck mounted his horse and rode out to start the cattle moving.

Cass had not heard what was said in the exchanges he had witnessed, but words had been unnecessary. Irrational emotions surged through him as he recalled the way Carter had touched Purity's cheek. He had wanted that touch to be his.

Cass silently cursed. It had been a morning of revelations. He had made a mistake, leaving Purity after her near fall. She had been shaken and vulnerable, but the reality was that he had been shaken as well—by the unexpected realization that in the split second before his arm had snatched Purity back from harm, fear had forced a glimpse of his true feelings for her.

He had seen another truth in the eyes of Carter and Buck when they talked with Purity. Both men would kill for her.

Despising the weakness against which he had no defense, Cass swept the lithe length of Purity's body with his gaze as she mounted. He felt her strength as she turned her mount toward the stream of cattle moving past. He saw the sun glisten on the golden braid lying against her narrow back. She turned, and he saw the fine line of her profile etched against the glare of the sun. The locket at her throat caught the sun's rays, glittering briefly, and its glow struck a heated chord within him.

Purity's chin rose a notch higher. He caressed it with his gaze.

Her lips pressed determinedly closed. He tasted them in his mind.

The cattle moved forward at a brisk pace.

Cass spurred his horse into motion.

"Where did she go?"

Stan frowned, awaiting a response as Buck avoided his eye. Purity and the men had returned later than usual from the day's work. It had taken only one look to know that the lack of conversation was not due totally to fatigue. The supper table had been more silent than ever, and Purity had left without lingering to talk as she usually did. Something was up and nobody was saying anything. He didn't like it.

Ignoring Pete as the balding cook fussed nearby, Stan squinted at Buck.

"I asked you a question."

"I heard you. That don't mean I've got the answer."

"Buck, damn it . . ."

"Purity went outside! How should I know where she went? I've been in here with you!"

"You might not know where she's gone right now, but you know what's eatin' at her."

"Think so?"

"Don't bother lyin'. You ain't good at it." Stan's squint narrowed. "What's the matter? Did she tell you not to say nothin' to me about what's botherin' her?"

No answer.

"Tell him the truth, Buck!"

Buck responded sharply to Pete's unsolicited interjection. "Mind your own business!"

"This is my business just as much as it's yours! Just because I ain't out on the range workin', that don't mean I ain't as much a part of this spread as you!"

"All right, that's enough!" Stan's words brought the angry exchange between the two men to a halt. He pressed, "Out with it, Buck. What's botherin' Purity? It's my guess that it's the same thing that's got Baird twitchin', Treacher holdin' back on his teasin', and Carter lookin' like a volcano about to blow."

"You don't miss a trick, do you?"

"Sure I don't miss a trick. My brain ain't been affected. Not yet, anyway."

Buck met his gaze fully. "Purity ain't goin' to like this. She don't want you to worry."

"She made me a promise. She said if things got too much for her, she'd tell me."

"She says she can handle Thomas."

Stan went momentarily silent. "I was hopin' he wasn't the problem."

"Well, if you was, you were wastin' your time. Purity and him ain't gettin' along."

Stan strove for a ray of hope. "Maybe they ain't had time to work things out yet."

"They're not goin' to work things out, not them

215

two. Nobody else on this ranch is goin' to work out things with that fella, either. He ain't left Purity alone for a minute since the first day he rode out with us. There ain't a one of us who can stand much more of it."

Stan stiffened. "What's he been doin'?"

"It's not so much what he's been doin'."

Stan's bushy brows tightened. "What's he been sayin to her, then?"

"It's not what he's been sayin'."

"If it's not what he's been doin', and it's not what he's been sayin'—"

Buck's eyes went ice cold. "I got it in my mind that fella's goin' to do anythin' he thinks is necessary to settle whatever grudge he's holdin' against Purity and the rest of us. I ain't goin' to let it happen."

It occurred to Stan that he hadn't seen Buck look like that since the day when the doctor said he'd never walk again.

Stan's throat went suddenly dry. "All right. You've seen what's been goin' on. I ain't. There's only one thing I'm askin'. I want you to tell me when you're goin' to step in—because there's no way I want the weight of all this lyin' on your shoulders alone."

Buck nodded.

A dull ache began inside Stan. He unconsciously shrugged. "I can't help thinkin' that Cass could've been my son."

"No, he couldn't."

There was nothing more to be said.

* * *

"Hold still, girl."

The semidarkness of the barn was lit by a lantern hung high on a peg nearby as Purity ran her hands along her mare's trembling flesh. It hadn't missed her notice that the animal had continued to favor her right foreleg for the remainder of the day after she had fallen.

Frowning at the animal's short whinny of pain, Purity continued her examination more gently than before. She cursed softly when she found what she had been seeking. She had no doubt how the injury had happened . . . just as she did not spare herself the blame. She had been acting like a spoiled child, taking out her frustrations on everyone and everything except the person who had caused it. Her mount was suffering for her behavior.

Lowering her mare's leg to the floor, Purity reached for the bottle of liniment behind her. She soaked the cloth she had readied and secured it over the bruised skin. She straightened up, her regrets full-blown as she whispered, "I'm sorry, girl."

"You didn't do that right, you know."

Purity turned sharply toward the unexpected voice behind her. Cass's broad frame filled the entrance to the stall and Purity took a spontaneous step backward. To some, this man was Cass Thomas. But when their gazes locked, leaving them alone no matter the number of people surrounding them, she would always see Pale Wolf.

Purity forced a normalcy to her tone that she did not feel.

"I suppose you know a better way to ease the swellin' . . . just like you know a better way to do everythin' else I do."

"A poultice would be better."

"I'm not much good at makin' poultices." Unable to conceal the exhaustion that rang in her voice, Purity forced herself to say the words that were long overdue. "I didn't thank you for what you did today. You saved me from a nasty fall."

"You were riding like a reckless kid."

"I know." She glanced at her mare. "My mare is payin' the price for it, and that's somethin' I won't forget for a while."

"Payin' the price is always hard."

Purity's next words emerged unexpectedly, spoken without conscious intention as she rasped with sudden vehemence, "All right. You win! What will it take to convince you that neither I nor my men know anythin' about whatever happened to Flyin' Eagle?"

Her question took him by surprise.

Cass's response was automatic.

"The truth."

Purity's silence was revealing. He noticed for the first time the new depth to the shadows that ringed her eyes, the weariness of her gesture as she swept a gold strand back from a cheek that was devoid of its usual color. He heard the fatigue in her voice.

"Stan wants this partnership to work. He *needs* it to work—but it isn't. Things are just gettin' worse."

"You know what can change all that."

Purity shook her head. Cass was startled to see the

glitter of moisture in her pale eyes the second before she mumbled, "Oh, what's the use?"

Purity turned away unexpectedly. She was almost at the door when Cass caught her by the shoulder and turned her back toward him. He was angry, for so many reasons. He was angry because the moisture in her eyes had momentarily disabled him. He was angry because the shadows now partially concealed her face and he could not clearly read her expression. He was angry because he blamed himself for the frustration that had driven Purity to a reckless act that could have caused her injury, and because that realization would give him no rest. He was angry because without any effort on her part at all, Purity had insinuated herself into his life in a way he never intended . . . and because he knew that there was only one way to cure the malady that had beset him.

Purity's hand moved toward the locket at her throat. He saw her grip it tightly. Clearly she valued the locket above all else.

Cass reached instinctively for the hand that clutched her locket. He enclosed it in his own as he drew Purity closer and into the light.

"I want to know what happened to Flying Eagle."

"I told you, I don't know."

"I believe you."

Cass felt the surprise that rippled through her as he continued with words he could no longer deny. "I believe you don't know what happened to Flying Eagle. But I also believe you know that one of your men is responsible for his disappearance."

"That's not true!"

Elaine Barbieri

"Look at me, Purity." Cass drew her closer. Uncertain why the reflection of his image in her clear eyes gave him such deep satisfaction, he clenched her fist tighter. "I can help you find out what happened to your sisters."

"W . . . what?"

"If they're dead—"

"They aren't dead!"

Unwilling to challenge her, Cass continued, "I know someone who can help you discover what happened to your sisters—someone who can help you see what you otherwise couldn't. I can take you to him."

Purity stiffened. "There is no such person."

"Yes, there is."

"Who is he? *What* is he?"

"His name is Spotted Bear. He's a holy man—a shaman."

Purity swallowed, her gaze locked with his. "If he can do these things, why couldn't he tell you what happened to Flyin' Eagle? Why couldn't he tell you how to find him?"

"He did."

"He did?"

"He led me to you."

Purity attempted a step backward. "He was wrong!"

"You know in your heart that isn't true."

Sensing victory in Purity's lack of response, Cass pressed, "You said we need to work things out. We do. But I want the truth. I won't accept anything less." His voice dropped to a throbbing urgency that

220

echoed deep within him as he continued, "I'll exchange truth for truth, Purity. I'll give you the fate of your sisters for the fate of Flying Eagle."

Purity shook her head. "No, none of this is true. You just want to drive a wedge between me and my men. You want me to doubt them."

"Your doubt already exists."

"You want me to betray them!"

"Justice isn't betrayal."

"Even if they were guilty, what would stop them from denyin' it if I questioned them?"

"They won't lie to you."

Purity's gaze flickered briefly. She shook her head again. "No, I can't."

"Are you afraid of what you'll find out?"

Purity's eyes closed. Her dark lashes fluttered against her colorless cheeks before she looked back up at him abruptly. He heard the resistance in her tone waning.

"How do I know there really is a Spotted Bear? How do I know he can do what you say he can?"

"Because I'll take you to him first . . . tomorrow."

"Tomorrow!"

Purity was suddenly shuddering. Refusing to release the hand enclosing the locket, Cass slipped his other arm around her. With their hands clenched between them, he held her close. Imprisoning her in his gaze, he whispered with fierce intensity, "He'll help you, and you'll *know*, once and for all, what happened to your sisters. All your uncertainties will be settled and that ache inside you, the gnawing that gives you no peace, will go away. You'll be whole again, Purity."

You'll be whole again, Purity.

Cass's words startled her. They echoed eerily in Purity's mind.

How had he known? How did he understand the emptiness within her that even she could not describe? How did he comprehend her feeling that her sisters were a lost part of her which she had to reclaim before she could feel truly whole?

The translucence of Cass's eyes took on new depth. Purity felt his gaze draining the last residue of her resistance as she rasped, "You're tellin' me the truth—this shaman *can* tell me about my sisters . . . ?"

"Yes."

Purity took a shuddering breath. "If I question my men about Flyin' Eagle and they say they don't know anythin' about what happened to him . . . if you're wrong . . ."

"I'm not wrong."

"But if you are?"

Cass's gaze flickered. "All I want is the truth."

The truth.

Nothing more.

The fierce pounding of her heart stole Purity's breath. Hardly recognizing her voice as her own, she responded in a ragged whisper.

"All right. Tomorrow."

*   *   *

"You aren't goin' to let her do it, are you, Stan?"

Incredulous, aware that Buck awaited his response, Stan looked at Purity where she stood, pale and determined beside his bed. Numbed by the unexpected announcement that she would be leaving with Cass at dawn for an unknown destination, Stan had yet to reply.

Not as speechless as he, Buck took an aggressive step toward him, his color high. "Tell her she can't go!"

"He can't stop me, and neither can you, Buck." The fervor in Purity's eyes was unmistakable. "Cass is goin' to help me find out what happened to my sisters."

"Your sisters?"

"Yes."

"How's he supposed to do that?" Buck gave a skeptical snort. "Is he goin' to read a crystal ball or somethin'?"

"He knows somebody . . . a shaman." Purity took a short breath. "This man can help me. Cass is goin' to take me to him."

"Where's he goin' to take you? Who is this shaman? How do you know he didn't make all this up?"

"I believe him."

"*Why* do you believe him?"

"He has no reason to lie."

"No reason?" Buck's eyes widened. "Cass Thomas is the man who roped you from your horse and held a knife to your throat last fall, remember? He didn't need a reason for what he did then, and he doesn't need a reason now! Did you forget what these past

223

few days have been like? Did you forget what you said to me this mornin'? Think, Purity!"

"That . . . that's all in the past, Buck. Cass and I have come to an understandin'. Everythin's changed."

"You may have changed, but *he* hasn't! There ain't no compromise in that fella, Purity! You know that as well as I do! I'm not goin' to let him take you off somewheres—"

"You don't have any choice. I've made up my mind."

Beyond words, Buck turned abruptly toward Stan. "Tell her the truth, Stan! Tell her that Thomas just kept diggin' until he found her weak spot, and now he's takin' advantage of it. Tell her she can't go. If you don't, you'll lose her!"

"I ain't goin' to lose her!" Stan dragged his thin frame up higher in his bed. His voice held no trace of the shock that had formerly held him speechless as he commanded, "Tell Cass I want to see him in here . . . now."

Purity took a step toward him. Stan suddenly realized that he had never seen her beautiful face paler or her determination more fixed as she stated, "I've made up my mind. I'm goin'."

Stan's fury became scalding heat. "Get him in here!"

Purity opened her lips to speak, then turned abruptly toward the door. Waiting until it had closed behind her, Stan ordered, "Get out, Buck. I want to talk to Cass alone."

"I ain't goin' nowhere."

"I said, *get out*."

Buck turned away without further protest.

Buck drew the door closed behind him. The echo of the sound was still reverberating in the silent room as Stan stretched a steady hand toward the nightstand beside him and withdrew his gun from the drawer.

"Come on in. That's right. Shut the door."

Cass briefly assessed the wasted figure in the bed in front of him. Stan's countenance was drawn and pale. The full head of gray hair that appeared to shrink his face was tousled, and his nightshirt was wrinkled and in disarray, as if he had been awakened from his sleep. Propped up in his bed as he was with two pillows supporting him, he looked pathetically frail.

But Stan's hand was steady, and his gun was leveled directly at Cass's heart.

It occurred to Cass as he pushed the door closed behind him and advanced into the room that he should not have expected any less.

"That's far enough." Stan's hard gaze pinned him. "Now, tell me, where is it that you think you're takin' Purity tomorrow?"

Cass did not immediately reply. Instead, he studied the old man more intently. He had intentionally avoided contact with Stan since arriving at the ranch. He had known exactly what he must do from the first moment he had seen Purity's face. In that same instant he had also known that any friendship which might develop between the old man and himself could only prove a hindrance to his purpose. No, there was no way he would willingly have submitted to Stan's probing scrutiny.

"I'm waitin' . . ."

But the present situation demanded more than he had formerly been willing to give. He replied emotionlessly, "What do you want to know?"

Stan's white lips narrowed. "Damned if you ain't a cool one! You know what I want to know. Where do you intend takin' Purity?"

"I won't answer that question."

"No, huh?" Stan's jaw twitched. "I'll give you three seconds to tell me why."

"Because I don't want anybody coming after us. That would only cause trouble."

"Trouble for who?"

"Trouble for everybody concerned."

"You don't want trouble."

"No."

"And you just expect me to sit back and accept that."

Cass did not reply. He noted the slow tensing of Stan's jaw. The old man's hand tightened on the handle of his gun as he pressed, "How long do you expect to be away?"

"Two weeks, more or less."

"Purity says you're goin' to take her to some shaman who can tell her somethin' about her sisters." He grated harshly, "That's a damned lie!"

Cass's jaw tightened. "No, it isn't."

"Injun mumbo-jumbo! You don't believe it any more than I do!"

"You forget that you're talking to an 'Injun'."

"No, I ain't talkin' to no Injun! I'm talkin' to a man who signed a partnership with me! I'm talkin' to a fella who's supposed to be here makin' sure this ranch gets back on its feet! I'm talkin' to a person who's supposed to be workin' alongside Purity at this ranch, not takin' her away to who knows where, to see some shaman—with no guarantees involved!" Stan's gray face twisted into lines of true menace. His gun hand began trembling. "You didn't really think I'd let you take Purity off alone somewhere, with no protection at all, did you?"

"She'll have protection."

"Yeah?"

Stan's finger twitched on the trigger as Cass moved closer to the bed. "Jack and I signed a contract with you. I intend to live up to that contract, but legal papers aside, my father feels he owes you a debt. He wants to pay it, and I have no intention of dishonoring that intention."

"I'm not interested in contracts right now, or old debts of honor, neither!"

Cass stared into Stan's eyes. It occurred to him that if he were in the old man's place—were Purity's life in possible danger because of a man he held in his sights—he would have pulled that trigger long ago. That thought steadied his gaze as he said levelly, "I won't harm Purity. I'm taking her to someone who may be able to answer some questions about her sisters, just as I said."

"And all this stuff about Flyin' Eagle?"

Cass struggled to withhold the bitterness that

sprang to his lips. "Purity says she doesn't know anything about him. I believe her."

"You do." Stan's eyes narrowed into a squint. "Since when?"

"Since today."

"What happened today to change your mind?"

"That's my business."

"That so?"

Stan's reply was unrevealing, but his hand had stopped shaking and his trigger finger was gradually relaxing. Cass noted a subtle change in Stan's tone as he continued, "So you believe Purity when she says she don't know nothin' about Flyin' Eagle." He nodded. "That's good,'cause I'll tell you right now, if it's one thing Purity never did take to, it was lyin'." Stan voice sharpened. "I ain't forgettin' what you did on that trail drive last fall. You made a mistake when you attacked her . . . a bad one."

Cass's eyes narrowed. "I paid for whatever mistake I made then, but if that's your way of asking if I'd ever put a knife to Purity's throat again, the answer is no."

"No, huh?"

"And if you're also asking if Purity will be safe while she's under my protection, the answer is *yes*."

"I've got your word on that?"

Cass nodded.

"Let me hear you say it, boy!"

"You have my word."

Stan's jaw tightened. "That ain't enough! I want to hear you swear to it . . . *on your mother's honor*."

Cass's gaze narrowed. "On the honor of an Injun squaw?"

"On the honor of the woman both of us loved."

The old man's scrutiny deepened as Cass paused, then responded. "I swear . . . on my mother's honor."

Stan's gun hand dropped wearily to the bed. He barked gruffly, "Get out of here. And tell Buck to come back in. I have to talk to him before I go to sleep, or you might never make it till mornin'." At the responsive tightening of Cass's jaw, he added, "Don't worry. I'll take care of it."

Cass turned toward the door. His hand was on the knob when a relieved sigh sounded in the silence. It occurred to him in that fleeting second that he was truly uncertain if that sigh had been his own.

Pale fingers of dawn stretched across the night sky as Purity emerged from the front door, her saddle-bags in hand. She frowned at the sight of the chestnut mare saddled and waiting beside Cass's gelding, and at the pack horse loaded nearby. She looked at Cass where he stood beside the animal, working at the hitch.

Purity's throat tightened convulsively. Cass's head was uncovered, his hair held in place by an Indian headband. He was dressed in buckskins that molded the powerful stretch of his shoulders and the lean, muscled length of his body with exacting perfection. She saw the laborious dedication of a female hand in the clothes he had chosen to wear, and she saw the ease with which he wore them. But she saw more, too. She saw challenge in the bold declaration

229

of his heritage and an allegiance he had no desire to disguise.

A cold chill crawled up Purity's spine. Dressed as he was, Cass looked exactly as he had that first day, when she found herself lying on the dusty ground, his startlingly light eyes looking down into hers and his knife at her throat.

Somehow relieved when Cass did not look up at the sound of her step, Purity turned toward the door as Stan appeared in the opening. Ashen and unsmiling, he manipulated his chair out onto the porch. A wheel jammed, halting his advance and he cursed softly as Pete stepped into sight to ease him forward.

Pausing a few feet from her, Stan glanced at Cass and frowned, then turned to squint up at her. "You take care, you hear? Buck'll take over while you're gone, but you make sure you don't waste no time gettin' back here. Hell, there ain't no way I'll enjoy lookin' at his homely face the way I do lookin' at you."

Purity leaned toward Stan. "You know I have to do this before anythin' can finally be settled here, don't you, Stan?"

Stan's eyes searched hers. "Yeah, I suppose I do."

Aware that the time had come to say good-bye, Purity felt a sudden flash of panic. Stan looked so weak. Damn, what had she been thinking when she'd agreed to this wild goose chase last night? How had she allowed Cass to convince her to leave Stan when he needed her most?

Those thoughts were interrupted at the sound of Cass's step behind her. Sensing his silent strength at her back, Purity responded flatly to the question in Stan's gaze. "Don't worry about me. I'll be all right."

Pressing a kiss on Stan's cheek, Purity turned quickly toward her horse and mounted. With Cass beside her, she nudged her mount into motion.

Chapter Seven

The darkening of the sky overhead was unexpected. Roger was annoyed. The morning had been clear when he started out.

Scowling, Roger surveyed the landscape around him. The new green that spring had raised would spur a fresh wave of optimism on the surrounding ranches, optimism that was doomed to failure for most. As far as he was concerned, all ranchers were fools, working year after year in pursuit of a dream that, if it was realized at all, often came when they were too old to truly enjoy the fruits of their labor.

His scowl became a haughty smirk. His father and he were too smart to allow themselves to lead such a hard life. It was so much more pleasant to sit back without shedding a drop of perspiration, to await the day when the fruits of other people's labors fell into their hands. The only effort they had to make was uttering the proper words of condolence as they held back their smiles.

It was a source of cold amusement to Roger that so many of the ranchers disliked his father and him, while many of their wives were accommodating in so many ways.

Roger's smirk faded at the memory of the afternoon a few days earlier that he had spent in Penelope Thurber's bed while her husband was conveniently engaged in the north sector of his ranch. He wondered why he had even bothered. Penelope was a slut. He wasn't the first she had entertained in her husband's absence, and he would not be the last. The only enjoyment he had actually derived from the frantic heat of their few hours together was the perverse satisfaction he felt the next morning when Tom Thurber appeared at his bank to negotiate a loan . . . and he had refused it. He wondered what Penelope thought of that, but the truth was that he didn't care.

There was only one woman who filled his thoughts, and she filled them to the point of obsession. That was the only reason he was now making an uncomfortable trip to the Circle C, aware as he was of the dangers involved.

Roger's handsome face creased into lines of angry frustration as Purity's image flashed again before him. He saw her beautiful visage twisting into lines of ridicule as his pleas echoed in the seclusion of his office. He heard her mocking words. The conniving witch had played him well, but the game was not yet over!

Almost two weeks had passed since Stan Corrigan introduced his new partners and the foreclosure notice had been lifted. Roger had waited with anxious anticipation, hoping that the letter of credit Jack Thomas had provided would ultimately be refused. But it had not. The wire confirming the funds in Thomas's account had come posthaste, and Roger's hopes had been cruelly dashed.

The remembered image of Cass Thomas's proprietary hand on Purity's arm when he steered her out of his office was another blow. But the heaviest toll by far was the persistent mental image of Purity lying in that half-breed's arms.

His stomach revolting, Roger spat out the bitter taste of bile that rose in his throat, then took a deep breath. But rumors were rife in town. The Circle C riders had made no secret of the malice they bore Cass Thomas. So explosive had the situation become after Jack Thomas departed the Circle C, that an innocent comment made to the usually even-tempered Nash Carter had almost led to bloodshed.

It had rapidly become the general consensus of opinion, however, that if blood were to be shed in the end, it would most likely be the blood of the half-breed, who had endeared himself to no one.

Roger refuted that last thought with a low grunt of sound. They were wrong—all of them. Vengeance would be taken, but *he* would be the one to take it. Purity would pay for the humiliation she had dealt him, and he would personally see to it that the half-breed regretted every hour she had spent in his arms.

His body reacting with a familiar hardening to the

stimulus of his thoughts, Roger cursed as the Circle C ranch house came into view. The truth was that he was desperate to determine the true status of affairs there, and rumors would not suffice. He needed to know, and he *would* know how things stood the moment he saw Purity's face. He would formulate his plans from there, because while all else remained uncertain, one fervent resolution remained unequivocally burned into his mind.

He would not be satisfied until he'd brought Purity Corrigan to her knees.

Roger indulged that thought for long moments. He then straightened his shoulders and affixed a smile on his lips.

That smile did not waver as Roger approached the Circle C ranch house. He saw movement at the doorway the moment before Stan rolled out onto the porch, a frown on his face and a shotgun lying across his lap. His greeting was not long in coming.

"Stop where you are! You ain't welcome here, Norris!"

The feeble old bastard . . .

Roger continued his approach.

Raising the shotgun with speed that took Roger by surprise, Stan growled, "I'm warnin' you one last time."

"All right!" Despising the perspiration that appeared on his brow as the old man pointed the gun at his midsection, Roger responded tightly, "Whatever the reason for your animosity—"

"Don't play dumb with me! You know damned well why this gun is pointed your way." Stan's pale face tightened. "Don't go foolin' yourself that the fact that I'm sittin' in this chair makes a difference, neither. You'd do better to keep in mind that I ain't got much to lose if I shoot you dead here and now. If you're half as smart as you think you are, you'll turn that damned horse of yours around and high-tail it out of here!"

Filthy old coot . . .

"This isn't a social call. It's business, about the loan."

"We settled all that in town! There ain't nothin' we got to talk about until the next payment is due!"

"I have a receipt for the certification of Jack Thomas's letter of credit. I need to deliver it directly into Cass Thomas's hands in his father's absence."

Stan's eyes narrowed. "He ain't here."

"I'll wait."

"Oh, no, you won't, not unless you think I'm goin' to let you sit there for two or three weeks until he comes back."

Roger frowned, disconcerted. "I'd like to talk to Purity, then."

"No."

"I'll wait here."

"No!"

Roger felt a slow fury rising. "I said I'll wait for her, and there's no way you're going to stop me!"

"There ain't, huh?" Stan smiled. "Aside from the persuasion of this gun I'm wavin' at you, I doubt if you'd like sittin' there on that horse for two or three weeks until she comes back."

"What are you saying?"

"I'm sayin' she ain't here, neither. And it wouldn't do you no good if she was, because she wouldn't give you the time of day."

"What do you mean, she's not here?" Slow fury gradually turning to rage, Roger spat, "Are you telling me she went somewhere with Thomas—that they'll be gone two or three weeks?"

Stan's scrutiny intensified. He responded with slow deliberation, "That's right."

"Where did they go?"

"That's none of your business."

"I asked you—"

Roger's words came to an abrupt halt as Stan raised his gun a notch higher with a growling command.

"Get out of here, Norris. Purity ain't here, and where she's gone, you ain't goin' to get to her—especially not with Cass Thomas ridin' beside her."

"That half-breed—"

"Get off my land!"

"You'll regret this, Corrigan!"

"That day'll never come."

Roger turned his mount and kicked it savagely into motion. He did not look back to see the satisfied smile that dawned on Stan's face as he turned toward the ranch house door to say, "You can come out now, Pete. I know you're there. And you can put down your gun. He's gone."

Neither did Roger hear the balding cook grunt harshly, "Why'd you tell him about Purity and Thomas leavin' together? It was none of his business, nohow!"

Nor did Roger see Stan's hard smile as he replied, "If you saw his face, you'd know. It's called gettin' even."

Instead, jealousy raging, Roger whipped his mount into a gallop as soon as the Circle C ranch house faded from sight. Cursing as the first drop of rain struck his shoulder, he glanced upward at the black clouds swirling ominously overhead. He swore a harsher vengeance at the second, and when the heavens opened up, he made a solemn vow.

The frigid deluge continued its unrelenting assault as Purity's mount plodded along the muddied trail. The storm had begun shortly after noon and had not yet abated, although daylight was waning. Wracked by another uncontrollable shudder, she grimaced as the persistent stream from the brim of her hat ran its unerring course down the back of her neck to soak her shirt underneath. Her teeth began another round of chattering, and she realized with bitter amusement that the physical misery of the past hours had had one positive effect. It had effectively supplanted in her mind the uncertainties that had begun plaguing her as soon as the Circle C had faded into the distance a few days earlier.

Purity sighed. The time Cass and she had spent on the trail since then had passed in uncomfortable silence. The sense of menace which had formerly influenced all exchanges between them had disappeared, but in its stead another, indefinable tension had arisen, which showed no signs of lessening. So intense had that tension become that the slightest brush of Cass's hand raised her discomfort anew. She was increasingly conscious of his presence whenever he was near, yet an invisible barrier had grown between them.

Attempts at conversation had resulted either in clipped responses on Cass's part, or in animosity, as had been the case the previous night when a simple question had resulted in a stinging glance from Cass that still burned. Angry, she had snapped, "I think it's about time you let me in on your secret."

Cass's head had jerked up toward her and his light eyes had narrowed.

"Where exactly is this Kiowa camp you're takin' me to?" she'd asked, but his silence had forced her to press, "I don't like bein' kept in the dark! You expect me to trust you, but you don't trust me enough to tell me where we're goin'!"

He had faced her fully then, eliciting a strange breathlessness within as he responded tightly, "Trust has nothing to do with it. I already told you that the camp is in north Texas, on land the government set aside by treaty. Exactly when we'll reach it will depend on what we run into on the way."

Prophetic words.

Purity glanced at Cass riding beside her. The brim of his hat was pulled low over his forehead and his shoulders were erect. He showed no sign of the weariness and discomfort eroding her endurance. Yet, she knew that the slicker he wore was no more effective than her own in keeping out the wet, and that the chill of his soaked clothing underneath increased, as did hers, with every passing hour.

Purity took a steadying breath that emerged as a shiver. The truth was that she didn't like spring storms, and she didn't like being at their mercy when on the trail. Faded memories became too vivid with the sounds of heavy rain. Remembered echoes of pelting drops striking the canvas cover of her family wagon grew clearer, as did recollections of deafening thunder booms and flashes of lightning that lit the interior of the wagon as if it were day.

Taunting her with a sadness that still tore viciously at her heart was the memory of her father's smile when he spoke to her sisters and her that last time.

I know my girls love each other, just like I love them. Take care of each other. Promise?

I promise.

I promise, too, Papa.

Me, too.

I love you, Papa.

Then her own rasping question after her father had left.

Where's Papa takin' us, Honesty?

Across the river . . . to the doctor.

Good,'cause I'm sick.

Me, too.

And Honesty's final reassurance.

Don't be afraid . . .

Purity reached unconsciously for her locket, suddenly realizing that her fingers were so stiff that she could hardly close them around it.

Spring rain, frequently colder than snow . . . and often more deadly.

A new round of quaking beset her, turning Cass

toward her with a frown. "It's getting late. We'd better stop."

Purity shook her head, her reply spontaneous. "No, it's too early. We still have another hour of daylight."

Cass's response was a look that communicated his thoughts more clearly than words.

Julia stared at the outline of a rider in the distance. Her heart leaped to a wild pounding as she reached up a trembling hand to smooth her hair.

Oh, please . . . please . . . let it be him! Time was slipping by so quickly.

The rider came closer, and Julia's heart fell. It was Barry Holmes. She should have known. Their foreman's horse was the same color and size as Jack's, and there was some similarity between Jack's and Barry's stature, but Barry was heavier than Jack, and he sat a horse differently. Cass was the only man she had ever known to ride a horse with Jack's fluid ease.

Barry continued his approach, but Julia turned away from the window. The truth was that there was very little resemblance between Jack and their foreman, even at a distance.

Wishful thinking, that's all that it had been.

Julia forced a smile, determinedly willing away the breathlessness that beset her. The room was bright with sunlight, despite the dark clouds in the distance. It was storming to the east. She wondered if Jack was traveling in the rain right now, on his way back to her.

Blinking back the moisture that sprang into her

eyes, Julia looked around her with slow deliberation. She kept a lovely house. It was clean and pleasantly decorated with items she had painstakingly sewn and crocheted over the years. The kitchen always smelled of good food and fresh baking. She had made it a point to learn the favorite foods of every man on the ranch so she might show them all favor in turn, but it had always been Jack and Cass on whom her attentions were devotedly concentrated.

She loved them both—perhaps too much. She had sacrificed her pride and moral integrity for that love, hadn't she?

Pain sliced deeply as Julia faced the tumult within. What would her father say if he knew? A man of God and of unyielding moral principle, he would doubt-less lambast her for allowing the hypocrisy of her life to continue.

Living with a man under a bond of marriage ne-gated by a previously given vow . . .

Concealing her knowledge of her husband's dou-ble life because she was afraid to lose him . . .

Keeping another woman from her rightful place in the house where she stood now . . .

Allowing her husband to suffer the pain of a deceit he did not carry easily . . .

Selfishness.

Julia brushed away a tear. But her selfishness was borne of love, was it not? And in truth, her awak-ening to the realization that her husband was no longer hers alone had come so gradually.

Jack's strange periods of preoccupation; the unex-plained absences which had grown more frequent and of longer duration over the years; his inexplicable anxiety when winter approached and the weather worsened, when he would leave with his pack horse heavily laden and a lame excuse for his absence that never truly deluded her; the sadness she sensed within him when he took her into his arms, and the pain she glimpsed in his eyes when he said he loved her . . .

But he did love her! She knew he did! She could not have borne it if she was not convinced that was true.

And then there was Cass. It was not in his nature to give love easily. For that reason, the love he had given her was all the more precious. She was uncertain when the roles between Cass and her began reversing themselves, with Cass providing the comfort that she had once extended him, but she had accepted the change willingly, with pride, because he was her son.

Whispering Woman . . .

The pain stabbed deeper and the questions returned.

Did Jack know that he whispered that name in his sleep? Did he realize that the despair he often felt was mirrored in his eyes? Was he aware that she despised herself for the anguish her silence inflicted upon him?

Would he return to her?

Oh, Jack . . .

Julia took a deep breath, then reached a trembling hand for the sack on the table. She scooped out a handful of flour and sprinkled it lightly over the dough on the board in front of her. Managing to subdue her unsteadiness, she worked automatically as her mind followed the same anguished track.

Why did she torment herself so? Jack and Cass had been gone less than three weeks. Jack would return. He always did. And when he did, she would greet him with love, as she always did. It was just that time had become so precious, and she—

Julia's head jerked upward at the sound of a horse drawing up in front of the house. She heard footsteps on the porch, and her knees went weak as she approached the door. Forcing a smile, aware that her disappointment was irrational when she opened it to see Barry standing there, she accepted the envelope he handed her as he spoke.

"Old John Nickels gave me this letter for you when he passed by, ma'am. He said you mentioned you were expectin' one, so he figured it might be important."

Julia glanced at the flowery hand scrawled across the envelope. Momentarily weak, she took a short breath. Clenching the missive tightly, she murmured, "Thank you, Barry." Pausing, she continued more strongly, "I'll be going into town tomorrow morning. I'd appreciate it if you'd get the wagon ready for me early. I'd like to reach town before noon."

Barry's leathery face drew into a frown. "I'd be happy to, ma'am, but the boys are spread real thin with Jack and Cass bein' away. It'll be hard to spare somebody to go with you."

"Oh, that won't be necessary." Julia made her smile brighter. "I can manage fine by myself."

"I don't know that Jack would like that. He told me—"

"I'll be fine. I'll only be gone a few hours."

Barry nodded. "Yes, ma'am."

Julia's smile faded as she stepped back and closed the door behind her. It disappeared as she opened the letter with trembling hands.

The downpour continued.

Clenching his jaw as he allowed his gaze to linger for long moments on Purity's quaking form, Cass turned to scan the nearby terrain. The rain was heavy and constant, a relentless torrent that had appeared unlikely when they first undertook their journey, when the sun was shining and the days were warm.

Purity shuddered again, and Cass cursed softly. She was chilled to the bone, her energy spent. Long hours in the saddle and nights with little sleep were taking their toll. He knew she had not been sleeping well because sleep had eluded him, too. Aware of her every move where she lay across the fire from him each night, he had allowed his gaze to linger on her. He was not sure whether fear, uncertainty, or the insecurity of her approaching encounter with the past kept her wakeful. He only knew that it had taken all the strength he could summon not to cross the short distance between them and take her into his arms.

His thoughts halting as the angry sky overhead unleashed a new deluge, Cass scanned the surrounding landscape with more urgency. His gaze stopped on a small grove of trees nearby. Reining up under its limited protection minutes later, grateful that lightning presently played no part in the storm, he dismounted.

Purity dismounted beside him. Her cheeks were pallid and her lips blue with cold, and a slow fury rose within him. So depleted was her strength that she was barely able to stand, yet she had not said a word.

Damn her stubbornness! Damn the determination even now visible in her eyes! And damn his own folly in pressing onward through the storm when he should have stopped, when he should have—

Purity shivered again, and Cass's control snapped. He addressed her tightly. "Wait under that tree over there, out of the rain. I'll take care of setting up camp."

Purity turned sharply toward him, snapping back through chattering teeth, "Stand over there yourself if the rain bothers you! It doesn't bother me."

Cass closed the distance between them in a blur of movement. Sweeping her from her feet, he quelled her protest with his superior strength and strode across the soggy ground to place her on her feet under the tree he had indicated. The rain hammered ever harder as he grated, "Stay here. I don't need your help."

Unrolling the canvas from his pack, Cass secured the roof of their makeshift shelter, but minutes later he turned to see Purity working at the straps of the pack horse, ignoring the rivulets that streamed down her face as she struggled to relieve the animal of its load.

Beside her instantly, Cass silenced Purity's protests with a glance as he again swept her from her feet, this time depositing her on the canvas floor of the refuge he had hastily erected. Crouched beside her, his head brushing the protective cloth above their heads, he ordered in a low tone that would brook no argument, "Stay here! You've had enough. You're cold and you're exhausted, and even if you're willing to let stubbornness replace common sense, I'm not!"

Her lips stiff, Purity managed to spit in return, "I'm fine! I've traveled through worse storms than this one a dozen times!"

"Not with me, you haven't!"

Purity's gaze narrowed. "I can pull my own weight . . . here, or anywhere else."

Cass growled, "Don't force me to do something I'll be sorry for."

Pale eyes flashing, Purity hissed, "I'm not afraid of you!"

Cass struggled to maintain control.

On his feet in a second, he strode from the shelter. Returning, he dropped a package of supplies beside her. "Make a fire and heat some of the water from that canteen for coffee if you want to make yourself useful."

Purity glared.

"Do it, damn it!"

Halting her intended protest as Cass loomed closer, Purity ripped open the pack and picked up the matches inside. Her light eyes challenged him. "Matches, but nothing to light."

Cass growled, "Just sit there!"

Looking back a short time later, Cass saw the glow of a fire beneath the makeshift shelter.

Stubborn witch . . .

Stubborn bastard . . .

Her gaze narrowed, Purity pushed aside the canvas covering to see that Cass had settled the horses nearby and was making a last-minute check to secure their camp.

She dropped the flap abruptly, then glanced down at the coffee pot in her hand. Cursing, she dumped the grounds into the water swirling within and smacked it down into the middle of the struggling flames.

Another tremor shook her and Purity closed her eyes, cursing again. She was angry, and she didn't know why. She was cold, despite the cover over her head and the bedrolls carefully stretched out atop the canvas floor. Her shaking would not stop. She was wet and cold outside, and hungry and suffering on the inside . . . suffering with a need that tore at her innards more than any longing she had ever known.

Her misery intense, Purity did not hear Cass's approach until the moment the flaps separated to admit him. Refusing to look up, she did not recognize his intent as he stripped off his slicker and tossed it roughly aside. Closing her eyes, she did not know that he had knelt beside her until the moment he drew her into his arms. Nor was she aware that tears streamed down her cheeks until he brushed them away with his palm, until he covered her mouth with his.

The heat of him . . . the warmth surging through her . . . the glow that started a new trembling deep within . . . the fire that ignited within her heart . . .

Purity was shuddering.
Cass halted her tremors with his warmth.
She was crying.
He stopped her tears with his heat.
She was aching. . . .
That aching reverberated deep inside him, calling out in a voice he could no longer deny.

The pounding rain overhead contributed to a moment that was suddenly serene as Cass whispered against her lips, "No more anger. No more conflict. Just what we feel . . . right now. Let me love you, Purity."

A shudder shook Purity as he drew her closer. Her cheeks colored with a sudden flush, and he cooled them with his touch. Her lips parted with words that would not come, and he brushed them with his own. The womanly heat of her melded to him, and he was lost.

The joy of her . . . the beauty . . .

Kissing her fully, deeply, Cass tasted the moist hollows of Purity's mouth. His kisses grew searching as he abandoned himself to the myriad emotions within. He drew from her, consuming the bliss of this woman he had failed so miserably to displace from his heart. He traced the line of her jaw, the curve of her ear, the slender column of her throat, a hunger unlike any he had ever known pressing him onward.

Stripping away the damp shirt and undergarment molding her sweet flesh, he caressed the soft swells exposed to his sight with trembling hands. Her breasts were beautiful, the crests erect and pink as he lowered his mouth to them. He tasted them. He laved them with his tongue. He suckled them gently. He drew deeply on the tender flesh, worshipping the burgeoning crests; the soft groan that escaped Purity's lips sent a jolt of pleasure through him.

Cass slid himself back up on her, needing words that would dismiss forever the anger and violence between them—words born not of the heat of the moment, but from the depth of Purity's heart.

Desire held momentarily in check, Cass rasped, "Tell me you want me, Purity. I need to hear you say the words. I need to know that you want me . . . that you need me as much as I need you. Purity . . ."

Holding his breath, his body aching with yearning, Cass waited.

Cass's words pierced the golden haze that had overwhelmed Purity's mind. She returned the intensity of his emerald gaze.

Didn't he know how she felt? Couldn't he see? Didn't he realize that the nameless misery afflicting her had not been a physical anguish? Couldn't he tell that he had halted it with his touch? Didn't he recognize, as did she, that she had come home to his arms, that she now knew they had walked a path toward this moment from the first day their gazes had touched, and that in that first moment, he had somehow become a part of her?

Did she want him?

Oh, yes, she did.

Did she need him?

Caution nudged but was dispatched by a wisdom instinctive to the moment, the sudden certainty that need was not weakness when it was shared.

The full glory of that understanding suddenly clear, Purity's voice was a broken whisper as she rasped, "I want you to love me, Cass . . . yes, I do."

Joy surged to thundering life as Cass slipped his arms around Purity to crush her close.

Unfastening her trousers, Cass slipped them from Purity's legs, leaving only a scrap of cotton underclothing between them. The coarse garment assumed the beauty of lace against her faultless skin as the visual wonder of the woman lying before him filled his senses.

Her hair was a fairer gold than any he had ever known, her skin a creamy hue that was velvet to his touch, her silver eyes filled with yearning. Her long limbs and gentle curves formed a sweet perfection not yet fully revealed.

Stripping away the final impediment to his gaze, Cass curled his fingers into the warm, golden nest revealed at last. Purity's breathless gasp echoed in his mind. Her breathing grew short, matching his own as he separated her thighs and stroked her warmly. A responsive moistness touched his palm, and he longed to taste it. Lowering his head to the heated delta, he brushed it with his lips.

That first taste spurring a greater need, Cass slipped his hands underneath Purity to cup her rounded buttocks in his palms. Raising her to him, unconscious of her short protest, he tasted her again, then slid his tongue deep within the precious slit. Passion encompassed him in a fiery mist as he found the bud of her passion and fondled it gently. It was sweet and warm, the womanly core of Purity that was his alone.

Her soft moans and the flush of ecstasy that shivered through Purity fed the flames consuming him as Cass separated her thighs further to expand his intimate assault, allowing no respite until her shudders grew greater, her breathing wild.

"Cass, please . . ."

Purity's rasping plea raised his gaze to hers. Apprehension and anticipation mingled in her gaze, and an aching tenderness rose within him. He whispered, "I need to love you completely, Purity. Give to me, darling."

Hesitating only a moment longer, Cass pressed his mouth full against her. He drew deeply from the font of Purity's passion, stroking, devouring, consuming. Sensing the rapid escalation of her excitement, he knew unsurpassed elation as Purity's body quaked with passion, as he accepted her body's sweet homage.

Purity's eyes were closed, her breathing ragged

when Cass separated himself from her and stripped away his clothes.

Lying full upon her as her quaking stilled, Cass waited only a moment longer before pressing himself inside her. Her heard her soft gasp of pain at the moment of penetration. He closed his eyes, his exhilaration supreme as her body closed around him so hot and sweet that it stole his breath.

The rhythm of loving began slowly. It accelerated as Purity's arms slipped around him. It deepened as elation swelled. His heart thundering at the moment fast approaching, Cass looked down at Purity to see her face flushed, her eyes bright with wonder. Her lips parted with the whisper of his name, and he thrust full within her, gasping her name in return as culmination burst upon them.

The silence within the makeshift shelter was broken only by the patter of the rain and the crackle of a fire reduced to embers as Cass raised himself above Purity at last. The moistness of mutual passion was slick between them, binding them in a way he was loathe to sever as he cupped her cheek with his palm and waited with unexpected anxiety for her eyes to open. The fragile lids lifted slowly, and the glow within lit his heart.

His words came unbidden. "You're *mine*."

The persistent hoot of an owl penetrated the silence of the night. Looking upward toward the center of the tepee, where the smoke hole allowed a glimpse of an overcast sky void of stars, Jack frowned. Rain was on the way.

Sleep eluding him, Jack glanced at Whispering Woman where she slept beside him, the sight of her sweet consolation in the midst of so many uncertainties. His thoughts returned to the disquiet he had left behind him at the Circle C. He knew he had made the right move in accepting the partnership Stan offered him. He had had no choice, but he was also certain that the ranch would soon be on its way to financial stability despite a few remaining problems. He was certain that Cass could correct those problems. The resentment against him was another matter with which Cass would have to deal, but Jack was not truly concerned about the outcome. His son had been tested harshly by life, in countless ways—in some that he knew would remain ever undisclosed. Cass had survived those trials to emerge stronger and harder.

Paternal pride surged.

Cass . . . who had often angered him, but who had never disappointed him.

Cass . . . his mother's joy, who would always be Pale Wolf in her heart.

Whispering Woman moved in her sleep, adjusting her naked flesh more comfortably against him in a posture of easy familiarity and love, and Jack smiled. These moments they were together had become more precious to him as the years passed—priceless jewels that glittered brightly along the trail he had traveled, adding inestimable richness to his life.

Jack studied Whispering Woman's still face. The graceful contours of her cheek and the magnificence of her small, perfect features never failed to astound him, but it was not her physical charms which so greatly moved him. The indefinable thread of wisdom and joy that impelled her in all she said and did had enchanted him from the moment when he heard her first speak her name. That thread had bound itself inexorably around his heart, never to be severed.

Jack tightened his arm around Whispering Woman spontaneously. Regretting his action the moment she stirred, he whispered, "Go back to sleep, darlin'." He kissed her lips lightly. "Everythin's all right."

Whispering Woman opened her eyes slowly. Attuned to his thoughts in a way of which only she was capable, she responded softly, "Yes, everything is well. I lie in your arms, and the joy of the moment is ours. It will remain forever with us."

Jack nodded, voicing the thought he could no longer evade. "I leave here tomorrow. This night is our last together for a while."

Whispering Woman's frown was fleeting. "Tomorrow and all the other days that follow will pass, and then you will return to me."

"But the time in between, darlin' . . ."

Tears glittered briefly in Whispering Woman's dark eyes. "In our hearts we are always together."

True words . . . loving words . . .

Jack took them deep within him as he closed his arms around her.

The silence of night was broken by a sound . . . a roar that was terrifyingly familiar.

She knew what it was!

It was growing louder . . . closer. A wall of water was rushing down the river to sweep away their foundering wagon!

Chastity was screaming. Honesty was calling her name. Mama scrambled toward them. She reached for them, but the river came between them.

The world was tumbling. Liquid darkness enveloped her, drowning her screams. There was no light, no sound . . . no life.

No!

"Purity . . . wake up, you're dreaming."

Trembling, Purity awoke with a start at the sound of the familiar voice. Disoriented, she heard rain pounding against a canvas roof over her head. She felt a strong arm tighten around her. She strained her eyes in the semidarkness created by the smoldering fire. She made out a sharply contoured face . . . dark hair brushing the powerful shoulders of the man lying beside her as he raised himself above her. She saw his eyes . . . light eyes, eyes that were startlingly green.

Pale Wolf.

But the name that sprang to Purity's mind stirred no fear as warm lips brushed hers lightly, as a gentle hand caressed her cheek, as his strong arms folded her closer. Instead, it stilled her trembling.

"Go to sleep," Cass whispered softly against her ear. "You're safe. Nothing can hurt you now."

Yes, she was safe in Cass's arms. The rain and the world were held at bay when she lay against him.

Turning fully into his warmth, Purity closed her eyes.

* * *

The mumble of curt conversation nearby . . . occasional footsteps echoing in the silence . . . the bark of a dog in the distance . . .

The camp stirred slowly to life beyond the walls of Whispering Woman's tepee.

Whispering Woman glanced up toward the smoke hole to see the light of morning dawning. She looked at her husband as he secured his pack and drew himself to his feet. He faced her, his expression sober. The time had come.

Standing beside him, her controlled expression allowing no hint of the emotions that raged within, Whispering Woman walked into his arms. She dared not let him know that the ache within her heart grew greater each time they parted. She dared not tell him that she dreamed of a time when they would never have to part again . . . for she knew that her pain would only increase his own.

Whispering Woman drew back with a small smile. She whispered, "We will be together again soon."

Her husband kissed her then, leaving her for a home where another woman awaited him with as much love as she had for him. She consoled herself with that love, knowing its value although it stood between herself and the man who held her heart.

"I love you, darlin'."

Her husband's words were like brilliantly colored beads that hung tenuously on the slender thread that was her life.

"I'll be back as soon as I can."

Her husband's mouth touched hers lightly, then

settled, imparting with its loving fervor the courage that was rapidly deserting her.

Accompanying him outside where his saddled horse awaited, Whispering Woman spoke simple words from the bottom of her heart.

"My husband . . . you are with me always."

A knife of pain slashed her as her husband mounted.

She waved farewell as blood drained silently from the wound.

The light of morning awakened Purity to a silence that announced the cessation of the storm, to intimately sensitive flesh that renewed memories of the passionate night past, and to Cass's naked warmth stretched full against her underneath the blanket covering them.

Unable to avoid his gaze any longer, Purity looked up. Her breath caught in her throat as his eyes linked with hers.

Cass wound his fingers in her hair, and her heart pounded. He whispered her name, and her lips parted. His mouth touched hers, and a loving languor engulfed her senses. She gasped as he slipped himself deep inside her . . . and the cadence of loving began.

The morning sky was bright and clear when Purity walked across their temporary camp at last. Her clothes were damp, her body ached, and a strange lethargy seemed to have invaded her senses. She covered a yawn with her hand as she attempted to shake it off, scanning the camp behind her. Their temporary shelter dismantled and packed, their fire cold, the horses loaded and readied, little physical evidence remained of the glorious night of loving past.

Glancing covertly at Cass as he stood beside his mount, Purity recalled his hoarse words of passion as their flesh had joined and culmination was near. She remembered the look in his eyes when all was still and the intimate moments they had shared were still fresh between them. She recalled that she had never felt stronger, more alive, or more alert than when she was in his arms.

But, somehow, as they had dressed and eaten in the stark light of morning, a silence had gradually slipped between them.

Cass turned toward her abruptly, his sober countenance unrevealing. Again clad in buckskin, with an Indian headband around his forehead, he did not allow his gaze to linger as he spoke.

"The Kiowa camp isn't much farther. We should reach there in another day or so."

Purity nodded.

"Let's get going."

Purity nodded again. Her anxiety returned with the abrupt assault of reality. Nothing had changed. Cass was Pale Wolf—a man intent on vengeance. She had made a bargain that had not been altered by the lovemaking they had shared. Her meeting with the shaman lay before her, and then she must keep her part of the agreement.

A strange sadness welled up in her. No, nothing had changed at all.

"We have to get going."

Snapped from her thoughts, Purity turned to see Cass standing beside her. Speechless when he picked her up unexpectedly, swung her up onto his saddle, and mounted behind her, she glanced behind them to see her mount secured with the pack horse on a lead tied to his saddle.

To the silent question in her eyes, Cass responded, "You're tired this morning. It'll be easier this way."

Purity's frown was spontaneous. "I'm not any more tired than you are."

She was unprepared for the flush that suffused her as Cass's gaze dropped briefly to her lips. The sudden huskiness in his voice sent a tremor down her spine as he whispered, "Humor me, Purity." His mouth softened. "The truth is, I want you near me a little while longer."

Her throat suddenly tight, Purity closed her eyes as his lips brushed hers. She leaned into him, accepting his support as he drew her back against him. Still unable to speak as he nudged his mount into motion, she allowed no further thought as he wrapped his arms around her.

Chapter Eight

Julia adjusted her shawl, then pulled her bonnet forward to shield her eyes from the glare of the early morning sun as her wagon moved forward at a steady pace. The headache that had not abated for the past few days was with her still. She had lost patience with her fruitless battle to overcome it and had managed an early start on her delayed visit to town. She could not wait any longer.

Glancing absentmindedly at the outbuildings alongside the road which announced that she had arrived at the outskirts of town, Julia breathed a sigh of relief. She would soon be riding down the main street. She would accomplish her business as quickly as she was able, and would then head directly home.

Home.

Julia thrust back the sadness that thought suddenly evoked. The Rocking T was a prosperous, well-run ranch, and the house that Jack had built on it was among the nicest in the county, but it was an empty shell without Jack and Cass. She knew that part of her anxiety in leaving the ranch at this particular time was because she expected them home any day, and she wanted to be there to welcome them. She consoled herself with the thought that if all went well, she would be back before noon. She had grown accustomed to the pattern of their arrivals and departures over the years, and it seldom varied. They never arrived before midday.

Drawn by the thought she had avoided all morning long, Julia looked at her handbag where it lay on the seat beside her. She then averted her gaze, grateful for the distraction of familiar voices as she entered town.

"Good mornin', Mrs. Thomas!"

Smiling, Julia dipped her head toward the tow-headed young fellow skipping along the boardwalk, dragging his younger brother behind him. She responded, "Good morning, William. I hope your mother is well."

"She's fine, Mrs. Thomas." His round face flushed, William called out as the wagon rapidly outdistanced him, "Are you goin' to bring some of them peppermint sticks to church this Sunday, like you did last week?"

Amused, Julia called over her shoulder, "You just make sure you're at church to find out."

The morning street traffic grew more brisk, and Julia drew back slightly on the reins, her lagging spirits rising as greetings continued to sound around her.

"Good mornin', Julia. Right nice day!"

"Good morning, John." The blacksmith was a dear man. "Yes, it is."

"Howdy, Mrs. Thomas! Nice to see you this mornin'."

"Good morning, Jacob." She smiled warmly at the burly tradesman. "Nice to see you, too."

"Julia, dear, what a surprise! What are you doing in town today? You stop by for tea before you leave, you hear?"

"I surely will if it's not too late." She had always liked the minister's wife. "Thank you, Georgina."

Yes, she had made a good life for herself with Jack, one she had never envisioned before that sunny October day when they met.

The pounding in her head grew worse as she followed the painted storefronts with her gaze, and Julia felt the rapid draining of spirits that had risen a few minutes earlier. She drew back on the reins, slowing her wagon's pace to little more than a crawl as the building she sought came within view.

Man prescribes and the Lord provides.

Had it been Father who had said that?

Julia reined up her wagon and alighted.

They had been traveling since dawn. The temperature had risen rapidly with the sun until the heat of the day had become a relentless burden. Purity was hot and tired, and her back ached. Reaching for her canteen, she unscrewed the cap and raised it to her lips. She seemed to have acquired an unquenchable thirst.

Glancing toward Cass where he rode beside her, Purity draped the canteen back over her saddle horn, noting that he apparently suffered no similar difficulty. In direct contrast with herself, he rode effortlessly, seeming to grow stronger, more attuned to his surroundings as the morning progressed.

Suddenly she understood. Cass was Kiowa, and he was coming home.

Purity struggled to restrain her trembling. Somehow, she had allowed that thought to escape her during the two nights of loving recently past. Lying in Cass's arms had seemed so right, and she had turned to him with the naturalness and ease of breathing. But the world their intimacy had created was disintegrating more completely with every mile that now passed. She was a stranger to this new world they were entering, and reality could no longer be held at bay.

Was she on a fool's errand after all? Could a shaman called Spotted Bear, a man she could not be sure truly existed at all, really help her learn her sisters' fates?

And if he could, would she be able to face it if she discovered that her sisters had not survived?

Tears threatened.

She blinked them away.

"Purity . . ."

Purity turned spontaneously toward the sound of Cass's voice. Unaware of her pallor and visible anxiety, she was surprised when he leaned toward her unexpectedly, cupping the back of her neck with his hand as he drew her mouth to his.

Cass's kiss was light, fleeting. Purity felt his reluctance as he drew back. "Just an hour more and we'll reach the camp." Then, unexpectedly, he said, "Tell me about your sisters."

No, she didn't want to talk about them. It was too difficult.

Purity adjusted her reins, then shrugged. "I don't remember much. I was too young when the accident happened."

"When your parents were killed."

She nodded, adding despite herself, "They drowned. I know they did. They would've found us and brought us all back together again, if they hadn't."

"But your sisters . . ."

"They're alive."

Cass's gaze narrowed at her adamancy. "How can you be so sure?"

"I just am."

"Tell me."

Purity swallowed. No one had ever pressed her for explanations before. As much as Stan loved her, he had never given her protestations enough credence to question her. Buck and the others had always avoided the subject because they didn't want to upset her.

A defensive note entered Purity's voice. "I'm sure because I see them sometimes. Honesty is beautiful. Her hair is black and her eyes are a deep blue when she's angry." She gave a short laugh. "Honesty would never let anybody get the best of her." Purity's brief smile dimmed. "Chastity's different. She was always more sensitive to people's feelings, always sympathetic with that curly red hair and soft voice."

Cass looked deep into her eyes. "You miss them. You need to know what happened to them—one way or the other—so you can put your mind at rest. You know that whatever you discover will be better than never being sure."

Purity closed her eyes at the abrupt realization that in gazing so deeply there, Cass had somehow seen directly into her soul.

"Purity . . . listen to me." Cass's whisper raised her trembling lids. "Just a little while longer and the waiting will be over."

Yes, a little while longer.

Whispering Woman walked back along the narrow path from the stream, her thoughts wandering as the overflow from her bucket left a spotted trail behind her. She had risen early, earlier than most other days. Impatient with her sleeplessness, she had chosen not to remain abed where she was assailed by thoughts she was unable to strike from her mind.

Whispering Woman withheld a sigh. Her loneliness was always more difficult, her emptiness more profound after her husband's visits ended, when she awakened each morning without the warmth of his arms around her and the sound of his voice in her ear. Flying Eagle, her beautiful son, had helped to fill that emptiness, bringing a joy to her days that had helped her to bear the pain of separation.

Whispering Woman's step slowed. Pale Wolf and Flying Eagle, her two sons . . .

Pale Wolf, her firstborn, was so different from his brother in many ways. He was tall, where Flying Eagle had been of medium height. He was strongly muscled, where Flying Eagle had been slight. He was pleasing to the eye, with his father's blood clearly manifested in light eyes that always drew attention to him. Flying Eagle had had no exceptional physical features, just a goodness of heart that glowed in his quick smile.

It occurred to Whispering Woman that she was truly uncertain when Flying Eagle's quick smile first began to falter. She had spoken to Pale Wolf about the gradual change in his brother. She recalled that her elder son had been as concerned about Flying Eagle as she. The bond between the brothers had been formed the first day of their meeting. It had grown stronger over the years, with Pale Wolf assuming responsibility for the guidance of his younger brother after Buffalo Hunter died. It had never entered her mind, however, that Pale Wolf's devotion to Flying Eagle might one day almost cost her elder son his life.

Sadly, she had never discovered the reason for the fading joy in Flying Eagle's eyes. When Pale Wolf had been returned to her, with his life all but drained from his wound, she had only known that if his heart stopped beating, hers would stop as well. And when he had survived to grow strong again, when he had pledged his vengeance, she had accepted his resolution as a burning need which she shared.

It was only after Pale Wolf had regained his health and returned to his father's ranch that she had finally allowed herself to mourn the son she had lost.

Raising her chin, Whispering Woman did not look at the scars of the cruel gashes on her arms and legs that she had inflicted in her anguish. Flying Eagle's life had been stolen from him. Her only ease from the ceaseless torment of his death had been to suffer as Flying Eagle had suffered, to spill her blood as Flying Eagle's blood had been spilled. She had sheared her hair in her suffering, and returning to the hilltop each day, she had wailed, crying out and gnashing her teeth.

And as she did, a part of her had died as well.

Whispering Woman briefly closed her eyes. Love had been her salvation—her love for the only son left to her, and her love for the husband of her heart.

Sadness welled in her as Whispering Woman neared her tepee. She looked down at the fire she had prepared and the pot awaiting the water she carried. She poured it inside. Her husband's generosity allowed her to live more comfortably than most. She did not hesitate to share her bounty with those around her, but she held herself apart. She was young, with many years left to her. Gray Fox and Laughing Bear had approached her many times, offering her the comfort of their bodies. She had spurned them.

Despite the protestations which she whispered to her husband in order to ease his heart, she was empty without him.

A sixth sense suddenly caused Whispering Woman

to look up. She stared into the distance where the morning sun shone bright and clear.

The horizon was free of movement, but in Whispering Woman's heart a soft singing began.

Cass stared into the distance, searching for signs of the Kiowa camp. Purity's anticipation had become an anxiety that grew stronger with every mile, until he had begun to feel it, too.

Purity sighed, and Cass turned toward her. Unconscious of his perusal, she wiped her shirtsleeve across her forehead, then pushed an errant gold strand back from her face. He noticed that her skin was pale, that her eyelids were heavy and her shoulders weary. The heavy braid that lay against her back glittered in the sun, as did the tendrils that the heat of the day had curled at her hairline. Her visible fatigue raised a feeling of tenderness within him. He longed to brush back those tendrils with his lips, to hold her close, lending her his strength. He longed to tell her that she need not be afraid, because he would be with her—but he dared not.

The moment of truth was fast approaching. With it came uncertainties that Cass strove to deny.

Purity was tinder to his flame . . . but would that flame survive what was yet to come?

Revelation.

Bloodshed.

Resolution.

Each stood before him, stepping stones toward the retribution he had vowed.

Suddenly, Cass saw the outlines he had been seeking—tepees standing proudly in the sun. A spontaneous inner warmth filled him, and Cass glanced at Purity.

She had seen the outlines, too.

But she was not smiling.

Her shoulders stiff, her anticipation held rigidly in check, Purity surveyed the Kiowa camp as she and Cass approached at a steady pace. The camp was smaller than she had anticipated. Thirty or forty tepees stood carefully spaced apart. Outside some of them, women stirred cooking pots in the bright sunlight of morning. A short distance from the structures, a group of young Kiowas looked up from their horses to squint in the direction of the newcomers. Women working at a hide shelter in another area of the camp turned to follow the young men's gazes, and scantily clad children playing nearby looked up as well.

Heads turned toward them from all areas of the camp as a stray dog raced aggressively forward, startling Purity's mount. A gruff Kiowa command from Cass halted the dog in its tracks as she struggled to draw her mount under control.

Watching as the dog trotted back toward the camp, Purity was intensely aware that a crowd was slowly gathering. Her discomfort expanded as Cass reined up his horse and dismounted. Following his lead, she dismounted as well. At once she noticed an older woman who stood in front of those assembled. The woman was slight, petite in stature, her features delicately composed and appealing despite the ragged cut of her hair and the scars visible on her slender arms.

His expression sober, Cass urged Purity forward, and her heart began a slow pounding. She was a stranger here . . . a former enemy of these people. She saw no warmth or welcome in their eyes when they looked at her. She wondered why she had not bothered to take that possibility into account, and she wondered if she would be made to pay for that lapse.

Cass halted in front of the small woman, and Purity's racing thoughts halted as well. There was something familiar about her, the shape of her eyes . . . the slope of her cheek. . . .

The woman's voice was a low, pleasing whisper of sound as she spoke words to Cass that stopped Purity's thoughts abruptly.

"Welcome home, my son."

. . . my son . . .

Purity looked up sharply at Cass, astonished as he laid his hand on the woman's shoulder and spoke in a voice deep with warmth. "I've brought someone with me for a visit, Mother. Her name is Purity Corrigan."

. . . Mother . . .

The woman turned toward her then. Her voice a gentle whisper, she said simply, "Welcome."

Purity's breath caught in her throat.

Cass looked at her then, and her thoughts were confirmed without the need for words.

* * *

271

Whispering Woman's words of welcome went unanswered as Purity turned angrily and strode back toward her horse.

Grasping her arm before she had walked more than a few yards, Cass swung her toward him.

"Where do you think you're going?"

"Back to the Circle C!"

"Don't be a damned fool!"

Purity's short laugh was hard. "Oh, I may have been a fool, all right, but I'm not a fool anymore!"

"Aren't you?" Aware of the curious gazes that followed their every word, he grated, "There are better places for this conversation than this."

"Where?" Purity's expression tightened. "When I'm lyin' underneath you and you have me too damned confused to think straight?"

"Confused? Is that how you felt?"

Purity's pale eyes iced. "Enthralled . . . mesmerized. Does that make you feel better?"

Cass shook his head. "No, there's only one thing that will make me feel better"—he dropped his gaze unconsciously to Purity's lips, and Purity's pale skin flushed—"but this isn't the place for it."

"Damn you!"

Grasping her arm, Cass turned her toward the path to the stream. He heard low laughter from the onlookers behind him, and he knew they were amused by the antics of the angry white woman. He also knew the sound infuriated Purity even more as she hissed, "Let go of my arm!"

"No."

"I told you—"

"You're wasting your time, Purity. There's no way I'm going to let you leave this camp right now, not this way. You want to talk, so we're going to talk."

"I *don't* want to talk! I know everythin' I need to know!"

"No, you don't!"

"All right." Purity was shaking with rage. "I know everythin' I *want* to know!"

"That isn't true, either."

"Let me go, Cass . . ."

"I will." Cass paused. She didn't know what she did to him when she looked at him that way, with that combination of hatred and desire that set his heart to racing. His own conflicting emotions under tenuous control, he pressed, "You have my promise. If you still want to leave after we've had a chance to talk, I'll take you back."

Purity stared.

"I give you my word."

Purity remained silent.

"Purity . . ."

"All right!"

The heat of curious eyes burned into Cass's back as he drew Purity with him toward the wooded path nearby.

"Let go of my arm."

Cass released her, and they walked in silence until they reached the stream, where he faced her abruptly. "Ask me whatever you want to know."

Purity trembled, her blazing eyes assaulting him. "That was Whisperin' Woman, wasn't it?"

"Yes."

273

"Why didn't you tell me? How could you have kept all this a secret from me—from Stan—when you knew how much Whisperin' Woman meant to him?"

"I'm good at keeping secrets. I've had a lot of practice."

"Unnecessary secrets that caused needless pain!"

"That isn't true."

"Isn't it?"

"These secrets were meant to *spare* unnecessary pain."

"Meaning?"

"Meaning Julia—whom Jack married when he thought my mother was dead. Meaning my mother—who loved Jack all her life, and who still loves him. Meaning Flying Eagle—"

"Flyin' Eagle." Purity closed her eyes briefly, then opened them to reveal tears. She rasped, "He was your brother, wasn't he?"

Pain stirred sharply, momentarily inhibiting Cass's reply.

"I should've known." Purity's eyes again blazed. "That's why you knew how I felt about my sisters— the way I miss them, the ache inside me that won't let go, that need to discover what happened to them, at any price. Why didn't you tell me who Flyin' Eagle was?"

"Would it have made a difference?"

"Yes!" Purity shook her head. "No! I mean . . ."

Purity's voice trailed into a silence fraught with confused frustration. Compassion rising, Cass stroked back the gold wisps framing Purity's cheek. "Sit with me now, Purity, so I can tell you how—"

"No." Purity shook off his touch. "It's too late. Keep your secrets. That's what you wanted, wasn't it?"

"No, it isn't."

"I don't want to hear anythin' you have to say!"

"You do."

"No, I—"

"You want to know, and I have to tell you, for my own sake as well as for yours." Cass paused. His voice became a low, unintended plea. "I never meant to deceive you or mislead you, Purity. Let me explain."

Sitting abruptly on a nearby log, Cass drew her down beside him and slid his arm around her. Purity's eyes were a liquid silver that melted his heart. He brushed their trembling lids with his mouth.

Her lips were parted, an appeal he could not ignore, and he covered them briefly with his own. Drawing back, his mouth only inches from hers, Cass started to speak.

Julia glanced upward, frowning as she measured the position of the sun in the cloudless sky with a practiced eye. She frowned at the realization that it was at least an hour past noon.

Frowning, she slapped the reins against her horse's back. She had not expected her visit to take so long, but she was gratified that all would soon be settled at last. It occurred to her that she had been in limbo for too long, floating in a sea of uncertainty. But all was settled now. It was just a matter of time until she would—

The Rocking T ranch house came into view, raising a familiar swell of emotion that stopped her thoughts abruptly. The dirt road before her glowed like a golden ribbon in the afternoon sun as it wound its way through a sea of new green, leading her home.

Home, where her heart abided. Surely it was the most beautiful sight in the world.

Julia surveyed the serenity of the scene . . . cattle grazing in the distance, riders moving leisurely among them, horses trotting in the corral outside the barn.

Julia's musings stopped. The horse drinking in the trough beside the house . . . it was black with a blaze on its forehead.

A happy sob caught in her throat and Julia slapped the reins against her horse's back once, twice. Not satisfied until the wagon was rattling along the road at a breakneck pace, she ignored the rush of air that knocked her bonnet awry. Trembling with anticipation, she drew the wagon up beside the corral at the same moment that the door of the house opened, and a familiar figure stepped into view.

"Jack . . ."

His name escaped her throat in a sob of pure joy, and Julia turned to step down from the wagon. Stumbling in her haste, she was caught by the strong arms of the man she loved.

Embracing him, holding him tightly against her, Julia heard the concern in Jack's voice as he drew back, his eyes searching her pale, tear-streaked face.

"What happened, Julia? Is somethin' wrong?"

"No . . . no." Suddenly embarrassed by her revealing display, Julia shook her head. "Of course not. Everything's fine, now that you're back." She paused, exerting a greater attempt at self-control. "Oh, Jack . . . I missed you so."

Jack's expression softened then, in a way she knew well. And when he slipped his arms around her, the anguish ceased.

She was back in Jack's arms, where she longed to remain. . . .

The sound of Cass's voice faded, leaving a silence between them as Purity struggled with her confused feelings. Not a trace of emotion was visible in his expression despite his tale of a love his father had lost and then found, of another love that his father held in too high an esteem to discard, and of a path his father had accepted, rather than chosen. She had sensed Cass's distress when he spoke of the life that had resulted . . . the anger . . . the torn loyalties. She had suffered the depth of Cass's anguish when he spoke of the brother he belatedly came to know and love. She had not pressed him for details about Flying Eagle's disappearance, knowing it was an open wound that still caused him pain.

Purity's response to Cass's sober narrative came unbidden. The words left her lips before she was aware of her intention to speak them. "Do you love me, Cass?" she whispered.

The green eyes that had once terrorized her dreams caught and held hers. She saw the warring within him, the hesitation, and the moment of ultimate surrender in his single word of reply.

"Yes."

His response freeing her, Purity whispered, "I love you, too. I loved you from the beginnin', without realizin' it at all—I know that now. I was terrified that first day, but the fear that I felt when you held your knife at my throat, when your blade pricked my skin, was nothin' compared to the fear I felt when I saw your life's blood drainin' onto the ground." Purity paused, continuing hoarsely, "The horror of that moment played over and again in my mind. I wanted to erase it. I tried to, as best I could, but you wouldn't let me. You hated me."

"No, I never hated you."

"You told me I'd made a mistake when I let you live."

Cass's gaze did not waver. "That might yet be true."

"You're sayin' that in spite of everythin' that's happened, you mean to follow through?"

Cass's silence tightened a cold knot within Purity as she rasped, "You said you love me, but you don't love me enough to put aside your vengeance!"

"I want justice, not vengeance."

"Don't you realize that if what you say is true, if one of my men is responsible for Flyin' Eagle's death, you could be in danger at the Circle C?"

"Purity, listen to me." His voice earnest, Cass whispered, "Neither of us knows what will come of all this, but we both know that it's too late to turn back. All that's left for us to do now is to go forward, one step at a time. The next step is Spotted Bear. I'll take you to see him tomorrow."

"Tomorrow?" A chill ran down Purity's spine. "No, not tomorrow. I . . . I'm not ready."

"Yes, you are. You've been waiting for this moment all your life. I'll take you to Spotted Bear in the morning—when the earth comes alive again and all things become clear."

"Cass . . ."

"But when I do," Cass continued softly, "all debts are cancelled. You owe me nothing in return."

"We made a bargain!"

"I took advantage of your need."

"Did you, Cass?" Purity searched the chiseled features so close to hers. "Or did I take advantage of yours?"

The futility of their exchange suddenly clear, Purity responded instinctively to the love newly discovered within her. "I'm tired of talkin', Cass. I told you I love you. I've never said those words before. I want to prove to you how much I mean them."

Not waiting for Cass's reply, Purity touched her mouth to his. Her lips clung. A threatened love newly acknowledged and cherished surged as she whispered, "Let me prove it to you now, Cass."

Purity's lingering kiss was halted as Cass stood abruptly and swept her up into his arms. She did not speak as he carried her deeper down the wooded path without a word of reply, to a place where the thick grass pillowed her head as he laid her upon it, where the verdant cushion cradled her as their bodies touched and his lips met hers.

The joy of the moment overwhelmed her. The heat of the sun warmed their flesh as love flared brighter, as Purity opened her heart to Cass and took him deep inside her.

Passionate moments soared to flame.

The loving subsided.

But the joy remained.

Walking back up the same path they had earlier walked in anger, Purity emerged with Cass within view of the camp, to find Whispering Woman seated beside her tepee. A subtle glance between mother and son removed the lines of concern from the older woman's face, replacing anxiety with understanding as she repeated simply, "Welcome home."

"What do you mean, the water hole was fouled?"

Stan stared at Buck, anger deepening the grooves in his ashen face. He had known something was wrong the minute he heard Buck's horse returning so early in the afternoon. One glance at the graying cowhand as he dismounted and faced him soberly across the ranch house porch had confirmed his thoughts.

Buck's whiskered jaw hardened. "I mean the water hole is fouled, just like I said. Hell, by the time we got there, there was fourteen steers lyin' on the ground moanin' and thrashin' about. It don't look to me like they're goin' to last the day."

"What do you suppose done it?" Stan shook his head. "Purity said that water hole wasn't lookin' good, but she said Cass, Nash, and her took care of cleanin' it up before she left."

"They did."

"So, what in hell happened?"

Buck's eyes hardened. "To my mind, it ain't *what* done that water hole in. It's *who*."

Stan stiffened. His knobby hands tightened on the armrest of his chair. "All right, I'm tired of riddles! Out with it! What's goin' on?"

"Well, if you want my opinion, somethin' underhanded's goin' on, that's what!"

"What're you talkin' about?"

Buck took an earnest step forward. "This ain't the first of the unexplained things that've been happenin' around here in the past few weeks, and I got an idea it ain't goin' to be the last." At the narrowing of Stan's eyes, he continued, "Like that corral that was knocked down a week ago, and them calves that were scattered. We had a hell of a time gettin' them calves out of that ravine they was hidin' in, but once we did, we got them to move docile enough. It didn't make no sense to me at all the way that corral was damaged when they escaped. Even if somethin' did scare them into breakin' through, they wouldn't have run that far. Hell, they was so scattered that we thought we'd never find them again! What with one thing and another, we lost a couple of days gettin' them back and ready for brandin' again."

"That don't mean—"

"That ain't all, Stan." Buck hesitated, then continued, "Unless our herds are takin' to shrinkin' overnight, I've got the feelin' somebody's been helpin' themselves to our stock, too."

Stan's hands began twitching. "So how come you ain't said nothin' about all this until now?"

Buck frowned.

"Out with it!"

"Because I wanted to be sure!"

"That ain't it, and you know it!" Cursing his inability to rise from his chair, Stan hissed, "You was afraid to tell me, wasn't you! You was afraid it might push me into apoplexy or somethin' if you did."

"Don't go gettin' yourself upset, Stan."

"And don't you go coddlin' me like this chair puts a kink in my brain or somethin'!" Stan continued hotly, "You was goin' to wait for Purity to come back before you did somethin' about all this, wasn't you?"

Buck did not reply.

"Damn it all, Buck, what was you thinkin' of!"

"I'll tell you what I was thinkin' of!" Buck took another aggressive step. "The fellas are upset. It's been takin' everythin' I have to keep them in line. Hell"— Buck shook his head—"Nash just about set his mind to ridin' out after Purity and that half-breed after they left, and Baird wasn't far behind him in his thinkin'. There's no tellin' what would've come of that! I had a damned hard time talkin' them out of it. As far as they're concerned, you was crazy for lettin' her go anywheres with that bastard! I had to keep them all on a short rein, and when a few head was missin' here and there, I figured it wasn't worth stirrin' up a hornet's nest at first. When that trouble happened with the corral . . . well, the boys was mumbling for days after that. I'm tellin' you, it's a good thing Thomas was nowheres around, or the fellas would've been lookin' to him to be at the bottom of it."

"That don't make no sense and you know it! Cass is a partner in the place, damn it! He'd only be hurtin' himself!"

"The boys don't like him, and they don't trust him. As far as they're concerned, he'd put a knife in their backs as soon as look at them. It's their thinkin' that he'll do anythin' he thinks he needs to do to get even for what happened on the trail drive last fall."

"Sure, like stealin' some beeves from himself . . ."

"You're forgettin', half them beeves are yours and Purity's."

"You're crazy . . . and so are they!"

"You wasn't there last fall, Stan." Buck's gaze tightened. "You didn't see Thomas—lyin' there half dead like he was and swearin' his Injun vengeance with them light eyes of his burnin' . . ."

"That's all over! Cass gave me his word."

Buck's mustached lip twisted into a sneer. "Yeah, the word of a half-breed."

Stan's agitation exploded. "Yeah, that's right, the word of a half-breed!"

Struggling to rein in his emotions Stan looked up at the cloudless afternoon sky for long, silent moments before turning abruptly back to his frowning foreman. "All right, maybe the men have a right to what they're thinkin', *even if they're wrong*, but that's all beside the point now. Cass ain't nowheres around here now, and Purity ain't either."

Buck nodded. "Yeah, the boys are gettin' itchy about that, too. Thomas said they'd be gone two weeks, maybe three, and they're already on the lookout for them."

"By 'the boys', you're meanin' Nash and yourself, no doubt . . . and maybe Baird."

Buck's anger was spontaneous. "Don't you go sellin' them fellas short! Every last one of them's got feelin's for Purity, one way or another. Hell, even Treacher's been grumblin' about you bein' crazy, and sayin' somebody should go out after her."

"That'd be a mistake."

"I ain't so sure."

"Well, I am, and I'm the boss of this damned place!" Glaring, Stan demanded, "Let's get back to the subject! Cass ain't nowheres around here, so he ain't got nothin' to do with what's been happenin'." Stan paused. "Has there been trouble like this at any of the other ranches hereabouts?"

"Ain't a word been said around town that I know of."

Stan nodded. "All right, first things first. The water hole . . ."

"The boys are keepin' the rest of the stock in the area away from it. I came back for the wagon and some wire so we can fence it off."

"All right. Get that done. Then I want you to go into town with Nash to talk to Sheriff Boyle."

"Hell, that worthless old fart . . ."

"He's the law."

"He's in Norris's pocket!"

A smile touched Stan's lips. Unconsciously sitting back, he gave a low snort. "So, the truth is comin' out at last. You never thought Cass was behind all of this. You think it's Norris."

Buck's eyes narrowed. "Yeah, I think it's Norris.

Hell, he salivates every time he looks at Purity, and he didn't take it lightly when she told him to move on. Pete says he was just about blind with fury when he came here and found out Purity took off with Thomas."

"Pete told you that, did he?" Stan's lips tightened. "He always did talk too much. Well, anyway you look at it, the sheriff is the law around here, and what I said still goes. You get back out to the water hole and fence it in like you said you was goin' to do. Then, after you give Sheriff Boyle an earful, I want you to do some nosin' around town to see what you can find out."

"I don't need to take Nash with me for that. I can handle it myself."

"Yeah, you can, but you ain't got no baby face that makes every one of them gals at the Purple Slipper want to pour her heart out to you. And you know as well as I do that if there's any talk circulatin' about what's goin' on, them gals will know. Besides, that'll give Nash somethin' else besides Purity to think about for a while."

Buck gave a short laugh. "Then maybe you'd better send Baird along with him. He could use some distractin', too."

"You just make sure Baird gets back out there workin' the cattle where he belongs! Hell, I ain't losin' a day's work for *three* men! I ain't no good samaritan or nothin'!"

"All right." Scrutinizing him for long moments, Buck questioned abruptly, "How long are you goin' to wait?"

"For what?"

"You know damned well what I'm talkin' about!"

Stan nodded. He did, all right.

"She ain't been gone three weeks yet."

"How long are you goin' to wait?"

Stan's expression hardened. "I'm goin' to wait three weeks—not a day longer. If she ain't back by then, I'm goin' to send you, Nash, *and* Baird after her."

"I thought you said you don't know where they went."

"I don't . . . exactly. But what I do know is that Cass is Kiowa. There's a Kiowa camp not too far from the Rockin' T, and it don't take no genius to figure out that's probably where he's headin'. If he ain't there, somebody at the Rockin' T will be able to tell you where to find him."

A smile twitched Buck's mustache. "I guess you ain't gettin' feeble-minded after all."

"Yeah, and don't you forget it."

Watching as Buck strode toward the barn, Stan strove to avoid the endless doubts that he dared not acknowledge, doubts that had badgered him since the moment Purity and Cass had disappeared from sight.

Why *had* he let her go?

He was still uncertain.

Whatever the reason, he only knew that he regretted that decision more with every passing day.

Stan saw Buck emerge from the barn with the wagon fully loaded. He followed the wagon's progress as Buck turned out onto the road and gradually disappeared from sight.

Stan spoke abruptly. "Do you think I made a mistake lettin' Purity go?"

He heard Pete's low snort behind him, then the sound of his booted steps on the porch as the cantankerous cook walked out and faced him with a scowl. "Why're you askin' me that now, when it's too damned late to do a thing about it?"

"There you go again, answerin' my question with a question!"

"Why do you always say that?"

Stan glared.

"All right, here's your answer, whether you like it or not. Yeah, I think you made a mistake! That fella you sent Purity out with ain't Cass Thomas—not really. He's Pale Wolf, and he's an Injun to the core."

"That don't make him no different than any one of us here!"

"Don't it? You can say that because you didn't see his face that day last fall. Hell, there was hardly a drop of blood left in his body by the time they brought him back to the camp for me to doctor! And I'm tellin' you now, I still get chills when I think about the look in his eye when he glared at Purity."

"Did he threaten her?"

"He did."

"What did he say?"

"He was talkin' too soft. I couldn't hear him."

"You couldn't hear him."

"I didn't need to hear him! I saw his face, and I saw Purity's! And I told myself then, that if the need came, I'd shoot him dead myself before I'd let him touch a hair of her head!"

Oh, hell . . .

Stan released a weary breath. He wasn't up to this. He was tired and feeling weaker by the minute. The way things were going, if Purity stayed away much longer, he might not be here when she came back.

Suddenly ashamed of the direction his thoughts were taking, Stan straightened his shoulders and clamped his jaw tightly shut. Damn it all, he'd be on the porch waitin' for Purity when she came back if he had to make a pact with the devil to do it! Because the truth was that he'd spend eternity in hell before he'd desert Purity when she needed him!

Pete's presence beside him momentarily forgotten, Stan stared into the distance, his gaze intent.

He'd wait one more week.

Night had come to the Kiowa camp. All was silent. The fire in the fire pit had been reduced to embers from which little curls of white smoke drifted lazily upward toward the smoke hole in the roof. Purity followed them with her gaze. Sleep was slow in coming despite the long day's journey that had started at dawn and delivered her to the tepee where she now lay.

Apprehension crawled up Purity's spine at the thought of the new day to come. Strangely, she had sensed a growing apprehension within Cass as well. She had also sensed that his anxiety was not for himself.

Purity closed her eyes against the fears suddenly

threatening to overwhelm her. She grasped her locket and held it tight, seeking the images that would relieve those fears, but they were lost in the shadows of her mind, unwilling to emerge. She looked toward the entrance to the tepee at the sound of a step beyond, her hopes falling when no one came in.

Cass had not yet returned after leaving earlier to meet with some of the men of the camp. Purity recalled the warmth with which Cass had been greeted by them. She remembered the resentment she had seen in the eyes of some younger women, those who looked at Cass with an interest poorly concealed. It was easy to see that he was accepted fully in this camp, despite the light eyes and superior size that betrayed his father's heritage.

Half-breed.

Enigma.

The man she loved.

Glancing across the fire, Purity saw that Whispering Woman lay on her sleeping bench, as silent as she had been most of the day. A strange reticence had held Purity silent as well, despite the opportunity for conversation while Cass hunted game for his mother in the absence of her husband.

Jack Thomas . . . Whispering Woman's husband.

Jack Thomas . . . Julia's husband as well.

She wondered so many things. Her thoughts returned to Stan and the love he cherished for the small woman opposite her. She wondered if—

"You are not sleeping." Whispering Woman's soft

voice broke the stillness between them. "Is something wrong?"

"No . . . yes . . ." Purity paused, then asked abruptly, "Do you remember Stan Corrigan?"

The fire's glow illuminated Whispering Woman's smile. "Your father is a good man. I knew him when I was little more than a child."

Purity's resentment increased. "He remembers you very well. He thinks you are dead. The thought pains him."

Whispering Woman's smile faded. "If not for your father, my life would be very different from what it now is. I will always keep the memory of him in my heart."

"If he knew you were alive, he would be very happy."

Whispering Woman did not immediately respond. Instead, her dark eyes studied Purity for long moments before she whispered, "What will make *you* happy?"

Startled by Whispering Woman's unexpected question, Purity replied, "I am happy."

"No, you are not. You are as Pale Wolf. The past shadows your happiness."

Pale Wolf. Yes. Cass Thomas did not exist in this place.

Whispering Woman continued more softly than before, "Pale Wolf wishes to help you because, although his own future is uncertain, your happiness has become his own."

"I know."

"The path he travels has already brought him close to death."

Purity blurted, "You're his mother! If you see the danger, why don't you tell him it's wrong to risk his life for somethin' he can't change?"

"Is it wrong for him to seek the person who took his brother's life?"

"It's wrong if he must die for it!"

Silence again stretched between them before Whispering Woman responded, "Were it Flying Eagle who had seen his brother's bloodied blanket . . . were it Flying Eagle who knew his brother's soul would not rest until the truth of his death was known . . . were it Flying Eagle whose steps you now awaited outside this tepee instead of Pale Wolf's, my reply would be the same. A man must listen when the voice within him speaks. Pale Wolf has heard that voice, and he will obey it."

Purity clutched her locket tighter.

"My son has taken you into his heart as he has taken no other. You have helped ease the unhappiness of his past." Whispering Woman paused. "I ask you to let him do the same for you. It will give him joy. You need have no fear about what tomorrow will bring because Pale Wolf will be with you."

Purity could not respond.

The silence of the tepee closed around Purity as Whispering Woman closed her eyes.

Uncertain how much time had passed when she heard a sound, Purity looked to see the entrance flaps separate as Cass entered. She watched as he laid his bedroll beside hers and stretched out full upon it. She waited expectantly until he turned toward her and took her into his arms.

Cass's warmth was heavenly against her.

His arms held her close.

Purity closed her eyes.

"This man's name is Spotted Bear."

The new day dawned. Cass's deep voice seemed unnaturally loud in the silence of the Shaman's tepee.

Purity stared at the wizened old man who turned toward her as Cass spoke. He was small and thin. His long white hair hung raggedly against bony shoulders curved by the weight of years. The skin of his face was dark and leathery from the sun. His forearms, exposed by the stained buckskin garment he wore, were sinewy, his hands small, his fingers curved by time into talons.

Spotted Bear's eyes narrowed in silent scrutiny, and Purity swallowed against the lump in her throat. The penetrating fervor of his gaze chilled her. Then he looked up at Cass and questioned harshly, "Why do you bring this woman to me? She is not Kiowa. Her spirit is in conflict with our ways."

Cass responded levelly. "She seeks your help."

"She is not Kiowa!"

Spotted Bear's adamant statement rang sharply in the silence of the tepee. She saw the growing animosity in his gaze.

His voice deepening, Cass responded, "This woman is not Kiowa—but she is *my* woman."

The impact of Cass's declaration shuddered

through Purity as he continued, "Her spirit is troubled. She comes to ask you to help her as you once helped me."

The old man's gaze darted back to Purity. The resentment of years resounded in his voice as he grated, "You speak to me with truth—but I am unaffected. The white man does not feel our need, and I do not feel his."

Purity's sense of loss was acute as the aged shaman turned away. She saw his shoulders stiffen as Cass spoke again.

"This woman is not Kiowa, but *I* am Kiowa, and her need is mine."

Silent, Spotted Bear turned back toward her. He stared at her for long moments, then addressed her in a gravelly voice.

"I see the truth of Pale Wolf's words. Your hair is gold and your skin is light, but your spirit is joined with Pale Wolf's in ways that are not only of the body." His gaze lowered. "I feel the power of the medicine bundle you wear."

A slow shuddering began inside Purity as she responded hoarsely, "I don't know what you mean."

"It is your bond to those you have lost. It closes the years between. You value it greatly."

Purity reached automatically for her locket.

Spotted Bear's eyes reflected his satisfaction. Motioning them to be seated near the fire, he did not speak again as he walked laboriously toward the darkened corner. He returned minutes later, all trace of resentment gone as he stood opposite them to address Purity across the flickering flames.

"You seek your loved ones—two who share your blood. I have sensed your approach since your arrival on Kiowa land. The visions of those lost to you are elusive, but I will restore them."

Closing his eyes, Spotted Bear began a low chanting. His low, droning monotone rose above the crackle of the fire, striking an unexpected chord of affinity within Purity. The cadence of his song stirred a strange awareness within her. Her thoughts assumed the primitive rhythm of the sound, her gaze becoming riveted as the aged shaman moved in his dance. Her captivation complete, she was hardly conscious of the moment when Spotted Bear gestured across the fire, releasing a fine dust into the flames.

The fire flared brightly, filling the interior of the tepee with a smoky mist as Spotted Bear addressed her.

"Breathe deeply, Pale Wolf's woman. Close your eyes and see the visions awaiting your view." Noting her hesitation, he admonished, "Gaze with a warrior's heart—without fear."

Courage unexpectedly failing her, Purity fought the images forming before her eyes. No . . . she could not bear the truth if it stole her sisters from her forever!

"Purity . . ." It was Cass's voice. She felt his touch on her arm, his breath on her cheek.

Courage gradually returning, Purity breathed deeply of the smoke, accepting . . .

She saw it then—the river! Brown with mud, it was still swollen from the storm, its surface glittering in the brilliant red and gold of the setting sun. She saw the riverbank. It was littered with debris—jagged pieces of wood, a broken wheel, torn articles of clothing, a calico dress that was vaguely familiar.

Purity's heart began a rapid pounding.

She saw a figure lying on the bank. It was a little girl with long dark hair that was wet and tangled. Her white nightdress was covered with sandy residue and plastered against her thin body.

It was Honesty!

But she was lying so still.

Someone was walking on the riverbank—a big woman with flashy red hair. When she spotted Honesty, she stopped abruptly. The woman crouched beside Honesty, frowning as she touched her cheek.

Honesty remained motionless. Then she stirred abruptly and opened her eyes.

Elation sang within Purity!

Crying out in protest as the image faded, Purity caught her breath as other fragmented pictures began swimming before her mind.

She saw Chastity! The long red strands of her hair were darkened by the water in which they floated as she lay at the river's edge. Chastity's nightdress was soaked and stained, and the small foot protruding from its hem was cut and bleeding.

She did not seem to be breathing.

Two ladies with large feathered hats were walking along the riverbank. She saw one, then the other start toward Chastity. They kneeled beside her, then turned her over. They brushed the hair from her face and pounded her back, but it was no use! Their actions grew frantic. Then Chastity suddenly began sputtering, and opened her eyes.

Chastity was crying, but she was alive!

Joy quaked through Purity in deep, pulsing sobs. Her sisters were alive! They had been rescued, just as she had known! She would—

Honesty's face flashed suddenly before her—an adult Honesty, beautiful as she had always expected Honesty to be. A big man appeared beside Honesty, joining her as they approached their horses. They mounted, and as the big man took her hand, Honesty turned directly toward her and *smiled*.

And Purity knew. Honesty was coming. They would be together soon.

She saw Chastity, then—tall and slender and fully grown! She was so pretty with her great hazel eyes and curly red hair. But she was hesitant in her approach. She was insecure. Purity longed to reach out to her, to take her hand. She saw a man step up beside Chastity. The man spoke to her and Chastity listened intently . . . but there was something strange about him. The man was not what he seemed.

Chastity's image faded as abruptly as the ones before it, and Purity's frustration emerged in a groan of protest that halted as another vision appeared.

It was Stan—as she had never seen him. His thin face was gray and his eyes were strangely dulled. He struggled to still his trembling hands as he stared into the distance. She saw fear in his eyes!

The vision blurred into a kaleidoscope of whirling images—water swirling . . . cattle stampeding . . . guns blazing.

She heard Stan call her name!

"Purity . . ."

Purity forced her eyes open with a start, her heart racing. The smoky mist was clearing, drifting slowly upward toward the outlet of the tepee as the aged shaman gazed wordlessly at her over the flames. Beside her, Cass grasped her arm, his voice deep with concern.

"Are you all right, Purity?"

"Yes."

Cass's arm slipped around her as Purity stood up. She turned toward Spotted Bear as the old man drew himself to his feet as well. Forcing aside a new feeling of urgency, she addressed the old Indian, speaking two words that came from the bottom of her heart.

"Thank you."

Now, Purity knew what she must do.

Chapter Nine

Purity scanned the horizon, her heart skipping a beat. Oh yes, she recognized the terrain—the slope of the ground under their horses' hooves, the sweet smell of the moist air, a sky that looked more blue, a sun that appeared more brilliant than anywhere else she had ever been.

Home.

They would soon be on Circle C land.

Purity glanced at Cass where he rode silently beside her. He was frowning. She did not need to question the reason for that frown. They had left the Kiowa camp almost a week earlier. They had traveled at a gruelling pace, rising before dawn and continuing until dark without an appreciable halt.

Cass had not protested her determination to return home. Nor had he questioned her urgency. Her own words to Whispering Woman before leaving had been brief and sincerely remorseful. Mounting immediately afterward, she had averted her gaze as Cass spoke softly to his mother, aware of the distress Whispering Woman concealed at their abrupt departure.

The hardship of Whispering Woman's life had never been clearer to Purity than at the moment when she glanced back to see the older woman bid farewell to her son, just as she had bid her husband farewell only days earlier. Two men Whispering Woman loved . . . two men who could not acknowledge her, who were held apart from her by a twist of fortune beyond their control. It occurred to Purity that fate had been inordinately unkind to that quiet woman.

The first night of their return journey she had confided to Cass all she had seen in Spotted Bear's tepee. Cass had listened, his russet skin warm against her, his pale eyes intent. She knew he did not doubt her conviction that Honesty was even now traveling toward her. She knew he shared her concern for Chastity and the uncertainty of the images that had flashed before her. And she had seen his face tighten when she mentioned Stan and her sudden conviction that something was dreadfully wrong at the Circle C.

Cass had grown increasingly silent as they neared Circle C land. She sensed the return of his former hostility and she wondered what that change would mean. Foremost in her thoughts, however, was the smoky image of Stan's face . . . the confusion and the gunfire surrounding him . . . and the fear.

Purity blinked back tears. She needed to see Stan, to talk to him. She needed to put his mind at rest, to tell him that her sisters' fates were no longer a mystery to her, that she could go on with her life with true confidence that she would find them someday. She wanted to tell him that Cass and she had been united in a common goal in the smoke of Spotted Bear's rough hide shelter. She wanted to reassure him that she knew now, whatever the future held, that she would never be alone because—

Purity paused in her thoughts. What was that noise, that sound like distant thunder?

Purity's eyes grew wide in sudden realization. She glanced at Cass to see her thoughts confirmed the moment before they both dug their heels into their mounts' sides and raced forward.

Choking dust obscured the bright sunlight, and the din of pounding hooves resounded across the land.

Galloping alongside the stampeding herd, Buck sought to penetrate the grainy mist with his gaze. Recognizing the need to turn the wild-eyed beeves as they trampled their way across the flat terrain, he shouted to the riders barely visible in the melee.

"Baird, Treacher, hold the curve! Nash, Pitts—up front with me to turn them!"

Amidst the deadly hooves and snorting, wild-eyed beasts, there was no time to think, only to react. But—the herd was switching direction. It was swerving toward them!

Baird was losing ground. Treacher's mount was stumbling. And then there were sudden gunshots ahead.

The wave of bodies swayed. Gunfire—again and again!

The bellowing herd swerved again, turning abruptly in the opposite direction.

Pushing his mount into the flow, Buck forced the curve, pressing it tighter as the herd doubled back on itself with increasing confusion. Their pace slowed, the agitated cattle protested loudly, scrambling, raising new clouds of dust that temporarily obscured two figures riding into view.

Cursing when he identified them, Buck spurred his mount in their direction.

Adrenaline still pounding through his veins, Cass reined up beside Purity where she drew to a halt near the milling herd. His chest heaving, he scanned her face to see excitement still bright in her eyes, and anger flushed hotly. He was about to speak when Buck drew his horse to a sliding stop beside him.

His expression livid, the graying foreman wasted no time in greetings as he shouted, "Bastard—what did you think you was doin', lettin' Purity ride out in front of that herd!"

Purity snapped, "Wait a minute, Buck!"

"That's right, wait a minute!" His self-control tenuous, Cass responded in a voice that cracked like a whip. "What I *let* Purity do is none of your business!" He gestured toward the hundred or more head still bellowing loudly. "What in hell happened, anyway?

How did you let the herd get away from you like that!"

"I don't answer to you, Thomas!"

"Don't you?" Acutely aware that Carter, Baird, and Treacher had drawn up alongside, and that Pitts was fast approaching, Cass felt the heat within him rising. His voice hardened. "I'll give you one minute to think that over."

"All right, that's enough!" Purity entered the volatile exchange. "Let's get some things straight, here. Cass didn't *let* me ride out in front of that herd. Nobody *lets* me do anything! I did what needed to be done to turn those beeves, and I didn't need anybody to tell me to do it! If any one of you sees it any other way, let him say it to my face, right here and now!"

Buck blinked. Cass saw the new flush that suffused the foreman's face just before his horse snorted unexpectedly, drawing up his leg and dancing with pain.

Cursing loudly when he was forced to dismount, Buck reached for his gelding's leg as Cass grated, "This isn't the time or place for this conversation. These cattle need to be turned back onto Circle C land—now."

Buck glanced up sharply. "This horse of mine ain't got another hour's work in him. Looks like I'll be headin' back and leavin' that job to you."

"No, you won't." Inching his mount closer to Purity's, Cass lifted Purity from her saddle and deposited her in front of him. He felt her resistance as he settled her there. He heard her grunt and felt the protest she suppressed as he curled his arm around her, continuing flatly, "Take Purity's horse. She'll ride back with me."

Buck's gaze jerked toward the possessive curve of Cass's arm. His angry color darkened. "Is that the way *you* want it, Purity?"

Cass waited. He felt the conflict raging inside Purity. "Just get that cattle back on Circle C property!" she snapped. "I'll talk to you all back at the house."

Aware of Nash Carter's jealous scrutiny as he drew Purity back against him, Cass addressed the fellow sharply. "Round up my pack horse, Carter, and bring him back with you."

Cass spurred his mount forward when they rode in silence until out of sight of the men. Purity looked up at him, her expression tight. "Why did you do that?"

Cass scrutinized the small, perfect features turned up to his. Her obvious anger raised his own. His response was curt.

"I did what I needed to do."

"Did you? Buck could've used the pack horse to finish out the day. You gave him my mount deliberately." Purity's look was determined. "I won't let you use me against them, Cass."

"That wasn't my intent."

"What was your intent?"

Cass held Purity's gaze with his. He felt the agitated pounding of her heart beneath the palm he rested against her ribs. How could he explain that fear had spread like hot fire through his veins when she had ridden out in front of that herd unexpectedly with her gun blazing? How could he make her understand that a future of barren emptiness without her had flashed before him in that fleeting second? How could he make her comprehend that when the excitement of the moment was past, he had seen in her eyes no regard at all for the risk she had taken with her life, and that in that moment, his fear had turned to rage?

That rage with him still, Cass exploded, "Buck was right, damn it! You did a crazy, fool thing, riding out in front of that herd! You could've been killed!"

"You rode out right beside me!"

"That's not the point!"

"Isn't it?"

"No!" His chest heaving, Cass grated, "Don't ever try that again."

Purity's jaw tightened. "What makes you think you have the right to give me orders?"

"Purity, dammit . . ." Agitation soaring, Cass slipped his hand into the gold hair at her temple, holding her fast as he grated, "You're mine, Purity. Get that through your head. Even if that goes against your grain, that's the way it is . . . the way it was meant to be from that first moment I saw you. I know that, and you know that. And I'll be damned if I'll take the chance of losing you because of a reckless moment!"

Purity's eyes narrowed. "I don't take your orders, Cass."

Still holding her fast, Cass covered the rigid line of her lips with his. He felt the anger in her resistance. He felt the anxiety she suppressed. And he felt the hunger and the need that matched his own as her lips gradually softened and separated under his.

Tearing his mouth from hers, his breathing ragged, Cass rasped, "Don't ever put me through that again."

Her gaze understanding, Purity whispered, "I'm sorry. I didn't mean to scare you, Cass." A smile touched her lips. "But I did what I needed to do."

His own words used against him. They resounded in Cass's mind.

They shuddered through him with a strange premonition as he searched Purity's gaze for long moments, then drew her back against him without responding and nudged his horse forward.

"Come on, put some effort into it!"

His body damp with perspiration, his eyes spitting fury, Roger labored over the buxom woman lying beneath him. Her dark hair was lush, her bold features brightly painted, the female heat of her accommodating as she met him thrust for thrust. Cursing aloud, he pumped harder, pounding the woman's flesh with his body, furious as his flagging member diminished more with every stroke.

Grinding his teeth with bitter agitation as the futility of his effort became apparent, he pulled back from the panting whore with a snarling sneer.

"You can stop your pitiful efforts! And you can be sure I'll let Sophie know that your half-hearted endeavors weren't worth the price this afternoon!"

Standing beside the mirror minutes later, Roger put the final touches to his appearance before stepping back to assess his reflection. Meticulous tailoring and grooming aside, he didn't like what he saw. His face was lined with frustration and tight with a wrath that would not abate. He glanced at the woman reflected in the mirror beside him. Standing boldly naked, she smiled and stroked her pendulous breast. She whispered, "You gave up too soon, Mr. Norris. There were a lot of things I could've done to help your distress."

"Distress?" Roger's handsome face flamed. "As cheap as you are, and as common, I suppose it is beyond your comprehension that a man could lie with you as I did a few minutes ago, that he could look at you as I do now, and feel *nothing* at all! That's the crux of it, you know. You're inferior and crass—"

The whore's face hardened. "You didn't think I was so 'inferior' a month ago, when you spent half the day on top of me, enjoyin' every minute of it!"

"I must've been drunk!"

"Maybe you should try drinkin' again, *Mr.* Norris! Maybe then you'd be able to stiffen up them parts of you that ain't worth a damn to a real woman!"

Roger laughed aloud. "You wouldn't be referring to yourself as a real woman, would you, Flossie? You aren't, you know. You're nothing more than a receptacle, an object used to accommodate a man's baser needs."

"Am I? Maybe that's true, *Mr.* Norris. But from what all the girls have been sayin', you ain't been able to get it up enough these past few weeks to let us do any accommodatin' at all!"

"Harlot!"

"Yeah . . ."

"Slut!"

"That's right." Flossie's painted features drew into a cutting smile. "And you ain't even man enough to take advantage of it."

Roger's hand struck out unexpectedly, contacting Flossie's jaw with a sharp crack of sound that sent the startled whore staggering backward. Twitching with rage as she fell against the bed with a grunt, he struck her again, his rage changing to satisfaction as blood trickled from the corner of her mouth and she sobbed aloud.

Holding her frightened gaze, he grated, "So, you've finally managed to give me some satisfaction after all." Stepping back, he paused a moment longer. "Perhaps I'll tell Sophie that I will visit with you again. Would you like that, Flossie?"

The frightened whore sobbed in earnest as Roger demanded, "Answer me!"

"Y . . . yes."

"Good. I'll be sure to keep that in mind."

Leaving the naked woman whimpering behind him, Roger drew open the door and stepped out into the hall. He slammed it closed behind him, Flossie's tears forgotten as he strode down the hall in rapid strides.

"Damn her . . . damn her . . ."

But it was not Flossie's flamboyantly painted face that filled his thoughts. A tall, slender woman with gold hair that glittered in the sun, silver eyes that challenged him, and a mouth that drove him wild with yearning was the true source of his torment. Roger cursed again. The traitorous part of his anatomy that had failed him only minutes earlier hardened at the thought of her. It pressed to bursting against the tailored fit of his trousers, a physical discomfort that caused him to curse anew. It had been that way since the day when he learned that Purity had left with the half-breed. Haunted by the image of her lying in Cass Thomas's arms, he had sought distraction, only to have that same haunting image emasculate him almost as efficiently as a blade.

In saner moments, he had questioned his obsession with the golden-haired witch, but then he recalled the sensation of her tight, womanly body pressed against his, the fluid grace of the long-limbed stride which so fascinated him, the aura of female power that surrounded her. He ached to control that power, to make it his. He yearned to feel those long limbs wrapped around him as he plunged inside her again and again, to see those light eyes glow with the same hunger that nagged so viciously inside him, *to hear her beg for more*—as he intended she would when he had her under him at last.

The time would come. He had already instituted his plan.

Roger paused at that thought. If his father knew . . .

Roger's low snort was a caustic comment he had never dared put into words. His father, whose only true passion was for the numbers rapidly building in the account under his name . . . His father, who had never really desired any woman, including his mother, who had gone back East ten years earlier and never returned . . . His father, who would say he was a fool.

Pausing in a shadowy portion of the hallway, Roger breathed deeply until his body was under control once more. Stepping out into the open at last, he started down the staircase, only to draw to an abrupt halt at the sight of a burly, unkempt fellow climbing the steps toward him. He inwardly cringed as the fellow addressed him.

"I figured you was here, Norris."

"Did you?" Pausing for a cautious glance around them, Roger continued, "What are *you* doing here? You're supposed to be tending to some details for me, aren't you?"

Slater's expression grew sullen. "You told me to report how things was goin'. Well, that's what I'm doin'. Besides, there's a little matter of payment for services done."

"Keep your voice down, fool! I paid you promptly for the other matters you took care of for me, didn't I?"

"Yeah . . . well this job's done, too. Me and the boys drove that herd the Circle C riders was gatherin' right off their damned land, then we got out of there fast, before they had a chance to see what started them critters runnin'. Hell, by the time them beeves stop, they'll be so scattered, it'll take them old boys days to get that herd together again."

"You're sure no one saw you?"

A smile twitched Slater's moist lips. "Me and the boys ain't amateurs. We just disappeared into the dust when them critters got up some speed. We saw that foreman tryin' to scare up some of his men to go after them, but they didn't stand a chance of turnin' them."

A satisfied smile tugged at Roger's lips. "I'll meet you in the shack with your money in a few minutes."

"In an hour would be better." Slater gestured toward the floor above. "I got some business upstairs."

His nostrils twitching at the rancid odor rising from Slater's armpits, Roger nodded, adding perversely, "You might try Flossie. She'll be glad to see you, I'm sure."

Roger proceeded down the stairs.

"All right, what in hell happened out there this afternoon?" Stan demanded.

The question reverberated as Purity glanced at the expressions of the wranglers silently assembled. The men had been late in returning. The sun was already setting and their faces had been longer than the shadows they had cast as they dismounted and approached the house.

Stan had been waiting for them. He had barely allowed the door to close behind them before assaulting them with the question that still went unanswered.

It occurred to Purity as she saw the anger burning in Stan's eyes, that aside from his pallor and unnatural thinness, he bore no resemblance to the frightened image of her vision. She recalled with surging warmth the happiness that had brightened those eyes when she had walked through the ranch house door earlier, and his surprising strength when he hugged her tight. She remembered his attentiveness when she related the visions she'd had in Spotted Bear's tepee. She had also seen the questioning look in his eyes when Cass came to stand at her back, too close for casual friendship.

"I asked a question, Buck, but I ain't gettin' any answers!"

Stan's voice startled Purity from her thoughts. She noted Buck's open resentment as he glanced at Cass. It was obvious that Buck didn't like being questioned in front of Cass.

"I want an answer, Buck."

"I don't have an answer, damn it!"

Stan's frown tightened. "What in hell is that supposed to mean?"

"It means that the boys and me rounded up them beeves like you told us to. We wasn't expectin' no problems. Hell, there wasn't nothin' to make us expect they was goin' to bolt when we left them to graze. But the next thing we knew, they was up and runnin' like the devil was at their heels."

"You didn't see nobody, or hear no gunshots . . ."

"Yeah, we heard gunshots, all right." Nash's angry interjection was a direct accusation as he stared heatedly at Cass. "Those beeves were runnin' wild, trampling everythin' in their path when Thomas let Purity get out in front of them with only her six-gun to turn them!"

Purity snapped, "Is that what Cass did, Nash? He *let* me get out in front of those beeves?" She took a furious step forward. "I thought we had this settled! I thought every one of you knew by now that I'm the

311

Elaine Barbieri

boss here. That means *nobody* tells me how to handle a herd. I know what to do, and I do it—myself—without anybody's advice!"

Stan turned toward her, his pallor deepening. "You didn't do what Nash said, did you, Purity? You wouldn't do nothin' that damned foolish."

Purity stared him down.

"Damn it, girl, are you crazy? Do you realize what could've happened if your horse panicked—or if he went down? Hell, you could've been—"

"No." Cass spoke for the first time. "I wouldn't let that happen."

"You're a big talker, all right"—Nash took another aggressive step—"but talk's cheap. All I know is that we didn't have no trouble on this ranch until you showed up here. Then when you took yourself conveniently out of the way, all kinds of crazy things started happenin'."

"Crazy things? What are you talkin' about?" Purity's question went unanswered, and she turned toward Stan. "What's goin' on, Stan? You told me everythin' went fine while we were gone."

"You're askin' the wrong man if you want to know what's goin' on." Nash replied hotly. "You should be puttin' that question to the fella you was travelin' with. He might be foolin' you, but he ain't foolin' any one of us. He's got an axe to grind here, and he ain't goin' to be satisfied until it's red with blood!"

Choosing to ignore Nash's response, Purity refused to surrender Stan's gaze. "What kind of trouble did you have? What have you been holdin' back?"

Stan shrugged. "Nash is exaggeratin'."

The men mumbled their reaction to Stan's statement, but Buck responded hotly, "Exaggeratin'? Yeah, maybe . . . if you call a poisoned water hole exaggeratin'; if you call cattle disappearin' at a steady rate exaggeratin'; if you call broken fences, missin' equipment, and every other damned manner of annoyance that can set hardworkin' men farther behind exaggeratin'! That stampede today—hell, that was the biggest exaggeration of all!"

Cass straightened up slowly. "Did you report this to the sheriff?"

Stan frowned. "Yeah . . . for all the good it did."

Cass's expression hardened. "I'll take care of it tomorrow."

Purity turned to survey the faces of the men around her. "Do any of you have anythin' to add to what's been said here?" When there was no response, she said, "All right, then I guess we're finished. Pete's got supper ready."

Waiting until the men had shuffled out of the room, Purity turned toward Stan again, her delicate features tight. "Why didn't you tell me what was goin' on?"

Stan scrutinized her silently. She saw his thin face twitch, and then he shrugged. "I don't know, darlin'. I suppose because you had just come home . . . because you was happy, and because it just felt too damned good to see your smile."

Her throat suddenly thick, Purity was grateful that Pete entered the room at that moment, distracting Stan's attention. "If any of you is expectin' to get somethin' to eat tonight, you'd better make it quick," he growled. "Knowin' them fellas in there like I do, they ain't goin' to leave much behind them."

Purity addressed Pete gruffly. "You and Stan make a good pair, keepin' your secrets from me."

Ignoring Pete's dour expression, Purity turned back to Stan. Her mouth softened. "You're a stubborn old coot, you know that? The only thing is, you seem to forget that I'm stubborn, too." Her voice grew softer as she added, "Don't worry about anythin'. I'll ride into town with Cass to talk to the sheriff tomorrow."

"Don't bother." Stan waved a hand in disgust. "You'd only be wastin' your time. That fella's as worthless as a barrel of shucks. He won't get off his tail for nothin' short of an earthquake . . . and you know how many of them damned things we have around here."

Leaning over Stan abruptly, Purity kissed his lined cheek. "That may be so, but you can bet I won't let him off easy." Her throat again tight, Purity looked up at Pete. "Get this chair movin'. It's time this old dog got somethin' to eat."

"Always givin' orders. I always said you should've been a man." Stan turned abruptly toward Pete. "Well, you heard what the lady said. She likes playin' boss, so we'll humor her."

Stan turned unexpectedly to address Cass. "As far as that stampede this afternoon goes, I'd read the riot act to you for lettin' Purity ride out in front of it— even if you was right behind her—but I know there was probably no way you could've stopped her, short of shootin' her dead. I suppose there's a lesson for you to learn in that, somewhere."

Not waiting for Cass's response, Stan signaled Pete to wheel him away.

The squeak of his chair's wheels brought abrupt tears to Purity's eyes. She turned abruptly toward the door. The sound of Cass's step behind her turned her briefly toward him.

"No, please. You'd better get somethin' to eat. I'm not hungry."

Not waiting for his response, Purity walked out into the darkness of the yard.

Julia stared out the living room window as darkness began falling. The last brilliant shades of pink and gold were fading from the horizon . . . the *empty* horizon. Sighing, she turned back toward the kitchen to find Jack watching her.

"Is somethin' wrong, Julia? I've never seen you lookin' so anxious as you have since I got home."

"Is that what I've been doing . . . looking anxious?" Julia's cheeks flushed. "I didn't mean . . . I mean I was just . . ."

Her words trailing to a halt, Julia suddenly could not think of a word of reply. She whispered, "I suppose I was just hoping Cass would come home soon."

"I thought I explained all that, dear."

The arm that Jack slipped around her was meant to comfort. She wished with all her heart it was meant to show more. She looked up at him, not caring if he saw the love in her eyes.

"I couldn't take the chance of leavin' the Circle C in the hands of a woman," he continued. When Julia

315

blinked, Jack gave a self-conscious laugh. "Not that woman, anyways. She's little more than a girl, and she thinks she can outride, outrope, outshoot, and outthink any man."

Julia blinked again. "Well, can she?"

Endearing himself more to her than he would ever know, Jack responded earnestly, "I really don't know. I know that Stan thinks she can. The men are behind her, all right, but I'm thinkin' they might be more than a little bit influenced by her pretty face and all that blond hair, not to speak of those pants she wears that are just a little too tight to suit me."

"Pants!"

"She's not a conventional woman, Julia."

Julia considered that thought. "Perhaps that's good."

Jack smiled. "You do surprise me sometimes."

"What does Cass think of her?"

Jack's smile faded. "I don't know. They had a rocky beginnin'. Things weren't goin' too smooth when I left."

"Well, Cass will straighten things out if he puts his mind to it. There's a kindness inside him . . . a sensitivity that makes him able to look right down inside a person."

"Kind and sensitive . . ." Jack shook his head. "I don't think you'll find too many fellas on the Circle C who'd agree."

"Then they're wrong!" The anger that surged through Julia made her temporarily dizzy. Holding herself erect with sheer force of will, she declared with all the adamancy her gentle soul would allow, "No woman could have a better son than Cass."

"I know."

"I . . . I wish he was home, Jack."

Julia felt the slow perusal of Jack's gaze. She wished she could tell him. She wished she could explain. Julia sighed inwardly.

"I love you, Jack."

She waited for the words of response that did not come. But she knew the concern in Jack's eyes was not feigned when he spoke at last.

"You're lookin' tired, dear. I'm tired, too. Maybe we should both go to bed early."

To lie beside Jack . . . to feel his arm around her . . . to know he loved her although the words were so hard for him to say . . .

"Yes, I am tired."

Julia slipped her hand into his.

The barn was silent and still as Purity ran an exploratory hand down her mare's leg. Relieved to find her sound again, she looked up as the animal nuzzled her arm.

"So, you missed me." Purity laughed, more pleased than she cared to admit by the animal's show of affection. "Well, I'm glad to be back, too. Three weeks is a long time to be away." Her smile fading, Purity continued, "I'll let you take me into town tomorrow since your leg's healed. You could use the exercise, couldn't you, girl?"

"Purity . . ."

Purity turned toward the entrance of the barn. She straightened up, frowning as Nash emerged into the

light and walked toward her. The confrontation in
the living room a short time earlier had upset her.
She didn't want to talk. She was about to tell him
that when Nash neared and the misery in his dark
eyes silenced her.

Taking his opportunity, Nash began hesitantly. "I
had to talk to you for a few minutes, Purity."

Feeling the rise of a familiar warmth as Nash
looked at her with his boyish features drawn into
lines of concern, Purity realized abruptly that she
had missed him. She replied as gently as she could
manage, "It's not a good time, Nash. I'm in a pretty
foul mood."

But Nash was not listening. He frowned unexpectedly. "You shouldn't have ridden out in front of
that stampede the way you did this afternoon."

Not him, too.

"I don't want to talk about it, Nash."

"You could've been killed."

"You think so? Just answer one question, Nash. If
you thought you could've stopped that stampede
with a few shots, would you have done what I did?"

"Maybe."

"Yeah. You know you would've done the same
thing."

"But that would be me takin' the risk, not you."

"What's the difference?"

"You know what the difference is."

Immediately regretting the opening she had provided him, Purity shook her head. "I said I don't want
to talk about it."

"I know." Nash closed the distance between them.

"What you really don't want to talk about is the feelin's I have for you."

"Nash, you don't understand. Some things have changed."

"Maybe I do understand." Nash slipped his arm around her. The pain in his brown eyes halted her withdrawal as he continued intently, "Maybe that's why I ain't goin' to ask you what you mean. Words don't mean much, anyways. Feelin's are what's important . . . like how much I missed you when you were gone."

Damn . . .

Resentment entered his tone. "I wanted to come after you when you left. So did Buck and Baird and a few of the others. There wasn't a one of us who liked the idea of you goin' off with Thomas like that, no matter what he promised Stan about takin' care of you. But Stan was hoppin' mad. He said you knew what you were doin' and you could take care of yourself. But all I could think about was you bein' alone on the trail with that Injun . . . and it hurt so damned bad."

A slow ache started inside Purity. She tried to smile. "Stan was right, Nash. I knew what I was doin'. I made my decision. Cass and I—"

"I don't want to hear no more!" Nash's face grew tortured. "You're home now, and things are back the way they was. You've got me—all of us—to stand behind you. There's not a one of us who'll let you down."

"I know."

"You don't need him, Purity! You never did! He's

319

smart, I'll give him that. He knew how much you were bothered about findin' your sisters, and he took advantage of it. But if it's findin' your sisters that's still botherin' you, I'll help you! I'll take you anywhere you want to go—do anythin' you want to do." Nash drew her closer. "Just let me show you how I feel. I can make you happy. I know I can. Hell, there's nothin' I've wanted more than that for as long as I can remember. And there's nothin' I wouldn't do to—"

"Take your hands off her, Carter."

Jumping at the sound of Cass's voice, Purity looked up to see Cass standing at the entrance of the stall. She saw the stiffening of his body as Nash's hand tightened on her waist and her heart began a rapid pounding.

"I said, take your hands off her."

Nash drew her closer.

No, she didn't want this. She whispered, "Let me go, Nash."

"No."

Uncertain what happened in the moment that followed, Purity gasped aloud as she was jerked free of Nash's embrace and whirled back against the wall of the stall behind her. There was a loud crack and Nash hit the ground with a thud. A chill chased down her spine as Cass stood looking down at Nash. She saw the anger in his eyes as Nash drew himself to his feet. Cass addressed him in a hard voice.

"Stay away from her, Carter."

"Bastard!"

Stepping between them, Purity halted Nash's intended rush forward. She refused to budge.

"Purity's home now!" Nash rasped. "Whatever happened is over and done! You're not goin' to take advantage of her anymore!"

"Cass didn't take advantage of me, Nash."

"Didn't he?"

"No."

"Maybe you think he didn't, but I know better. Bastard . . ."

Purity swallowed at the emotion that choked off his words.

Tears rising to her eyes, Purity whispered, "I'm sorry, Nash."

"It doesn't make any difference, you know." Nash shook his head, his gaze holding hers. "It doesn't change the way I feel about you. Nothin' could."

"Get out of here, Carter."

Purity glanced at Cass. His expression was unrevealing, his emotion betrayed only by the heaving of his chest as she snapped, "I'll handle this."

"No, you won't." Cass's warning was soft and deadly. "Get movin', Carter . . . now, before it's too late."

"What will you do if I don't—pull a knife on me, like you did on Purity that first day?"

Cass's jaw tightened.

"Or maybe you'll sneak up on me in the dark, like the rest of your breed!"

Purity couldn't tell which of the men attacked first. Knowing only that Cass and Nash had collided, she heard pounding fists and grunts of pain that were halted abruptly by a sharp command.

"Stop! Right now!" The barrel of Buck's gun glinted in the meager light as a sudden stillness prevailed. Cass turned menacingly toward him and Buck grated, "Give me the chance I'm lookin' for, and I'll take it, Thomas."

Her heart pounding, Purity ordered, "Put that gun down, Buck."

Ignoring her, Buck commanded, "Get out of here, Nash."

Wiping the blood from his lips, Nash grated, "I'm not goin' anywhere."

"I told you to get goin'!"

Nash did not move. Purity saw the shift of Cass's eyes. She knew what was coming, and she couldn't let it happen.

"Let's go, Cass." Purity felt the chill of his gaze as she continued, "This has been a mistake. You know that as well as I do. We can't afford to fight among ourselves."

Cass did not respond.

"Cass . . ."

Purity saw the tick of Cass's jaw. She pressed, "I don't want any trouble. Let's go."

Cass dropped his gaze to hers. She saw the fury burning beneath the ice there, and she held her breath for long seconds before Cass turned toward Buck. "You can put your gun down."

Grasping her arm, Cass steered her toward the door, ignoring the gun still leveled in his direction.

Walking stiffly, Purity controlled her rising emotions as they walked across the yard. She waited only until the ranch house door closed behind her before

322

she jerked her arm free of his grip and rasped, "You didn't have to do that! I could've handled Nash."

"You think so?" Cass paused, his gaze cold. "I wasn't going to wait to find out. The next time he touches you, I won't bother with a warning."

"I can't let this happen, Cass."

Purity strode toward the stairs. She pushed open her bedroom door moments later and locked it behind her.

Her throat tight, Purity closed her eyes at the decision she knew must be made.

Julia was silent, but she was not sleeping.

Lying beside her in the bed they had shared for many years, Jack closed his eyes, seeking the sleep that eluded him also. Unable to bear the strained silence between them a moment longer, he turned toward Julia and slipped his arm around her. She was trembling. Cursing his weakness, he pressed his lips to her cheek, then whispered, "Are you all right, dear?"

"Yes, Jack. I'm fine. I . . . I just can't seem to sleep tonight."

Jack drew her closer, his emotions conflicted by the comfort he felt when she turned her womanly softness against him. Somehow, that comfort remained. He supposed the reason was simple. Julia had brought serenity and peace into his life when only turmoil abounded. Her gentleness and capacity to love without asking anything in return had not diminished with the years. It was a source of bewilderment to him how his feelings for Julia could be so separate and different from the love that Whispering Woman brought to life with just a look . . . a word . . . a touch.

Whispering Woman's image returned before his mind's eye at that moment, and Jack softly groaned.

"Is something wrong, dear?"

Julia's question hung on the silence.

What could he say, that he had lived a lie with her for years because he had not possessed the courage to tell her a truth? That the lie had grown harder and more difficult to accept as the years passed? That part of his guilt lay in the realization that his silence had forced Cass to deny to the world the mother and brother he loved? Could he tell her that he knew the death of Flying Eagle tormented Cass even more *because* he had never acknowledged him? Could he tell her that if Whispering Woman were a different woman, one who had chosen to press her case, he might actually have cast aside all the years Julia had given him so selflessly?

And, could he tell her that even now, as he held her in his arms, feeling her love and taking comfort from it, he was unsure what the next year would bring?

"You didn't answer me, dear. Is something bothering you?"

Jack laid his cheek against Julia's hair. The fragrance of lilacs rose from the graying strands, a scent so different from Whispering Woman's natural, musky fragrance. He responded with a partial truth.

"I'm worried about Cass. There are problems on the Circle C that he might not be able to overcome."

Julia was momentarily silent. "Maybe you could send a telegram . . . bring him home for a little while and talk to him about them."

"I don't think he'd come."

"Why? Because of the girl you spoke about?"

"I'm not sure."

"He'd come if you asked him to."

"There are things Cass needs to settle there, things only he can handle."

Jack felt the tremor that shook Julia. "You're frightening me, Jack. There's something you aren't telling me. Cass is safe, isn't he?"

"I suppose . . . yes, of course."

"Jack . . ."

Jack's short laugh was touched with irony. "I doubt if anyone at the Circle C would believe for a moment that someone fears for Cass's safety. I think they feel it's the other way around."

"Cass would never hurt anyone!"

"Julia . . ."

"He's kind and—"

"—sensitive, yes, I know."

"He's been the greatest joy to me. I'm so proud that I had a part in raising him. Did I ever thank you for that, Jack, for entrusting Cass to me? I truly cherish his love."

Jack swallowed against the tightening in his throat.

"I wish he was home, Jack."

"He'll be home before you know it."

"No mother could be more proud of a son than I am of Cass."

"I know."

"Do you suppose he realizes that?"

"Yes."

"D . . . do you suppose a prayer might bring him back sooner?"

"You know more about prayers than I do, dear."

Julia's laugh was a short hiccup of sound. "I suppose I should."

"You could try if it means that much to you."

"Yes. I will."

Silence.

"Goodnight, Jack."

"Goodnight, dear."

The conflicts within him never stronger, Jack pressed his mouth to hers.

"I love you, Jack."

Silence.

Reluctance.

No longer able to withhold the words, he whispered softly in the darkness.

"I love you, too."

The room was shadowed and silent. Purity's breathing was a shallow whisper of sound as Cass undressed and slid into the bed beside her. She did not stir. Her sleeping features were illuminated by the pale light streaming through the window.

Cass indulged himself in her beauty.

Then jealousy returned, surging hotly. Carter was right. If the other man persisted, blood would be spilled.

Cass frowned. He didn't want that. Purity would

suffer needlessly. It would be difficult enough when she was forced to acknowledge the truth at last.

But Purity was lying safely beside him now. He brushed her lips with his, and the anguish faded. He pressed his mouth more deeply, and the hunger grew.

She stirred. . . .

A familiar warmth enclosed her. A remembered touch brushed her lips. The taste was sweet. The joy all-encompassing.

Purity turned to it. She stretched herself against its heat. She separated her lips to welcome it in.

Purity opened her eyes, to meet Cass's pale-eyed gaze. Reality returned, bringing with it a familiar torment. She drew back, silently cursing the regret she felt as she spoke.

"What are you doing here, Cass?" She glanced toward the door of her room. "How did you get in?"

His shadowed expression was unrevealing. "You should know by now that a locked door wouldn't keep me out."

Purity swallowed against her mounting agitation. This was the man she loved. They could share moments of ecstasy in this solitude that shut out the world around them.

But painful reality was only hours away. It would come with the sun. It glinted on the faces of the men she trusted and who trusted her in return. And it shone with a vengeance still to be served in the green eyes now filled with yearning.

The gnawing ache within her expanded.

"I want you to leave, Cass."

"You don't mean that."

Purity forced coldness into her voice. "Yes, I do." She struggled to maintain the chill. "We're back home now, and everythin' is changed. It was all a mistake . . ."

"A mistake?"

"You came here, and everythin' happened too fast for me to think. I was confused. I don't even remember why I told you about my sisters, but you believed me when no one else did. You helped me when no one else could. You became my guide, my protector, my friend when I was at my lowest. I was afraid, and I leaned on you. I wanted you to hold me, to lend me your strength. I wanted you to make me believe what others made me doubt. I wanted you to stop the fear growing greater inside me with every day of our journey. You did that, Cass. You gave me strength, and you kept me strong enough to face my uncertainties. I can never thank you enough for that."

Purity took a shuddering breath. "But we're back here now . . ." She paused, the ache within increasing. "I can't stand with you against my men, Cass. I can't let myself believe that Buck, Pete, Nash, Baird, or any of the other boys could be responsible for your brother's death. They don't deserve that. I can't do it, and I won't!"

Purity felt Cass's heart pounding against hers. She saw a tic in his cheek as he maintained his silence. But she was unprepared for the throbbing timbre of his voice as he whispered, "You said you love me."

Cass's words broke her heart.

"Did you mean what you said?"

Emotion filled Purity's throat, blocking her response.

"Tell me."

"Yes, I meant it."

"Have your feelings changed?"

Purity's reply was a rasping whisper. "Here and now? No. There's no conflict between us here, no hatred. But there's no reality, either. There's no wrong or right. . . ."

"No, that's not true."

Cass touched his mouth to hers. "To return my kiss is right, Purity."

He stroked her cheek. "To know my touch is right."

He drew her closer. "To indulge the beauty when our flesh meets is right."

His lips brushed hers, and then he whispered, "To believe there is no one else in the world when I hold you in my arms could never be wrong."

"No . . ."

"Look at me, Purity, and listen." His eyes seemed to mesmerize her. "Your breath is my breath. Your heartbeat is mine. We are one now, Purity."

"But tomorrow—"

"Tomorrow is hours away."

Cass's voice trailed off in the darkness. His words echoed in her mind, a litany of love she could not silence as his mouth closed over hers.

His kisses bemused her.

His touch set her on fire.

She sighed, and he took the sound deep inside him.

She tried to speak, and he swallowed the words.

She attempted to say that she wished tomorrow would never come.

But their bodies blended and the words were swept away . . .

. . . as the night shadows lingered.

The night shadows lingered. The silence was strained. A harsh whisper shattered the stillness.

"He knows, I tell you!"

"No, he doesn't."

"I can see it in his eyes!"

"There's no way he can know for sure."

"He won't give up until he finds out who did it!"

No response.

"We've waited too long already."

Silence.

"Did you hear what I said!"

"Yeah, I heard you."

"Well?"

Chapter Ten

He was feeling very well, indeed.

Roger walked along the boardwalk of the dusty main street. He had just emerged from the barber shop. His hair was freshly cut, his mustache was neatly trimmed, and his face was smoothly shaved. It never ceased to amaze him that a fellow with the limited intelligence and coarse manner of Willard Pratt could have such a delicate touch with a razor. For that reason alone, he had listened to the barber's inane conversation with cultivated patience.

He was also aware that the fellow's ceaseless gossip had at times proved of value—as it had the time when he learned that Jesse Parker's wife was openly dissatisfied with her husband. Roger's low snort reflected his amusement. Sally Parker had not been much to look at, but she had been inordinately grateful for his attention, so much so that he doubted the bed linens had yet cooled.

And then there was Asa Malone, who had come to the bank asking for another extension on his loan with the promise that he would be able to meet the payment in three months. Fool! Had he really expected that the sickness spreading through his herd could be kept a secret from the town barber?

And, of course, there was Bart Slater, who had walked into the barber shop a few weeks earlier, and who Pratt had confided was an unscrupulous sort who would do anything for money. Roger had made it his business to strike up a conversation with Slater shortly afterward . . . which had resulted in a covert business arrangement, the effects of which were still being felt on the Circle C.

Roger sneered. Asa Malone's ranch had been forfeit, Sally Parker had provided hours of entertainment . . . and he would soon have the Circle C on its knees.

Thank you, Willard Pratt.

Of course, he could not thank Pratt for his knowledge of Jack Thomas's financial affairs. He had made his own, personal inquiries, which had revealed that although the Rocking T was stable, Thomas's funds were not unlimited. It had been immediately obvious to him that the Circle C must soon begin to pay for itself or both ranches would be in trouble. It pleased him to believe, now that he taken a personal interest in the direction of Circle C affairs, that the Circle C would be the first to go.

Roger's step grew more brisk at the thought of the

stampede he had arranged the day before on the Circle C. Such an unfortunate incident—especially since those cattle had doubtless stampeded directly into a herd of diseased cattle which had somehow escaped Asa Malone's ranch. Roger smiled. He supposed he could have arranged for those same cattle to have been placed *on* the Circle C, which had already been inspected and found free of contamination, but he was not fool enough to chance such a maneuver.

Roger's smile faded as a familiar agitation returned. The truth was that he was becoming impatient. It could be several months before the disaster he had engineered reached fruition—weeks of waiting, endless days and nights passed in expectation of the day when Purity's tall, slender form would stride through his doorway again, when he would see to it that she cast aside the arrogant half-breed who had barged into his office and into Purity's life.

The thought of Cass Thomas infuriated Roger. He'd have the breed taken care of then! He had already decided that. He would never be suspected, and a shot in the dark would probably be applauded, considering the fellow's popularity.

Roger's step slowed as the bank came into view. His anger deepened at sight of the unshaven, burly fellow waiting outside the bank's entrance. Halting beside the man, Roger hissed, "What are you doing here, Slater? I thought I made it clear that I didn't want to be seen with you in public."

"Looks like you didn't." Slater raised his hat and wiped a stained bandanna across his sweat-beaded forehead. "Hell, it sure is hot this mornin', ain't it?"

"Out with it, you fool! What do you want?"

Slater's yellowed teeth flashed in a smile. "You ain't goin' to like this."

Roger began a slow seething.

"I told you that me and the boys didn't wait around for anybody to see us after we got them beeves runnin' yesterday. Well, looks like they didn't run as far as we thought they would. Them wranglers must've stopped that stampede short somehow."

"What are you saying?"

"I'm sayin' that when me and the boys went back to check things out, them sick critters was just where we left them, and there wasn't a single head of Circle C cattle around."

"How can that be?"

"That was what me and the boys was wonderin', especially when we went lookin' and saw that the Circle C herd was drove back onto Circle C land and split up so that there wasn't no way we stood a chance of stampedin' them again and makin' it look like an accident."

Roger's heart began a rapid pounding. "You're lying. You did this purposely . . ."

"Now wait a minute . . ."

"You want to be paid for the same job twice!" Roger grew livid. "Well, that isn't going to happen!"

"I don't like the way you're talkin'."

"Get away from me, Slater."

"I'd watch what I said if I was you."

"Get away from me before I call the sheriff!"

Slater sneered. "That ain't likely!"

"Just try me!"

"I don't need to. You just made a bad mistake."

"Did I?"

"That's right. You wouldn't like it much if I walked up to that pretty lady ridin' into town over there, and told her what you had me and the boys doin' on her ranch while she was gone."

"Pretty lady . . ." Roger turned to scan the street behind him as Slater rambled on. His gaze halted abruptly when Purity rode into his angle of view. Agitation flamed when he saw the man riding beside her.

"And they might not think it was so—"

"Shut up!"

"What did you say?"

"You heard me. Get away from me! You've gotten all the money you're going to get from me. And I wouldn't go talking out of turn, either, because aside from incriminating yourself, you just might find it injurious to your health."

"I don't like what I'm hearin' . . ."

"I don't care what you like!"

"You think you're big enough to take me on?"

"I don't have to be. Money avails me of resources unaccessible to the average man." It was Roger's turn to sneer. "What would you say your life is worth, one hundred dollars—maybe two?"

"You slimy bastard . . ."

"Get away from me—now!"

His unshaven face hot, Slater turned with a curse and strode away.

Roger entered the bank with a stiff smile, his pace

accelerating as he approached his office door. Once inside, he cursed aloud, then strode to the window. Concealed there, he stared out into the street.

There she was, damn her! Her hair was lighter, an almost silver gold as if bleached by the sun—and the creamy skin of her cheeks was darkened to a golden hue, making her eyes appear all the lighter in contrast. She drew her mount to a halt and swung down from the saddle. Those long legs . . . that firm, slender body . . . the pure, womanly power of her . . .

Roger swallowed against the moisture that had gathered in his mouth.

Salivating . . . she had him salivating!

Roger took a deep breath.

The half-breed dismounted beside her. He looked down at Purity. Damn that look in that bastard's eyes—as if she belonged to him!

Damn him to hell!

The dusty street was bright with morning sun as Cass dismounted beside her. Purity glanced up at him, remembering that she had awakened with his clean, male scent still fresh on her bed linens although she was alone. She had hastily dressed and gone downstairs to find him talking to Stan in the living room. But he had not betrayed by so much as a glance the intimate hours of the night past.

Gratitude had surged within her at the realization that Cass had freed her to resume a semblance of normalcy and mend fences with the men. She had approached Buck first, on the pretext of discussing the chores of the day. Encouraged when the stiffness between them gradually faded and the spontaneous warmth was restored, she had approached each man in turn. She had sensed the hair on the back of Cass's neck rising as she made a special effort to restore Nash's smile. Uncertain whether that effort would prove to be a mistake, she knew only that she was truly pained to cause Nash distress, and that she had badly needed to restore peace between herself and the men who had supported her without question when she had needed them so badly.

Cass and she had left the ranch shortly afterward to see Sheriff Boyle as planned. She had felt Stan's scrutiny when they left. Stan, who was weaker than he would acknowledge, stronger than most would think, and whose eye was as keen as an eagle's.

When they had turned out of view of the ranch house, and when Cass leaned toward her abruptly and drew her mouth up to his, she realized she had been waiting for that moment.

But Main Street eventually came into view, and with it harsh reality returned. Responding to that reality as Cass looked down at her, Purity stated flatly, "I'll do the talking. Sheriff Boyle will expect me to." A smile tugged briefly at her lips. "The boys say he thinks I'm a high-handed woman."

Cass did not smile. "I'd say there's some truth in that."

"He said I'd never be able to handle the Circle C."

"He isn't as smart as he thinks he is."

Purity shrugged, suddenly frowning. "Anyway, he's the only sheriff we've got, and I'll be damned if

I'll let him sit on his tail when somebody out there's playin' games with the ranch's future."

"I'll straighten him out."

Purity's frown deepened. "I'll handle it, Cass."

Not waiting for his reply, Purity turned toward the sheriff's door.

Julia moved uncertainly around her sunny kitchen. Another headache . . . worse than the last . . . She closed her eyes briefly. It would not abate.

Turning toward the mound of beef she had cubed so carefully, she dumped the meat into the pot nearby. The vegetables had also been cubed and the spices added. She would simmer the meat, make a pie crust, and she would have Jack's favorite dish baked and ready for their evening meal.

I love you, too.

Jack's words, whispered in the darkness of the previous night, returned as they had countless times since she had risen that morning and watched Jack ride out with his men for the day's work. She treasured those words all the more for the difficulty Jack had in speaking them.

Uncertainty nudged. Did he know?

No. She shook her head, regretting the movement as the pounding increased. That wasn't possible.

The aroma of searing meat rose, filling the room, and a sudden nausea assailed her. Walking quickly to the side door, Julia jerked it open and breathed deeply, her heart pounding. No, not yet, please.

Her breathing returned gradually to normal and the unpleasantness passed. Julia managed a smile.

No, the good Lord would not disallow her only chance at repentance. He would not be that unkind.

Swallowing against the tightness in her throat, Julia looked up to see movement in the distance.

A rider was approaching. She waited.

She was still standing in the doorway when the rider dismounted and placed a telegram in her hand.

Sheriff Boyle puffed with annoyance, his full cheeks ballooning almost comically, his bloodshot eyes shifting as he made no effort to conceal his irritation.

"How many times do I have to say the same thing, Purity? Whatever trouble you're havin' at the Circle C, there ain't nothin' to say it's anythin' but a run of bad luck like a lot of other ranchers in these parts are havin'!"

"Bad luck?" Purity pressed angrily, "Does it make sense to you that bad luck would poison a water hole?"

"You ain't got no proof that the poisonin' wasn't from some natural drainage."

"I had cleaned that water hole out with the boys a few days earlier."

"Maybe you should've done a better job!"

Cass's low-voiced interruption was sharp. "I'd watch what I said if I were you, sheriff!"

"I can handle this, Cass!"

When Cass fell silent, allowing her to continue, Purity turned back to the rotund fellow aggressively denying her claims. "I'm not goin' to argue that point. I know I'd be wastin' my time. I just want to point out a few other things to you . . . like the stock that's been disappearin', a little at a time."

"It's easy enough to lose a head or two, here and there."

"The equipment that's been damaged and stolen."

"Did you try questionin' some of your own fellas? Could be most of that stuff was mislaid."

"The corrals that have been damaged . . . the fences that have been knocked down . . ."

"Them things happen sometimes when beeves panic. You know that!"

"And the stampede . . . out of nowhere."

"I'd say you'd better give them hands of yours a talkin' to. They shouldn't let things like that happen."

Her chest heaving, Purity stared at Sheriff Boyle. "Stan was right, as he usually is. He said I'd be wastin' my time tryin' to get you to move your lazy hide."

"Wait a minute!"

"No, you wait a minute!" Stepping forward, Cass took Purity's arm. He allowed only a moment for his cold-eyed gaze to register before he grated, "You had your chance."

Outside on the boardwalk moments later, Purity was still flushed with anger when Cass turned her toward him and stated flatly, "You knew what to expect."

"Yes, but that doesn't make it any easier to take."

"He made a mistake that he's goin' to regret."

"What are you sayin'?"

"I'm saying he doesn't leave us much choice in what we have to do."

The determination in his gaze disallowed protest

as Cass propelled Purity up the street. Her strides matching his, she walked beside him in tense silence until they turned into a storefront a short distance away. She paused as Cass stepped up to the counter and addressed the bespectacled clerk gruffly.

"I want to send a wire."

The clerk nodded and slapped a form down in front of him.

Frowning, Purity watched as Cass picked up the pencil and began printing in clear block letters:

TO: CAPTAIN JOE BARNES
    TEXAS RANGERS
    SAN ANTONIO, TEXAS

Observing tensely from the window of his office, Sheriff John Boyle frowned as he watched Purity Corrigan and Cass Thomas walk back up the street, mount up, and ride out of town. He didn't like what he had seen. That Purity Corrigan had always been too big for her britches, and he never did trust a half-breed. He didn't like the look in that big fella's eyes when he spoke, either—that threat that somehow didn't need to be put into words.

Sheriff Boyle shook his head. Hell, how did he get into this mess in the first place? A word or two exchanged in the Purple Slipper . . . a favor or two that had netted him favors in return . . .

Cursing softly, Sheriff Boyle wiped the sweat from his brow, then reached for his hat and walked out onto the boardwalk. He hesitated only briefly before turning toward the telegraph office. He emerged minutes later, his face twitching as he strode across the street, straight toward the Citizens First Bank. He did not stop on entering, but walked directly to a familiar office door and knocked sharply.

"Come in."

He knew by the look on Roger Norris's face that he had been expected, and that Norris was irritated.

"So?"

Sheriff Boyle's face twitched again. Reluctant to admit to an alliance that was of long standing, he removed his handkerchief from his pocket and wiped a new sheen of sweat from his forehead. "Hot mornin', ain't it?"

Norris glared.

He began uncomfortably, "You mentioned when I saw you at the Purple Slipper some weeks back that you was interested in what was goin' on at the Circle C . . . because you hold the mortgage on the ranch and all."

"Come on, out with it, Boyle! It doesn't take you that long to get to the point when you're looking for a loan that you don't intend paying back, or if you're looking for me to put a good word in for you at Sophie's Place!"

"I didn't come here to discuss that." Sheriff Boyle's puffy features drew into lines of concern. "I just thought you'd like to know that Purity Corrigan and that half-breed partner of hers came into my office and that they were lookin' for me to investigate some things that are goin' on at the ranch."

"Well?"

"I told them the same thing I told that foreman of

theirs a couple of weeks ago—that I didn't have time
to waste investigatin' somethin' that was nothin' at
all."

"So?"

"They wasn't too happy. I watched them. They
went straight from my office to the telegraph office."

"Come on, out with the rest of it, damn it!"

"That big fella sent a telegram to the Texas Ranger
post in San Antonio, to one of the captains there.
Seems like he must know the fella because he asked
him to come up here and investigate doin's at the
Circle C." Sheriff Boyle's beefy shoulders jerked nervously. "He wrote somethin' about the sheriff's office
turnin' a blind eye to what's goin' on."

"Bastard . . ." Roger grimaced. "Did you tell the op-
erator to tear up that message?"

"Hell, no! I couldn't do that!"

"Idiot!"

"I don't like you callin' me names, Mr. Norris!"

"Get out of here."

"And I don't like—"

"I don't care what you like. I told you to get out!"

Barely withholding the retort that sprang to his
lips, Sheriff Boyle jerked open the door and strode
across the interior of the bank. Emerging onto the
street, he glanced first one way, then the other, and
then headed back to his office.

Seated at his desk minutes later, Sheriff Boyle put
his feet up on the desk and leaned his ample proportions back in his chair.

His furious expression belied his casual posture.

His soft tone belied his resolution as he said, "All

right, Mr. High-and-Mighty Norris, you're on your own."

He had made a mistake, and he knew it.

Cursing softly, Roger struggled to overcome his agitation. Withdrawing a spotless handkerchief, he patted his forehead dry, infuriated by the odor that rose from his armpit as he did.

Disgusting!

It was *her* fault! Purity Corrigan had made him *common!* She had infused him with *common* emotions—jealousy being the foremost and most torturous. She had forced him into *common* acts—unlawful acts that might yet rebound upon him!

All without any satisfaction at all.

Yes, he had made a mistake when he'd sent Bart Slater packing. He didn't have time to find another wretch like him to do his bidding.

Roger considered another thought. It was probably just as well. With that telegram on its way, time was growing short. He should have known that if he wanted something done right, he'd have to do it himself.

"I told you it wouldn't do no good!"

"You were right."

Cass was standing a few feet from the porch where Stan had parked his chair an hour earlier, awaiting the men's return at the end of the day. Cass had been the second person in from the barn, and he had wasted no time approaching the house. Of course, the first one in had been Purity, but Stan had let her pass without more than a few words in greeting. He hadn't wanted to press her for information. It was Cass he was after—Cass with his guarded expression that revealed so little. Not that Purity had been much different after they returned from town that morning.

Damn it all, the two of them had been about as forthcoming as a cigar store Indian, with neither of them offering much more information than the fact that Sheriff Boyle had been no help at all. They had both ridden off immediately afterward to join the men where they were working.

Holding Cass with his gaze, Stan pressed, "You didn't tell me much about what happened in town this mornin'. I figured we'd go over it one more time."

Cass's light eyes narrowed. "We told you that the sheriff wasn't any help at all, just as you predicted."

Stan gave a low snort. "Yeah, and what else?"

"What do you mean?"

"You're not goin' to stand there and tell me that's all there was to it, because I don't believe it! I know Purity, and I've seen enough of you to know that neither of you would accept that as easy as you did if you didn't have somethin' else in mind."

Stan squinted. He could almost believe a smile picked briefly at Cass's lips. He pressed, "Well?"

The men had gradually drifted back toward the house. One by one they had gathered around Stan until they were all assembled, listening. Aware of it, Stan was also aware that each and every one of them had put all they had on the line for the Circle C, and they deserved to know what was going on as much as he did.

He pressed with less patience than before, "I don't hear nothin', but I know I asked a question."

Cass responded with a tightening of his jaw, "There was no use arguing with the sheriff. A little more said, and there would've been trouble."

Stan did not need to ask for an explanation. The sheriff's attitude toward Purity was well known. His blood began a slow boil.

"So, what are you goin' to do about it?"

"I already did it."

"Meanin'?"

"Meaning I sent a telegram to San Antonio—to the office of the Texas Rangers there."

"You did." Stan gave a hard laugh. "What makes you think they're goin' to bother with somethin' like this when our own sheriff won't even come out to give a look?"

Cass paused. "Captain Barnes is an old friend of my father's."

Stan considered that thought. "When do you think he'll get here?"

"I don't know. As soon as he can spare a man, I suppose."

"Hell, that could be never!"

"I don't think so."

Stan pressed, "Anybody know you sent that telegram?"

"I suppose. We didn't try to hide it."

"Well, maybe that'll do the trick by itself. There ain't many I know who'll mess with a Ranger."

When Cass did not respond, Stan continued, "In the meantime, I guess we might as well eat that supper Pete has waitin'."

Cass walked past him into the house, and the thought struck Stan that the men had been unnaturally silent throughout their exchange. They were still silent as they filed past him.

He didn't like it. He wasn't sure why. But he didn't like it.

Time was growing short. Too short.

Julia stood stock still in the midst of her kitchen. She listened to the sounds emanating from the dining room beyond her kitchen door. Forks scraping, soft conversation in deep, manly tones—music to her ears. She had already put a mountain of fresh biscuits on the table, and the orange honey and apple butter she had especially prepared. She would next carry in the four large beef pies that lay glossy and steaming on the table in front of her. For dessert she had also made Jack's favorite—rice pudding from a recipe in a cookbook that was her mother's only legacy to her.

Julia considered that thought. No, it was not her mother's *only* legacy.

Julia forced away her sober musings. She then straightened her spotless apron, ran a hand over her tightly bound hair, and picked up the first of the meat pies. She walked briskly into the dining room, her expression brightening as grunts of appreciation sounded around the table.

Her eyes darting briefly to Jack, Julia smiled. He

347

smiled in return—a display that had become too rare of late. She cherished that smile because she knew it was true.

A gift . . .

Julia walked back into the kitchen, her heart filled to bursting.

Pete entered the dining room, scowling in his usual manner as he placed another platter of steaming beef on the table. Cass surveyed the men seated around him. Their expressions were not much better. It had been a difficult day, with the men resenting every order he issued after he arrived back from town. Purity's efforts to ease the situation had been in vain. Buck had been civil, but Carter's self-control had been tenuous.

He supposed Stan would never realize that the timing of his questioning a few minutes earlier had been choice. It had allowed him to study the effect of his words on each of the men. He knew they were all concerned about the incidents occurring on the ranch. He knew they wondered who had instigated them—whether he really had reason or opportunity to arrange them as Nash had accused him—and that they also wondered what would happen next. His clash with Nash and Buck the previous night had increased the tension on the ranch and heightened the personal animosity against him. He sensed that the news of the telegram he had sent had not been well received. The question was, why?

Whoever was behind the incidents on the Circle C, Cass was satisfied that he had taken a step toward resolving the problem. He had his suspicions who was responsible. He had not forgotten Roger Norris's expression when he'd walked in on Purity and him in Norris's office that first morning. Norris had been humiliated, and he had known in that moment that Norris would not let it end there. But he doubted Norris would continue his harassment once the word got out that a Texas Ranger was heading in their direction. The fellow was arrogant and prideful, capable of financing such dirty work in a bid for revenge, but he was not a fool.

Cass frowned. The next debt to be paid would not be handled so easily.

One look around the table confirmed that the men were united in their distrust of him. But the distrust was mutual. There was one difference. He was Kiowa. He would not relent.

Pete returned to the room, carrying another platter. Pete was an old-timer on the Circle C who obviously felt as much a part of the spread as Stan himself. He was difficult to read. His consistently gruff manner did not allow the true depth of his feelings to be judged.

Horton and Pitts were two quiet fellows who left no doubt as to their feelings about him. Everything he did was suspect in their eyes.

Treacher's opinion of him had been clear from the first. His animosity and his mouth were bound to get him in trouble sooner or later.

Rome was a crack shot, capable of bringing down a rider with a single bullet. And he was too quiet, too watchful.

Carter's jealousy was a furious force. Despite his youthful appearance, he was dangerous.

Buck was loyal to the Circle C and everyone on it, but otherwise the man was a puzzle, despising him one minute and tolerating him the next.

All were hard men. And all were capable of acts of violence if the circumstances demanded.

Which one?

He could feel the hatred building.

He needed to know.

Night had fallen.

Purity lay awake in her bed. She heard her door open and she waited.

A shadowed outline . . . a glint of russet skin . . .

Cass slid in beside her and she turned into his arms.

Night had fallen. Whispers hissed on the shadows.

"Did you hear what that half-breed said?"

"I heard him."

"He knows, I tell you."

Silence.

"That's why he sent for a Ranger!"

No reply.

"If we're goin' to do somethin', we're goin' to have to do it quick."

"I know."

"He won't give up, I tell you!"

"I know!"

"We can't afford to wait!"

"You're right.

"When?"

Chapter Eleven

It was a beautiful morning. The sky seemed a brighter hue than Julia had ever seen it, and the sun more brilliant.

Julia stood in the small bedroom that she and Jack shared. She remembered the love she had felt flow silently between them as they had lain side by side.

Yes . . . love.

She smoothed the surface of the bed and looked around her. The room was neat and spotless, the coverlet cheerful, the pillows fluffed and ready to welcome a weary head. Jack's spare change of clothing hung freshly washed on the hooks in the corner.

Julia nodded with satisfaction.

Walking slowly down the stairs to the main floor minutes later, she surveyed the other rooms with the same critical eye, knowing that freshly baked bread lay on the kitchen table, that vegetables had been prepared on the kitchen stove, and that the smokehouse was stocked with meat. Yes, everything was ready to welcome the men home.

Julia approached the small desk in the corner of the living room with trepidation. She glanced at the envelope she had placed there an hour earlier. She touched it with her fingertips, her throat tightening as she remembered the difficulty she had had in composing the letter inside.

It was so difficult to say good-bye.

The pounding in her head began anew, and Julia briefly closed her eyes, realizing that she had needed that reminder as her determination momentarily weakened. She glanced upward, offering a silent prayer of gratitude for that guidance.

Her step steady, Julia approached the door. She picked up the bonnet lying on the chair nearby and put it on, careful not to tie it too tight lest the pounding increase. She allowed herself a last, lingering glance at the room behind her, then picked up the suitcase near her feet and walked outside, closing the door behind her.

The wagon was waiting where she had left it at the hitching post, and Julia placed her suitcase in the back. She climbed up onto the driver's seat, a sob she could not suppress sounding deep in her chest, despite herself. Forcing her chin high, she controlled the flood brimming in her eyes. She was leaving, never to return, but her distress did not stem from her own sorrow. What truly pained her was the torment she knew Jack would suffer when he returned with the men at the end of the day and found her gone. She regretted that almost as much as she regretted leaving. Her only consolation was in the thought that his anguish would be temporary as compared to what he would suffer if she stayed.

Dear Jack . . .

She loved him so.

With a snap of the reins, Julia set the wagon into motion.

"You ain't my boss! I ain't doin' it!"

"Nash!" The reproach in Purity's tone was lost on the furious wrangler as he faced Cass angrily. The Circle C wranglers halted in their work beside a rough corral of bawling calves, watching as the two men squared off.

Purity strode toward them. She should have expected it. Nash had come in from the bunkhouse for breakfast that morning at the exact moment she had started down the stairs with Cass descending directly behind her. She had regretted that lapse of caution the moment she had seen his face. Nash had been silent through breakfast, but his silence had not lasted long. The tension had erupted into conflict with the first order Cass had given him and had increased along with the heat of the day until relations between them had reached the boiling point.

Purity snapped sharply, "I won't stand for this, Nash."

Nash turned toward her, fury blazing. "I ain't takin' this fella's orders, Purity, and that's the way it is!"

"You think not?" His anger barely controlled, Cass grated, "You'll take my orders, or you won't be taking anybody's orders here—not anymore!"

"You can't fire me. I don't work for you!" Not a trace of intimidation evident in his demeanor, Nash faced the bigger man boldly. "I work for Stan, just like I've been workin' for him for the past eight years! I earned my place on this ranch. I didn't come in here, makin' threats and pushin' my weight around like you! And I didn't come in here takin' advantage of somebody who don't have no choice but to let you stay!"

Cass took a quick step forward that was halted as Purity snapped, "No, Cass! Please . . ."

Grasping Cass's arm, she felt the rage shuddering through him as he rasped, "No, not this time . . . not even for you."

"Cass . . ." Purity's voice dropped to a low plea. "Give me a chance to straighten this out."

"Don't you go beggin' him for me!" Struggling to shake off Buck's restraint, Nash continued hotly, "Let's settle this thing here and now!"

"No!" Her eyes blazing, Purity reiterated, "The answer is *no*, do you hear me, Nash? I won't have our workday interrupted for battles among ourselves. There's too much to do with all the things that have been happenin', and I'm not goin' to let anyone fall into the trap that someone seems to have done such a good job of setting."

"Someone?" Nash sneered. "You're holdin' the arm

of that *someone,* and everybody here knows that but you."

Her face suddenly flaming, Purity grated, "Really? But *I'm* the one who counts here, because *I'm* the boss, and *I give the orders!*"

A small smile twitched at Nash's lips. "That's all right with me. I'll take your orders any day of the week."

Purity realized she had stepped into a trap of her own making.

Glancing at Cass, she saw the fury he concealed behind the ice in his gaze. She released his arm, abruptly aware how little her restraining hand had meant in terms of physical control as she turned toward the silent wrangler standing a few feet away.

"Horton, I want you and Nash to ride out to check the property line again. I don't want a single head with a Circle C brand strayin' over it." She added in afterthought, "Make sure you keep a sharp lookout on the way."

Turning back, Purity saw the resentment in Nash's expression. She replied to it coldly. "Don't say it, Nash. You go where I send you. *I'm* the boss here, remember?"

Purity saw the rapid heaving of Nash's chest. She saw the grievance he did not express. She felt the pain of it, and she regretted it with all her heart as she ordered, "Get goin'."

The dust raised by Nash's furious departure was still billowing as Purity turned to meet Cass's cold expression. She knew what it said. It said that he had compromised for the last time.

Cass turned abruptly away. He picked up a branding iron and ordered, "Treacher . . . Pitts, get those calves ready. Buck . . . Baird, check those irons. Rome, scout up some more fuel for those fires. They're practically cold." The taut lines of his face tightened. "We're going to get every one of these calves branded before we leave here today!"

Purity kept her silence for the long second before the men moved to do his bidding.

And Purity knew.

The time had come to make a choice.

"What in hell is this?"

Roger slapped the sheet of carefully tabulated columns down on Walter Graham's desk. Saliva sprayed from his mouth with the vehemence of his words as he leaned toward the senior bank clerk and spat, "These aren't the figures I asked you for! I want the deposits for *last* month, not *this* month!"

"Y . . . you asked me for this month's deposits, sir."

"Are you challenging me?" Roger leaned closer to the cringing employee. "Are you tired of your job, is that it, Graham?"

"No, sir."

"Then get me the figures I asked for!"

Looking up, Roger became acutely aware of the disapproving looks of bank customers standing nearby—Elizabeth Flagg, the overweight, homely housefrau that she was; Homer Williams, a debt-ridden rancher who had the nerve to frown; Marjorie Perkins, the haughty wife of Jonathan Perkins, owner of the town's mercantile establishment. His sneer deepened. He didn't care what they or anybody else thought!

Storming back to his office, Roger slammed the door behind himself and walked to the window. He scanned the street, still trembling from an inner agitation he could not seem to shake. Suddenly aware of the tall, feminine figure he was unconsciously seeking, he cursed aloud.

Witch! He was obsessed with her!

Roger took a shuddering breath, then raked a trembling hand through hair that already showed the results of several previous such assaults. A night of restless twisting and turning had followed another frustrating evening at Sophie's, where her most experienced girl had been unable to provide him the release he had been seeking. His male organ had lain limp and useless in those experienced hands, just as it now lagged in his trousers, just as it remained immune to any manner of arousal other than the thought or sight of a particular long-legged, golden-haired witch.

Frustrated beyond his endurance, he had again taken solace in a bottle of brandy, which had resulted in a painful, tardy awakening that had not allowed time for his morning visit to the barber. He had not even noticed that his fine white shirt was spotted from the previous day's wear. So foul was his mood, he did not care that his jacket was stained from the profuse perspiration that had plagued him all morning long, that his trousers had lost their crease, and that in his headlong rush to the office he had stepped in a particularly large patch of canine excrement that was still stuck to the bottom of his shoe. The worst torment was brought by the thought that as he suffered his rapacious need, Purity was lying in the arms of another man—a common, arrogant half-breed whom she had chosen over him!

Roger paused at that thought, the reason for his obsession suddenly clear. Purity Corrigan was the only woman who had ever provided the slightest challenge to his mastery. She was the only woman who even approached being his match. She was . . . the only woman for him.

Roger's thoughts drew to a halt at the sound of a familiar step outside his door. He turned toward it as the door was thrust open to reveal his father's rotund figure. Closing the door behind him with a sharp click, Willard Norris approached him slowly.

"Are you insane?" His expression rabid, Willard Norris continued with increasing vehemence, "Do you realize the public spectacle you made of yourself a few minutes ago?"

"Spectacle?" Roger's short laugh was tight. "Who was there to witness it? Just a fat, homely housewife and—"

"—and Marjorie Perkins, the biggest gossip in town!"

"I don't care what she thinks . . . or what anyone else thinks!"

"Well, *I do*!" His gaze scathing, Willard Norris spat, "Look at yourself! Your grooming is appalling! Your clothing is wrinkled and unclean! And . . . what is that smell?" Willard looked down at his son's feet, his eyes narrowing in sudden realization. "Revolting!"

Roger took a spontaneous step backward. "I had a restless night and I awoke late this morning."

"From the look of your eyes and the smell of your breath, you slept with a bottle!"

Roger's gaze narrowed. "Whoever or *whatever* I take to my bed is my business!"

"No, it isn't, it's mine!" Advancing aggressively, Willard Norris halted only inches away, close enough that Roger could feel the heat of his father's quivering bulk as the older man poked his face into his and grated, "It's that woman, isn't it?"

Roger shook his head. "I . . . I don't know what you mean."

"Don't lie to me!" Livid, Willard Norris hissed, "I saw the way you look at Purity Corrigan. You're obsessed with her! Damned fool that you are, you've allowed your carnal desires to overwhelm your good sense until you can think of nothing but her!" Pausing, he grated, "I never thought you could be such a fool."

Allowing a moment for the full impact of his words to be felt, the elder Norris ordered, "Handle it! Do whatever you have to do to get your satisfaction with that woman! Bring her to her knees, then chew her up, spit her out, and grind her into the dirt with your heel . . . and then move on! This is not a suggestion, Roger. It's a warning. Straighten yourself out, and do it now! I will not accept less!"

The massive rolls of his chest heaving, Willard Norris stepped back. "Get out of here . . . now! Clean yourself up and make your choice, but don't come back to this bank tomorrow in this same sorry state. Because, son or not, I'll throw you out on your ear if you do!" The elder Norris paused, his gaze tightening, "Heed what I say. I won't warn you again."

Twitching in the aftermath of his father's verbal assault, Roger watched him leave the office as abruptly as he had come.

Roger's twitching increased as he stared at the door his father had closed behind him.

"Corpulent ass . . . malevolent brute . . ."

Roger snatched his hat off the stand nearby. Yes, he'd leave now. He'd clean himself up and he'd make his plans.

Roger paused at the door, a decision made. And he'd make sure that if he couldn't have Purity, no one else would.

Jack sat his horse wearily as the animal plodded forward. He did not have to look at the men riding beside him to see that they were as tired as he. They had all had a particularly difficult day. A rampaging bull, a dead horse . . . He had known that bull was a bad one, but he was still uncertain what had made it attack. The animal had charged them when they approached. The herd had panicked and bolted, blocking the retreat of Walsh's mount, and when the bull charged again, Walsh was trapped.

Jack sighed. He knew he'd never forget the sound of that gelding's agonized whinny when the bull's horns ripped into his chest.

They had finally gotten the bull under control, but

there had been no saving Walsh's mount. A good, hardworking animal lost. The incident had cast a pall over the entire day. He despised such waste.

As the ranch house came into view, Jack raised his head. He squinted into the distance, then scanned the horizon, a knot slowly forming inside him. Everything seemed normal . . . except there was no smoke coming from the house chimney.

That was strange. Julia should be cooking. It was a source of particular pride to her to have the evening meal ready when they returned.

Jack spurred his horse forward.

The house was silent when he entered, and Jack's heart began a heavy pounding. He walked toward the kitchen.

"Julia?" He walked faster. "Julia?"

Upstairs in a few racing steps, he called again. He was descending the stairs, panic beginning to invade his senses when he saw an envelope on the corner desk. He had it in his hand when he saw Holmes standing anxiously in the doorway.

"Did you find her?"

He shook his head, somehow unable to respond as he ripped open the envelope. Julia's neat, even hand leaped up at him and Jack's throat choked tight. Lowering himself into the nearest chair, he read:

"Dearest Jack,

It is so difficult to say good-bye. But the time has come for total honesty, something that has been neglected between us in recent years. I know the truth will cause you pain. I fear it will anger you and make you think poorly of me. I can only hope that time will temper any ill feelings that may result, and you will remember that all I did, I did because I love you. That truth has never changed, dearest Jack. It never will.

First, I must thank you for the invaluable wealth you bestowed upon me—a wealth of love and joy, of expectation and fulfillment. I had never expected to know a man's love when we met. You gave that to me so selflessly. I could not bear a child, and you gave me yours to cherish. There was not an hour of the day during our lives together when I did not realize the true worth of those gifts. I strove to repay you for them in all I did. Sadly, I failed you.

I cannot say I truly recall the exact moment when I realized you had found Whispering Woman again. There was no change in the quality of love you gave me. But the sadness and the torment . . . dear Jack, I saw it in your eyes! I felt it expand within you. I tried so hard to believe I was wrong.

Disclosure came in the oddest way. Do you remember the fair we attended several years back? You didn't see the traveling man who sat briefly in the empty chair beside me while you and Cass competed in the games. He was a friendly fellow who enjoyed talking. He didn't know who I was, but he remembered you and Cass. He said he had seen you both at a Kiowa village the last time he was there. He said that you and he were a pair that would be difficult to forget, and he remarked that when he saw the *three* of you together, the resemblance between Cass and his mother was notable. He described her so clearly to me that I almost felt I could see her. He told me she was beautiful and that her name suited her because she spoke in a voice barely above a whisper. I knew she could be no other.

The traveling man left before you both returned to my side, and in that moment, I accepted fully the future course of my deception.

I cannot tell you how difficult it often was to receive your praise, to hear you say that I was generous and kind when I knew I was not. I knew you kept Whispering Woman's return to your life a secret from me with noble purpose, that your gentle heart would not allow you to take from me the life I had embraced so wholly. The motives for my duplicity were not as virtuous. I was selfish because I could not bear to surrender the life you had given me. I was deceitful in allowing you to believe I was ignorant of the truth. I was unkind in allowing others to suffer for their generosity toward me. And I was cowardly, because I did not believe I could face living without you.

Even in this moment of reckoning, I cannot claim honor, my dearest. Rather, the Lord made his choice known to me, and I have but embraced it and the opportunity He has given me for redemption.

You see, I am dying, Jack. I recognized the

symptoms gradually manifesting themselves—
the headaches I could not escape, the weakening
and trembling of my limbs, the nausea. My father had described the manner of my mother's
death to me as a warning, since my grandmother died in the same way. I denied the signs
until it was impossible to escape the truth any
longer. Strangely, I was almost relieved when
Dr. Zimmer confirmed my condition, and it was
then that I accepted the Lord's hand in all that
had come about.

It was then that I wrote to the ministry with
which my father was loosely affiliated. I knew
the Lord would provide for me to discover his
whereabouts, despite the years that had elapsed
since we were in communication, just as I knew
that part of His plan was that my father would
still be alive and that he would accept me back
wholeheartedly and agree to provide care for me
until the end.

Do not worry about me, Jack. I will be well.
Please absolve yourself of any unwarranted
guilts. Your goodness did not warrant the needless pain I caused you. Whispering Woman did
not deserve to have her place usurped by a
woman lacking her inner strength and benevo-
lent spirit. Cass should have been spared the
pain of denying his mother to the world when
she was returned to him so miraculously, and
he should not have been made to suffer the hardship of torn loyalties because of the affection he
had grown to feel for me.

Purity

Dearest Jack, I realize now that we were not intended to be together to the end. The life you gave me was a precious and unexpected gift which I accepted joyfully, but which I was not meant to keep.

Please explain all this to Cass, and tell him I treasure the love he gave me, more than he will ever know. Tell him that it was one of the greatest joys of my life to call him son, and that in my heart he will always be my son. And, tell him, please, that I beg his forgiveness.

My final request of you is a difficult one, Jack. Whatever your reaction to this letter, however conflicting your emotions, please allow me to take this final step out of your life. Please grant me this opportunity for atonement, and remember that I take it, however belatedly, with love.

I will ask my father to contact you when the time comes. It should not be too long. I await that time fearlessly now, unburdened and filled with loving memories that will sustain me.

You gave me so much, Jack. You gave me a home, a son, a life that was beautiful beyond my fondest imaginings, but greatest of all your gifts was your love. I will cherish the memory of it all my life. Thank you. Forgive me if you can. I will always love you.

> Your wife,
> Julia"

"What's the matter, Jack?"
Jack did not acknowledge Holmes's inquiry as the

frowning foreman stood in the doorway. With tears trailing down his cheeks, he was unaware of the moment when the fellow stepped back slowly, then drew the door closed behind him. Overwhelmed by pain almost more than he could bear, he could do no more than lower his face into his hands.

Another sundown.
Another night.
But this night was painfully different.

Purity lay abed, waiting for the sound of Cass's step. Stan had retired to his bedroom at the rear of the living room hours earlier. The tension in the house was too much for him. It was beginning to wear him down. She knew the greatest tension came from the men's resentment of Cass. Working side by side for seasons on end, the men had become too close not to stand united. The clash between Cass and Nash that morning had been a turning point. She had seen it in their eyes then as they recognized the possibility that she might actually turn against them.

And then there was Cass . . . His silent conviction that one of the Circle C men was responsible for the death of his brother did not waver. He would suffer no one and nothing to stand in the way of justice. The men felt that threat. They would not tolerate it much longer.

Purity reached unconsciously for her locket. She felt closer than ever to her sisters because of Cass. She felt their presence more warmly. She had seen the past clearly and was now able to look toward the future with renewed confidence that she would meet them again someday. But she also realized that this was a time when she could not allow herself to wonder what Honesty would do, or how Chastity's gentle soul would react. This decision was hers alone to make.

Purity's thoughts came to an abrupt halt at the sound of Cass on the stairs. She heard no hesitation when he reached the landing and turned toward her door.

Sitting up in bed as Cass approached, Purity followed his progress toward her in the semidarkness. Yes, she loved him. His gaze met hers and his mouth softened as he reached up to unbutton his shirt.

The ache within her almost more than she could bear, Purity whispered, "No, Cass. Don't do that."

His hand stilled.

"It's no good," she went on, "You know that as well as I do. We were able to separate our tomorrows from today for a little while, but the hours have a way of catching up. We can't avoid them any longer."

Cass took a step closer. "This time is ours alone, Purity."

"No." Purity's throat choked tight. "I can't pretend anymore, Cass. I can't be one person when I lie in your arms, and another when daylight dawns."

"I don't understand . . ."

"I'm tellin' you I love you, Cass. But lovin' you won't work in this time and place. Too much stands between us. The men on this ranch have given Stan years of loyalty. They supported me when neither Stan nor I had much to offer them, and they deserve

367

the same loyalty in return. I can't stand by, pretending I don't know that each word out of their mouths is being measured by you, that you're laying those words side by side in your mind as stepping stones on a path toward vengeance. I can't betray them like that!"

"Is justice betrayal?"

"I don't know." Purity shook her head, tears brimming. "But what I do know is that I can't be a part of it."

"You aren't."

"Yes, I am. The men feel it. I feel it."

"What are you saying?"

"I'm sayin' I can't take you into my bed at night and pretend at first light of dawn that those hours when we lie together have no influence on me at all. They do. They're colorin' the way I regard my men . . . and the way they regard me."

"No . . ."

"And I'm sayin' I can no more ask you to abandon what you believe you must do than you can ask me."

"Purity . . ."

"Please Cass"—Purity took a shuddering breath—"I want you to leave."

She saw the sudden slump of Cass's shoulders. She felt the yearning that reached out to her with an almost palpable force as he whispered, "I don't want to go."

"Oh, Cass, don't you see . . . ?" Purity's voice broke on a sob. "I don't want you to go, either." When Cass took another step toward her, she appealed softly, "Please . . ."

The shadows of the room shifted, allowing her a glimpse of Cass's expression. She read in it an anguish that matched her own.

The next moment he was gone.

The night shadows undulated in the breeze. They played against the figure moving stealthily at the rear of the Circle C ranch house. They allowed a shaft of moonlight brief passage to illuminate a face tight with malevolent determination as Roger cautiously scanned the yard.

His heart pounding with an excitement that was strangely exhilarating, Roger studied the bunkhouse, dismissing the possibility of threat there. He had seen the light dim, had waited until there had been no sound or movement within for more than two hours.

Approaching the ranch house, Roger glanced upward toward Purity's bedroom, his lips tightening. The house had darkened even earlier. He had allowed mental images of Purity readying herself for bed to play across his mind in the time since. He had indulged them with an enjoyment untinged by bitterness, because he knew that whatever the outcome of this night, neither the Circle C nor Purity Corrigan would ever be the same.

Roger smiled, steadying his grip on the oversized metal containers he carried. He had been cautious, leaving his mount and pack horse hidden a distance away where they could be neither seen nor heard. He had approached the house with the stealth of a hunter, because that was his mission this night . . . to hunt down his prey.

Roger's smile broadened. Yes, he had wasted time in the petty harassment of the Circle C that he had ordered over the past few weeks. It had netted him more aggravation than satisfaction. He wondered why it had taken him so long to realize that the step he now took would provide instant retribution for the indignities he had suffered. He consoled himself that it would only be a little while longer before those indignities were razed from his mind forever.

The darkness enveloped Roger as he reached the rear of the house. His smile became a leer as he uncapped the first container and splashed kerosene against the wooden frame. He was liberal in his dousing, generously saturating the dry wood before continuing a steady path around the house. He emptied one container, then opened another, cursing under his breath as he rounded the final corner to discover that he would have to be less extravagant if he hoped for full coverage.

Done at last, Roger stood back for a final look at the darkened structure. How many years was it that Stan Corrigan bragged his house had been standing? Twenty? Twenty-five? Roger shrugged. It was of little consequence. It would not be standing much longer.

Roger withdrew a newspaper from his pocket. He rolled several sheets tightly into thick wands. His hand trembling with excitement, he struck a match to the first one. His eyes widened as the flame caught. The thrill that chased down his spine emerged from his lips in a choked laugh as he tossed it against the rear wall of the house.

Combustion was instantaneous. The flames raced across the base of the house, barely allowing him time to reach the next side to strike another match.

Glorious! Magnificent!

Roger ran to the front to toss another blazing wand, then to the fourth side of the house to follow the fiery kerosene trail.

The flames rose higher, licking up at the darkness, and Roger was possessed of sudden glee. He wanted to shout, "Are you sleeping now, Purity!" He wanted to deride, "Do you think you have beaten me now, Stan Corrigan!"

But instead, he snatched up his empty containers and slipped back into the shadows.

Purity coughed. She moved restlessly. She came slowly awake to the realization that her room was filled with smoke.

She heard the crackle of flames. She felt the heat. She saw the terrifying glow at her window.

On her feet in a moment, Purity stumbled toward the door. Her eyes burned. Her throat ached. Her chest was so heavy that she could hardly breathe.

Smoke barreled into the room as she opened the door, and a stunning reality was suddenly clear. The entire house was ablaze!

She staggered forward weakly and was caught by a strong hand. Looking up, she recognized Cass's broad outline in the smoke, but she could not see his face.

She reached for him.

* * *

"Purity . . ."

Purity fell limply against him as Cass struggled for breath. He had gone directly to his room after Purity's emotional appeal hours earlier. Pacing for hours, he had battled the conflicts within, finally lying down atop the bed, where he had awakened what seemed moments later to see smoke filtering through his window. He had been on his feet in a moment.

Clutching Purity's limp form closely, Cass glanced into her room to see that it was densely filled with smoke and that flames licked at her windows. She had almost been overcome.

"Purity?"

Purity looked up and Cass felt her response. His heart racing, he slipped his arm around her and turned toward the staircase. He felt her determined effort to support herself as they descended blindly. He heard her rasping whisper as they neared the first floor. He felt her pull toward the rear of the house, muttering Stan's name as they stepped onto the bottom landing, but he drew her relentlessly toward the door.

Intense heat . . . flames leaping higher . . . smoke thickening, obscuring his path . . .

He wavered, suddenly uncertain of his direction.

He heard shouting, then a crashing sound as the front door was thrust open. Smoke billowed toward the opening, briefly directing him as he locked his arm around Purity and moved forward in a rush.

He heard shouts as he burst out into the open. He felt Purity's sagging form pulled from the possessive circle of his arm the moment before he fell to his knees, gasping for air. Beside him, Purity was struggling for breath, her face blackened with smoke. She grasped Pete's arm as he crouched over her, gasping, "Stan is still inside!"

But Buck was already at the door. Glancing over his shoulder, Cass saw him disappear within the smoke. He saw Carter follow as the flames encircling the structure leaped ever higher.

Coughing, Cass drew himself to his feet. His strength rapidly returning, he shouted to the men forming a water brigade nearby, "The house is lost! Saturate the front entrance. That's Buck's only chance to get Stan out!"

The men scrambled to do his bidding, halting briefly as two figures stumbled out through the doorway. Squinting against a sudden firestorm of stinging sparks, Cass dashed forward to relieve Buck of Stan's weight as he staggered.

Purity struggled to his side when he laid Stan's limp form on the ground. Beside him, he saw Buck sag to his knees. He heard him rasp in a voice hardly audible over the escalating roar of the fire, "Nash went down . . . he's still in there . . ."

On his feet, Cass looked at the flaming structure. He reacted instinctively, unaware that Baird was at his heels as he dashed inside.

Smoke stung his eyes, blinding him.

Heat seared his lungs, stealing his breath.

His foot struck a soft object on the floor and Cass stumbled. Baird appeared beside him in the smoke and Cass grasped his arm, rasping, "Carter's over here. Help me get him out."

Gasping . . . straining . . . the door only inches away.

Breaking out into the open at last, Cass heard shouted words he could not quite comprehend as Carter was wrenched from his grip. Baird staggered out beside him and they both fell to their knees beyond the reach of the flames. Cass strained for breath, his chest heaving. He heard Purity beside him. He felt her arms encircle him. He heard tearful words, incoherent words as she clutched him close.

Stan's violent coughing brought Purity back to his side. His mind again clear, Cass drew himself to his feet and glanced around him. Carter was lying nearby. His eyes were closed, his boyish face was blackened with smoke . . . but he was breathing. The house was completely engulfed by flames now. The roof swayed in a deadly dance as it was consumed before it crashed to the ground in a blaze of glittering sparks.

Momentarily overwhelmed, Cass glanced away, his averted gaze coming to an abrupt halt on a figure moving in the darkness just beyond the rim of light.

He strained his eyes.

He could not be certain—

The flames surged brightly, briefly illuminating the face of the man concealed in the shadows as he turned, then faded into the darkness.

"Cass . . ." Purity was again at his side. "Stan's having trouble breathing. I'm afraid."

Cass turned to the men nearby, commanding

gruffly, "The house is lost! Forget it! Rome . . . Pitts . . . Treacher, get started wetting down the bunkhouse. Horton, get the wagon! Pete, get blankets and a pillow from the bunkhouse so we can take Stan to a doctor. And get something for Purity to put on." He glanced at Carter; the young fellow still labored for breath. "Get a blanket for Carter, too. We're taking him with us."

Cass kneeled beside Stan as he struggled to speak. He urged, "Don't waste your breath trying to talk, Stan. Purity and I will get you to a doctor as fast as we can."

Unable to discern Stan's insistent reply, Cass leaned closer. "I can't hear you."

"I said . . ." Stan fought for breath. "D . . . don't tell me not to talk when I've somethin' to say!" Stan's hand clamped over his arm when he attempted to draw back. Cass heard him add with a breathless rasp, "Thanks."

The wagon rattled up beside them. Cass felt Purity press close against his side as he ordered, "All right, let's go!"

"Buck, bang on that door and wake up the doctor! Tell him we're bringing Stan and Carter in now."

Darkness prevailed on the street of the sleeping town as Buck sprang wordlessly to his bidding. Jumping down from the driver's seat, Cass secured the reins before turning to the back of the wagon. Their anxious entourage had traveled from the ranch as quickly as the moonlit trail and their passengers' safety would allow. Driving with Buck seated beside him, with Purity and Pete installed between Stan and Carter's prostrate forms in the back of the wagon, they had maintained a tense silence. Once they'd arrived in town, they had driven directly to the doctor's office.

Purity spoke softly as Cass approached, her smoke-blackened face still streaked from tears now held tightly in check. "Nash is feelin' better, but Stan's still havin' trouble breathin'."

Cass looked up at Pete. "We'll take Stan in first."

Still buttoning his trousers, the doctor met them at the door. He frowned, directing them to a cot in the rear as he questioned gruffly, "What in hell happened?"

"A fire . . . the house is gone."

Purity's halting reply tightened the knot within Cass as they settled Stan nearby. Determination quickened his step as he returned to the wagon to see that Carter had pulled himself up to a seated position. Carter drew back as Cass reached for his arm, but his voice was devoid of its former hostility as he said, "I'm all right. I can make it by myself."

Waiting in silence until Carter was standing steady, Cass returned to Purity's side, and they watched from a corner of the room as the doctor worked over Stan. Uncaring that Buck and Pete stood closeby, that Carter observed through slitted eyes, Cass slid his arms around Purity and drew her back against him. She leaned into him, and Cass lent her his strength.

Purity stiffened in his arms as the doctor halted his examination and turned toward her, his expression unreadable. Cass felt the new trembling that began within her the moment before the doctor shook his head. "Don't let this old goat fool you. He isn't going to die yet. All he needs is a little less excitement and a little more fresh air, and he'll be all right."

Cass sensed the sob Purity withheld. He knew the physical effort she expended when she drew herself erect and approached Stan slowly. He watched as Purity crouched beside Stan and took his hand.

Retreating, waiting only until Purity began speaking softly to Stan, Cass slipped out the door.

Cass walked silently along the darkened street, seething with cold fury as fragmented facts flashed through his mind: The fire . . . hot and searing . . . immediately intense; the ring of flames totally encircling the house; the unmistakable odor of kerosene.

Yes, it had been a simple plan.

Arriving at the edge of town, Cass approached the bachelor's quarters he sought . . . reputedly filled with all the luxuries that money would allow. He walked to the rear of the house, tested a window, then slipped inside. Slivers of moonlight lit a silver path toward the parlor, where Cass paused, looking at the staircase to the upstairs bedrooms. He took a step forward that was halted abruptly by a familiar voice from the darkness.

"So, you're here at last."

Roger stepped out of the shadows, his eyes eerily bright, the gun in his hand glinting in the meager light as he held it leveled at Cass's chest. He continued malevolently, "You really are an ignorant savage, aren't you? You didn't need to come in the window. I left the door conveniently open for you and you didn't even try it." He snickered softly, "Did you really believe I was stupid enough not to realize you saw me at the fire tonight? Did you really think I'd be fool enough to come back here and go right to my bed, pretending I knew nothing about it?"

Roger took a step closer, his refined features rigid with hatred. "You thought you'd be in your element here, didn't you? Sneaking around in the darkness is natural to your breed!"

Refusing to be bated, Cass remained silent as Roger gave a short laugh. "What? Nothing to say? Why? Because you played right into my hands? Because you provided me with the perfect opportunity to claim that you sneaked in here in the middle of the night with deadly intentions and that I shot you in self-defense? Not even that Texas Ranger you sent for will be able to dispute it!"

Roger rasped, "I'm untouchable! I always have been! My father will lend his influence and the sheriff will back me up on anything I say! And when all is said and done, Purity will eventually come to me." Pausing, Roger added with rancor, "I want you to picture it—Purity lying naked in my arms . . . willing . . . receptive to my every whim . . . giving me everything she ever gave to you . . . and giving more, *much* more . . ." A snort of laughter escaped his lips. "Picture it, damn you! I want that picture to be your last thought!"

Anticipating the moment, Cass leaped sideways into the shadows as Roger pulled the trigger and a gunshot shattered the silence. The sound rebounded as Roger fired again, then again.

Gasping aloud, Cass hit the floor with a resounding thud.

"Fool! Did you really think you could get away?"

Silence.

His gun poised, Roger started forward. "Bastard . . . where are you?"

Springing at him from the darkness, Cass hit Roger with the full weight of his body, pinning him to the ground at the same moment he swept his knife from his waist. His heart pounding, Cass pressed the blade to Roger's throat and spat, "You were right after all, Norris. Stealth is natural to my breed. I *am* in my element in the darkness."

His eyes bulging, his heart hammering, Roger gulped. Cass felt the tremors of fear that coursed through Roger's shuddering body as he rasped, "Your plan almost succeeded, Norris. A few minutes longer and Purity might have been overcome by the smoke in her room. I might not have been able to find her in time." Cass took a breath. "Bastard . . . you lit the fire under her window first, didn't you! You splashed kerosene around the base of the house, but you almost ran out by the time you reached the side of the house where I was sleeping. You didn't know which room I was in, did you, Norris? Or maybe you didn't know I was sleeping upstairs at all. That was your mistake . . . because the smoke wasn't as heavy in my room. I wasn't as badly affected as Purity, and I was able to bring her out safely."

His blood pumping hotly, Cass spat, "Bastard . . .

you wanted her and you couldn't have her, so you tried to kill her!" He paused, continuing with scathing intensity, "You failed . . . but I won't. You called me a half-breed. Yes, that's what I am, and that's what I want *you* to remember. I want *your* last thought to be that it's a half-breed's knife that you feel at your throat, that it's a half-breed's blade that will make your blood flow—"

"No, Cass, please!"

Cass stiffened at the sound of Purity's voice. He pressed the knife tighter to Roger's throat as he turned to see Purity in the doorway with Buck beside her. He ordered sharply, "Get out of here, Purity!"

"No, I won't!" Beside him, Purity made no attempt to strike away his blade as she whispered, "Pete saw Roger at the fire, too. He didn't want to say anythin' because he was afraid of what you'd do. He went to get the sheriff. He'll be here in a minute." Tears suddenly filled her eyes as she rasped, "Don't do this, Cass. Roger will win out after all, if you do. As much as I love you, it won't make any difference because the damage will be done!" Cass heard the ragged breath Purity took as she rasped, "He isn't worth it, Cass! Please, don't let him win."

Rage pounded through Cass's veins. He looked down at the man lying rigidly beneath him. Shuddering with fear, his color ashen, Norris was frozen into immobility as Cass pressed his knife closer. . . .

Muttering a low curse, Cass released him abruptly. He stood up, dragging Norris to his feet beside him. He glanced with contempt at the rank stain that marked the crotch of Norris's trousers, then thrust him toward Sheriff Boyle when the lawman appeared in the doorway.

Roger drew himself erect, fighting to conceal his visible shuddering as he addressed the sheriff shrilly. "I want you to arrest this man, sheriff! He broke into my house and tried to kill me! He—"

"Save your breath, *Mr.* Norris!" Cutting him off abruptly, the sheriff continued, "Pete told me what you done, and as far as I'm concerned, you was only gettin' what you deserved! There's no way you're goin' to talk your way out of this one."

"I demand you call my father! I demand—"

A shove from the sheriff halted Roger's protest, moving him out of sight as Cass turned toward Purity. He slipped his arm around her, claiming her for all to see as he drew her with him toward the door.

Out on the street a new dawn was shedding its pale light over the town. Cass waited only a few minutes before he turned to Buck abruptly. The honesty and revelations of the moments past seemed to call for one more confession.

"You did it, didn't you, Buck?"

Leaning against Cass's side, Purity was startled by his unexpected question. She glanced between Cass and Buck, realization dawning as Buck held his direct gaze. She caught her breath, her thoughts confirmed as Cass pressed, "You know what happened to Flying Eagle."

Buck did not respond.

"Why did you do it?" Cass spoke softly, without

381

emotion. "Flying Eagle wasn't much more than a boy."

"He was a man, and he had a gun!"

Purity's eyes closed briefly, a sickening feeling twisting inside her as Cass responded, "Flying Eagle wouldn't have hurt anyone."

Surprising him, Buck hesitated in reply. His lined face drew tight as he shook his head. "I don't know. That may be so. It all happened real fast . . . in the space of a few minutes. I was ridin' towards the remuda when I saw some steers wanderin' off. I chased after them and got separated from the herd, and that's when I saw an Injun drivin' off some of our stock. I hollered out and he started the steers runnin', and when I started after him, he turned and fired." Buck paused. "He missed. I didn't."

Purity felt the jolt that shuddered through Cass, as if Buck's bullet had struck him as well. His arm dropped away from her. She sensed his body tensing as Buck continued, "He was dead when I rode up. I figured there might be trouble because I knew there was a powwow goin' on thereabouts, so I dragged the body off where nobody would see it right away."

The sickening ache within Purity became true pain as Buck looked at her, his voice thickening. "I'm sorry, Purity. I figured it would be best if you didn't know." He turned back to Cass without waiting for her reply. "Purity was with Pete at the chuck wagon, helpin' him fix a wheel. My horse had been limpin', so she had let me use hers to get another one from the remuda. I was ridin' it when everythin' happened. Right afterward, I got another horse like I originally rode out to do. I took Purity's back to her as quick as I could. She was still workin' on the wheel with Pete. She hardly knew I was gone."

Buck glanced at Pete, who had come to stand a short distance away. Pete shrugged. "Buck told me what happened after Purity left. I went out with him later and we buried the body."

Purity saw the remorse that twisted Buck's lips as he addressed Cass directly. "I'm sorry. I can't argue right or wrong about what happened. I can only tell you the way it happened. I didn't see no choice but to fire back when them bullets came flyin' by me, and with so much at stake here on the Circle C, and with Stan dependin' on that cattle drive, I couldn't afford to take a chance reportin' what happened." Buck paused. "When you rode up and dragged Purity from her horse and I saw you with a knife to her throat, I figured that powwow was breedin' bad blood for the white man, and that the best thing we could do would be to get away from the area as fast as we could."

"Buck . . ." Purity's voice was anguished. "Why didn't you tell me what happened?"

Buck tried to smile. "What good would it have done, darlin'? It was over and done, and there was no changin' it. As far as I could see, the best thing to do was to pretend it never happened at all." Buck turned back to Cass, "Truth is, it really didn't make no difference to me that that fella was an Injun when I saw him drivin' off our stock. I would've reacted the same way if he was a white man, and after he fired the first shot, I would've fired back just as straight."

Pausing, Buck continued on a softer note, "There's somethin' else that needs to be said, too, now that everythin's out in the open. Me and Pete didn't like the way things was goin'. With everythin' comin' to a head the way it was around here, we was about to make a decision. I ain't goin' to lie to you. I'm not real sure what we might've done if all this hadn't happened tonight."

Halting again, Buck swallowed against the emotion that rose in his throat. "What I'm tryin' to say is that you proved what's inside you tonight, Cass, to me and everybody else on the spread. You deserve the truth, so I told it to you—all of it. As far as I'm concerned, whatever way you want to handle it now is all right with me."

His expression unreadable, Cass remained silent, but Purity felt the conflict inside him—the loss, the torment, the rage. It washed over her in successive waves, her heart joining his with an abrupt certainty that she had made her choice at last—to stand beside Cass as she did now, whatever course he took.

Purity slipped her hand into his.

Silence.

Uncertainty.

Seconds stretching into hours.

Her heart almost stopped with joy when Purity felt Cass's hand tighten around hers. She held her breath as he slowly turned his back on the two men watching him, drawing her along with him as he walked away.

The pale light of early morning grew gradually brighter as Cass stopped abruptly in the shadows of an overhang and turned toward her. Closing her eyes as Cass slipped his arms around her and drew her close, Purity whispered words that came from the bottom of her heart.

"I'm so sorry, Cass. I didn't know."

"I did." Cass's response was tortured as he whispered against her hair. "When I finally admitted to myself that I believed you didn't know anything about Flying Eagle's disappearance, I knew either Buck or Pete had to be involved in whatever had happened. Any of the other men would've told you if they had had a run-in with an Indian. I knew Buck and Pete were the only men on this ranch who would take the chance of making you angry by keeping a secret from you, especially if they felt it was safer for you that way."

Purity whispered, "I wish I had known. I wish I could've stopped it. I wish . . ." She took an unsteady breath. "I wish I could change it all . . . that I could make it all right again."

"I'm sorry, too. I'll be sorting out what's right and what's wrong for a long time, but there's one thing that's clear to me—clearer than it's ever been before."

Drawing back, Purity felt the impact of green eyes that had once chilled her with their menace. She felt the heat of a hard body which had once held her threateningly captive with its weight. She felt the caressing touch of fingers that had once gripped her hair painfully tight. And she heard a deep voice that had once promised a sinister retribution whisper softly, "I love you, Purity."

A singing began in Purity's heart as Cass continued, "Whatever's right or wrong, that truth won't change. And I won't take the chance of losing you."

Cass lowered his mouth to hers. She felt the warmth of his kiss, the love, the commitment in the words he had spoken.

The kiss lingered. It deepened. Passion swelled. Pulling back abruptly, his breathing ragged, Cass spoke three words that stirred a soaring hope.

Three words filled with love.

A wealth of beauty was contained in those syllables.

Three words.

"Let's go *home*."

Epilogue

Captain Joe Barnes of the Texas Rangers read again the telegram he had received a few days earlier. A big man with a sweeping gray mustache and a lined complexion reflecting long years spent on the trail, he turned toward his office door at the sound of a familiar step approaching. He responded to the knock and waited as the door opened. He spoke curtly to the man who entered.

"It's about time you got here."

The tall ranger frowned. "I only arrived back in San Antonio yesterday." His frown darkened. "I'm ahead of schedule by a couple of weeks."

"You've been gone for months. Crime didn't take a holiday, you know."

"I didn't take a holiday, either."

"I know. How did it work out?"

Elaine Barbieri

"Fine."

"That's good, because I've got somethin' for you to take care of."

The big fellow shook his head. "I'm still on leave."

"This can't wait." Captain Barnes held up the telegram in his hand. "This wire is from a fella named Cass Thomas. It doesn't say much about his problem, but if this fella is askin' for help, I know it's somethin' that needs to be taken care of."

"Send somebody else."

"Everybody else is already out on the trail."

"I have some things to do before I go back on duty."

"I'm *askin'* you to do this . . . as a favor. I'd do it myself, but I can't leave here right now."

The big fellow did not respond.

Captain Barnes scrutinized the man standing across from him as he awaited a reply. It was no mystery why most people were intimidated when they first saw him. He was tall and powerfully built, with those black eyes that seemed to see right through a man. Captain Barnes supposed that was one of the reasons the fellow was one of the best rangers he had ever had under his command.

Captain Barnes prompted, "Well?"

Hesitation lingered a moment longer before the ranger responded, "I still have some time comin' to me."

"You can take it as soon as you get this taken care of."

"All right."

Captain Barnes handed him the telegram.

"This is all you have?"

"That's right."

Captain Barnes smiled as the big fellow pulled the door closed behind him. He couldn't really blame the man for hesitating, with a new wife waiting for him at home. The talk was that his wife was a damned beautiful woman, too, and a real handful in more ways than one—a former dancehall dealer with a virtuous name, of all things!

Barnes gave a short laugh. Well, if anybody could handle her, that fella could. Wes Howell was one of the toughest lawmen he had ever known, just like his father before him.

The rough hide shelter was devoid of sound.

Standing motionless within, Whispering Woman looked around her. Her supplies were ample, her shelter comfortable, and her privacy was honored. But her tepee was empty, and her heart was empty as well.

The ache within Whispering Woman deepened. She had not seen the husband of her heart for more days than she could bear to consider. She had not felt his touch for more nights than she would allow herself to count.

She hoped Pale Wolf's woman had found the answer she sought in the smoke of Spotted Bear's tepee.

To seek loved ones without finding them was torment indeed.

To await a loved one who lay in the arms of another was a pain beyond bearing.

Unable to endure her thoughts a moment longer, Whispering Woman stepped outside her tepee and looked up at the afternoon sky. Loneliness swelled. Flying Eagle was lost to her forever. Pale Wolf's life kept him apart from her. Her husband had returned to another.

A mother with no sons.

A wife with no husband.

A rider approached in the distance, and Whispering Woman's thoughts were interrupted. She was aware of the tricks her mind played, allowing each rider to assume the appearance of her husband.

Whispering Woman's gaze lingered as the rider neared. Yes, his mount had the look of her husband's, and he rode much the same way that her husband did. The tilt of his head was the same . . . the measure of his shoulders . . .

Whispering Woman fought to subdue a rising excitement as the rider continued his approach. She forced herself to stand silently as his features grew clearer.

Anticipation sharpened, escalating to a roar of sound that drowned out the noise of the camp around her, leaving only her perception of the man approaching.

She caught her breath with sudden certainty.

It was he!

Willing herself to remain still despite her elation, Whispering Woman watched as her husband drew his horse to a halt and dismounted. She saw joy mixed with pain in his sober gaze as he approached her. He halted beside her, and Whispering Woman listened with all the love in her heart as he took her into his arms and spoke at last the words she longed to hear.

"Darlin', I've come to take you home."

Night had fallen. The low canvas shelter was heated by the warmth of two bodies lovingly sated as Purity lingered in Cass's arms.

Flesh to flesh, heat to heat, Purity slipped her arms around Cass's neck, separating her lips under his. She felt his kiss deepen, and she indulged it. She felt his stroking hand, and she pressed closer.

Purity smiled when they separated at last. Purity Thomas . . . she liked the sound of that name. They had been married a few days earlier in front of the new ranch house, which was still under construction. She supposed they could have waited until the ranch house was finished and a formal reception could have been held there, but Cass didn't want to wait, and neither did she. It seemed important to both of them, somehow, to effect without delay their own closure on the terrible events of the past.

The wedding had been a simple affair. Having lost all her personal belongings in the fire, she had chosen to wear a new pair of work pants, a fancy new shirt, and a new pair of boots for the ceremony. Cass had given her the boots as a wedding present. They were hand-tooled. Her single concession to tradition had been the bouquet of field flowers she carried.

Later, as they lay in the privacy of a canvas-covered wedding bower stretched out under the stars, Cass had said she was the most beautiful bride he had ever seen. She had known his words would remain with her always. And as Cass had taken her into his arms, as he had pressed his mouth to hers with whispered words of love, she had suddenly realized that nothing else really mattered at all.

She did have some regrets. She wished both Cass's parents could have been present for their marriage. It occurred to her that having a new daughter-in-law might come as a shock to Jack when they were finally able to get in touch with him—most especially a new daughter-in-law by the name of Purity. She could hardly wait to see his face when he found out.

Stan had been present, however. Seated in his chair, the rigors he had suffered in the fire almost forgotten, he had been grinning from ear to ear. Buck and Pete, with the past placed firmly behind them where Cass had decided it should be, had stood solemnly to his rear. Carter had stood nearby, silently and sadly observing, but she sensed that he and the remainder of the men had finally given their approval to the half-breed who had come amongst them.

Whatever their thoughts, the men had made fast work of the wedding supper Pete prepared over an open fire, and Purity had then known that the worst was over.

Of course, there was still Roger Norris to be taken care of. She was pleased that Willard Norris had been unsuccessful in getting his son out of jail. She supposed Sheriff Boyle had refused to submit to the pressure the elder Norris exerted because of the wire he had received stating that a Texas Ranger was on the way to look into the situation. She hoped the ranger would arrive soon.

Aware of the massive job ahead of them, Cass had decided to wait until the remains of the old ranch house were cleared and a new one raised before making the journey to tell his mother what he had discovered about Flying Eagle's death. He had confided that both his mother and he had sensed a change in Flying Eagle during the last months of his life—a growing agitation that had climaxed the day of the powwow when Flying Eagle had left the gathering enraged at the hunger his people suffered in some camps on the reservation. Cass confided that it was Flying Eagle's fury that had caused him to follow his brother when he did not return. The depth of his own personal rage had come from the tormenting knowledge that he had not reached his brother in time.

Cass and she had both lost so much—but they also had much to be thankful for. No lives had been lost in the fire, and amidst the holocaust, they had found each other. She had lost some things that she could never replace in the blaze, but her most precious material possession had survived it all.

Purity reached up for her locket. And, strangely, through all the furor and excitement, she felt a growing certainty that her sisters were closer to her than they had ever been, that the time was fast approaching when she would see them again.

Purity clenched the locket tighter. She looked up when Cass's hand closed around hers, seeing the same light in his eyes that she saw whenever he looked at her now. It was love, unguarded and exposed, a sight more beautiful than any she had ever known. She hoped her sisters had found a love like hers. She wished it with all her heart.

Purity was unaware of the tear that rolled down her cheek until Cass wiped it away. She heard a new depth of commitment in his voice as he murmured against her lips. "Don't worry. We'll find them."

She believed him. She knew they would.

"I love you, Purity."

Cass's voice was a solemn whisper in the silence.

Sliding her arms around his neck, she told him she loved him too. She told him with her lips, with her body, with her heart, with all she had to give . . . without speaking any words at all.

DANGEROUS VIRTUES:

ELAINE BARBIERI *Honesty*

Honesty, Purity, Chastity—three sisters, very different women, all three possessed of an alluring beauty that made them...DANGEROUS VIRTUES

When the covered wagon that is taking her family west capsizes in a flood-swollen river, Honesty Buchanan's life is forever changed. Raised in a bawdy Abilene saloon by its flamboyant mistress, Honesty learns to earn her keep as a card sharp, and a crooked one at that. Continually searching for her missing sisters, the raven-haired temptress finds instead the last person in the world she needs: a devastatingly handsome Texas ranger, Sinclair Archer, who is sworn to put cheats and thieves like herself behind bars. Nestled in his protective embrace, Honesty finds the love she's been desperately seeking ever since she lost her family—a love that will finally make an honest woman out of her.

_4080-8 $5.99 US/$6.99 CAN

DANCE of the FLAME

ELAINE BARBIERI

**Elaine Barbieri's romances are
"powerful...fascinating...storytelling at its best!"
—*Romantic Times***

Exiled to a barren wasteland, Sera will do anything to regain the kingdom that is her birthright. But the hard-eyed warrior she saves from death is the last companion she wants for the long journey to her homeland.

To the world he is known as Death's Shadow—as much a beast of battle as the mighty warhorse he rides. But to the flame-haired healer, his forceful arms offer a warm haven, and he swears his throbbing strength will bring her nothing but pleasure.

Sera and Tolin hold in their hands the fate of two feuding houses with an ancient history of bloodshed and betrayal. But no matter what the age-old prophecy foretells, the sparks between them will not be denied, even if their fiery union consumes them both.

__3793-9 $5.99 US/$6.99 CAN

Dorchester Publishing Co., Inc.
65 Commerce Road
Stamford, CT 06902

WHO WROTE THE BOOK OF LOVE?
ELEVEN OF THE TOP-SELLING ROMANCE AUTHORS OF ALL TIME— THAT'S WHO!

MADELINE BAKER, MARY BALOGH, ELAINE BARBIERI, LORI COPELAND, CASSIE EDWARDS, HEATHER GRAHAM, CATHERINE HART, VIRGINIA HENLEY, PENELOPE NERI, DIANA PALMER, JANELLE TAYLOR

From the Middle Ages to the present day, these stories follow the men and women whose lives are forever changed by a special book—a cherished volume that teaches the love of learning and the learning of love!

ALL PROFITS WILL BE DONATED TO THE LITERACY PARTNERSHIP!
JOIN US—
AND CELEBRATE THE LEARNING OF LOVE AND THE LOVE OF LEARNING!

_4000-X $6.99 US/$8.99 CAN

Dorchester Publishing Co., Inc.
65 Commerce Road
Stamford, CT 06902

Please add $1.75 for shipping and handling for the first book and $.50 for each book thereafter. NY, NYC, PA and CT residents, please add appropriate sales tax. No cash, stamps, or C.O.D.s. All orders shipped within 6 weeks via postal service book rate. Canadian orders require $2.00 extra postage and must be paid in U.S. dollars through a U.S. banking facility.

Name_____

Address_____

City _____ State_____ Zip_____

I have enclosed $_____in payment for the checked book(s).
Payment <u>must</u> accompany all orders.☐ Please send a free catalog.

NO ANGEL'S GRACE

LINDA WINSTEAD

From the moment Dillon feasts his eyes on the raven-haired beauty, Grace Cavanaugh, he knows she is trouble. Sharp-tongued and stubborn, with a flawless complexion and a priceless wardrobe, Grace certainly doesn't belong on a Western ranch. But that's what Dillon calls home, and as long as the lovely orphan is his charge, that's where they'll stay.

But Grace Cavanaugh has learned the hard way that men can't be trusted. Not for all the diamonds and rubies in England will she give herself to any man. But when Dillon walks into her life he changes all the rules. Suddenly the unapproachable ice princess finds herself melting at his simplest touch, and wondering what she'll have to do to convince him that their love is the most precious gem of all.

_4223-1 $5.50 US/$6.50 CAN

Dorchester Publishing Co., Inc.
65 Commerce Road
Stamford, CT 06902

LEIGH GREENWOOD

**"I loved *Rose*, but I absolutely loved *Fern*!
She's fabulous! An incredible job!"**
—*Romantic Times*

A man of taste and culture, James Madison Randolph enjoyed the refined pleasures of life in Boston. It's been years since the suave lawyer abandoned the Randolphs' ramshackle ranch–and the dark secrets that haunted him there. But he is forced to return to the hated frontier when his brother is falsely accused of murder. What he doesn't expect is a sharp-tongued vixen who wants to gun down his entire family. As tough as any cowhand in Kansas, Fern Sproull will see her cousin's killer hang for his crime, and no smooth-talking city slicker will stop her from seeing justice done. But one look at James awakens a tender longing to taste heaven in his kiss. While the townsfolk of Abilene prepare for the trial of the century, Madison and Fern ready themselves for a knock-down, drag-out battle of the sexes that might just have two winners.

____4178-2   '$5.99 US/$6.99 CAN